BACKSLIDE

a

novel

by

Steve Elam

5-1-13 Dean,

Thanks for letting me use your name on the back cover!

SM Elam

Copyright

This book is a work of fiction. References to real people, events, establishments, sponsors, organizations, or locales are intended only to provide a sense of authenticity, and are used fictitiously. All other characters, and all incidents and dialogue, are inventions of the author's imagination and are not to be construed as real.

Book design and cover artwork by Dylan Glover.
For book and CD cover design, contact Dylan at: sidd229@live.com.

Second Edition

ISBN-13: 978-0615628974
ISBN-10: 0615628974

Praise for

BACKSLIDE

*****

"Elam's book reads like a movie!"
Chris D – IT Specialist – NY

"America's enemies just got a new BAD idea."
Dean A – Fmr. SEAL Team One Rangemaster – AZ

"The action had me kicking and swinging!"
Andrew W – Martial Arts Instructor – WA

"Reading Backslide was PURE pleasure!"
Holly J – Dental Assistant – WA

"Suspense, drama, action...couldn't put it down!"
Kevin A – Machinist – MI

"Where has this author been...I want more!"
Beverly M – CEO – TX

"Backslide offers excitement and energy!"
Cher M – Financial Counselor – WA

"Thrilling! Backslide delivers the goods!"
Chad U – UPS Driver – MI

"I read Backslide twice...best book in years!"
Rick K – CNC Operator – MI

"Finally, an explosive thriller with no 'F' bombs"
Arlene V – School Bus Driver – PA

"A thriller both men AND women will love!"
Mary C – Homemaker – WA

"Couldn't stop reading Backslide...I lost sleep!"
Lynda E – Ultra Hair, Owner – MI

"Meat and potatoes novel. Elam serves up a healthy portion of kick-ass guts and glory!"
Jasmine V – HR Assistant – WA

... and it's just beginning!

ACKNOWLEDGEMENTS

The saying goes that no man is an island. That's especially true when writing and self-publishing a novel. It takes scores of people sacrificing time and treasure to produce a successful story. So it is with great joy that I acknowledge a few of the dedicated folks who supported me along the way....

Rick Kacos was my navigator from the beginning. Not a week passed when I didn't burn up his phone with text messages. He kept me on track whenever I doubted and provided an eagle eye for details.

A big vote of thanks goes to Washington State Senator Jerome Delvin. Even before the novel was complete Senator Delvin stuck with me, dutifully reading each new chapter between floor votes and then emailing comments back. Senator Delvin's background in Police, SWAT, Bomb Squad, and mountaineering could make for his own action novel!

I wish to thank Beverly McChesney for helping me pare down my manuscript and for her helpful advice. Also deserving kudos for my novel's weight loss are Vicki and Dick Mills. Vicki is a published author and educator on computer technology. She knows how tough it is to write a book. Her positive CAN DO spirit spurred me onward during the last mile when I needed prodding the most. Dick taught me the meaning of "less is more," which I hope to continue improving on. My daughter Novella Elam gets a giant hug for taking on the herculean task of editing.

A big shout out goes to Buzzy Martin, author of *Don't Shoot! I'm the Guitar Man* (currently in production as a motion picture). Buzzy provided advice and constant encouragement.

I wish to thank my life-long friend, Chris Dreyfus. Chris can reduce a matter to its basic elements and put them all back again better than before. Chris' inventiveness helped me maintain focus in the story.

Where would I be without Dylan Glover? His rock-solid dedication to Backslide made the difference. His cover artwork is awesome. His sense of humor kept me laughing during the grind of novel writing.

Many others contributed to helping Backslide sound authentic. Rachael Kacos approved the female "voice" (best not to have lady characters sounding like dudes!). Rhoda Greenman-Bat encouraged me to develop characters so thoroughly as to smell them (now that's realism!). Cher McCarson is responsible for me pushing harder on the romance element in my story (probably not enough…next novel, Cher!). Bob Elam has a special genius for critiquing a novel and its numerous plot points and story elements (he made sure I left no shoe untied!). Black belt and martial arts instructor Andrew White gets a karate chop for helping with the fight scenes (AW speaks softly and carries a big kick!). Arlene "R" Vietmeier was especially helpful with proofreading and suggestions on tone and language (keep it classy, she said!). Dina Elam made it clear she hates thriller novels but LOVED Backslide for its rich drama (now that's an endorsement!). And also special thanks to Nadine Salter for her finishing touches prior to final printing.

A special thanks to Dave Komejan for providing technical support and converting Backslide into various e-book formats. Dave is a WIZ!

Shawna Glover was a godsend. She assisted me during the darkest days of writing. We spent untold hours reading and debating the story. Her good cheer and steady encouragement kept me going.

And there are my buddies who bust my chops…reverently so of course. My best friend, Dean Ulrich, has acted to keep me grounded my entire life. Dean helped me keep wording and phrasing down to earth. Tim Heavner has been forever encouraging me to take a good product to market. Bruce Linscott was the neighborhood storyteller who passed a bit of his talent on to me. And the rest of the gang: Mark Dood, Mark Egolf, Scott Terrill, and Mike Rinard who lent their personas to the story. Basically, we're all legends (in our own minds!).

Our journey in life is also a spiritual one. I want to thank Pastor Melvin Dahlgren of the South Bay Christian Church in San Jose, CA, for his personal examples of peace, love, and devotion, Godly elements we can all draw from. On a similar note, I want to thank my Godwin Heights High School football coach, Lyle Berry, who taught me the meaning of teamwork early on in my life.

The love and support of my dear family has made it possible for me to write Backslide. They've all contributed in countless ways. Al and Julie Elam and daughter Shandi; Lyndon and Teresa Espinoza Elam; sister Tami Elam; Keith and Patricia Talsma; the entire Chiechi clan, especially Gina, Doug and Mary; and Westley, Jasmine, and Jewel "Pinkie" Vomenici.

For years my children heard me talk about wanting to write novels. To finally do so is owed in great measure to them. Their love is the wind in my sails. Novella, Eva, Jasmine, Nathalie and Jed—you all are the greatest children a man could ever wish for.

And the greatest thanks of all to my dearest Donna…where it all began with a dream.

Thank you all for believing in me!

To My Fathers

* *

John Henry Elam

&

Vito Trifone Chiechi

"WE cannot direct the wind,

but we can adjust the sails"

— Anon.

~

PARABELLUM

Word coined by German arms maker DWM from the Latin:

si vis pacem para bellum

"If you desire peace, prepare for war"

— Patrick Sweeney

PROLOGUE

RICKY JENKINS KILLED THE MOTOR. The truck gained speed coasting down the hill. He tightened his grip on the steering wheel and struggled for control. The plan seemed good when leaving the dormitory, but now he wished he'd tested it first. What if he woke up Mr. Richards after all?

He wrestled the truck to a stop alongside the white picket fence, breathed a sigh of relief, then reached across the seat and pushed open the passenger door.

Clarice Richards sat on the porch, hands folded on her lap, her lush golden hair flowing onto creamy shoulders. She rose up, smoothed wrinkles from her pink dress, and tiptoed to the truck.

The most beautiful girl in all of Texas!

Ricky sure wished for a magic chariot instead of the old Chevy. Clarice had made a promise. He'd waited a long time, forever it seemed. Their day had finally come.

They drove through Gladewater to the juncture of US Route 80. Ricky chose west toward Big Sandy. Ten minutes later they approached the new Texas Waterland Family Park and were forced to stop. An eighteen-wheel tanker truck momentarily blocked the road.

Ricky grumbled at the delay.

Three miles beyond the park entrance, Ricky turned onto a ranch-access road. He maneuvered the truck along a sandy two-track that hugged a half-mile of cattle fencing, passed by a white bull atop a hill guarding his grass kingdom, then veered across a green pasture and into the thick forest beyond.

As the young lovers reached the tree line, they were greeted with dozens of NO TRESPASSING signs.

Clarice's face twisted. "Isn't this Texas Waterland property?"

"Yeah, so what?"

She looked at Ricky. "So we shouldn't be here."

"But it's just not right," Ricky protested.

"That's progress, darlin."

"I don't care. I used to go to the old reservoir every summer with my brother, Billy Ray. Besides—"

"Besides what?" Clarice pleaded.

Ricky struck a proud pose. “You’re looking at the newest employee of the Texas Waterland Family Park.”

“You mean it?”

“Yup. I wanted to surprise you.”

“Well, you did.” Clarice scooted closer to Ricky.

Ricky put his arm around Clarice. “Good, because we’re gonna’ have fun this summer.”

They pressed deeper into the woods until at last the forest opened up. A large body of water appeared before them, the Loma Reservoir. Ricky spotted his objective and drove to a sunny clearing beside a high bank overlooking the water. This part of the reservoir had a sandy beach, at least it used to. He hadn’t been back here in years, not since Billy Ray killed....

He stopped the truck. A dust cloud caught up and settled to earth. They looked all about, ensuring their privacy, and then faced each other. Smiles appeared, a giddy one for Ricky, a nervous one for Clarice. They felt tickles in their stomachs.

Ricky exited the truck and hurried to Clarice’s door. He escorted his princess to the shade of a mature oak. Clarice spread a blanket over soft earth and smoothed the wrinkles from their simple bed.

He pulled her up. They joined hands and faced skyward. Morning sun filtered through the trees, dappling their faces with light.

The place was perfect.

They sought acceptance in each other’s eyes. It was granted.

Slowly, deliberately, they removed each other’s clothing. First off was Ricky’s varsity shirt, then Clarice’s pink dress, until finally they stood before each other as nature intended of lovers—unashamed.

Ricky Jenkins lowered Clarice Richards onto the blanket. Birds sang in lofty trees. Squirrels chattered and dashed about. The leaves of the oak tree rustled reassuringly. They made love to the chorus of nature all around them.

They lay naked in the warm air, looking up at a blue sky through the opening in the trees. The sun had risen in the Texas sky and so had the temperature. Time had sped by too quickly.

Ricky took Clarice’s hand. “Let’s go for a swim.”

Off they ran, down the bank and into the water, laughing and screeching in playful delight. They dove in hand in hand. They splashed and frolicked, kissed, and kissed more.

Birds hushed in mid-song. Squirrels hurried away. A blue heron fled its perch and swooped down above the lake, leaving swirls in the morning mist.

Ricky hadn't heard them approach. They stood silent on the bank—two men, outfitted in military gear, guns pointed at their naked bodies. One man held a cell phone to his mouth.

Clarice screamed!

Ricky shouted, "Who are you!"

The men said nothing. They didn't move. Beyond the obvious, there was something strange about them, but what?

Ricky strained to discover. Then it struck him. They looked Chinese. "What do you want? Do you speak English?"

No reply.

Moments passed…moments that seemed like hours. Ricky's mind raced to make sense of it all. Finally, he did the only thing that came to mind. He rose up out of the water and began a march toward the soldiers, or whatever they were. Before managing a single step, a hail of bullets churned the water around him. He froze. No bullets had caught flesh.

The soldiers had missed intentionally!

Ricky lowered himself into the water. He turned toward Clarice. She treaded water further off shore. A look of terror possessed her. They made eye contact and her screaming stopped.

Ricky made his decision. He mouthed a single word, *Go*.

Clarice was paralyzed by fear and made no attempt to flee.

"Go!" Ricky yelled. "Swim out of here!"

Clarice blinked rapidly. Logic thawed her fear-numbed brain. She began swimming away from shore, but made slow progress.

A black Ford Bronco drove up among the lethal gathering. Out stepped a tall man with broad shoulders and stylish blond hair. He wore matching khaki vest and trousers. To Ricky, the man looked like a game warden—but American!

"Wh…who are you people?"

"Who are you, mate?" the blond man shouted back.

An Australian accent? Ricky was shocked!

"You kids are trespassing."

"No I'm not. I'm on Texas Waterland property."

"Precisely, Lad. You're trespassing."

Ricky's face twisted in confusion. "You all work for the park?"

"That's right." The man's steel gray eyes stared hard.

"Me too. I'm Ricky Jenkins. I'll be working in the ticket office."

Clarice heard the exchange between Ricky and the blond man. She stopped her attempt at escape. The gunmen looked at each other. The blond man extended a hand and received a cell phone.

After a short conversation, he handed the phone to its stocky Asian owner and then hopped down the bank to the water's edge.

"Why didn't y'all say so before?" The foreign accent was replaced with perfect Texas drawl. "Name's Wiggins, head of park security. Now come outa' there."

Ricky hesitated, embarrassed by his nakedness. He glanced at Clarice treading water fifty yards off shore. She was tiring from her effort to stay afloat. He turned back to Wiggins. "Am I in trouble?"

"No law 'gainst swimmin' in your birthday suit I know of."

"Then what's the rush?"

"This area near the water plant is extremely dangerous."

Ricky's eyes shifted rapidly, struggling to grasp the whole picture.

"Don't be shy, we're all men here...except for her." Wiggins pointed at Clarice.

Ricky decided everything was all right. What choice did he have, Clarice was sinking deeper into the water. "Okay, but y'all turn your backs when Clarice comes out of the water."

"Of course, that's what gentlemen do." Wiggins squatted at the water's edge and held out a hand. "Let me help you up outa' there...before the snakes get ya."

Ricky moved to shore.

Suddenly, the outstretched hand struck with the speed of a viper, snatching Ricky by the hair and yanking him forward.

Wiggins spoke into Ricky's frightened face, the Texas drawl gone, "You and your *sheila* picked a very bad day, mate!" Then he jammed an object into Ricky's mouth and plunged his head under the water.

Clarice at first thought Ricky slipped and the blond man had tried to help. But after seeing Ricky's head shoved violently underwater and the frantic kicking of his feet, she knew he was in mortal danger. She tried to scream and choked on brown water. She began swimming to Ricky, and then realized she could do nothing to help. The once stoic soldiers laughed and beckoned her to shore.

Ricky's white legs kicked. His arms thrashed about. His movements slowed until all motion ceased.

With a final grasp at reason, Clarice turned away from the man she loved, whom she was powerless to save. She sucked in a deep breath and resumed her fitful task. She thought to swim for the opposite shore where morning mist still lay upon the water.

Wiggins left Ricky's naked corpse floating at the water's edge and scrambled up the bank. He grabbed the Asian man's cell phone as before and hit a single digit. "Release them, it's feeding time."

Done with giving orders, Wiggins pulled a rifle from the Bronco. He calmly put the gun to his shoulder, found the girl in the crosshairs of the scope, and pulled the trigger. The gun bucked against his shoulder.

Clarice felt something sting her buttock. Adrenaline masked the pain. She stopped, took her bearings, another breath, and swam toward the far shore. Something was wrong. She sensed an impending doom and ordered her muscles to swim faster.

Drawn by movement and the scent of blood, a school of ravenous piranhas slammed into Clarice Richards. The tranquil waters of the Loma Reservoir burst into a frenzied boil. Then mere moments later, the feast ended, the food source devoured.

Serenity returned to the dark waters.

A wooden rowboat appeared out of the mist. Standing in the bow, donning a conical straw hat and draped in black silk, was an ancient oriental man. His white hair and wispy beard fluttered in the breeze of the moving boat.

1

EASTHAM PRISON
HOUSTON, TX

The lights came on and the squawkbox announced the start of a new day in hell. A prison guard marched along the metal catwalk dragging his riot stick across the iron bars. Yawning prisoners moaned and cursed the man's heritage. He halted in front of one particular cell.

"Jenkins, you ready?"

"Yeah…I guess so."

"Then get your ass in gear! The parole board don't wait on white trash like you, boy." The guard raked his stick across the cell bars and then moved on to another inmate and another tongue-lashing.

Billy Ray Jenkins placed a Bible under his pillow and hopped down from his bunk. He shaved, brushed his brown hair, and pulled a fresh uniform from under his mattress where it was being pressed. He slipped into the formless clothing. The uniform was designed to depersonalize prisoners. However, the light-weight material did little to mask his broad shoulders and muscular arms and chest, the results from years of lifting weights in the exercise yard. At least the white cotton contrasted nicely with his hazel eyes.

He faced forward to await the opening of the timed bars.

The parole board consisted of two men and a woman—Dragon Lady, as inmates called her. They busied themselves with stacks of paper—Billy Ray's prison record, criminal history, staff evals, heavily redacted military record, parole request form completed in triplicate, and God only knew what else.

As if on cue, the board members lifted their heads in unison. Dragon Lady motioned to a solitary chair facing the members. "Please be seated Mr. Jenkins." She peered over rimless glasses. "Let us begin. Has your rehabilitation progressed since we last met?"

"Yes, ma'am, it has."

"That sounds encouraging. However, it's my understanding you never accept help, that you're a loner. Is that correct?"

Billy Ray considered her question. It could take a lifetime to answer. He searched for an explanation and came up empty.

"Well, is that correct?"

"I guess it is, ma'am. For most of my life I never wanted help."

"Why on earth not?"

"I was... just feeling sorry for myself. But things are different now. We've worked hard to change that." Billy Ray angled a glance at the black man in a dark suit and white collar of a priest. Their eyes met and he was rewarded with a warm smile.

Dragon Lady continued, "Given your past record, the State of Texas can ill-afford to return you to society where you might cause considerable harm to persons or property."

"I understand your concerns, ma'am. I truly believe I'm ready to go home."

The middle-aged man in a business suit and checkered tie was next to speak. "Young man, what do you have to offer society if you're released?"

The man's role was to protect the interests of an overburdened Department of Health and Human Services by ascertaining the employability of prospective parolees. Billy Ray knew that mouthful meant keeping him off the state's teat any way possible.

"With all due respect, sir, I'm not a young man. I want to get on with life before it's too late."

The bureaucrat's face reddened. "You being smart with me?"

"No, sir. I'm physically fit and in good health. If nothing else, I can sell my strong back."

The man was unimpressed. "Manual laborers don't make much money. Most end up on state assistance. As you stated, you are no longer a young man." The bureaucrat pressed the matter. "I mean, what skills do you possess?'"

"My military training. I can do things—fix things."

"Oh really..." the man stole a glance at his notes, "like machine guns and bombs? It seems your training only armed you with the ability to hurt people and break things."

"Much more than that. SEALs are trained in various subjects to enable unit autonomy. My specialties were chemical and electrical engineering."

"You make it sound like SEALs are a bunch of Harvard grads."

He'd heard such criticisms before. In fact, many SEALs were college educated and could have entered Ivy League institutions had they applied. Several SEALs were even former Olympic athletes. No doubt this man's cynical attitude stemmed from the secretive nature of America's Special Operations Forces. He chose to consider it a compliment instead. "I'm only at liberty to say my training was comprehensive and intense."

"Don't play rock, paper, scissors with me, Jenkins." The man leaned forward. "You must admit, a dishonorable discharge just might screw the pooch with prospective employers."

In times past, Billy Ray would've bristled, even bit back. Instead, he pointed at the man's stack of papers. "You have a report confirming that I completed a two-year correspondence course at Texas Lutheran University. I earned my degree. Added with military training, I should qualify for entry-level work at the very least."

The Human Services man shuffled through his notes. "Theology? Not what I'd call a how-to-make-a-living degree."

"No, sir. I consider it my how-to-live degree."

It was the final board member's turn. The Reverend Moses Greer was an imposing figure. Inmates called him "Mosey." He was a giant physically and spiritually. Mosey was the founder of Texas Faith on Parole Program, which operated in conjunction with the TDCJ. He had a heart of gold and soul on fire. His expectations for you were two-fold—grace and repentance. Most inmates at Eastham claimed to be innocent. That mattered little to Mosey. His take on life was that everyone was guilty of something. He had an impressive record of steering scores of "innocent" inmates on the road to redemption.

In a deep baritone voice, Mosey said, "Billy Ray, how's your day?"

"Better than most, Reverend. How about yours?"

"Same as you, better than most, I pray. Did you finish reading the Bible I gave you?"

"Mostly...." Billy Ray's voice trailed off.

"How far did you get?"

"The Book of James. I've been stuck there for awhile."

"Any verse in particular?"

Billy Ray gave a concerned look. "James 1:27."

"Why?" Mosey leaned forward, interested in his problem.

"It kind of explains where my warring comes from, and..." Billy Ray searched for words, "what to do about it."

"And what is that? What will you do if you're paroled?" Mosey moved smoothly to the business at hand.

Billy Ray felt a wave of clarity sweep over him. He answered without hesitation. "Serve the fatherless and widows and help them battle *their* afflictions." With one simple statement a massive weight lifted from him, his mission clear at last.

"Thank you, Billy Ray." Mosey crossed himself and said to the other board members, "I'm finished."

"Prisoner 49508, please stand," Dragon Lady ordered.

Billy Ray did so. The chains around his ankles rattled.

"You were tried, convicted, and sentenced to fifteen years confinement at hard labor for the crimes of marketing illegal drugs and malicious mischief resulting in the death of one Brenda Lee Payne...."

Billy Ray barely heard Dragon Lady's words. Instead, visions of Brenda Lee's smiling face came to mind. Then those same visions degenerated into the horror-stricken look of a drowning victim, eyes bulging in terror, face stretched in panic. Dead.

Dragon Lady's voice came back to his ears. "Court records show you refused counsel and offered no defense at your trial. In fact, the record states you ignored all instructions by the presiding judge and remained speechless, even to the point of contempt. You've now served ten years of your sentence. It is the opinion of this board that you be... set free."

Billy Ray's knees nearly buckled. And yet, he felt no joy.

"Any last comments from the board?" Dragon Lady asked.

The Health and Human Services man shook his head. The Reverend did likewise, then changed his mind.

Mosey rose from his chair. At six feet eight inches and three hundred solid pounds, he towered over all. He cleared his throat. "Billy Ray, if you wish to know true freedom, seek out the innocent, serve the fatherless and widows, relieve them of their burdens. This is 'pure religion undefiled before God,' sayeth James, the Brother of our Lord."

Billy Ray felt his attention captured by this man. In Mosey, he recognized a true warrior.

The Reverend expanded his chest. Passion blazed in his eyes, God's power in his deep voice. "You've accepted the gift of our Lord, so hear my warning. You'll be forever lost if you backslide."

2

The Greyhound bus picked up speed leaving Houston. Billy Ray stared out the window at the passing countryside. Mile after mile of fence posts strobed across his view with hypnotic rhythm. Focus on the present blurred until all that remained were the ghosts of his past. Images played before his mind's eye like a bad film strip. Scenes filled with pain, disappointment, and finally, of loss....

It seemed any good thing he attempted only led to pain. The cycle always repeated, good intention met with ridicule, ending in grim results. As when his drunk father beat his mother and showered her with vile insults. If only he hadn't helped her with housework, or wiped away her tears, maybe his father wouldn't have punished her. The neighbor kids would line up at the windows of his house to peek in on the latest whoopin' Rodney "Switch" Jenkins was givin' the wife. He hated them. He hated his father, too.

Martial arts were meant to instill self-control and help channel his emotions—the inner rage—and did, for a time. Then one night after Big Sandy defeated their Gladewater rivals, he spotted his school's star player knocking around a Gladewater cheerleader. His blood boiled over. Martial arts to be thanked, he hesitated. Then the Big Sandy player tore off the girl's uniform, threw her onto a bleacher, and began taking what was wanted. Something deep inside snapped. He beat the kid bad enough to put him out for the season. Brenda Lee Payne testified that Billy Ray Jenkins saved her from both harm and disgrace. And because her father was the sheriff, it came as no surprise when all charges were dropped.

Perhaps it was then that Brenda Lee saw something different in him, something to be loved. Their relationship marked the beginning of love for them both, and a hopeful future. But it was not to be.

Sheriff Roy Payne saw to that.

Word around town was that if he hadn't enlisted in the service on the day he turned 18, the sheriff would've shot him at first sight. The Navy brought respectability to him and his family. He was accepted to and successfully completed the Navy SEAL program. His paychecks even provided relief to his mother. She managed to hide the money from his alcoholic father, though only for a time. One night, Rodney stormed home from the bar looking for money. Lela wouldn't give it to him. He beat her up and even hurt little Ricky, and then tore the house apart in search of the hidden cash. If not for a call to the sheriff by the parents of a young window-peeker, Lela Jenkins might've died from her injuries. He was gone by the time the sheriff arrived. No one ever heard from Rodney "Switch" Jenkins again.

Life had gotten better for his mother and Ricky, even for Brenda Lee and him. Although he only managed a homecoming once a year, he and Brenda Lee grew deeply in love. Letters were heartfelt. He would read them again and again until the paper crumbled in his fingers. Eight years had elapsed since leaving home and the woman he loved. He had just reenlisted for his third tour and was granted a fat bonus. He could now afford a wife and a home. He bought a large diamond while on assignment overseas. It was all arranged. He arrived stateside and brought the ring with him. They would meet at their favorite place, "God's little garden in Texas," Brenda Lee called it. Among the rolling hills of East Texas and the Piney Woods, their place by the tranquil waters of the Loma Reservoir on the Ambassador Ranch had no equal. He would ask Brenda Lee this night to be his companion for life.

They would be free.

His plane had been delayed. He arrived late to their special place. Brenda Lee was nowhere in sight nor was her car. The bedroll was spread out, there was the picnic basket, and even a beer can still cold to the touch. But where was she?

He walked to the bank and listened. Maybe she'd gone in for a swim. All was quiet. He turned to leave and that's when he heard it, a strange noise. First once, then a second time...glub-glub. He couldn't tell where the noise was coming from, the night was so dark. He fetched a flashlight from his car. Back at the water's edge, he shined the light up and down the shore. Nothing. He was about to give up when it happened again. He hurried to the spot and pointed the light into the water. Submerged some twenty feet from shore was the perfect outline of a car roof. Colorful petroleum rings bubbled to the surface.

Panic struck! Panic like he'd never felt before, not deep beneath the ocean rigging explosives, not in the snake-infested waters of the Amazon, not atop the scorching sands of Africa, nor even in firefights when he lost buddies. This panic ripped his heart out!

He dove into the water alongside the car, flashlight in hand that thankfully stayed lit. Brenda Lee was in the car. She wasn't moving. He tried frantically to get in. No luck. The doors were locked and the windows rolled up for the air conditioning. Again and again he took the breath of life to her. It went undelivered.

Billy Ray finally found a large rock, broke the glass, and pulled Brenda Lee's lifeless body to shore. He sat for hours rocking his dead angel. It killed him to know he hadn't been there to save the woman he loved.

He somehow managed to drive to Doc Hastings. Together they called the sheriff.

The autopsy revealed Brenda Lee Payne died as a result of drowning. Toxicology tests confirmed the existence of high levels of barbiturates in her system, and what the coroner guessed to be six ounces of alcohol. Also found in a heart-shaped locket alongside his picture was a rock of cocaine wrapped in plastic. The coroner was curious to know if the sheriff was aware of his daughter's drug habit...or that she was pregnant.

Sheriff Payne arrested Billy Ray, charging him with selling drugs, reckless endangerment, even murder if it could be made to stick. But the worst charge of all was for rape.

He offered no resistance when the sheriff cuffed him, only stood in stunned silence as the Miranda warning was read loud and slow. Hatred filled every word uttered by Roy Payne, but he'd ceased hearing voices, only saw lips moving in a fog.

Neither did he resist when on the way to jail the sheriff turned into a pecan orchard, nor when getting dragged from the car. He didn't even resist when Payne kicked him and slugged him and beat him with a night stick, over and over again, until too winded to go on. He was feeling none of it. He was past feeling.

Only when the exhausted sheriff pulled a gun, crammed it in his mouth, and the deputy intervened, did he finally protest. He parted swollen, bloodied lips and cursed the deputy for interfering....

The airbrakes snorted and the bus came to a stop at the tiny Gladewater depot. Billy Ray made no attempt to exit. Passengers bumped him on their way past. He struggled for a long while to clear his mind of the painful memories from a decade ago.

"Hey, mister, you gettin' off?" The bus driver stared at him.

The dark clouds finally parted. Billy Ray crossed himself, stood and retrieved his seabag. As he did so, a Bible verse came to mind. It was the Prodigal Son.

He was back.

3

FBI FIELD OFFICE
DALLAS, TX

The Special Agent in Charge for the Dallas division of the FBI poured a last cup of tea for the day and returned to his desk. Nothing was more important to Chris Dreyfus than keeping America safe. The Federal Bureau of Investigation had 56 field divisions located in major cities throughout the United States. Each was headed by a Special Agent in Charge or SAC. So large was Texas, the state hosted three field offices. His Dallas Division had a backyard totaling 137 counties that covered 125,000 square miles and was home to more than nine million people.

His career with the FBI had run the traditional route. He hailed from the East Coast, had attended preppie schools, and had risen through the detective ranks in Baltimore. In age, he was nearing the senior discount on the Denny's menu and, he hoped, retirement on a boat in Florida.

He carried the tea back to his desk and turned his attention to reading the latest threat assessment from headquarters. There was a new monster on the prowl, a "super meth." Several people had already died from the drug. Besides the deaths in Texas, there'd been cases on both coasts. Strangely, there were no known *living* users of the new product. The worst could be yet to come and his investigators had nothing to go on. No one had a clue where the new drug was coming from. The matter needed attention. However, most of his agents were spread thin investigating the enormous flow of traditional products entering the U.S. from Mexico. He could only spare one agent from his Field Intelligence Group. He chose the best man for the job—a real pit bull—perfect for chasing down the new mystery drug.

Dreyfus called out, "Hey, Johnny, anything new on the wire?"

"UFOs and missing honey bees."

"Smartass! We don't do X-files."

Agent Johnny Lam scrolled through the text on his computer screen. "Wait...here's something. Give me a minute."

Like his boss, Lam had a good nose for trouble and a sixth sense for detective work. However, similarities ended there. Lam was a Texas native, born and bred in the steamy bayous near the Louisiana border. He came to the Agency in less traditional fashion, from the military. As an Army Captain in the Green Berets, his exploits in the jungles of South America were legendary. He'd distinguished himself countless times battling ruthless drug cartels during joint operations with the U.S. Drug Enforcement Agency. He was fearless, determined to engage the drug lords on their own turf—to the death when necessary.

On style, Dreyfus and Lam were yin and yang. On results, they were trigger and finger.

"Here it is, boss, a drowning in East Texas…19-year old male."

"For a second there, I thought you said drowning."

"I did."

"Then call the Red Cross. We don't do drownings, either."

Lam rolled his eyes. "There were drugs in the victim's system. I flagged notices involving that new drug."

"Rapture?"

"That's the one. According to the report filed by Upshur County Sheriff Roy Payne, the kid drowned while high on Rapture."

"This new drug's a killer," Dreyfus said.

"It's weird stuff, too. Kinda' makes LSD look like a smart pill."

Lam had read the coroner reports on the deaths involving Rapture. The facts were shocking. The new designer drug shared much of the chemical structure of methamphetamine, but was faster acting, longer lasting, and exponentially more potent. The departure from meth was that Rapture also incorporated a powerful hallucinogen. None of the deaths from Rapture thus far had been a result of toxic overdose. Instead, five of the deaths were from accidents, like the drowning victim in Big Sandy, while two others had actually starved to death.

Dreyfus held up a sheet of paper. "This just came in. The lab has a new theory about Rapture. They think the drug is still evolving, that an additional compound may yet be added."

"As in *accessorized?*"

Dreyfus looked worried. "Something like that. The lab won't speculate, except to say it won't be good."

"Like the drug is a gun and the accessory—"

"A silencer," Dreyfus finished Lam's words. "Guns have functions, good or bad. Attach a silencer and the use becomes predetermined."

"Murder!" Lam said. "If you're right, we better find out where the drug's coming from before the bad guys figure out what they have."

Dreyfus' look worsened. "What if the makers of Rapture already know and they're test-marketing the product?"

"Then I'd say that puts them one giant leap ahead of us."

"You got that right. Now you know what I know, or think."

"That would suggest a conspiracy, something far greater than peddling drugs for the sake of cash."

Dreyfus pointed to his nose. “That’s what my sniffer’s telling me. But I can’t take theories to headquarters, I need something firm.”

Lam felt his mind spin. The idea of a drug having a purpose beyond lust for money was nearly unfathomable. It flew in the face of the usual profit motive. Drug dealers had at least that much in common with legitimate businesses, profits suffered when products killed. Good guys or bad, the bottom line was the same—money.

“What if you’re right and we did nothing until it was too late?”

Dreyfus looked hard at Lam. “My nose is also telling me we’re running out of time.”

Lam felt a chill. “This could become a national disaster.”

They stared at each other, both considering the dangers of Rapture and how little information they had to go on.

Dreyfus broke the silence. “We need to find out who’s behind this drug and punch a big hole in their plans.”

“Then I’d better get hot.”

“You know I can’t afford to pull any of the troops in on this without firm evidence. So you’re on your own.” Dreyfus changed track. “Back to that little matter in Big Sandy...dig a little deeper. Let me know what you find.” Dreyfus turned his attention back to the stacks of paper on his desk.

Lam spent the next hour studying reports of the drowning incident in Big Sandy, making phone calls, and reading relevant files. One file in particular held his attention, the background for Billy Ray Jenkins. He was amazed. No way was this coincidence. He didn’t believe in happenstance any more than he bought the story of a chubby fellow in red pajamas snaking down chimneys at Christmastime. He also had to question what the cops in East Texas were smoking. And that went double for the folks at Eastham prison. It didn’t take a good nose to figure out what came next.

There was going to be trouble in the Piney Woods.

4

April showers bring May flowers. It might be that simple in northern states, but not in East Texas. April brings back heat, with May comes bugs and humidity, and June is anyone's guess. Beads of sweat covered Billy Ray's forehead from lugging his seabag the half-mile down Main Street in Gladewater and to the nearest tavern, a place called the Frontier Inn.

The dark, air-conditioned building was a welcome relief. The lunchtime crowd had vanished after refreshing themselves on chicken gizzards, home fries, and cold beer. The heavy drinkers and pool players hadn't yet arrived. He made his way to the end of the bar, dropped his bag beside a stool, and sat. He motioned to the bartender, who busied himself wiping down the bar. "I'll take whatever's cold, Guinness if you have it."

"No Guinness. We don't get many Irish folk passing through." The bartender stopped wiping the bar. "How 'bout a Lone Star?"

"What the heck, Lone Star it is...so long as it's cold."

Billy Ray allowed his eyes to adjust in the dim lighting. A few people were scattered about the tavern speaking in hushed tones or not talking at all. Only one other person sat at the bar, slumped forwards, withered fingers clutching a glass of warm beer. The man looked familiar, then Billy Ray remembered the name, *Jonesy*.

Jonesy was the town drunk. Most people called him Four Eyes due to his seeing double most of the time. With the abuse the old man heaped on his body, Billy Ray thought it a miracle Jonesy was even alive. He had to be pushing ninety on the age meter.

The old drunk once told Billy Ray to call him Jonesy, like his friends had done. Afterward, Jonesy had wept.

Jonesy wore a battered US Marine Corps hat. The emblem on front had long-since faded. Jonesy had always been a mystery. The tarnished ring on his bony finger only deepened that mystery. It bore the insignia of the United States Naval Academy. A former US Marine officer, Billy Ray guessed. He was also left guessing at what in the man's past had made him check out of life. Just what kind of pain was Jonesy trying to forget?

Billy Ray sympathized with the old man. Jonesy was the example of what he'd become if he didn't bury the past and get on with life.

The bartender returned with a bottle of beer and frosted mug and slid them across the bar. Billy Ray fished a twenty from his wallet. "I'll just be having the one beer. How about you making sure the old man gets a hot meal when he wakes up."

"Sure thing, mister. That's nice of you. Ol' Four Eyes don't mean harm to nobody, that's for sure. What did you say your name was?"

"I didn't."

"Have it your way." The man ambled away wiping the bar.

On a whim, Billy Ray fished a quarter from his pocket and went over to the jukebox, at least he thought it was a jukebox. It had buttons and lights, looking more like a NASA computer. If the new technology wasn't shock enough, then the price was—fifty cents a song or three for a dollar. He scanned the artists, names like Grip, The Whines, AKA 360, Vito and the One Eyed Jacks, Lady Gaga, and dozens more. But no Hank Williams, no Bob Seger & The Silver Bullet Band, no Lynyrd Skynyrd. What had the world become? A decade had been more like an eternity. Time stood still for no man, least of all a convict. Even art had marched on without him. He felt like Rip Van Winkle.

Billy Ray gave up and plodded back to the bar. What had he expected, that the world would stop and wait for him, that the good people of Gladewater and Big Sandy would line the ten miles of US Route 80 to celebrate his return? There would be no welcome mat for him. Not in a million years. He was hated in both towns. That, in part, was why he hadn't told anyone of his release from Eastham.

The other reason for coming home unannounced was more subtle. His mother never visited him at the prison. Even her letters stopped several years back. She loved him, he had no doubt, and merely stated in her final letter how she could bear it no longer. And why she'd relocated to Gladewater so soon after his trial was a mystery to him. She would only say there'd be no running from trouble—his or hers. He didn't know what that meant, only that the Payne family lived in Gladewater. In his opinion, her move was like jumping from the frying pan and into the fire. But maybe she'd been right, Ricky was sure doing well.

Ha! Little Ricky.

The boy was a young man now. There'd been a photocopy of a college report card in Ricky's last letter, he was a four-point-oh student. Billy Ray tipped his beer at the thought. Maybe there was hope for the Jenkins family after all.

Jonesy awoke from his stupor and interrupted Billy Ray's thoughts. "Hey, I know you from *shumwhere….*"

He turned to see Jonesy pointing a crooked finger.

"Yeaahh…I do know you."

"I know you too, Mr. Jones."

"Call me Jonesy, my friends did."

For a moment the old drunk's eyes caste a faraway look before refocusing on the present.

"Okay, Jonesy it is. So how are things?"

"Same old crap, boy, jus' a different day," he said and then launched into a coughing fit.

Billy Ray waited for Jonesy to recover.

Jonesy wiped phlegm from his mouth with the end of his tattered coat sleeve. "You ain't been 'round for awhile."

"Nope."

"I know why you're back, then."

Billy Ray hadn't a clue what Jonesy was getting at. Alcoholics could look through things as if they weren't there.

"Yeah, and you won't like it none, neither."

"I don't know what you're talking about, Jonesy."

"I saw them. Nice kids they were."

The old drunk was rambling. Maybe the ghosts of his past were back. More likely, it was just a brain rotted by decades of booze. Time had no meaning for severe alcoholics. Past and future had their confluence in the present.

A lot like himself.

After all, a quarter of his life had just been wasted in prison. And, except for a few blissful moments with Brenda Lee and the years on the SEAL teams serving his country, the rest hadn't been worth much. He couldn't tell whether time had stopped or was about to catapult him naked into an uncertain future.

"I fought the Japs…Koreans too. I'd do it again if I had to. I jus' don't trus' 'zem bastards," Jonesy slurred.

The bartender finished cashing out the last of the afternoon crowd and began wiping his way in their direction.

Jonesy brought his swaying body under control and struck a proud pose. "I got medals too, like you." He rewarded himself with a swig of beer.

Billy Ray attempted a new subject. "How about I buy you some food?"

Jonesy paid no attention and continued with his war stories. "Fought in the Pacific in dubya dubya two…and in Korea."

At the mention of Korea, the old warrior's eyes misted over. There was a long pause. Billy Ray thought the conversation was over. Then Jonesy slapped the bar.

"I know they ain't Japs, they're Gooks!"

That got the attention of the bartender, who hurriedly worked his towel down the bar until standing opposite of them.

Jonesy looked around, as if about to tell a secret. "I've been watching them. Those guys are Koreans, I just know it. Except for the big fella."

Billy Ray didn't know what to say. His first conversation on the outside and it was with an old drunk consumed by booze and history. Fortunately, the bartender took the lead.

"You talk too much, Jonesy. I told you before there ain't no Koreans around these parts. You must be talking about the Chinese restaurants." The bartender set a bowl of peanuts in front of the old man. "Now let the new guy drink his beer in peace, will ya?"

Jonesy knocked the bowl onto the floor. "Hell there ain't no Gooks!" He pointed at the door. "Right over there. And they joined up with the Mexicans. They're up to no good, I say!"

Billy Ray wondered what in the world Jonesy was talking about. Certainly, the old man was delusional. He was about to give up on all the nonsense and leave when a name stopped him in his tracks.

"I told Sheriff Payne, too. Those Gooks killed them kids."

"You don't know that, nobody does. Besides, there's no trace of the Richard's girl. She probably was never even with the boy."

"She was!" Jonesy shot back. "I saw those kids together. Drove past me this morning laughin' and carryin' on like a couple of lovebirds. And the girl's pretty hair flyin' all o'er the place."

Jonesy's talk upset the bartender. "The sheriff declared it an accident!"

Billy Ray felt perplexed. "What are you two talking about?"

"Oh nothin', just a local matter. A boy was found drowned this morning back behind the new waterslide park. Apparently he'd been joyridin' under the influence when his truck went off into the water. By the time anybody got to the boy, it was too late."

Tragedy! Drowning! Vehicle in the water! A dead body!

The past attacked Billy Ray's mind. He stared at the bartender.

"You all right, mister? Looks like you seen a ghost."

He took a swallow of beer, anything to chase away the demons.

The bartender wiped the bar. "Haven't seen you around before."

Billy Ray found his voice. "Probably not."

"Ol' Four Eyes seems to know you." He laid down the towel and extended his hand. "Name's Harper, what's yours?"

"Billy Ray—Billy Ray Jenkins."

Harper's hand went limp. He pulled away and took up his towel and compulsive wiping. "You relation to Ricky Jenkins?"

"Yeah. He's my baby brother. Why?"

Harper looked stunned. "He's the boy who drowned."

Billy Ray's world caved in.

Harper attempted to rescue the situation. "I'm real sorry. We're all real sorry, Mr. Jenkins. Word is your brother was a good boy."

Billy Ray ran out of the tavern.

The drunk came alive. "You dumbass, Harper. He didn't know."

Billy Ray sprinted the two miles to his mother's house. He'd never run so fast in his life. His clothes dripped with sweat. He raced past a Cadillac in the dirt driveway with an I HEART JESUS bumper sticker. He vaulted onto the porch, nearly ripped the screen door off its hinges, and stumbled into his mother's living room.

From a threadbare couch, three heads turned. Each registered shock at seeing Billy Ray standing before them. On one side of Lela Jenkins sat a woman extending a compassionate arm. On her other side was a balding man in a black suit and maroon tie. The minister and his wife. They looked as if the devil entered the room.

"Billy Ray?" Tears streamed down his mother's cheeks.

"Yes…mama." He fought for breath.

Lela moved to get up from the couch, faltered, and fell back. He went to her. They explored each other's faces. Then the instinctive love mothers feel for their children overrode all other considerations and with shaking arms, took Billy Ray into her bosom.

He pulled back. "Is it true, Mama? Is Ricky dead?"

The preacher answered for Lela. "Mr. Jenkins, yes, it's true. He was discovered this morning at the Loma Reservoir, drowned."

"No! Not again!"

5

Deputy Sheriff Tom Dixon entered the office carrying two styrofoam cups. He slid one of the drinks across the desk to Payne, who sat with feet on the desk reading the Huston Chronicle.

"Here you go, Roy. Non-fat latte just the way you like it."

Payne closed the newspaper and sat upright. "Thanks, Tom."

The men took a moment to sip their drinks.

"And to what do I owe this tasty treat?"

"Now, Roy, how long we known each other, huh?"

"Since high school." Payne lifted his cup. "To the glory days."

Dixon raised his coffee. "And how long you been sheriff?

"A long time…and it'll be more after November."

"So then, to the past and to the future."

"And to wrapping up this drug case so quickly," Payne added.

They toasted.

"By the way, Roy, guess who's back in town?"

"I give up. The devil?"

Dixon checked himself. Maybe Payne wasn't far off the mark. "It's Billy Ray Jenkins. You think he knows yet?"

Payne calmly sipped his drink, offering no answer.

Dixon had anticipated the sheriff coming unglued. He persisted, "So what do you think about that?"

A cunning smile formed on Payne's face. "What do I think? Well…" he drew out the word, "I think it's time."

* * *

"I think you'll want to see this, boss."

Dreyfus turned his attention to Lam. "What is it?"

"Looks like we got something. Our latest Rapture victim has a brother serving fifteen at Eastham for drugs…could be our connection. The file states our convict was a war hero, Navy SEAL, with a chestful of medals, even the Navy Cross."

Dreyfus let out a low whistle.

"Only the Medal of Honor is higher than a Navy Cross."

"Didn't I see that once on the History Channel?"

Lam ignored the sarcasm. "It's all here in his service record, though some things are blacked out due to his having been a Special Forces guy."

"Sounds like one tough cookie. What's he in for?"

“Manslaughter…death of an adult female…Brenda Lee Payne.”

That got Dreyfus’ attention. “Could you repeat that?”

“Brenda Lee Payne, none other than the daughter of Sheriff Roy Payne. Take a guess how she died.”

“I give up.”

“Drowned.”

“That’s too much coincidence.” Dreyfus leaned forward. “Why do you say the convict was this and was that, like it’s past tense?”

After reading the police reports and Jenkins’ file, Lam knew a trip to East Texas was needed. But since there was no legitimate reason to involve the FBI, and ass-covering being what it was, he needed Dreyfus to order his involvement.

He dropped the bombshell. “Jenkins was paroled this morning.”

“What? Dammit, Lam, find out what’s going on down there. Stink as this does it’s not our business. Be discreet, we need the local guys for help on the bigger picture.”

“So ordered so done, boss. I’ll keep it on the down-low.”

“Report back when you know something.”

Lam headed for the door.

* * *

Billy Ray rose to his feet. He wasn’t sure if he was the same person anymore. Their grieving was interrupted by someone knocking outside.

“I’ll get it.” Pastor Dahlgren made for the door.

“Thank you, Melvin,” Lela said from her place on the couch, exhaustion evident in her voice.

The spring on the screen door squeaked. Muffled voices came from the porch. Billy Ray could just make out the pastor’s voice asking for respect for the grieving family. Then a flurry of whispers rose to an audible crescendo.

Billy Ray opened the door. “What’s going on out here?”

Dahlgren stood before two strangers. A slim man in yellow shirt and brown slacks stepped forward, his white leather shoes glistened in the afternoon sun. With a well-oiled motion, the man reached into his breast pocket, retrieved a business card, and thrust it at Billy Ray.

“Name’s Ballerd—Clive Ballerd. I want to ask you questions about Ricky Jenkins,” he announced way too cheerfully.

“We don’t want what you’re selling. Please move on.”

Ballerd acted offended. “But you have to talk to me, I’m a reporter with the Gladewater News.” He pointed at his partner who carried a video camera. “Citizens have a right to know what’s going on here.”

"I don't care who you are. Go away and leave us in peace."

Billy Ray turned to leave.

The reporter grabbed Billy Ray's shoulder. "What about the drugs in the boy's system—"

Ballerd failed to complete his sentence. With lightning speed, Billy Ray snatched the offending hand, twisted his body and yanked forward and down. Ballerd somersaulted through the air and landed on his back with a thud. Straddled atop his chest, an iron grip around his throat, was the bringer of death—Billy Ray Jenkins.

The cameraman jumped back in fear. The preacher gasped.

Lela rushed to the porch. "Billy Ray, let him go!"

Ballerd gurgled. Spittle formed at the corners of his mouth.

Lela placed a gentle hand on his shoulder. She spoke softly, "You need to let the man go, Billy Ray. He won't hurt me."

Life replaced death in Billy Ray's eyes. He released his grip from the man's throat and stood up.

Ballerd fought his way to one knee and then the other. Pastor Dahlgren rushed forward to assist and they struggled to a standing position. Ballerd looked to be in a state of shock as he feebly smoothed his clothing, the cheerful demeanor now gone.

Billy Ray pulled himself together. "You're timing is terrible and so are your manners. What's this crap about Ricky?"

The reporter acted deaf to the human voice. It was the cameraman who answered. "The police confirmed the presence of drugs in your brother's system. I'm very sorry to say," the cameraman offered with all the sincerity he could muster, plus an additional step backward, "drugs were also found in the boy's college dorm room."

"That's bullsh—"

"Billy Ray, that's enough!"

Lela took control. "Mr. Ballerd, I'm sorry for your trouble. This is a bad time for us. Please come back another day."

The reporter turned and left. The cameraman apologized and fell in behind his partner. They got into a yellow Jeep Cherokee and tore out of the driveway. Billy Ray turned to find his mother and the Dahlgrens staring at him.

Lela placed a tray of iced tea on the table. Her hands trembled, but she declined help. Billy Ray had witnessed her strength countless times. This time, however, she looked near the breaking point. Losing Ricky could be the death of her.

He had to do something, but what? What could he ever do to bring Ricky back? The answer was, nothing. He'd never felt so helpless. All his mother had left was a convict son.

He hung his head in shame. "I'm sorry for overreacting with that reporter, Mama. I really am trying to change my life."

"Perhaps you should let the Lord have a try with you, son," said Pastor Dalhgren.

Billy Ray looked up, not at the pastor, but at his mother.

"I am."

The pastor cocked an eyebrow at that.

Lela sat down. "We're both under a great deal of strain right now, son. I guess we each have different ways of dealing with it."

"I promise you. I'll deal differently with matters from now on."

As though realizing for the first time that Billy Ray was there, Lela placed her drink on the table and stretched forth her arms. "Welcome home son. I've missed you terribly."

Billy Ray vaulted into his mother's arms once more. He felt an iceberg melt from around his heart. Reverend Greer had counseled him to trust people again. Erasing the scars from his mind, the pent-up anger in his heart, would take a miracle. But on his knees, before his mother, he swore an end to the warring in his soul.

Peace would begin with him.

6

Joseph Wiggins faced the wall of surveillance monitors. He tracked the progress of a stainless steel tanker truck as it turned into the entrance of the Texas Waterland Family Park. The truck motored beneath a massive bronze arch sculpted to resemble a wreath of olive and live oak, and having a five-pointed star the size of a Volkswagen hanging beneath. The structure depicted the Seal of Texas, the Lone Star State.

Texas Waterland was his brainchild, and would open for business in less than a month. The park was being advertised as the "Granddaddy of all waterslide parks." It would be the most high-tech aquatic facility of its kind, with scores of exciting slides and attractions.

The property was vast, encompassing eleven square miles. Two-thirds of the land remained undeveloped, surrounded by forest on two sides and bordered on another by the Loma Reservoir, which supplied water for the park's extensive needs. The developed portion amounted to three square miles of concrete and steel, buildings and shops, and dozens of waterslide attractions, many having no equal anywhere in the world. Marketing brochures boasted that the parking lot alone could host a NASCAR event.

Traversing the grounds posed special challenges for customers and employees alike, and was solved in several creative ways. Above ground, families could ride an open-air Monorail that circled the park. Or they could float on rubber rafts in the lazy river to access their favorite rides and attractions. If one didn't care for heights or getting wet, a scaled replica of an old steam train could ferry the masses, complete with an occasional "Great Train Robbery" for the delight of the kids. For the healthy and the brave, several miles of footpaths coursed throughout the park.

The business of operating the vast facility was conducted below ground by utilizing a system common to theme parks. Tunnels and access hatches provided quick access to all areas by vendors, employees, and security. Electric scooters and golf carts were the savior here. The level of organization and coordination was staggering, utilizing scores of closed circuit cameras, digital monitors, and even electronic traffic signals.

Finally, there existed a third level far underground completely unknown to park employees and the public. Activities here filled a different task—one ominous and foreboding.

Wiggins' phone rang.

"It's here," the guard reported.

“Send it on.” Wiggins hustled out of the secret command center beneath the Texas Waterland security building.

The tanker drove along a utility road that circumnavigated the park at the rear of the property, ending at the loading docks of the water treatment plant on the shores of the Loma Reservoir.

Wiggins joined seven other men, all Asian. They wore blue overalls zipped to the collar and protective masks and gloves, as would be expected when transferring caustic chemicals for purifying the vast amounts of water.

He marveled at his operation. When Texas Waterland opened in a month, it would be the largest park of its kind in the United States. Chemical needs for a waterslide park were enormous—purification, sanitation, substances for manufacture and repair of plastic polymers, even explosive pyrotechnic compounds for firework displays. A dozen tankers cycled chemicals and waste through the park each week. Transfer operations on the loading dock were understood by all to be a legitimate hazard. The area was cordoned off as required by law and all unauthorized personnel ushered from the premises.

Not visible beneath Wiggins’ overalls and those of his men were special impermeable hazmat suits, the kind worn by such people who work with level-4 viruses or highly toxic pharmaceuticals. In this case, a secret tank inside the container truck held a second substance, deadly if allowed to mingle with the surrounding chemicals. Also hidden from sight were five snipers with high-powered rifles positioned strategically around the park. Additional men scouted the terrain around the Loma Reservoir. Once assured the perimeter was secure, Wiggins gave the order to proceed.

And so went one crucial phase of operations in what was the largest clandestine drug lab inside the borders of the United States.

Above ground would be the delightful squeals of children and families. State inspectors had given their approval. Texas Waterland Family Park was being hailed as “the safest place in the sun for wholesome family fun.” The words had been set to music in an advertising jingle and broadcast in all major radio and television markets throughout the United States.

Below ground was a factory of nightmares. Men labored at producing a product that would revolutionize the drug market—Rapture.

Wiggins had guided the development of the drug so to satisfy the cravings of a lusty nation and reap billions of dollars in profits for his employers. Yet, he could care less about money. He had a more devious intention for Rapture.

Destroy America!

7

The funeral would be held at the small cemetery on the outskirts of Gladewater. Billy Ray had managed to save a little money over the years. Added to money from Ricky's meager student life insurance policy through the junior college, he was able to purchase a grave plot. Unfortunately, the money hadn't been enough to keep his brother from being cremated.

Lela mentioned that Ricky had been hired the previous week by the Texas Waterland Family Park in Big Sandy, and perhaps they provided life insurance for employees. It took Billy Ray three calls before reaching a manager in the business office. It turned out that there was a small policy covering employees both on and off the job. However, in the case of Ricky Jenkins, it was understood from the sheriff's report that the incident involved illegal drugs. Texas Waterland was a family corporation with an image to uphold, and extending benefits under such circumstances would be inappropriate.

Billy Ray slammed the phone down, wishing it was the man's head. He checked his anger. He'd promised peace, first to God in the loneliness of his prison cell, then to Mosey who saw something worth redeeming, and now to his mother. He was all she had left. He'd change. He'd handle things with more tact and diplomacy.

But drugs . . . . No damn way Ricky was using drugs!

They'd talked about drug and alcohol abuse on one of Ricky's visits to Eastham. There was sincerity in Ricky's voice when he'd said he hated both for what they'd done to his family.

He had never told Ricky the truth surrounding the incident with Brenda Lee. Except for the Reverend Greer, he'd never told anyone what really happened. What good was a prison confession? The State of Texas would never retry his case. The time for defending himself had come and gone. Perhaps his incarceration would serve some good by motivating Ricky to choose the right path in life.

Lela entered the living room to catch Billy Ray staring at the phone. "You okay, son?"

"I'll be fine. Let's go, Pastor Dahlgren is waiting outside."

Lela wore a black dress. Billy Ray was halfway there, having on the same black denim pants and gray pullover shirt he'd worn home from prison. Thankfully, Pastor Dahlgren had lent him a dark sport coat. The coat was tight and the sleeves too short. He'd just have to leave it unbuttoned and not lift his arms.

Ten minutes later, Pastor Dahlgren turned into the cemetery. A narrow blacktop snaked through the property and up and down several hills. They came to a stop beside an old hickory tree near the rear of the property. A fresh mound of red earth lay beside a beckoning black hole.

It irked Billy Ray that he was unable to afford a grave nearer the front of the cemetery. But upon further reflection, he decided a resting place beneath the outstretched branches of the mature tree held deeper meaning than showing one's station in life by how close to the front you were buried. The hickory tree had character so, too, had Ricky.

Several people stood beside the grave. He was told how Ricky had been well-liked. Whether because of the early hour or that summer vacation had begun for students, no young people were in attendance. More than likely, the specter of drugs had kept them away. The gathering was small.

Services began with Pastor Dahlgren asking all gathered to move in close, then led the small group in prayer. The prayer was one inspired from the heart. The pastor had known Ricky. The message reflected the goodness that had lived within the young man. Pastor Dahlgren ended the ceremony by reciting Psalm 23 from the Bible.

Oh how many dark nights in his prison cell had he whispered the encouraging words of the 23rd Psalm.

Billy Ray began mouthing the words aloud with Pastor Dahlgren. To his surprise, his mother was staring at him. Her eyes were filled with tears for Ricky's loss. And yet, miraculously, a smile appeared as she listened to him. Her look said it all—she'd also gained a son.

Services ended. The tiny crowd formed a line and paid their respects to Lela. Each in turn offered words of comfort. Some parted company immediately and headed for their cars. A few people glanced at the rugged looking man at Lela's side.

"This is my son," Lela told an elderly couple. They smiled politely and then left.

A tall man stepped forward. He had thinning gray hair and a sunburned forehead. "Billy Ray?"

"Yes—" Billy Ray looked closer at the man. "Mr. Heavenor?"

"In the flesh."

"It's been a long time since I swept your floors."

"Yup. I'd say about twenty years. Lots of dust off the prairie since then. Those floors still need sweeping if you need a job."

"I'm no teenager, but you never know, it might be sweeping floors at Heavenor Hardware & Sports is the only work I can get."

"First off, call me Gus. Mister makes me feel old. Second, you were always handy with tools and such. I'm sure we could find something more for you than sweeping floors. That's my job." Gus winked and moved off.

When Billy Ray turned back he felt his breath sucked from his lungs. He blinked to clear his sight. The vision was real.

"Hello, Billy Ray." Her voice was like warm honey.

"Rebecca? Is it really you?"

"I'm so sorry this is what you came home to." Tears welled up in Rebecca's eyes. She reached forward and hugged him.

It was like holding an angel. Rebecca Payne looked a lot like her sister. Her emerald green eyes and tanned complexion were perfect compliments to her auburn hair. She also carried the same pleasant figure as Brenda Lee had. Even her smile sparked memories so dear he was afraid to think on them for fear of losing them forever. He held their embrace longer than appropriate for two near-strangers standing beside a grave, but couldn't help it. Something deep inside ached to recapture a thing thought lost forever. He opened his eyes and released his arms. "Sorry, Rebecca. For a moment you reminded me of—"

"I know...I miss her too," she said warmly and then departed.

Rebecca had been the last person in line. Billy Ray watched her walk down the road to an awaiting patrol car. Leaning against the vehicle, arms folded across a barrel chest, eyes chambered behind mirrored sunglasses—most certainly targeted on him—stood Sheriff Roy Payne.

He met the sheriff's gaze, but failed to penetrate the black lenses. No need. He could see into the man's heart.

Hatred prowled the darkness.

8

On the ride from the cemetery, Billy Ray's mind turned from Ricky to Brenda Lee. He didn't know how much longer he could bear the truth alone. Others had suffered for his silence. He'd wanted so much to love her—to protect her. He had to accept that she was gone.

It'd taken him years to realize that the living were unable to bear the weight of the dead, not without going insane from grief and heartache. The time was now for coming clean if his pledge of peace was to bear fruit. He'd start by confessing to his mother and then tell Rebecca the truth. After all, she'd suffered as much or more by losing a sister. The problem was not knowing how to begin with either woman.

Pastor Dahlgren pulled up to Lela's house. They all said their goodbyes. Billy Ray hooked his mother's arm for the trek inside.

They stopped.

A gray sedan parked in the driveway and a man in sunglasses, slick black hair, and mocha complexion sat on the porch. His suit jacket covered a similar build as Billy Ray, minus the prison biceps. The man stood and held out his hand. "Mr. Jenkins, I presume."

Billy Ray smelled cop and ignored the offering. The man used the hand to remove his sunglasses. *Smooth move, definitely not a local product.* The last thing he wanted was a detective pumping his mother for information. Still, he reminded himself to watch his manners. "Sorry, sir, that was rude of me. What can we do for you?"

"No apologies necessary." The man turned to Lela and opened his leather ID case. "Sorry to bother you at a time like this, ma'am."

Lela inspected the badge. "FBI? What's this about, Agent Lam?"

"I'd like to ask questions about your son's death, if that's okay."

"I suppose it would be all right. Let's all have a seat."

"I'll keep this short. I know this is a terrible time for you both." Lam began by pulling a notepad from his coat pocket. He flipped through a couple of pages. "I was wondering if you could shed light on why your son was at the reservoir the morning of the accident?"

"He didn't say. I suspect it was personal," Lela answered.

"Personal? What makes you say that?"

"My son and I had a good relationship and didn't keep secrets."

"I see." Lam made a notation in his book then proceeded. "If no secrets, then what makes you think Ricky went to the reservoir for personal reasons? Why didn't he discuss it with you?"

The harder line made Billy Ray straighten in his chair.

"I guess in a manner he did tell me, just not the details. You see, Ricky was in love with a girl at the high school."

"Clarice Richards?" asked Lam.

"Yes, Clarice. The very first time Ricky introduced us, I knew. I could see it in their eyes. They were in love. The last time I saw her was the Friday before—" Lela began choking up.

"...Before the accident, Mrs. Jenkins?"

Lela pulled a tissue from her purse and wiped her eyes. "I cooked ham and sweet potato pie. Ricky told me to plan on the following week too, that he might have a special announcement."

"And you never learned what that special thing was."

"My guess is he was going to ask Clarice to marry him."

Lam asked more questions and took notes. Lela hadn't seen Ricky and Clarice the day of the accident, but was sure of one thing, they were in love. Billy Ray felt sick. How could tragedy befall two brothers, ten years apart, both looking to establish love in their lives, only to be met with death?

Lam consulted his notepad. "The police report makes no mention of Clarice at the scene of the accident. Only your son's body was found inside the truck, already dead from drowning."

"Maybe so, but I spoke with Clarice's mother this morning at the funeral. It's been a week and there's still no word from her."

Billy Ray could hold back no longer. Mostly he'd been thinking Ricky's death was all part of a repeating nightmare. Nothing about the accident made sense.

"Maybe she exited the truck in time to save herself."

Lam sized up Billy Ray, then read from his notebook. "The sheriff found no evidence of a second passenger. It stands to reason that if the Richards girl had been in the truck she would've remained there until the authorities arrived."

"What do you mean by that?"

"It's like this. When the truck was pulled from the water the doors were locked and windows rolled up, except for the driver's side, which was cracked about an inch. There's no evidence of a passenger having been in the truck at the time of the accident. Furthermore," Lam pressed, "there's no possible way a body would've been in the truck, have been thrown clear, then swam back to roll up windows and lock doors." Lam stared at Billy Ray.

Billy Ray didn't flinch. Something about the accident stunk. Maybe this fed suspected more than he was telling.

"Agent Lam, how hot do you think it is right now? Would you say about 90-degrees?"

The agent looked disarmed by the question. "Probably."

"And here we are sitting in the shade, sipping cold lemonade, and it's not even 9am."

"Thanks for the report," Lam said.

Billy Ray pointed at Lam's notebook. "Does that little book of yours tell you the time of my brother's death?"

Lam flipped a page. "Between ten and noon. Your point?"

"I was in Houston the day of Ricky's so-called accident and it was hotter that day than it is today. That old truck didn't have air conditioning. And I damn sure don't think my brother would drive around with the windows up." He looked hard at Lam.

"Good point, Mr. Jenkins. But if the drugs played any part—"

Billy Ray came out of his chair. Prison taught him not to step toward an officer. He pointed a steady finger "You better check that one out too. My brother was no doper!"

He turned to leave.

"Billy Ray, sit down!" Lela demanded. She faced Lam. "I'm sorry for my son's outburst, but I side with him. Ricky didn't use drugs."

Lam proceeded cautiously, keeping a wary eye on Billy Ray. "How can you know for sure? There could always be a first time."

"There was a first time…just not with Ricky." Lela turned to Billy Ray. "Sorry son, you have a right to know." She said to Lam, "I knew Ricky well. He hated drugs. I know this because he hated Billy Ray for what he did to Roy Payne's daughter. I'm sure you have that in your book, too."

Billy Ray sat down hard.

Lela wasn't finished. "If you're a cop worth your salt, as I sense you are, you wouldn't come down here without knowing the lay of the land. So you must know Billy Ray spent the last ten years in prison for the death of Sheriff Roy Payne's daughter. And that, Agent Lam, had everything to do with drugs."

Billy Ray felt his heart exploding. His mind raced in a thousand directions. He wanted to retreat, but to where? What would hiding do for him now—what had it ever done? Ten years in prison had only caused pain for others, even hatred. The shame from the townspeople must've been intense for Ricky and his mother, but they'd risen above it, they'd been brave. So why not him? Why had he allowed himself to be railroaded? What had he been avoiding? He never even knew of Brenda Lee's drug abuse, nor her desperation. Was it the baby forming in her womb? Was it her father's torment? Did *she* even know?

Brenda Lee never once came to him, never mentioned any of her troubles. So many questions had consumed him for a decade, but no answers. Ultimately, he'd only been thinking of himself, wondering what he'd missed that could have saved her. She was gone. He could never know the cause for her pain. He could only discover the canker within his own soul, before it killed him, too. What was it to be, hiding behind a lie or living in the light of truth?

He chose truth, and then it clicked. Ten years after, too late for Ricky, the answer appeared, bursting forth with the light of a thousand suns, exposing the cancer eating away at his soul. The enemy had a name.

Resentment!

Brenda Lee had chosen drugs over him. His love for her hadn't been enough. Her horrible death, his self-blame, and then every other hurtful thing throughout his life had cascaded all at once—the trauma unbearable. Fight or flight? Neither. He'd chosen surrender.

Resentment had its victory!

"It wasn't me, mother." Billy Ray heard himself say. "I had nothing to do with Brenda Lee's death."

Lela ignored the visitor. "What was that, son?"

Billy Ray left his chair and knelt before his mother.

"I swear to you, I had nothing to do with Brenda Lee's death. I didn't even know she was using drugs. I tried finding out where she'd gotten them, but didn't get far behind bars." His voice shook, yet he proceeded, "The sheriff testified that I brought her cocaine. I brought her a wedding ring. I took her guilt upon myself...to guard her memory...to protect her…from her father…from Roy Payne."

Lela took his hand. "I know. I've always known. Rebecca told me."

"But Ricky died believing a lie."

"It was for you to set right. I never stopped praying for the Lord to show you the way."

Mother and son wept the cleansing tears of truth.

Lam made a notation in his book, then made his way to the car. He had much to think about on the long drive back to Dallas.

9

Lam pulled into the agency's Employee of the Month space next to the front door. It'd been awarded for cracking a messy drug smuggling ring. The short walk to the building's entrance was worth gold, silver, and diamonds. Okay, not that much, but the Texas heat was bad and his time for parking in the Batmobile spot was nearly up. July heat would be even worse.

He grabbed his briefcase and headed to the office. A welcoming blast of cool air met him at the door. He stopped by the cafeteria to grab himself and Dreyfus cups of tea. Friends or not, he was still the junior man. Good thing he liked tea.

Dreyfus was busy when he arrived. He placed the cup on his boss' desk and went and sat down. Lam removed his jacket and hung it on the back of the chair. The sweat rings under his arms began evaporating immediately. He gave Dreyfus another minute before beginning their howdy-do ritual of first busting each other's chops before getting down to the skinny stuff.

At last, Lam said, "Hey, Chris, this tea you've been buying for the office tastes great."

"What tea? The lab sent that up…claimed it was wastewater."

"The lab, huh? Better than the janitor."

"Watch out. I'm friends with him too."

As usual, Dreyfus was swamped with paperwork and paying only half-attention to him. But Lam appreciated his ability to multitask, which in copland meant concentrating on police work while matching dig for dig. In their line of work, you'd go nuts without gallows humor.

Before getting started on the debriefing Lam had a name to crosscheck. He flipped open his notebook to the last notation he'd made at the Jenkins home, Rebecca.

Rebecca who?

He'd seen the name somewhere. He scrolled down the computer screen to the official report for the Jenkins drowning incident. Because the Loma Reservoir bordered the jurisdictions of Big Sandy and Gladewater, both towns had begun the initial investigations. Then somebody with a modern education and handy-dandy GPS finally determined the accident site was in an unincorporated area, thus making the incident a county matter. The case was finished and signed by the long-time Sheriff of Upshur County, Roy Payne.

Lam began there, but came up empty. Surprisingly, the report made no mention of witnesses. He checked the Gladewater police report. There was a single notation referring to an unnamed witness, for what good that did. Lastly, he checked Big Sandy. No witnesses were listed in the document. He scrolled up again, thinking he'd missed it. He was about to give up when a handwritten notation in the margin of the scanned document caught his eye. No wonder he'd skipped over it. The name was there, "Rebecca." Her statement claimed the boy and girl had driven down Main Street at approximately 7:05am. There was no last name for Rebecca. He made a note to call the filing officer.

Before logging off, Lam noticed another eyewitness mentioned at the bottom of the Big Sandy police report. The witness' name was Edward Jones. His story was strange. Jones claimed to have seen two kids enter the property leading to the Loma Reservoir in a pickup truck. Jones further claimed that "a bunch of gooks" chased after the truck, then later hearing a single gunshot, large caliber, possibly a Remington M40 Sniper rifle. The filing officer submitted a disqualifying note in the margin that read how Jones was known to get drunk and wander through the woods playing war games, and that nothing Edward Jones reported could be taken seriously due to mental illness and alcoholism.

Well that sounded likely.

He didn't quite know what to make of the report. It was interesting reading, if nothing else. He decided to interview the filing officer as well on his next visit to East Texas.

Dreyfus paused his work and turned to Lam. "Okay, Johnny, I got a minute. Learn anything new in the Piney Woods?"

"The locals discovered a new snake. They're calling it a copper-mouth-rattle-head." Lam's deadpan said you could bank on it.

"Sure, Lam, sure. Any more factual tidbits, like maybe along the lines of criminal science?"

"This Big Sandy case has a bad smell to it."

"Was it a drug matter or not?"

Lam straightened in his chair. "I'm not sure…I mean it was. Trouble is, it feels more like a suicide or even murder than anything recreational. Also, a girl was said to be in the company of our Rapture victim. What's more, the sheriff has already suspended the investigation. Things don't add up."

"Feels like...? Your report sounds like an Agatha Christie story."

"Who's that?"

"Never mind. What's the evidence?"

"No hard evidence, just a hunch." Lam tapped his nose.

Dreyfus crossed his arms. "Okay, I'll accept gut feelings for now. Read me your laundry list."

"One dead young man, coroner's report says drowning, Rapture found in the body. The sheriff also recovered Rapture from the boy's dorm closet. One eighteen-year-old female, high school valedictorian, failed to show for graduation. Now five days missing."

Dreyfus showed a concerned look.

Lam continued. "The sheriff refuses to link the two incidents, citing lack of evidence. Everyone I spoke to claim the boy and girl were in a relationship and that both were squeaky clean."

"Has a missing persons report been issued for the girl?"

Lam huffed on his fingernails and rubbed them on his chest. "As of three this afternoon, which just so happens to be the same time as my phone call to the sheriff suggesting he should think about issuing one. Only a suggestion, mind you. I certainly didn't want to tell the man how to police his beat."

"Good boy," Dreyfus said tongue-in-cheek.

"I merely called as one concerned parent to another."

"Right," Dreyfus nodded.

"And what would it hurt to go ahead and post the alert? A lot less than if he didn't and the girl turned up in a condition nobody cares to consider."

"Quite the diplomat, Agent Lam."

"I was Hillary in pants...even reminded the sheriff of this being an election year."

"What'd he say to that?" Dreyfus asked.

"He said, 'Oh.'"

"I see. Not a man to waste words."

"Nor time on a proper investigation," Lam threw in. "I hung up without leaving my name. Five minutes later the AMBER alert went out." Lam allowed himself a modest victory smile.

"And the other matter? Didn't you say the sheriff had a history with the family of the deceased?"

Lam shifted in his seat. "You said low-key. I decided not to touch that one. This Jenkins family thing is like a sizzling fuse. And at the end of that fuse is Sheriff Roy Payne."

Dreyfus had a serious look. "Strong words. All that in one visit?"

"I only scratched the surface and showed color."

"If the sheriff is purposely dragging his feet, that's a matter for Greg Abbott at the Texas State Attorney General's office, not the FBI."

"I'm with you, boss. I can't make a case for us getting involved. I handed out plenty of business cards and instructed folks to call me. Most of the good people of Big Sandy and Gladewater just looked at me as if I rode into town on the short bus. I bet half my business cards are in the trash by now."

"Half's not bad, Johnny. Imagine if your picture was on them, could've been a total loss."

"Good one. You done with me, boss?"

"What about the ex-con, did you speak to him?"

Lam rubbed the back of his neck. "I could just say he's a prick and be done with it. The guy was wound pretty tight. Although anyone of us would be a wreck if we'd just lost a loved one. So I gave him a pass on that."

"From what you said before, the man deserves a fair shake."

Lam continued. "He was rusty on social dainties. But hell, he's been locked in a cage for ten years. The man reminded me of my gunny sergeant in the Green Berets, a no-nonsense kind of guy. One you want fighting with you not against you. The more we talked and I considered his background the more I liked the guy."

"As I said before, one tough cookie."

"There's more, boss. I had a long talk with a pastor I know at Eastham prison. He told me quite a story about our ex-con. He holds this Jenkins guy in very high esteem. And I know for a fact that Moses Greer doesn't pass out attaboy ribbons."

"I've heard of Greer."

Lam normally avoided preconceptions, they could taint an investigation. He felt differently this time. "I came to believe something else today about Billy Ray Jenkins."

Dreyfus had his curiosity up. "And what's that?"

"The man never committed a crime in his life. And that goes double for his deceased brother."

The FBI agents stared at each other.

"Okay, Johnny, let's call it a day."

Lam hated mysteries. He never slept well after days ending with more questions than answers.

He was in for a long night.

10

Billy Ray had been given a month to secure employment after leaving Eastham. His time was up. The classifieds had come up empty as did several promising leads. He couldn't blame them—why take chances with an ex-con. It was time to take anything, even sweeping floors.

The Heavenor Hardware & Sports Store sat at the west end of Gladewater. Billy Ray parked his mother's car and made his way to the building. He hesitated at the door.

He hadn't passed through these doors in twenty years. Other than a new lighted sign bearing the store's name and some fresh paint, the place looked the same. It brought back memories. Gus Heavenor had been a good boss and was probably just being charitable now. Billy Ray almost turned to leave. But no, he'd promised to make a new start.

He opened the door and went back in time.

Everything was as he'd left it. Aisles ran end to end like rows of corn presenting countless choices of merchandise. Shovels and rakes stood at attention. Bags of animal feed lay neatly cross-stacked. Chemical fertilizers added their stinging odor to the air. Every tool and accessory imaginable occupied the shelves. The entire back wall was dedicated to hunting and fishing supplies. The place spoke to him.

Welcome back.

A skinny teenager sporting a green apron and toothy smile approached. "May I help you, sir?"

Billy Ray wondered if he was seeing a ghost of himself a quarter-century ago. "I'm looking for Gus Heavenor."

The boy pointed. "Out back, unloading supplies."

"Thanks...Jeff," Billy Ray read the name on the apron.

He headed for the rear of the store, passing down an aisle displaying a vast array of electrical parts: wire, fittings, connectors, switches of all shapes and sizes, and an assortment of tools for the trade. He felt at home among them all. Even the chemical smells called to him, bringing back memories of his days in the SEALs crafting and detonating explosives.

For obvious reasons, prison authorities hadn't allowed him near materials with potential to be weaponized. Washing dishes was deemed safe. Although, kitchens had chemicals that could produce a great deal of mayhem if compounded in correct amounts and subjected to certain external forces, such as heat, electricity, or microwave radiation.

If they'd only known.

Billy Ray opened the loading bay door. He was just in time to catch a backpedaling Gus Heavenor. "Let me help you with that." He grabbed the box that was about to topple the old salesman.

"Thanks, son."

"There must be plenty of strong boys around to do grunt work."

Heavenor straightened, rubbed a kink from his back, and swiped his brow with a handkerchief. "What say we skip this heat and discuss your idea over cold sodas?"

"I'd say, *hooyah.*" Billy Ray fell in behind the huffing store owner. They made their way to the upstairs office. Heavenor pointed at a stack of folding chairs. "Grab a seat." Then passed Billy Ray a frosty bottle of Cheerwine soda. "So how are you, son? How's your mother holding up?"

"We're fine, Mr. Heavenor."

"Good news, then."

Billy Ray lifted his eyes and met those of the older man. "I thought we could discuss that job you mentioned at Ricky's funeral." Life was a risk. He was ready to risk again.

"Thought you'd never ask." Gus Heavenor lifted his bottle for a toast. "Job's yours. Now let's drink on it and get down to brass tacks."

"What about—"

"Your record?"

"Yes. I'm only weeks out of prison."

"Not my worry. You're the one who let the state lock up an innocent man. Now let's bang bottles and get to business."

Billy Ray touched his bottle to Gus Heavenor's. They sealed the deal with swallows of pop.

"First off," Heavenor began. "I appreciate your politeness and all, but since we're going to be partners, you mind calling me Gus?"

Billy Ray chuckled. "Okay, Gus."

"Thank you. Now for brass tacks." Gus scooted closer. "I'm not much good for lifting, as you saw a moment ago. I'm also forgetting where I put things. Young Jeff downstairs is my nephew and only here for summer break. Mildred still runs the till and helps with bookkeeping, but she's my age and coming down with the same memory problem as me." Gus tapped the side of his head.

"I see your point."

"So how about I train you to run the store. It's about time I retire and spend my days down in the Gulf on a fishing boat. I'm looking for a partner. You interested?"

"Partners? I'm honored!" Actually, Billy Ray was blown away. "But, Brenda Lee—"

"Yeah, yeah...." Gus waved a hand. "I never bought that story neither. I've known you since you had as many pimples as young Jeff. Sure you had anger issues, but who wouldn't living with ol' Switch? Hell, son, it's a wonder you even survived."

He didn't know how to take Gus' admission. Could it be others in town held the same opinion?

"And since we're on the subject, Lela called me earlier to say you might have something to tell me about the incident."

Billy Ray tried to speak, but words caught in his throat. He fought the feeling. "Gus, I was innocent of those charges. I loved Brenda Lee Payne with all my heart. I felt I needed to protect her. I failed. When she died, everything in me died, too. Brenda Lee was gone, so were my hopes and dreams. I didn't care anymore what happened to me." He swallowed hard. "I see now how terribly selfish that was. Mom and Ricky needed me. So did my SEAL team. I had a lot to live for and lost sight of it all."

The two men stared at each other for a long moment.

Gus lifted the bottle of soda, drained the last of the liquid, and placed it in the tray behind him. He turned back to Billy Ray. "I suspected that was the truth from the very beginning. I knew you weren't guilty of hurting Brenda Lee. It was Roy Payne. It was your father, too. And it was your whole miserable upbringing. You finally shut down."

"But mom survived those years. Why not me?"

"Because she had context, you didn't. You've been sailing a course set by others. There's been too much loss and too much bloodshed. You need to know—"

"Need to know what?" Billy Ray interrupted. "Tell me."

Gus nodded. His look said brace yourself.

"It all began with Roy Payne and your mother...."

11

Joseph Karl Wiggins looked around his underground command center. He felt proud. His creation—his life's work—nearly complete. He would finally get revenge for his father's murder.

His father had been a great man who'd spent his life defending Marx's dream and Stalin's methods in their tiny South American country. Then came the fateful day when the CIA and their minions killed his father in a bloody coup.

His father's lifeless remains hung in the village square for three days. When finally taken down from the hangman's noose, the body was swollen and stinking and the eyes were gone. The picture of his father's rotting corpse swinging at the end of a rope, like the devil's pendulum, was forever seared into his young mind. Hatred branded his heart. An eternal stain blackened his soul.

Friends at the Soviet Embassy arranged travel for him and his Australian-born mother to Moscow to live with an uncle. He was forced to take his mother's maiden name. Keeping his birth name would've attracted unwanted attention. He was, however, allowed to bear the names of his father's heroes, Joseph and Karl, to honor Stalin and Marx.

His education began, his father's beliefs took root, and then came special training. He flourished. No lesson was too great if it could prepare him to destroy his father's killers. His handlers were impressed by his dark talents of espionage and murder. He became one of the KGB's greatest operatives, a bright star reflecting the best of the Soviet State, the hammer to crush and sickle to slash. And then came the fateful day when the USSR ceased to exist and his handlers in the KGB cut him loose to find his own way in from the cold.

That, he could not do. America had to be punished.

He approached his counterparts in the Democratic People's Republic of Korea. The North Koreans offered employment at twice the wages. His hiring paid immediate dividends to the DPRK. In two short years, he gathered valuable intelligence from every English-speaking country.

And then things changed.

He was ordered back to Pyongyang. The reason was simple, the nation was broke. The official state ideology of communist North Korea was *juche,* self-reliance. *Juche* was a gross understatement, however. The DPRK's cupboard was bare and always had been. North Korea had never possessed the necessary resources to stand alone from the rest of the world. The majority of financial assistance had come from the now-defunct Soviet Union. Their cousins to the north, China, had since sold out to Western-style capitalism.

The Dear Leader Kim Jung-il felt betrayed, left to wave the banner of true communism, alone against the world.

And then matters worsened.

Famines intensified. The DPRK experienced apocalyptic shortages of food. Citizens were ordered to eat but twice a day. Most were lucky to eat twice a week, and then only rice or rotting vegetables. Deaths mounted. An entire generation actually shrunk in stature from prolonged malnutrition.

Yet, from out of that desperate time came an ingenious idea—an amusement park in America.

Wiggins' handlers dismissed his idea as a cruel joke. They were too busy attending the nation's problems. Besides, why supply Americans with bread and circus while the Korean people suffered?

Wiggins knew the rains would come and that food would reappear in homes. Then it would be time to place blame where it belonged, on the United States.

So he spent the time perfecting his plan.

The rains did return. He was summoned to appear before Kim Jong-il. He presented his plan once more. Some of the Dear Leader's advisers labeled the idea unrealistic, others a fantasy.

He assured them the plan could work and bring badly needed money to the State, that their usual sources of hard cash from kidnappings and counterfeiting were both paltry and stupid.

The concept was audacious, yet simple. In fact, it was elegant. He argued anything was simple compared to famine.

The idea had come to him while watching a pirated Disney movie with the Dear Leader. The plan would be to offer decadent pleasures for the American masses at a waterslide park. All the while, hidden deep below ground, he would produce a product gluttonous Americans truly craved—escape from reality.

With assistance from one of the state's bright young chemists, he would create a super-drug based on the methamphetamine compound. The American government and her allies even ensured success of his plan and greatly multiplied potential profits by passing laws controlling precursor chemicals for methamphetamine. One chemical in particular, ephedrine, could be found growing wild in the North Korean countryside in the Ephedra plant.

With the stroke of a pen, the nations of the world turned a weed once slashed and burned into the DPRK's most valuable cash crop.

With a wave of the Dear Leader's hand, approval was granted. Rapture born. The operation was given a name, Blood Star.

Operation Blood Star would produce and distribute Rapture to the hungry American public and raise billions of dollars for the cash-starved Democratic People's Republic of Korea.

A location for the waterslide park was chosen and purchased using dummy corporations and intermediaries. Acquisitions were child's play, as nearly any local community across America salivated to swing deals to attract business. Avoiding local labor requirements had been as easy as stuffing cash in paper bags for union bosses.

Wiggins recruited and trained dozens of men. Each learned American-style English taught by "foreigners" carefully selected by the State and then kidnapped and forced into service. His men were tough and loyal, skilled in all methods of repelling undesirable forces. They were also experts at handling the highly-toxic ingredients used in making their new form of methamphetamine.

Six long years. The men were trained. His chemists had perfected Rapture. A Mexican Drug cartel was contracted to supply the drug to the American public. And the Texas Waterland Family Park was about to open. Operation Blood Star would begin reaping untold wealth for the DPRK and the Dear Leader.

At least that's what Wiggins had led Kim Jong-il to believe. He had not shared all. Nobody in Pyongyang knew of his true plan for America. Only he and his chief chemist knew. His objective for Operation Blood Star had a purpose far beyond financial gain. One final element to his grand design remained.

Rapture was about to receive a deadly attachment.

Revenge was near.

12

Billy Ray had a sudden feeling of dread. "Is Payne my father?"

"No, nothing like that," Gus replied. "Your mother and Payne dated for a week or two. Then Lela met Rodney. He and Payne were friends, and a one-two punch on the football field. People called Rodney and Roy the R and R railroad. "Your father got the nickname "Switch" after changing schools from Big Sandy to Gladewater. The move had caused quite a stir at the time. Rodney was the best running back in the state. Roy was a bruising lineman, and also an extreme bully, but more on that later."

Billy Ray listened intently.

"A scholarship was riding on their senior season. Your dad was a shoo-in. The scholarship would be his ticket out of poverty. School was about to start. Wealthy families returned from their summer vacation properties. Payne's family had property down by the Gulf. Your father had none of that and lived in a small trailer. For some reason, Rodney never told Roy about Lela. They showed up together at the homecoming dance a month into the football season. I'll never forget that night as long as I live."

Billy Ray could hardly believe his ears. This was history he'd never heard. He'd avoided his father—hated him even.

"When Rodney introduced Lela, Payne's face turned beet red. He stormed off, leaving his date standing among us. Poor girl probably still wonders what she did wrong.

"The real fireworks came when your dad drove us home. We spotted Payne on the side of the road, puking. Rodney stopped to offer help. Heated words followed. Then Dixon got out of the car and grabbed Rodney and Payne punched him in the face. I told the girls to wait in the car and went to help. Dixon released your dad and punched me. I went down like a bag of rocks. Payne and Dixon seemed to have had enough. They'd made their point. Your father and I would heal."

Billy Ray tasted acid in his mouth.

Gus went on. "And that's when it happened—"

"What?" Billy Ray leaned closer.

"Your mother got out of the car to rescue Rodney. Payne saw her coming. She shouted to leave Rodney alone, that she loved him. Payne went berserk and knocked her down. Then he had Dixon hold your father again. Payne said to your mother, 'Now we're going to crack the switch' and then stomped with all his weight on your father's knee. You could hear cartilage and ligaments snapping ten yards away. Your father fell next to your mother. Payne and Dixon got in their car and peeled away."

Billy Ray looked at his hands, they were balled into fists.

Just then the phone rang. Gus took the call. His face went slack. After a moment, he acknowledged the caller and hung up.

Billy Ray stood. "What's happened? Tell me!"

"She's going to be all right. Your mother fainted at the Dahlgren's house. They got her to the hospital right away."

Without a word, Billy Ray made to leave.

Gus put up his hands. "Billy Ray, stop! The doctor said she'll be fine. She's just exhausted and a bit dehydrated. She said to tell you she's fine and for you to finish the interview."

Billy Ray stopped, but didn't look to be in agreement.

Gus spoke firmly. "She insists, son, and so do I. She loves you and would never steer you wrong. So let's finish our chat."

He felt his pulse slow, and then sat down. "You sure she's okay?"

"Her words exactly. Cross my heart." Gus drew on his chest.

"It's just so much has happened. I worry about her."

"She's strong. She needs you to be strong, too. We all do."

"Okay, I'll hang in there. Now where were we?"

"Pretty much at the end...your father didn't get the scholarship. Your parents married after high school. I can tell you Rodney was good to your mother at first. Later...well, later alcohol took its toll. Something in him died back then. Not too long after, it took his love for your mother along with it.

"By the end—the end you know anyway—the only difference between your father and Roy Payne were their methods. Your father's was physical abuse. Roy Payne, on the other hand, had a badge to legitimize physical means and shield him from prosecution. Psychological abuse is Payne's weapon of choice. He's the devil's expert at emotional manipulation."

"Why didn't mother tell me any of this?"

"My guess is she wanted to spare you kids the bad history. She's the type to fix things when they're broke not just talk about it. Plus, I'm guessing that living with Rodney those bunch of years must've wore her down. In the end, nothing was bound to work. 'The children are punished for the sins of their fathers,' if I remember my scriptures correctly."

"Why wasn't Payne arrested for what he did to my dad?"

"Rodney's family brought charges. But Payne's family had connections and the matter was buried. Then Payne joined law enforcement where he's been protected ever since."

"Payne doesn't deserve to be dogcatcher!"

"Exactly. And now he's up for reelection to his ninth term as Sheriff."

"Not if I can help it," Billy Ray said.

Gus threw up his hands. "Hold on. Payne's a dangerous man. He's got the law on his side and plenty of patrons. And there's an evil streak in him. He won't rest until your head's on a platter!"

Billy Ray's shoulders sagged. He felt drained by Gus' story. Or was it something else? He'd hated his father. The story of his father described his own past. He saw himself in Rodney Jenkins. Indeed, the sins of his father—the wretched winds of resentment—had come to fill his own sails.

"What about Payne? Did he ever confront my parents again?"

"I don't know. Your folks moved over to Big Sandy around the time you were born. I lost track of them. I bought the store and spent the next bunch of years building up the business."

Both men remained silent for quite some time.

Gus offered another soda. It was turned down.

"Where does this leave us?" asked Billy Ray.

"I hope it leaves you with a warning, that Payne's a dangerous man."

"I caught that." Billy Ray massaged ghost pains in his jaw. "I mean the job?"

Gus got a twinkle in his eye. "With you minding the store and me fishing. Is it a deal?"

Billy Ray reached his hand across the table. "Deal."

"I'll be out of town tomorrow. How about we start tool school the day after, say about 7am?"

"How about noon? I have to register with my parole officer. He'll sure be glad to hear I have a job."

"Okay, noon it is. See you then."

The interview ended.

Billy Ray left with more than he ever dreamed possible. Not only had he gained employment, he now had missing pieces of his life. He'd come away with truth. Then like the finale of a hurricane, the tempest of hatred toward his father played out, leaving behind the debris of disappointment. He didn't know if he'd ever forgive his father for the abuse. He'd certainly try, but at least he understood matters more clearly. Resentment had spawned terrible bitterness in his father's life, and then bitterness consumed Rodney Jenkins until nothing human remained.

Billy Ray reached the door of Heavenor's Hardware & Sports. Time had caught up with him.

He crossed himself and walked out into the light of a new day. Never had he felt so determined to go forward.

To live at peace.

13

Billy Ray couldn't remember the last time he felt so light on his feet. Things were looking up. Flowers were his next priority. He stopped by the Piggly Wiggly grocery store to see what they had in stock. He wasn't sure which kind were appropriate. He was looking over the display when he felt a tap on his shoulder.

For the second time in a week, Billy Ray turned to see heaven staring him in the face.

"Howdy." Rebecca smiled.

"Hello." Billy Ray noticed the name tag. "You work here?"

"Actually, I rolled a bagboy for his apron. It gets me the employee discount."

"What a girl won't do for a sale!" He laughed, so did Rebecca. "Wait—a bagboy named Rebecca? East Texas has changed."

They laughed all the harder and embraced in a warm hug.

"It sure is good to see you smiling, Billy Ray."

"It feels good. Guess I've been storing it up."

Rebecca looked down. "I know what you mean."

"How long have you worked here?"

"Since my senior year of high school, about seven years. I'm the assistant manager now."

"Impressive."

"Maybe, but I graduated from the University of Texas in Tyler last week. I earned a master's degree. I'll be heading off to begin my career soon."

"Wow, congratulations!" He raised a hand for a high-five. Rebecca slapped it. "That's really awesome. A masters in what?"

"Psychology."

"Oh...well then, I'd better stop slobbering all down the front of me. It could give the wrong impression."

"Too late, cowboy. You're certifiable."

"I graduated last week too. But it was just an associate degree."

"Congrats back at you!" Rebecca offered her own high-five.

"So how was your graduation party?" Billy Ray asked.

"Actually, I decided against an open house." Rebecca's mood dipped and her next words reflected it. "I don't have many friends. With Mom and Brenda Lee gone, and just my father, I wasn't really up to a party."

Billy Ray's look said he understood.

"How about you—" Rebecca stopped, embarrassed.

Billy Ray covered for her. "Believe it or not, I did celebrate. The warden congratulated me personally. The two of us had coffee and doughnuts in his office and discussed my future."

Rebecca showed her appreciation by flashing a wide smile. "Well now, that's more than I did."

"Then how about we toast each other's accomplishments? We could go out for ice cream or something."

"I'd love to. How about the day after tomorrow? I'll have some time off before the long Independence Day weekend."

"Dang. I have to go to Tyler that morning."

Rebecca thought for a moment. "I have books to return to the U.T. library. What if we combined our trips? We could stop for a treat on the way back."

"Works for me," Billy Ray said.

"Me, too."

Somewhere in town a police siren blared. The harsh noise pulled them back to reality.

"Rebecca, what about your father?"

She had the same concern. She explained about making a break with her father two years back and how he'd demanded she live at home, but refused and moved into the college dorms.

Billy Ray could tell there was more to the story. "Is everything okay with the two of you?"

"Let's just say there was more to my leaving than merely spreading my wings."

"How so?" After what Gus Heavenor told him, he allowed himself to pry deeper. He and Rebecca weren't strangers, but ten years was a long time. She'd been in pigtails and braces back then. The person who stood before him now was a beautiful woman.

She hesitated, apparently deciding how far to discuss the matter, then looked in both directions, like somebody needing to share a secret. He'd seen the look before—in the mirror.

"My studies in psychology taught me a lot about myself," She began. "The more I learned, the more dark feelings and memories awakened."

"Your mom and Brenda Lee?"

"And what drove them to their graves—my father. He's a sick man, I'm convinced of it. Even his hatred for you and Ricky is weird, presenting more like jealousy."

Quite a first conversation, but Billy Ray was thankful to be having it. Based on Gus' story, she was hitting center mark. He had a window into the man's hatred now. But that didn't change the fact that Roy Payne was a problem best avoided.

"Maybe we should forget the ice cream. I don't want to cause trouble for you, Rebecca."

"We both know he'd never approve. But I'm twenty-five years old and live on my own. I don't need his approval."

"But—"

"I know," she interjected. "We don't need trouble for you, either."

He could almost scream. Payne was always perched on the edge of his happiness, ready to lower a boot and squash it like a bug. He didn't want trouble either. And yet he couldn't live life like this, nor could Rebecca.

"How about we ask somebody to ride along with us?"

"Like I said, I don't have many friends. Maybe they're afraid to be near me. Wait…my roommate is planning to take the bus to Tyler later this week. She could just ride with us."

"Excellent. Is seven to early? My meeting begins at eight."

"Seven works for me. And Shandi's an early riser."

"Okay. Where do I pick you up?"

She pointed to a building across the street. "We live above the bookstore. Just pull up and toot the horn."

"Great. See you then." He began walking off.

"Billy Ray, aren't you forgetting something?"

"Oh, yeah." He turned back to the flowers.

"She'd like the yellow ones."

"How do you know who they're for?"

"Word gets around pretty quick."

"Seems we're living in a fishbowl. You sure my mother likes yellow?"

"Positive. Ricky always bought her yellow flowers. He said it was her favorite color."

"Yellow it is then. See you day after tomorrow."

Billy Ray paid for a bouquet of roses and left.

14

His mother loved the flowers. She put them on the bedside table alongside the others. After catching her up on his interview with Gus, Billy Ray gave her a kiss and excused himself at the request of the nurse. He spoke with the doctor out in the hallway, who assured him Lela would be fine in a couple days after some much-needed rest. He thanked the man and left.

His plan now was to visit the parents of Clarice Richards and offer whatever encouragement he could. He'd met them only briefly at Ricky's funeral. Their faces had showed worry, but they'd done their best to comfort Lela even though their daughter hadn't yet come home or phoned. Three weeks had passed since her disappearance. By now the Richards had to be sick with worry. Sometimes, the *not knowing* was the worst.

Billy Ray stood on the porch of the Richard's home. It was almost evening time. He didn't know what the father's line of work was, or if Mrs. Richards had an outside job or was a homemaker.

His questions were answered when the front door opened and Mrs. Richards appeared. She had salt and pepper hair cut short, wore a beige blouse and tan slacks, and was wrapped in a pink flowered apron. She stood at the door wiping her hands on a kitchen towel and staring expectantly at him.

"Hello, Mr. Jenkins," she said after a moment.

"Hello, Mrs. Richards."

"What brings you by? Have you heard from Clarice?"

Billy Ray's heart sank. "No, I haven't. I'm sorry."

Mrs. Richards deflated. "Oh. How can I help you, then?"

"I wanted to see if I could be of any help to you, like with chores or something. I can fix things, anything you need."

"That's very kind of you. My husband is quite handy, as you can probably tell. He takes a lot of pride in the house and yard."

Billy Ray followed her look. Both yard and house were immaculate. The white paint on the picket fence was fresh. "Well, if you need anything at all, even just to talk, call and I'll be there." He began to leave. He reminded himself the Richards were grieving and didn't want to upset them.

"Mr. Jenkins?"

Billy Ray turned around. "Yes, ma'am?"

"How about a glass of iced tea? We could sit on the porch and talk, if you're not in a hurry." She showed a spark of hope.

"It'd be my pleasure, ma'am." He sat on the porch swing.

Mrs. Richards returned with glasses of tea and some fresh-baked cookies. "I'm sorry, but I've already sweetened the tea with a bit of honey. I hope you don't mind?"

"Not at all. I haven't tasted honey in...." He let the point drop.

"Don't worry, Mr. Jenkins. I'm not going to judge you. In fact, if you're like your brother Ricky, you'll always be welcome here."

"Thanks, ma'am. There couldn't be a better compliment."

"We thought the world of Ricky."

They sipped tea and nibbled on cookies, content with their thoughts and the view of the cheerful porch and manicured yard. Certainly this was a home where there was love.

Mrs. Richards broke the silence. "This is where they would sit." She pushed her weight against the swing until they were in gentle motion. "They were such good kids. I'd say about the best this town ever had."

Billy Ray let her do the talking. God knew how he felt about Ricky, and at least had the benefit of knowing where his brother was.

"Clarice was our...she...she was our only child." Tears welled up in Mrs. Richards' eyes.

"I'm so sorry."

She grabbed another tissue.

The last thing he wanted was to upset this dear lady, but he had to ask. "What do you think happened to Clarice?"

Mrs. Richards was too choked up to speak. She shook her head from side to side.

"I'm confused. May I ask you some questions?"

She nodded. A tear rolled down her cheek.

"Okay. Please stop me if I'm upsetting you. For starters, did you know Ricky and Clarice were in love?"

"Y–yes, I did." She pulled another tissue from the apron pocket for her eyes and took another swallow of the cold tea. She recovered. "Clarice thought the world of Ricky. We all did."

"My mother says the same thing. Do you think Clarice's disappearance had anything to do with Ricky?"

"How so?"

He was about to step on thin ice. "Maybe Clarice was pregnant and wanted to run away from everyone?"

"That's not possible. Clarice had made a promise to wait until her high school graduation before having sexual relations."

Billy Ray blushed at the woman's forthrightness.

"It was Clarice's idea. We promised that any baby of hers would be a baby of ours, no matter the circumstances."

"We could all learn from those kids," was all he could say.

"I trusted her and she trusted me." Tears returned. "She was more than my daughter, she was my friend." Mrs. Richards wept.

Billy Ray put an arm around her shoulders. After a minute she straightened, tried dabbing her eyes with an already-sopped tissue, then gave up and wiped her tears on a corner of her apron.

"Thank you, Mr. Jenkins."

"Please, call me Billy Ray."

"And you can call me Dolores—Dee to my friends."

"Thanks, Dee."

"It's pretty selfish of me to go off like that. I'm sure your family is broken up over Ricky's death."

"No apologies necessary. Burying my little brother was the hardest thing I've ever done in my life." Billy Ray's mind drifted to a scene in his past, another funeral, one he was not allowed to attend on account of his being handcuffed to a hospital bed, recovering from Sheriff Payne's beating. But no, he admitted, Ricky's death was harder. "I'm the one who should apologize. At least I know where Ricky is."

"I can't stand not knowing where my baby is."

"If you're right, and I believe you are, Clarice wouldn't feel any reason to run away."

The smell of baking bread filled the air.

Dee stood, smoothed the wrinkles from her apron, and wiped her damp cheeks with the back of her hand. "Soon after George and I married, Grandma Richards told me her secret to baking. 'If you can smell it, you should check it.' So..." she made a valiant attempt at cheer, "I better go check the oven."

"Before you go. Can you think of any reason why Ricky went to the Loma Reservoir the day he died?"

"Yes, I can. He was with Clarice."

Billy Ray shot up from the swing. "You're the second person who's told that to me." He remembered Jonesy's words. "But I thought Sheriff Payne determined there was no trace of Clarice having been with Ricky when he died."

"The sheriff thinks so. But I know Clarice left with Ricky."

"In the morning, about seven o'clock?"

"That's about right. George probably knows exactly, he keeps the alarm clock on his side of the bed."

"Did you tell the police?"

"I told the sheriff." Dee paused, determining how best to proceed. "Billy Ray, I may be a trusting mother, but I'm no fool, especially when it comes to love." She pointed at the road. "Ricky came coasting down that hill on graduation day with the motor off and the passenger door ajar."

Billy Ray looked at the road and tried imagining the scene.

"I could see Ricky's shamed face as I watched from behind my bedroom curtains. I'm sure Ricky thought George would shoot him, but he wouldn't have. Clarice had kept her promise. In fact, George always preached to his daughter that when her time came, to make it safe and make it special."

Billy Ray felt his heart exploding. "Anything else?"

"Yes. I believe Clarice and Ricky were about to decide on marriage, or already had. I'm certain they were heading off to make love." Dee opened the screen door.

"A final question, Dee?"

"Anything if it can help find my daughter."

"Were the windows of truck rolled up?"

Dee thought about it. "Clarice's window was rolled partly down. My last vision of her was the morning sun shining on her golden hair as they coasted away." Dee left for the kitchen.

Billy Ray made his way to the car deep in thought. Nothing made sense about Ricky's death and Clarice's disappearance. Payne must've missed something. Or was it possible his hatred wouldn't allow for digging deeper? He knew firsthand how hate could trump truth. It was clear that if he wanted to find out what really happened to Ricky, he'd have to discover it for himself.

He pulled away from the white picket fence, made a U-turn, and drove down the same hill Ricky had on that terrible day.

15

US ROUTE 80
NEAR BIG SANDY, TX

Cars raced past, illuminating Edward Jones.

Blinding white light….

Blackness....

The stars returned to light his way.

He didn't feel so wobbly. He'd left the Frontier Inn early. It was time for answers. It'd been three weeks since telling that cop what he knew about those kids getting killed. Nothing. Nothing on the news, and no word from the police. The officer had laughed at him. But he wasn't drunk and his meds hadn't taken effect yet. He knew damn well those Koreans did it. He'd been watching them for months, listening to their conversations, going into the field, gathering intelligence while appearing to be a delusional drunk. No way the gooks were gonna invade his town and start knocking off his people.

"No way!" Jonesy yelled into the night. If only his men were here. They'd go in there and clean out the whole stinking lot. Jonesy's eyes teared up at the thought of his men.

They were gone—his friends were gone. He'd taken a bullet in the leg the first day. Damn his luck! By the second night, most of his company had been killed. He'd ordered the bodies stripped of clothing and equipment for those still alive. He'd then made the corpsman carry him up and down the line on a stretcher so he could encourage his boys to fight on.

It was so cold. It hurt to fight. The bodies were frozen, stacked anywhere space allowed. There'd been no time to treat the dead with any greater honor.

The gooks were everywhere!

Jonesy felt wobbly again…the injury.

Spit on it. Keep fighting!

A vehicle passed, illuminating Jonesy walking along US Route 80. It made a U-turn on the deserted highway. The car neared, then slowed to a crawl. The high beams shined into Jonesy's eyes. A window lowered and a voice said, "It's him."

The bodies. His friends. The cold!

He'd tried to save as many as he could, he'd tried real hard. He'd been ordered to abandon their position, but refused that order. The gooks would have a turkey shoot on the 8,000 Marines behind him. So he'd ordered his company to stand and fight. It was a suicide order and every man knew it. When the battle ended six days later, only he and a few others had survived. Most of his 220 men were dead. He'd ordered his brave young Marines to fight to the death and they had.

The leg still gave him fits. It caused him to wobble when he walked. His men hadn't been so lucky.

Luck?

Huck-phew…he spat on the ground. He didn't feel so lucky. Hell, most of his men were kids—just like those teenagers the gooks killed at the reservoir!

That light again...so bright, almost blinding.

Was this the end? He'd always heard you'd see a light. Was God calling him home to his men?

Not men…just kids!

"They were just kids!" Jonesy shouted at the light.

A voice from inside the light said, "See, I told you the old man knows about those kids!"

How odd. God's voice sounded familiar.

"Harper?"

The vehicle shot forward and slammed into Jonesy. His body flew into the high grass between the road and the railroad tracks.

Blinding white light….

Blackness….

The stars were gone.

16

Between worrying about his mother and nagging thoughts about Ricky's death, sleep became impossible. Billy Ray got up, dressed, and grabbed a bite from the kitchen. He read his Bible until it was time to go visit his mother.

His plan for after the hospital would be to locate Jonesy. The old drunk knew something, he was sure of it now. Jonesy's story made more sense after what Dee had told him. There were now two witnesses who'd seen Ricky and Clarice together.

Billy Ray was pleased to find his mother asleep. God knew she needed the rest. He decided not to wake her, and instead turned his sights to finding Jonesy. He didn't have a first name or an address. Perhaps the old man had used this very same hospital in the past.

He left his mother's room and went to the business office to make an inquiry. He tried describing Jonesy to the young administrative assistant, but got nowhere. He turned to leave and was stopped by an older woman who'd overheard the name Jones and Billy Ray's description. The sign above her desk read Accounts Manager.

"You must be talking about Edward Jones," she said.

"About ninety years old, medium height, wears an old USMC cap. He may have alcohol related issues."

"I can't comment on the condition of our patients. But if you merely wish to visit Mr. Jones to check on his wellbeing, I guess I can provide you with an address. I'm not sure if he still resides there, however. He hasn't been admitted to this hospital for several years to my knowledge."

"Any help would be much appreciated."

"Well, then," she scribbled an address on a yellow post-it and handed it across the desk. "Here you go. Please tell Mr. Jones hello from us. He was quite the colorful character, as I recall."

"Thank you, ma'am." Billy Ray took his leave.

On the way to Edward Jones' home address, he paid a visit to the Frontier Inn on the chance Jonesy would be there. The place was closed. Posted hours indicated the tavern should be open. A hand-written note on the window apologized for the inconvenience and to come again later. He sat in the car looking around the area. Jonesy was nowhere in sight. He put the car in gear and drove off.

Jonesy's address matched a nice ranch-style house. There were mature shrubs and trees surrounding a large porch. His knock was rewarded by the twinkling eyes and smiling face of a tiny white-haired lady. She opened the door merely wide enough to peer out.

"Are you the pizza guy?" she said.

Billy Ray smiled. The woman had to be pushing the century mark in years, but still retained a youthful charm.

"No. I'm not the pizza guy. I'm looking for Edward Jones."

"He likes pizza too. We especially enjoy pepperoni with cheese."

"I'll try to remember that." He repeated the request. "Does Edward Jones live here?"

He heard a commotion from behind the door. A voice called out, "Who's at the door, Wilhelmine?"

"It's not the pizza man," Wilhelmine said.

The door opened fully and a woman about Billy Ray's age stood in the opening. "May I help you?"

She was medium height and had lovely brown hair with wide curls resting on soft shoulders. Her arching brows and full lips smiled in perfect harmony. A wine-colored blouse complemented olive skin, white slacks accented a nice figure.

Billy Ray forced his eyes forward. What was wrong with him, anyway? Was he going to gawk at every woman he saw?

"I was hoping to find Edward Jones. I was told he lives here."

"And who might you be?"

He blushed. "My name's Billy Ray Jenkins. I'm sort of friend of Mr. Jones. I was hoping to speak with him."

The lady's expressive eyes took on a look of worry. "I'm sorry, but he isn't here right now."

"Do you know when he'll be back?"

The pretty lady turned to Wilhelmine. "Dear, would you go check the oven?"

The elderly woman smiled up at the both of them. "Sure, darling. Wouldn't want the meat to burn, now would we?" She gave them an exaggerated wink, and walked off.

"Did she just wink at us?" Billy Ray thought out loud.

Embarrassment came over the lovely lady's face. She said, "Wilhelmine Van Luven, my adopted aunt. She loves to play the matchmaker. My name's Eva." She offered a hand.

The hand was warm and soft to the touch.

Worry returned to her face. "I'm concerned about Uncle Edward."

Now Billy Ray was concerned, too. "Is he okay?"

"I'm not sure. He didn't come home last night." Eva bit her lip.

"Has he stayed out all night before?"

"A few times, especially these past several months."

"What about the police, did you report it?"

"They no longer do anything. So I stopped calling."

Billy Ray offered to drive them around to search for Jonesy.

Eva shrugged her shoulders. "I wouldn't even know where to begin. If you're a friend, then you also know he drinks."

"Yes. He's had a reputation around town since I was a kid."

Eva looked at Billy Ray in a curious manner. "I'm not sure I've seen you around here before."

"Probably not, but I am from these parts. I was born over in Big Sandy. I haven't been around for a long time."

"Billy Ray Jenkins—" At once she caught herself. Her brown eyes warmed with compassion. "I'm so sorry…."

"Thank you, Eva."

"I didn't know Ricky personally, but I knew of him through common friends. He was good people."

"Thank you again. When Mr. Jones returns, could you please have him call this number? I want to ask him some questions about my brother. He told me a story the day of the accident about seeing Ricky and Clarice Richards together." He left off the seedier details of Jonesy's testimony.

"I remember my Uncle being upset. He kept mentioning something about 'them kids.' I thought he was talking about his war years again."

"So Edward Jones is your uncle?"

"Great Uncle, actually."

"I see. I've always liked him. And Wilhelmine is real sweet."

"I think the world of those two. I moved in with them a few years back to help out. I enjoyed it so much I stayed on."

Billy Ray wished to know more, but felt it inappropriate to ask. He brought his mind back to business and handed Eva his number.

He thanked her and left.

17

This time the Frontier Inn was open. Harper busied himself pulling chairs from the tables and placing them in position for the night's business. Billy Ray was the first patron to arrive. Harper didn't notice.

Billy Ray broke the silence. "Hey there."

Harper dropped a chair. "Dang, mister! You trying to sneak up on me?" He made the recognition. "Oh, it's you."

"Didn't mean to spook you."

"No problem." Harper stopped his chore and faced Billy Ray. "Sorry about the other day, dropping a bombshell on you like that. Didn't know you were related to the boy who died."

"Can't hold that against you, we'd never met."

Harper grunted and resumed his chore.

Harper acted oddly. He wasn't so easygoing as when they'd first met. Billy Ray chalked it up to embarrassment about Ricky.

"So can a guy get a cold one?"

"Take a seat at the bar. I'll be with you in a minute."

Billy Ray chose the same stool as the first time.

Harper finished with the chairs and returned behind the bar. He sat a frosted glass and, of all things, a bottle of Guinness beer.

"Hey, you remembered."

"Got to thinking tourists might want more than just the local stuff. There's a case in the cooler. If I'm wrong, you better help drink it."

Billy Ray gave a laugh. "I'll do that."

Harper continued his chores and appeared less uptight.

Billy Ray sipped his beer and waited. Ten minutes went by. "Say, where's Jonesy? I kind of expected him to be here."

Harper rediscovered his sour mood. "You mean Ol' Four Eyes? How would I know? Probably sleeping it off somewhere."

"Maybe so. When did you see him last?"

Harper grabbed a towel and began wiping an already clean bar. "You're jokin', right?"

"No," Billy Ray said bluntly.

"Oh. Well then, last night at closing time. In case you haven't heard, Jonesy's the first in and the last out."

"That's what I was counting on. I'm surprised he's not here. With you opening late, I figured Jonesy to be camping on your doorstep."

"Well, he wasn't. Maybe he went to another bar."

"Perhaps. This is the first place I tried."

"What you need that old drunk for?" Harper's face didn't hide much, the agitation was telling.

He was about to answer Harper's question when the tavern door swung open. Two men entered. One was short and stocky, the other tall with broad shoulders. The taller man looked to be forty-something or even older, it was hard to tell. He had an athletic build, wore a black pocket tee under a safari vest and khaki pants, and combed his blond hair stylishly to the side. The short and stocky man wore the same outfit as his partner. His most striking feature were narrow eyes. The man was Asian. They took a seat at the end of the bar.

Billy Ray turned back to ask Harper another question and stopped. Harper was frozen in place, eyes wide, a thin layer of sweat beading on his forehead.

"Harper, you okay?"

The mercurial bartender recovered. "Uh…oh yeah, I'm fine."

"As I was saying, when did you see Jonesy last? I want to ask him some questions about my brother."

Harper stared at the new customers. The man was flustered.

"Excuse me," a voice said.

Billy Ray turned around. The blond man stood before him.

"You look familiar. Have we met before?"

Billy Ray studied the man's face. "Not that I can recall."

"Well then, name's Joseph Wiggins," He said and thrust out a hand.

Billy Ray sized him up. There was strength about the man, and a good deal of refinement. The guy reminded him of a military officer. He took the offered hand. "Billy Ray Jenkins."

For a split second, he caught a flash of recognition in Wiggins' eyes, but assumed it was related it to Ricky's death. If that was the case, the man showed enough tact not to mention it. He peeked back at Harper. The man was petrified, towel dangling limp at his side. He could've spilled beer on the bar and it would've laid there until it evaporated.

Something was wrong.

"A pleasure to meet you, Mr. Jenkins."

Billy Ray faced Wiggins. "Same to you. By the way, I like your outfit. What do you do, if you don't mind my asking?"

"You mean professionally?"

"Yes. You a park ranger or something?"

"I'd have to say, 'or something.' My line of work is security."

"I see," Billy Ray said. Wiggins offered no further details.

The Asian man moved in beside them. "My associate and I were about to have a drink. Care to join us?" asked Wiggins.

First off, Billy Ray didn't drink with strangers. And second, something wasn't right. He thought he detected a foreign accent beneath the man's southern drawl. He couldn't put his finger on it. Something deep down sounded warning bells, like times in the jungle when the enemy was near or had booby-trapped an area. On one occasion the enemy hadn't even been human, but a jaguar. His field guide stated Jaguars were stalk-and-ambush predators, opportunistic in prey selection. His instincts had saved his life on that occasion as he'd rolled onto his back and pointed his bayonet just as the beast pounced, impaling itself, its wet dripping fangs mere inches from his throat.

Wiggins gave him the same impression.

Billy Ray calmed his inner voice. He had to find Jonesy. Maybe he'd gone to another tavern after all. If that were the case, it'd be best to catch the old man before the alcohol did.

"Appreciate the offer, but I need to cast off."

"Another time, perhaps." Wiggins again offered his hand.

This time the man's grip was more firm and suggested a great reserve of strength. He sensed Wiggins taking his measure.

He paid for his drink and left.

Two black Ford Broncos were parked next to his mother's car. He memorized the license plates and then pulled away from the Frontier Inn to go check the other taverns in town. There were three. Jonesy wasn't at any of them. The bartenders each reported never having seen Jonesy at their establishments. He wondered where Jonesy could be.

Billy Ray decided to call it a day. He looked forward to the next morning, seven o'clock would come early.

Not soon enough to see Rebecca again.

18

The drive to Tyler was a quiet one. After Rebecca's introductions and some initial chatter between Billy Ray and Shandi they each busied themselves for the remainder of the trip. Shandi wrote in a journal. Rebecca skimmed through textbooks to erase notes before returning them to the campus library. Billy Ray was content to enjoy the passing scenery of farms and ranches and rolling hills.

Upon arriving in Tyler, the Rose City of Texas, Billy Ray delivered the ladies to their respective destinations. He then drove to the address given him upon departure from Eastham prison. It turned out to be a small office suite in a strip mall. The name on the door read Cliff Michaels, CSO. The man was a Community Supervision Officer.

He arrived ten minutes early, took a seat next to the door, and waited. There was no receptionist just a single office with the door closed and a sign that read 'Meeting in Progress.'

He picked up a local newspaper. The first section was like most dailies, full of tragedy, as if good news was foreign to planet Earth. He skipped to the entertainment section on hopes of finding a fun activity he and Rebecca might enjoy together. The back page caught his eye. An advertisement touted the upcoming opening of the Texas Waterland Family Park. There were colorful maps of the park, descriptions of rides and events, and a photo showcasing the park's grand entrance, a silver star suspended from an immense brass arch. A group of men stood beneath, arms outstretched as if to say, "Y'all come in."

He had mixed feelings about this new amusement park after the way they'd treated Ricky's death. One of the men in the photo caught his attention. There was a head of blond hair, combed stylishly to the side. The man was several inches taller than the others in the photo. He wore an outfit resembling that of an African game warden. Billy Ray knew this man. It was the very same person he'd met at the Frontier Inn, Joseph Wiggins.

Something about Wiggins told Billy Ray to watch himself. There was a level of refinement to the man. And yet, Wiggins' manner suggested something else, something like a holstered gun or grenade with pin still intact—something potentially lethal.

His thoughts were interrupted when the CSO's door opened and a spirited conversation continued into the small lobby.

"Listen, Jack, you can do it the easy way or the hard way," said the man Billy Ray assumed to be Cliff Michaels. "It's your choice!"

"Like, it's your way or the highway?" Jack shot back.

"You got that straight. Do I need to draw you a map? It'll lead you back to the pen. Is that what you want, Jack?"

"No, Cliff."

"Then you'd better march your butt back to that employer and beg for your job back. Take a pay cut if you have to."

"But—"

"No buts! You know the terms of your parole require you to get a job and to keep the damn thing. You forfeited the luxury of cherry-pickin' employers when you broke the law. Do I make myself clear?"

Jack merely nodded his answer.

"Okay, then. I'll see you back here next week. Same time, same place, but you'd better be tuned to a different channel."

Jack let the door shut hard behind him.

Billy Ray stood at attention.

The CSO looked Billy Ray over for a moment. A curious look came over his face. "At ease, soldier."

"Actually, it's sailor."

"You gonna argue with me, too?"

"No, sir," Billy Ray said and relaxed some.

Michaels smiled. "I take it I've been assigned as your parole monitor."

"Jenkins, Billy Ray," he replied in military fashion.

The CSO was tall and slim, and wore gold-rimmed eyeglasses. He displayed a natural grin, except when angry, as 'Jack' had just discovered.

"Step into my office, Mr. Jenkins."

Billy Ray followed the man into a room no larger than a closet with every available inch occupied with bulging cardboard file boxes. He allowed Michaels to seat himself first and then followed in turn.

"I've been reading your file, Mr. Jenkins. Let me begin by extending my sympathy and prayers to you and your family for the loss of your brother."

"Thank you, sir."

"How you holding up?"

"The sun shines a little brighter each day, Mr. Michaels."

"Good to hear. It may take some time—it may take forever. My baby sister was murdered in the parking lot of an all-teen club twenty years ago. Not a day goes by that I don't miss her smiling face in this world." Michaels probed Billy Ray with a long look.

"Yes, sir. It's becoming the same for me, I reckon."

"I'll never forget my sister. But the living have a job to do. We must carry on with building the better world our loved ones would've wanted."

"Thank you, Mr. Michaels, I appreciate your insight. You've been there and know the pain."

"You're welcome...now on to business." Michaels reached down, pulled a file from a cardboard box, and sat it on the table between them. The manila folder had Billy Ray's name on the tab. Michaels arranged the materials and said, "Before we begin, Reverend Greer asked me to pass a message on to you."

Billy Ray felt his heart jump. "Mosey?"

"Moses Greer, the crusader of human redemption, and my former staff sergeant. I was a Major in the Marine Corps."

"I didn't know Mosey was a Marine. I thought he'd always been a minister."

Michaels nodded. "Actually, you'd be right on target. When time came for me to bump Mosey to E-7, he came to me in private asking to be transferred to the Chaplain Corps instead. To make a long story short, there were no openings for chaplains. So I watched as Mosey finished his enlistment and headed home to study in the seminary. Looking back on it, I'm proud of his accomplishments. He's a Christian soldier and a social warrior."

"Mosey helped me find my way back," Billy Ray professed. "What's his message?"

"It's a Bible verse. He said you'd catch the meaning. James 1:27."

Billy Ray smiled. "Tell Mosey I'm working on it."

"I'll do that the next time I hear from him. Now, is this going to be a long meeting or a short one?"

"Sir?"

"Do you have a job yet?"

"I was offered a partnership in the Heavenor Hardware & Sports store in Gladewater, starting just as soon as I get back to town."

"That's good news, Mr. Jenkins." Michaels made a notation in Billy Ray's file and then snapped it shut. "Meeting over."

Billy Ray shook hands with Michaels and let himself out. He appreciated being treated with professional respect, even as a parolee, no beating around the bush, just plain speaking.

He drove back to the campus to pick up the ladies. To stay cool, he let the motor run and the air conditioner perform its magic. He'd experienced extreme temperatures during his time in the SEALs, some of the worst heat and humidity imaginable. Even so, he'd still rather be hot than cold.

He'd never drawn a cold-weather assignment prior to his discharge. Word was that Antarctica was shaping up to be the new battle ground.

He spotted Rebecca rounding a corner of the library building. He watched her glide toward him—the grace in her movements and alluring sway of her hips stirring long-forgotten feelings. As a warfighter, he knew that pain indicated you were still alive. So what could be made of desire?

Maybe pleasure was the true measure of life.

"Billy Ray...?"

A rush of embarrassment overcame him. What was the matter with him, anyway?

"I'm sorry. I was thinking how pretty you are. I mean—"

"You're darned handsome yourself." Her smile glistened.

Relief washed over him. It was like getting caught in the cookie jar and then grandma offering milk instead of a swat.

"Thanks, Rebecca."

"I'm done with business here in Tyler. I'd love to take you up on that graduation treat. What you say we get some ice cream?"

"What about Shandi?"

"She said to go on without her, that she'd take a bus. So how about it?" Rebecca cast him a wide smile.

"It'd be my pleasure, ma'am!"

The idea was to stop at the Dairy Queen on their way out of Tyler. However, two school buses filled the parking lot and sixty kids ran helter-skelter jacked up on sugar while several adults did an imitation Old West roundup. It looked more like ranching cats.

They pulled away and headed home to Gladewater.

He was enjoying his time with Rebecca. She was smart. She was fun. And she was gorgeous. Her auburn hair, large green eyes, and curvaceous features were the songs of Sirens.

What an improvement over the past ten years!

19

They chatted on the drive back to Gladewater, each discussing plans for the future. Billy Ray's contribution was short—he didn't have any plans. Although, just discussing the future was a marked improvement. He'd buried himself in the past for so long he'd forgotten the thrill of looking forward. He told Rebecca about accepting Gus Heavenor's offer to run the store. She told him about opportunities she was considering, each requiring her moving away from Texas. He felt a sudden heaviness. What was the matter with him?

He had no right to feel this way.

He checked himself in the mirror to make sure his face wasn't betraying his heart.

He almost missed it.

The scene was strange enough to pull him back to reality. It happened a mile before the entrance to the Texas Waterland Family Park, where the elephant grass grew tall between the highway and the railroad tracks. A scrawny yellow dog struggled to drag an olive-colored jacket across the road. Billy Ray slowed to let the dog pass and got a good look at the coat. His blood ran cold. He'd last seen it on Jonesy!

Confirming his greatest fear, he spotted the old man's Marine cap lying partially obscured in the roadside weeds.

He turned onto the shoulder and shut off the motor.

"What's the matter, Billy Ray?"

"I'm not sure yet. Would you please go after that dog and get back the jacket he's dragging off?"

They exited the car. The smell was horrendous.

"Wow, what died?" Rebecca covered her nose.

"I'll tell you in a minute."

Billy Ray walked over to the hat. He retrieved a nearby stick, squatted on his haunches, and lifted the hat up off the gravel. The name Jones was written inside. He returned it to the exact position he'd found it and scanned the area for clues. There was a break in the Elephant grass just beyond the car. If someone was to trek into the gargantuan weeds, they'd do so at that point. He left the old warrior's cap and headed back to the car to retrieve a crowbar, needed for hacking his way through the grass and warding off snakes. He checked on Rebecca, now a hundred yards down the highway engaged in a tug of war with the yellow mutt, its teeth clamped tightly onto its prize. Then he stepped into the bush.

He'd seen dead bodies before, some left for days in the African sun. What Mother Nature did to dead matter was no pretty sight. If Jonesy lay in those weeds, the body could be in bad shape.

It took a good bit of effort to hack through the tall grass. He was only thirty feet from the car, but might as well have been a mile. Among towering grass as thick as tree branches, hissing snakes and scurrying rodents, the environment was extremely claustrophobic. He comforted himself knowing that at least there were no jaguars.

Jonesy had to be close. In addition to the stink of death, the insane hum of insects reached a crescendo—nature's buzzsaws. Pushing aside a freshly hacked clump of grass, it was obvious he'd reached his destination. Edward Jones lay in a grotesque heap. Dead.

The flies and hornets were relentless. Billy Ray pulled his shirt up around his face to fend against the smell and insects. It left no doubt whose body it was. Even bloated, the form held the appearance of an elderly person, a shock of white hair clearly visible. Also, the clothing was what he remembered. The most telling evidence was on the corpse's finger, a Naval Academy ring. He touched Jonesy's lifeless finger with the stick. The ring slipped off and fell to the ground. He stabbed the ring on the first try and inspected it. The ring bore Jonesy's initials. No doubt. No hoping against hope. These were the remains of the old warrior.

What happened to Edward Jones became clear. By the look and position of the body, Jonesy had been hit by a passing vehicle and tossed into the weeds like a bag of garbage. He scanned the area for more clues, but the dense elephant grass made the chore virtually impossible. What Jonesy's enemies had failed to accomplish in war, a careless motorist achieved in the blink of an eye. In fact, his body was so lightweight the driver may not have realized they'd struck a human. And with Jonesy wearing green BDUs the motorist may have dismissed the object as a young deer.

Billy Ray had suspicions, but forced himself to consider facts instead. Jonesy was usually drunk. If the tragedy happened at night, the old man would've been difficult to see by a motorist, especially one with a few beers in their own tank. Certainly, these were plausible explanations. But why now? The very man he'd been trying to find—a person capable of shedding light on his brother's death and the missing Richards girl—found dead on the highway. And another thing, what was Jonesy doing on the highway? This spot had to be five miles from the Frontier Inn and in the opposite direction of Jonesy's home. The body on this side of the road meant Jonesy had been heading toward Big Sandy.

He heard someone approach, but didn't allow it to interrupt his train of thought. He should have. The approaching body chose its footfalls too carefully. In times past he would've noticed.

Cold steel touched the back of his neck.

Billy Ray froze. He knew instantly what the object was. After all, he'd done the same to enemy combatants in the field. A gun.

"Don't move a muscle," a man's voice said. "Don't even twitch."

Billy Ray remained perfectly still.

The voice continued, "You're under arrest. Place your hands behind your back."

Before Billy Ray could respond, another voice spoke, it was low and gruff. "Lower your weapon. Place it on the ground. Now!"

The steel was removed from Billy Ray's neck.

There was the sound of movement.

"Don't even think about it, copper!"

"Okay...okay. Don't do anything stupid. I'm a deputy. You're committing a serious offense," said the shaky voice.

"Do it," the gruff voice demanded. "Or I'll smear you right here and now!"

It was Rebecca, purposefully disguising her voice. She'd made her way along the same track as they, and had brought some cold steel of her own. Billy Ray heard the deputy's heavy breathing as the man bent to place his gun on the ground.

"Billy Ray Jenkins, turn around."

He turned and faced the deputy. The man was young. Fear painted his face. The deputy looked about to wet himself.

Rebecca wasn't through. "Mr. Jenkins, pick up the gun."

Billy Ray watched the deputy's eyes go wide.

"Now take the gun..." she hung a long pause in the air, "and place it back in the deputy's holster."

He switched on the safety and placed the weapon where it belonged, all the while watching the deputy for signs of panic.

"Now extend your right hands and clasped them together."

They gripped each other like old drinkin' buddies.

Finally, in her normal voice, Rebecca said, "Billy Ray Jenkins, I want you to meet a friend of mine, Larry Bell."

They stood beneath the Texas sun, among the tall grass, flies buzzing madly, hands clasped, and looks of confusion twisting their faces. Bell's hand stopped shaking.

"Rebecca?" His voice cracked like an adolescent schoolboy.

Rebecca withdrew the metal object from the back of Bell's neck and stepped into plain view. She began lathering her mouth with an aluminum tube of lip balm while casting Bell a puppy dog look. She smoothed the moisturizer, puckered her lips, and then kissed Deputy Bell on the cheek.

Both men were too flabbergasted to talk.

"Now that you two have been properly introduced, mind telling me what's going on?" She motioned with the lip balm. "And who is that dead person?"

The deputy struggled to find his tongue.

Billy Ray had no such problem. "That's Edward Jones…or what's left of him. Now can we get the hell out of here?"

Just as they arrived back at the cars, Sheriff Payne's cruiser came screeching to a halt.

"Uh oh, here comes trouble," Bell said under his breath.

Rebecca gave Bell a stern look. "Keep your mouth shut with my father or I'll spread the word around the county of how a girl got the drop on you!"

Cowed by Rebecca, Bell turned to face his approaching boss.

As for Billy Ray, he did what he always did before meeting the sheriff.

He prepared for the worst.

20

Billy Ray sensed trouble. He always did around Roy Payne. The sheriff's black sunglasses aimed straight at him, like the holes of a double-barreled shotgun. More from reflex than fear, he backed against the car, placed his hands in plain sight, and waited. Rebecca did the same and stood at his side. Bell had the good sense to take up position in front of the two civilians, ready to participate in the interrogation.

Sheriff Payne marched toward the group, followed by his ever-present deputy and faithful lapdog, Tom Dixon.

After the history lesson from Gus, Billy Ray could never look at these two men again without being disgusted. To him, they were just bullies with badges. Nonetheless, they had authority. He kept himself in check.

The lawmen ignored Bell and stopped in front of Billy Ray. He noticed how Bell gave way to Payne, the alpha male more than duly-elected boss. He assumed such had always been the way for Roy Payne, and that the sheriff had come to expect it.

There was a long, uncomfortable silence. Payne's sunglasses remained locked and loaded on the target—him. Finally Payne said, "What's the meaning of this? What's going on here, deputy?"

The first question probably made no sense to the young deputy, but it did for Rebecca and Billy Ray.

Bell moved out from behind Payne. "Sheriff, there's a dead body in there."

"Something's dead all right…or will be soon."

"No, already dead. I saw the body." Bell missed Payne's double meaning.

"Why are these two here?"

"They found the body," Bell reported.

"Who does this car belong to?"

"It's registered to Lela Jenkins."

"How did it get here?"

"Sir?" Deputy Bell cast a puzzled look.

"Here…on the side of the road. Is that plain enough?"

Billy Ray knew Payne's game, he'd been baited by this man before. Rebecca knew it too. They held their tongues.

"Well, sir, I'm assuming Mr. Jenkins drove it here."

Wrong word.

"Assume? I don't pay you to assume, deputy! Did you check the man's identification or license and registration?"

"Well, no…I mean…not yet," Bell stammered.

Payne was about to lay into the young deputy when Rebecca stepped forward. She'd had enough of her father's manipulating ways. His torturing Bell had flushed her out.

"That's enough!"

Payne pointed at his daughter. "I'm not talking to you."

"Yes you are! You want to know if I was riding with Billy Ray."

Payne said nothing. No need, he was getting paid.

"You want to know what's going on between us. And you want to know why I'm not coming around to see you anymore." Rebecca fired a litany of statements. She could give as good as she could get. She stared hard at her father.

Payne didn't move a muscle. The only commotion came from the nervous twitches of the two deputies.

Billy Ray felt himself pulled backward in time. Emotions welled up from that…that time of death! He'd been powerless then to save his lover from herself. *No,* he corrected himself, *from her father!* He, too, had had enough. "Payne—"

Rebecca threw up her hand, cutting him off, the signal that this was her fight and she wasn't done. She knew her father's game as well as he did. Bait, hook, club, and gut. She stopped Billy Ray short of the hook.

"You should be ashamed of yourself, father. Why can't you just come right out with the questions? What compels you to browbeat people for information?"

"Listen here child—"

"I'm no child. I'm a grown woman!"

Stifling heat, embarrassment from the bystanders, the overpowering smell of death, all made for cruel theater. They were saved from further family venting when a Big Sandy Police cruiser pulled up. The officer secured the ear-splitting sirens, wrestled his overweight frame from the vehicle, and made his way to the gathering.

It was the long-time Chief of Police of Big Sandy, Wesley Harlan. "Howdy, Roy. What's going on here, these kids a couple a commies or something?" Before anyone could answer, Chief Harlan said, "Whoeee! Something's dead in that there thicket."

That broke the spell.

Dixon took control. "Chief, we have us a dead body in there."

"Brilliant deduction, Tom. Who is it?"

"Don't know yet."

"Then why all the yappin? These kids responsible?"

There was a pause, but Dixon did the right thing. "These good Samaritans actually found the body."

"Okay, so who is it?"

Dixon covered for Payne. "We were just about to find out."

"Uh huh." Harlan looked unconvinced.

All eyes turned back to Billy Ray and Rebecca.

Billy Ray pushed past Payne, ignoring the menacing stare. He pulled up near the break in the elephant grass. The four police officers followed. He pointed down at the green BDU cap. "If you check that hat, you'll find the name Jones inside."

Payne spoke to Billy Ray for the first time. "How would you know that?"

"I looked inside."

"Don't you know better than to disturb a crime scene?"

"Who says it's a crime scene?" Billy Ray countered.

Payne stepped close. "Don't get smart with me, punk!"

"Now just hold on there, Roy. We can't go treatin' helpful strangers like that," Harlan objected.

Dixon ran interference once more. "Actually, Chief, these two aren't quite strangers."

"What you mean by that?"

Bell piped up. "He's Billy Ray Jenkins and she's the sheriff's daughter."

Payne removed his sunglasses and shot the young deputy a withering glare. The junior officer melted back into the crowd.

Chief Harlan looked around at the gathering. "Is there something going on here I should know about?"

"No," said Dixon. "Just doing our jobs."

"Is that so? Then how 'bout we get crackin?" Harlan turned to Bell. "Got any yellow tape in your trunk?"

"Yes, sir."

"Good. How 'bout you fetch it and secure this area? The rest of us will move our vehicles out of the way." Harlan said to Payne. "See that mile marker?" He pointed to a post a hundred feet up the road. "It means this area's within my Big Sandy jurisdiction. Wouldn't you agree, Roy?"

Payne was slow to answer. A dummy could see the man hated losing control. "Incidents on the highway belong to me."

Harlan turned to Billy Ray. "Have you seen the body?"

"I have," Billy Ray said.

"How far from the road would you say it is?"

"About forty feet. Through that opening." Billy Ray pointed.

Harlan looked up and down the road. "I don't see any debris or skid marks indicating a traffic accident. Secondly, it sounds like the body lies beyond the easement line. That makes it my jurisdiction."

"We don't know that for sure, Wesley," Dixon said.

The chief gave the deputy sheriff a hard look. "What you say we get to findin' out. That all right with you, Roy?"

Payne merely nodded.

Sensing a shift in the action, Rebecca handed Chief Harlan the tattered Marine jacket. "I believe this belonged to Mr. Jones."

"Where'd you find it?"

"Fought a dog over it."

Harlan smiled and took the offered piece of evidence.

Sheriff Payne turned on his heel and left.

Dixon knew his boss well. "Deputy Bell was first on the scene, he'll take things from here." Dixon chased after Payne.

The heaviness in the air lifted. Even the chief let out a breath. He said to them, "You two wanna' give me a full accounting of what went on here? Leave nothing out."

It may have been luck. More likely, it was intercepting a police report over a scanner. Regardless, a yellow Jeep Cherokee with a Gladewater News logo on the side pulled up among the gathering. The passenger door opened and a tall skinny reporter jumped out and hustled to the assembled group of police officials and citizens.

Billy Ray turned to see the commotion. The reporter spotted him and skidded to a halt. It was the same man he'd treated to a near-death experience on his mother's porch, Clive Ballerd. The newsman dropped his used car salesman smile and stared directly in horror at his tormentor.

"So much for ice cream," Billy Ray said to Rebecca.

He turned to the reporter. There was something he had to do. "Mr. Ballerd, I wish to apologize. I think we stepped off the wrong side of the porch the other day."

Ballerd's face registered a double martini of confusion and fear. At last, he realized there was safety in the presence of a police chief, and found his voice. "What's happened here?"

"Hit and run," Bell volunteered.

That got a retort from Harlan. "You mind me doin' the talkin'? Now please go put up that yellow tape as I asked."

"Oh, yeah." Bell headed off to his patrol car.

Harlan faced the group. Billy Ray imagined the old lawman rolling his eyes behind his sunglasses. "Ballerd, this matter's fresh. I need to get a grip on things here. How 'bout you come back later?"

"Hit and run?" Ballerd blew through the caution light. The man gave a strong impression that subtle words and kind deeds had no affect nor ever would. "So where's the stiff, I want a picture."

"I'll make a deal with you, Ballerd," Harlan offered with notable professional effort. "Let me do my job and you'll get the story first."

"But I have a right—"

Harlan cut him off. "Or I can cite you for obstructing an official police investigation and you get squat. Now git!"

East Texas' version of a paparazzi turned on his shiny leather shoes and marched off. The jeep spit gravel as it pulled away. Billy Ray again imagined Harlan's eyeballs rolling over, wondering why the world was so full of nuts.

Harlan turned to the two witnesses. He removed his sunglasses. "So you're Billy Ray Jenkins. I heard you were…residing in the Houston area."

Billy Ray looked into eyes that betrayed nothing. "I was paroled."

"My condolences to you and Lela."

"Thank you, Chief. You know my mother?"

"I do," was all Harlan said.

Billy Ray and Rebecca spent the next half hour recounting events and exploring possibilities to Jonesy's demise. He noticed Ballerd hadn't taken full leave of the area, but merely moved his vehicle across the highway where it now sat like a vulture. Harlan finally let them go, but requested they appear at the station later to sign official reports. Then he drove Rebecca home.

As he pulled away and entered traffic, Billy Ray noticed in his mirror that an Upshur County Sheriff vehicle took his spot.

He gave himself one guess who was in the car.

21

Two hours past the time Billy Ray had told Gus to expect him, he entered his new place of employment. The young clerk, Jeff, was busy assisting an elderly customer decide between screws or nails for a project. So he made his way through the store and vaulted the stairs two at a time to the office. Gus was talking on the phone. The two made eye contact. Billy Ray took a seat and waited for his partner to end the call.

He had a lot on his mind. Much had happened since his release from prison and Ricky's death. Details were mounting. A new witness had come to his attention, Mrs. Richards. And now the untimely death of Edward Jones. He pulled a pen and a blank sheet of paper from his pocket. He had to get his thoughts written down. Beginning with Jonesy's death, he worked backwards in time. No detail too insignificant. He recorded every thought, every notion, and every suspicion. Too many items didn't add up—too many issues that didn't allow him to accept Ricky's loss, nor make peace with the ghosts of his past. Until he settled these disturbing issues and discovered the truth of Ricky's death, Clarice's disappearance, Jonesy's demise, and even the mysteries surrounding his own father, Billy Ray knew there'd be no moving forward with his life. There'd be no peace.

While Gus spent the next half hour ordering supplies over the phone, Billy Ray wrote steadily. His notes read like a mystery. Discordant details, coincidental facts, convenient timing…all parts to a growing body of truth. One thing was unmistakable, however, no way any of it was fiction.

Gus ended his call. "There you are. I'd begun to think you changed your mind about running this old bucket of bolts store."

"No, nothing like that," Billy Ray said and turned his notes around for Gus to read. "I'm afraid there's been trouble."

Gus' eyes reached the bottom of the list. "It can't be."

"It is. At least, I believe it is."

"What will you do?"

"Dig deeper."

"And then? You know Payne will have you keelhauled if you get anywhere near the yellow line."

Gus wasn't telling him anything he didn't know. If he so much as spit on the sidewalk, Payne would throw him in jail, especially knowing he and Rebecca were spending time together. But Gus was right to ask. Still, he had to know what really happened at the Loma Reservoir and if Jonesy was killed to silence him.

"I'm going to get to the bottom of this, Gus."

"Some advice, then. Tread lightly. Your own grave awaits you."

Billy Ray knew Gus was right. He'd only recently risen from a grave of his own making, one of despair and a decade-long odyssey of self-pity and resentment. And yet, he'd merely traded one hell for another—Ricky's death. Until he got the plain truth, he'd never be free. The grave would forever beckon.

"I have to know what really happened."

"Then be careful, son."

Only fools rush in.

He'd use the tools of his trade and find out what the hell was happening to their town, then put a stop to it.

He checked the time and then folded his notes and put them in his pocket.

Gus caught the movement. "Where to first?"

"Edward Jones' house. There are two very worried ladies waiting for him to come home. I don't like the idea of them getting the official treatment."

"That's good of you. I often wondered if your mother would get a knock at the door by a naval officer with hat in hand."

No, just Sheriff Payne.

22

The sun hung high in the sky throwing down some serious heat when Billy Ray exited the hardware store. He walked to his mother's car. As if the first half of his day hadn't been vexed enough, there was a traffic citation on the windshield. He plucked the ticket from under the wiper and read it. Taking up two spots in a parking lot? He looked down. The front wheels were cocked and barely touching one of the lines. The ticket was signed by Tom Dixon.

Wasn't Gus' parking lot private property?

He tossed it in a nearby trash can and got in the car. Then thought better of it and retrieved the ticket. There was no telling what obscure statute Payne would attempt to cite him for next.

He pulled up to the home where Jonesy had lived his days in peace. He felt a lump rise in his throat. It was a shame to lose an old warrior, a survivor of two wars, in such a way as this.

They guessed his mission, or maybe it was his remaining in the car so long that gave it away. Eva stood on the front porch of the house. She had her arms wrapped snugly around the elder woman, Wilhelmine. Their faces told the tale.

He dreaded what came next. He made his way up the steps and came to a stop in front of the women. Two sets of eyes filled with tears. They knew. Eva and Wilhelmine held each other and cried. He reached out as his own mother had done for him and embraced the women. "I'm so very sorry," was all he managed before his throat closed down.

It was a full minute before anyone spoke.

Wilhelmine went first. "When?"

Billy Ray cleared his throat. "Night before last is my guess."

They held each other in the shade of a pink Bougainvillea trellised above the porch. The afternoon heat enveloped them, buzzing insects audible amidst the silence of the group's despair.

Eva broke the sad spell. She pulled a tissue and wiped her eyes. "Let's go in the house. We'll be cooler and I have iced tea."

"Did you know I was coming?"

"We had a feeling Uncle Edward wasn't coming home this time."

Eva took Wilhelmine by the hand and they moved into the house. She directed them to sit and then headed to the kitchen for refreshments.

"Young man, where's Edward?"

There was no joy in Wilhelmine's face. He didn't know whether to answer or wait for Eva's return.

"Please, you can tell me," Wilhelmine insisted.

He took a deep breath. "By now, he's at the county morgue."

"What happened to my Edward?"

Billy Ray hesitated.

Thankfully, Eva returned. She set down a tray of drinks and took her seat. After a sip of tea, she said, "Yes, please tell us what happened. We knew this day would come, actually thought it had several times before."

He liked this woman. Eva displayed strength.

"I figure your uncle was hit by a car while walking along the highway toward Big Sandy."

"Did he...do you think he suffered?" Wilhelmine asked.

"I don't think so, ma'am. He appeared to have been killed instantly." The answer provided Wilhelmine a degree of relief. He explained the rest of the details as he knew them to be.

"You say he died at night, not early morning?" asked Eva.

"That's the guess so far."

"Billy Ray, how far from the Frontier Inn was he?"

"About five miles, I'd say. Why?"

"Because I can't think of a reason why he'd be walking on a dark highway, so far from home, and heading in the wrong direction."

Eva was on to something, he could feel it. "I wondered the same thing. His direction had him going toward Big Sandy. Any idea why?"

The women looked at each other. Neither one had a clue.

"His health had declined these past few years," Eva said.

"And his nightmares came back," added Wilhelmine.

Billy Ray considered each woman's statement. "Maybe he wandered off in the wrong direction by mistake."

"To my knowledge, he had no friends in Big Sandy, and certainly no medical or government needs." Eva turned to Wilhelmine. "Would you say that's true?"

"Yes, dear. We moved from Big Sandy years ago. Edward's Marine buddies are nearly all dead."

"There's nothing worth walking ten miles to see," Eva said. "The only thing between here and Big Sandy is the Ambassador Ranch—"

"And the new waterslide park, honey."

"Aunt Wilhelmine, I hardly think he'd go to a theme park at night. It isn't even open yet."

"It will be soon. Can we go see it?" Wilhelmine digressed.

Eva patted her hand. "Yes, we'll go when it opens."

"Oh, good. I have coupons."

Eva allowed for Wilhelmine's distraction. A little hope for happier days could only be good medicine.

She turned to Billy Ray. "I don't know why my uncle was on that highway, especially with his bad leg. The way it made him wobble, it always took twice as long to get anywhere."

"What was the matter with his leg?" Billy Ray wanted to know.

It was Wilhelmine who offered the explanation. "Edward was wounded in Korea. His leg was shattered by an enemy bullet. Didn't stop my Edward though," she added proudly. "He kept right on fighting to the very end. We met stateside at the hospital. I was his nurse." She paused, reflecting in her mind. "He refused amputation. That leg never did regain much use."

Just like a Marine.

Billy Ray appreciated having fought alongside men like Jonesy. But a bad leg, that was something he'd never known. He'd always assumed Jonesy to be stumbling around drunk. He peeked at his watch. "I must be going. Chief Harlan is expecting me over in Big Sandy soon." Billy Ray stood to leave.

Eva rose from the couch. "I appreciate you coming to talk to us. I was worried it'd be the sheriff...or his creepy deputy."

He noted the disgust at the mention of Dixon and could only imagine the source of Eva's comment. "I know how cold such news can be." He stopped at the door. "One more thing." He dug Jonesy's Academy ring from his pocket and handed it to Eva.

Tears welled up in her brown eyes. She took the ring and hugged him.

He let himself out and walked to the car, deep in thought. Eva had raised a good question about her uncle being so far from home. He did the math. To have been killed during the night, five miles from the Frontier Inn, Jonesy would have to hoist anchor hours earlier than Harper claimed, especially with a crippled leg. He could think of only one explanation.

Somebody was lying.

23

Nothing could be allowed to spoil his goal. His employers didn't know the full extent of his plan, nor would they. Wiggins didn't trust Kim Jong-il. Neither did the Dear Leader trust him, which explained why a special handler had been sent to America to observe the project and report back to Pyongyang. The handler was well-versed in all matters of drug trafficking, and had been contracted from a tribe near the Tai border, the once Golden Triangle of opium production. After effective government-sponsored eradication programs, criminal syndicates had turned to methamphetamine production. Expertise could be bought cheaply by the Koreans.

Nevertheless, he was too close to allow any interruption in his plan. The ends would have to justify the means. It was for that reason Wiggins now stood before the handler, being made to explain how a boy and his girlfriend managed to get so close to the very heart of their operation. And why an old drunk had been allowed to provide an eyewitness account to police. And now, that same old man's body had been found outside the park gates and put under investigation. The handler's other concern was allowing release of their drug into the American society and the resulting deaths, that Rapture was no longer a secret.

The handler was a chieftain among his tribe. He sat cross-legged on a rug. His black silk clothing spoke of his commanding position. His hands nested inside bell-sleeved cuffs and cradled in his lap. Long white hair crept down his leathery skin like winter fog. And his flat eyelids hung half-closed, as was his custom when angry. He spoke through an interpreter, a young Asian man, dressed immaculately in a business suit and polished Italian shoes that reeked of riches and refinement—the very thing Wiggins despised. He felt his anger rising, an overdressed dandy and old man in black pajamas in East Texas.

How out of place.

"Mr. Wiggins," the interpreter used highbrow English, "Master Pao demands to know how a child breached your defenses."

"The matter's been taken care of, mate."

The interpreter spoke to the handler so softly Wiggins could barely hear. After a lengthy discussion, he said, "Master Pao says he considers your fish with teeth like dogs an acceptable solution, but warns you not to draw attention from authorities."

"As I said, the matter's been fixed. The boy's death was made to look like an accident."

"Drug-related, no doubt. And your choice of drug?" The man remained placid, vocal tempo even, the perfect mouthpiece for Pao.

"The drug from our labs, Rapture."

"Fool!" the interpreter shouted. "You fail to see how this could draw attention to our operation!"

"Listen here, you little prick!" Wiggins felt his blood boil. "I placed the drug in the boy's school dorm to throw off the authorities!"

The old chieftain and his interpreter remained silent.

Wiggins persisted, "There was no way to know what those kids witnessed. We were unloading a critical shipment. And you," he pointed at the old man, "went out on the water in plain sight."

The young interpreter turned to the old man, then back again.

"Master Pao wishes to caution you. He says the tongue is a dagger best kept in its sheath."

Wiggins collected himself. He needed to remain calm. He was too close to his goal. He nodded. "Understood, mate."

The old chieftain's eyelids raised a fraction. He whispered to his interpreter. The young man said, "Master Pao wishes to know how you disposed of the elderly alcoholic."

"I thought it best to let the man's own drinking be the cause of his death. He was hit by a car while staggering on a dark highway, a nightly occurrence in America. Nothing points back to us."

"And your reason for releasing Rapture before our target date?"

"Simple, mate, the mention of Rapture in the press provides free advertising. Bad news spreads fast in America. The masses will be waiting like starving dogs to get the drug."

"And our defenses here at the park?"

"An army couldn't breach them without getting ripped apart."

Again, the young man turned to his master for instructions.

Wiggins waited patiently for their conference to end. He thought about the deaths, all unavoidable. The kids, the old man, and others who'd either stood in his way or come to know things that doomed them. There could be no witnesses. Not now. Not ever. Nor would he let anyone get in the way of his grand design—to make America pay for killing his father.

The two men ended their conference. The interpreter gestured with a sweep of his hand. "Master Pao thanks you for your foresight. He also wishes to share wisdom with you. It's best told in a story."

"Okay, mate, enlighten me."

"When the Vietnamese mongrels from the south came with their Yankee masters, our skies lit with fire, our ground shook with thunder, rivers ran red with blood." The man gestured wildly.

Wiggins rolled his eyes at the juvenile display.

"They came in a vast army of rapists. Their machines performed magic. Their soldiers had food, clothing, and comfort far beyond our standards. Yet they were no match for us. We poisoned them with our cannabis. Our women stole their spirits. Our warriors crushed them and chased them away like frightened children. Small bands of our brave men, sometimes only a single man, could occupy an entire force of these devils."

The old man stared at Wiggins through coal black eyes.

"Master Pao recognizes your genius for matching force against force, army against army, but wishes for you to learn from the black ghosts of his homeland who thrashed a superpower and devoured the dogs of the south."

"I'm all ears, mate. Your point?" Wiggins fought against a yawn.

"Beware the freedom of a single man against the rigid positions of a standing army. A single man can multiply his force manyfold through stealth, movement, and surprise.

"The Yankees had a few warriors who understood this and performed well in our jungles. They became the jungle even as our black ghosts. If by water, then as the fish that finds its way through darkness. If by land, then as the great cat who stalks silently to kill in an instant. And if by air, then as the bat, who rules the night sky."

Wiggins tired of the lecture. "Are you saying my security's no good?"

"No, Mr. Wiggins. You've anticipated the enemy well. If the Americans come in force, they will fail."

"What then?"

It wasn't the interpreter who spoke, but Pao. The old chieftain withdrew a frail hand from the silk sleeve and pointed in the air. Shock registered on Wiggins' face at the sight of the man's hand—there was but one finger among four stubs.

In clear English, Pao said, "Beware the army of one."

24

Billy Ray picked up Rebecca from her apartment. She slid into the front seat and belted in. He watched her movements, smooth and effortless. She wore a salmon-colored cotton blouse, faded blue jeans, and western boots. The scent of vanilla shampoo was intoxicating. Her lush auburn hair framed her face beautifully. Why couldn't the world just go away and leave them alone? There was something between them, something unspoken. He could sense more than their common loss of Brenda Lee.

Rebecca noticed Billy Ray staring at her. She said nothing, just smiled.

Time stood still. They stared into each other's eyes.

After a long moment, he brought his mind back to earth. "Let's just head west into the sunset."

"Mmm…tempting. We better go see Chief Harlan first."

The moment ended, the affect lingered on.

After two full hours rehashing the story with Harlan and signing papers certifying their testimony, Billy Ray and Rebecca were thanked for their time and allowed to leave.

They ran into Deputy Bell at the front door. He was talking to one of the Big Sandy police officers.

"Hi, Larry," Rebecca said.

"Oh…hello Rebecca." Bell's salutation lacked enthusiasm.

"Long day?" She gave him a wink.

Bell managed a grunted reply.

"All finished with your statement?" asked the second officer.

"We are."

"Kind of weird having one of the only two witnesses to the Jenkins incident end up dead."

Billy Ray jumped in. "What do you mean, officer?"

The cop looked at Rebecca and then back at Billy Ray.

Having been raised around police, Rebecca understood the cue. "Dylan Glover, this is Billy Ray *Jenkins.*" She added emphasis to the last name.

Glover took the hint. "Mighty sorry about your brother."

"Thank you." Billy Ray caught Rebecca's eye. She looked pleased. He appreciated her people skills. He also noticed Bell looking overly amused by the situation.

"Well gentlemen, gotta' go," Rebecca announced. "It's been a long day for me too. I think my lipstick's wearing off." She shot Bell another wink, which took the smirk off the deputy's face.

Officer Glover touched the bill of his cap. "Watch your back, Rebecca. I know your dad closed the case, but we don't need anything bad happening to the only other witness."

Billy Ray might have remained in the hall, jaw dangling, if not for Rebecca hooking his arm and escorting him out the door. Once in the car he turned to her. "Mind telling me what that was all about? What did Glover mean back there?"

"I saw Ricky and Clarice together that morning. I reported the matter. Dylan took my statement."

"Why didn't you tell me about this?"

"I haven't had the chance. Besides—"

"Besides what?"

"I wasn't sure how you would react. I was afraid you might do something...rash."

Rash!

Billy Ray felt incensed. The interior temperature of the car was stifling. Sweat broke out on both of their faces. He had to cool down, body and mind, and get control of himself. He turned to the business of starting the car and turning on the air conditioning.

Rebecca was right. He couldn't allow himself to overreact. That's how battles were lost. He faced her. This time he put his thoughts in order before engaging his mouth.

"We need to talk. I want the truth."

Rebecca took her time answering. She studied his face, determining what she was up against, what kind of man he was, and how much she could trust him. He could sense himself being analyzed, judged, and finally accepted. He got more than he bargained for—he got the whole load.

"All right, Billy Ray, you asked for it." Rebecca squared her shoulders and ran straight over tackle. "It was my day to open at the Piggly Wiggly. Ricky was my first customer. He bought a six pack of soda, a bag of ice, a rose in a glass tube, and one other item—"

"What?"

"Condoms."

"Condoms?"

"An entire box. The store was out of single packages. I remember how embarrassed he was when I held them up to read the price."

Billy Ray could imagine his little brother's red face.

"Ricky kept making sure nobody was watching us. He made a joke to settle his nerves, something about hunting big game."

"Sounds like Ricky."

"I joked back, reminding him that open season was four months away." Her shoulders sagged. "I can still hear his nervous laugh."

He felt a lump in his throat. He could hear Ricky's laughter too.

"Ricky asked me to keep the matter between us. I said I would. I wished him well and watched him get in his truck and leave."

Billy Ray considered how he would've been just like Ricky, except his purchases would've included alcohol. Ricky had chosen soda pop. His little brother not only hated drugs, but also detested alcohol, and both for the same reason. They'd torn his family apart.

He cleared his throat. "Rebecca, do you remember if Ricky's windows were rolled up or down on his truck?"

"Down," Rebecca said. "At least the driver's side. Ricky leaned out and waved to me as he drove off and I gave him a thumbs-up."

Again, the issue of the windows. Why would Ricky be found dead in his truck with the windows rolled up? The coroner found drugs in Ricky's system, some kind of new methamphetamine. He couldn't explain that. But he was ready to bet his life Ricky was no user of street drugs. Maybe somebody slipped the drug into Ricky's system. Maybe it was true Ricky drove his truck into the lake by accident. Then again, maybe somebody killed him, rolled up the windows, and pushed the truck into the water.

Billy Ray didn't know what to think. He wrestled with every possibility. Clarice was still missing. Might she have done the evil deed? If so, she couldn't have acted alone. He dismissed the idea. But where was she? Was she killed too, her body left in the woods or dumped in the reservoir? Ideas swirled in his brain like a tornado. He heard Rebecca's voice cutting through the storm....

"What fool would drive around here with their windows up, even at seven in the morning?"

Billy Ray focused. "Wait. You said you saw them both together."

"I did. About ten minutes later. They came driving past the store. Clarice looked at me as went by. I remember her long hair flowing in the breeze from the passenger window. The window was down."

"Did you know Jonesy also saw Ricky and Clarice together?"

"No, but I gathered as much from Glover's comment."

"Dolores Richards told me she watched Clarice get into Ricky's truck and drive off."

Rebecca nodded. "That makes sense. Clarice lives up the hill from the Piggly Wiggly. They must've just come from there."

"So what do you think happened to my brother and Clarice?"

"I don't know. That was the last I saw of them."

Billy Ray returned to his thoughts, but didn't get far.

"Wait…you said the truth. I think they were killed."

"What? Say that again."

"You heard me. Your brother and Clarice were murdered."

"But your own father, the sheriff of this county, determined otherwise and closed the case."

"I need no reminding who my father is." She stared at him.

He calmed down. "Sorry. I shouldn't have put it like that. Why do you think the sheriff concluded the case as he did?"

"That answer could take all night. Let's say I think he's wrong."

They sat quiet for a moment, processing each other's words.

"Truth is a two-way street. What do you think happened?"

"With what all I know now, I'm ready to believe my brother and Clarice were murdered. I think Jonesy's death was no accident, that somebody killed him to shut him up. I also believe a cover-up is taking place. It may or may not involve your father, but must involve a law officer somewhere in the system. I have my suspicions. And there's one more thing...."

"What?"

"The killers are still in the area." He looked into Rebecca's emerald eyes. "I believe you're in mortal danger."

"I considered that. So how can we find out what's going on?"

"Not *we*…me."

"I want to find out what happened, too!"

"If Jonesy was killed for being a witness, you could be next."

"What's so important about Ricky's death the killers feel the need to murder again and again? And why stage his death to look like a drug-related accident? What are the killers trying to hide?"

That got Billy Ray thinking.

Rebecca continued, "If some random creep killed Ricky and Clarice, they'd be long gone by now, before the police caught them. So why the staging? More importantly, why stick around?"

That was it!

There was no question in his mind about murder. Rebecca's look said she'd drawn the same conclusion. They stared at each other. He couldn't stomach the thought of Rebecca being in danger. If something happened to her…he couldn't finish the thought.

Before he could object, Rebecca slid close to him and put her arm through his and said, "I feel safe with you."

He joined the embrace. They held each other as if their lives depended on it. Rebecca felt good in his arms.

She pulled back after a long pleasant moment and kissed him on the cheek, then shifted in her seat and fastened the safety belt. "Okay, cowboy, I say we get to the bottom of this." She furrowed her brow. "And don't even think about dumping me off at home!"

He was dumbfounded. Between suspicions of murder, fear for their safety, and his deepening feelings for Rebecca, head and heart struggled for the lead. Neither had sleuthing skills nor resources for solving a murder, let alone three murders. On the other hand, what were their choices? Sheriff Payne had already closed the case. All they had left was to try.

"Where to next, Sherlock?"

Where indeed? Billy Ray thought. So much didn't add up, or was coincidental. He couldn't accept Payne's conclusion. However, belief wasn't enough, he needed proof—proof, which could prove impossible to obtain. He didn't think Payne would knowingly put his daughter in harm's way, either. So why should he? What right did he have risking Rebecca's life? Moreover, was he even the best person to protect her from an unseen enemy? The blood froze in his veins at the thought. He'd failed others in the past. He'd failed her sister. But who else did he dare entrust Rebecca's life to?

Nobody.

He would involve Rebecca. Keeping her close was the best way to protect her. Plus she wouldn't stay out of the picture, anyway.

"Okay, you win. How about a cold beer?"

"Great. I need a little cooling off," she teased.

"That's an understatement."

Rebecca stuck out her tongue.

25

The chime on Lam's computer sounded. It was the East Texas thing again. One of the witnesses in the Jenkins case was discovered along the highway near Big Sandy. He knew there was little possibility that yet another death in Big Sandy could be coincidental.

Normally, the death of an old man wouldn't attract much attention, least of all the FBI's. However, his nose was twitching. Something was happening in the Piney Woods. He just didn't know what.

Dreyfus had been called back East, to headquarters. Something big was going down. He hadn't elaborated, only not to expect him back for a few days.

Lam hoped it led to a big drug bust. God knew how out of control the methamphetamine problem was throughout the nation. Estimates ranged as high as twenty million Americans, ages twelve and up, having used meth during the past ten years, with nearly twenty percent of users becoming addicted. Eighty percent of all meth in the US was coming across the Mexican border. With Texas sharing 1,200 miles of that border, the Lone Star State was the soft underbelly for smugglers feeding the nation's drug lust.

Lately, however, there'd been a dip in meth activity. A strange hush had descended over the state. Even murders and kidnappings on the border were down. However, the law of supply and demand remained in full force. Meth prices were skyrocketing. Maybe the hard work busting cartel supply routes and dealers was paying off.

He could hope Dreyfus was getting a shiny medal for the Dallas office. But hard experience taught him not to hope in one hand and pee in the other. The bad guys could just be reloading.

He considered whether to wait and run the Big Sandy matter by Dreyfus. But his gut said bad guys lurked in East Texas. He made his decision. He closed the laptop, stowed it in a travel case, and headed out the door.

* * *

Wiggins snapped the cell phone shut. He'd just learned from his mole inside the police force that the Big Sandy Police Chief formally declared Edward Jones' death a homicide.

No worries, he'd expected such. Vehicular homicide in the United States was common. He also knew the evidence to prove homicide would be difficult to acquire—impossible in fact.

The only loose connection to the old man's death now resided at the bottom of a swamp inside the trunk of his car. Harper had been offered a handsome pile of cash for his tavern. *Two birds with one stone.* Wiggins allowed himself a smile.

A perfect plan would have the old man remain undiscovered. But time had been short. A roadside accident involving an elderly alcoholic provided the perfect cover. All other schemes would have met with greater scrutiny. No plan ever proved perfect. *No worries,* he reassured himself again.

Wiggins' reverie was interrupted by a chirping cell phone. He took the call and his smile vanished. "When?"

He listened for a full two minutes to the caller.

"Put them in position. Call me when they arrive."

The smile returned.

26

Billy Ray drove through the parking lot of the Frontier Inn. He gave up searching and chose the street. As he and Rebecca exited the vehicle, a black Ford Bronco caught his attention. Something glowed inside the menacing vehicle, a cell phone perhaps, but difficult to determine behind the tinted windows and glare of the overhead street lamp.

Rebecca came up beside Billy Ray. “Mind holding a lady’s hand, or will your drinking buddies think you've gone soft?”

He took her good-natured jibe and her warm hand. “I'd love to, madam. Besides, I don't have any drinking buddies.”

“Guess I'll have to do, then.” Rebecca winked at him.

“You'll do fine!” He squeezed her hand. She returned the favor.

They approached the door. An R&B song blared from the jukebox inside, something about *falling off the end of the middle.* A dozen Latinos lined either side of the door. They wore decorative Guayabera shirts and pressed slacks. All sported ornate western boots. They talked among themselves, some smoking cigarettes, but all casting their attention away from the approaching couple. Unseen by Billy Ray, one man's choice of dress presented a stark contrast to the others—webbed boots, black T-shirt, and multi-pocketed canvas pants. The man puffed a cigar, the smoke sumptuous, pervading. Beyond the sight of well dressed men, the sound of loud music, strong smells of tobacco and aftershave lotion, and even the feel of Rebecca’s hand, other more intuitive senses signaled alert. He struggled to interpret their meaning. His instincts said danger. His eyes and ears read all clear. The men posed no trouble and were distracted by their own company. As the door closed behind them, he heard a man say, “*Ese era el,* that’s him.” The loud music made it difficult to be sure.

They remained at the door, allowing their eyes to adjust. The place was packed. Billy Ray scanned the room for a seat. He wondered if there was a convention in town. But Gladewater?

“Looks like a popular hangout,” Rebecca said.

He pointed to a single stool at the front. “Let’s belly up to the bar.”

“Whatever ya say, *pahdnah*.”

He tightened his grip on Rebecca’s hand and led a path to the bar. Heads turned. How could they not? Rebecca’s fancy boots made her as tall as him. She was stunning in her faded jeans and salmon-colored blouse. Her auburn hair poured like wine onto tanned shoulders. Even her perfume left heads to swim in a wake of honey and vanilla.

They reached the open seat. Billy Ray helped Rebecca climb onto the stool and then took up a position behind her. He scanned the crowd for familiar faces, but recognized no one. He was surprised to see so many Latinos, and a distinct lack of females. In fact, he counted only two other women besides Rebecca. Then he remembered the upcoming event that might explain a large crowd and so many strangers on a weeknight. The Texas Waterland Family Park was about to open. Radio and television ads proclaimed a pre-grand opening and firework extravaganza for VIPs and park staff during the upcoming Independence Day weekend. Maybe these men were connected with the park in some way.

"What can I get you two?"

Billy Ray turned. The man working the bar wasn't Harper. Instead, he faced a man with Asian features.

Rebecca ordered a bottle of beer.

"Okay. And for you, mister?" The man spoke perfect English.

Billy Ray looked around. There was no trace of Harper. "A Guinness."

"Sorry, no Guinness."

"You all out?"

"We don't stock foreign beers."

"Okay. Make it what she's having then." Outwardly he smiled. Inwardly his instincts fired. Something was wrong. The bartender brought their drinks. He held out the money, the bartender reached for it. "Where's Harper tonight?"

It lasted only a microsecond, the man's face flashed worry. "Harper's out of town…a wedding, as I recall."

Again Billy Ray scanned the crowd. They were in trouble. He could sense it, like those times in the prison yard when a gathering storm was felt more than seen. He spotted a billow of smoke rising from a table near the door. Surrounding the owner of the cigar were the men who only moments ago had stood either side of the entrance. The cigar smoker was looking straight at him and Rebecca!

He turned back to the bar without betraying his discovery—a husky cigar-smoking Asian dressed in black clothing. It was the same man who'd accompanied the head of security during his visit to the Texas Waterland Family Park. The man was spying on their every move. He went on full alert. A casual observer would fail to see that every fiber of his body was cocked and ready to fire. His mind assumed the controlled manner of a jungle cat, still purring, but ready to pounce.

The bartender approached with the change. Billy Ray took the money and casually thanked the man in Korean, "*Kamsa hamnida*."

"*Chon maneyo,*" the bartender welcomed him without hesitation.

They stared at each other—the bartender knowing he'd made a terrible mistake, Billy Ray knowing he'd confirmed his suspicions...the man was Korean and was an imposter! Harper had lied about Jonesy's claim.

The Korean knew he'd been outed and shot a glance to the front of the room before hurrying away to the far end of the bar.

During their exchange one additional man had entered the tavern and taken up position near the door. The new arrival had a clear view of the room, specifically the man and his lovely lady at the end of the bar. The new arrival was tall, owned a muscular build beneath an identical black shirt as his cohort across the table, and one additional feature—stylish blond hair. It was Joseph Wiggins.

Signals passed. Five men stood and made their way toward the bar. Billy Ray caught the movement. He lifted his beer, took a sip, and bent forward to place the bottle on the bar. As he did so, he said quietly, "Start smiling and keep facing forward while I'm talking to you."

Rebecca began turning.

"Stop!" he forced through a whisper. "Do as I say. We're about to have visitors so put on a good act. Laugh out loud."

She tossed back her head and laughed. Billy Ray did the same and then said in her ear, "Just as soon as you can, make your way out of here. Get to the car." He reached around her waist, a lover's embrace, and slipped the keys into her pocket.

Rebecca went tense with worry, but she stuck with the ruse.

"Have the car started and the door open. If I don't come out, you get to the police immediately."

Rebecca laughed again and then whispered, "Who are they?"

"I think they're the ones who killed Jonesy." Billy Ray had to hold Rebecca down. "Trust me."

"I—" She didn't finish her sentence.

"Hey, *hombre,* eez thees your *chica?*"

Billy Ray and Rebecca turned.

The man who'd been sitting on the next stool over now stood and was joined by three others. Billy Ray spotted two additional men taking up position further out in the crowd, blocking any attempt at escape. He now realized just how much trouble they were in. He should've known an open seat in a packed house was unlikely. The fact that an end stool had been the only available seat, that their location offered no rear exit, and even reduced the possibility of witnesses, screamed setup!

What had he done?

He'd led them into a trap. The Ford Bronco, the men at the entrance acting as though a stunningly beautiful woman didn't exist, even the words he'd overheard signaling his arrival were all crystal clear now. He'd ignored his instincts. If not for discovering the Korean identity of the bartender, he would've been taken entirely by surprise. And even that only mattered because Harper had lied. How could he have let this happen?

What had he become?

He had to fix this. So he did what he was trained to do—think first and act second. He prioritized the threats before him, marking each man's position, confirming no signs of weapons.

Billy Ray answered the man casually, "Yes, she is."

"*Muy bonita,* very pretty," a second man said in Spanish.

"*Gracias, señor,*" Rebecca offered.

"Ahh," said the spokesman. "You're pretty, and speak Spanish?"

"*Poquito,* a little."

The third Latino spoke up. "*Cuanto cuesta tu puta?*"

Rebecca's smile vanished. Billy Ray kept his silly smile. Unknown to his attackers, he spoke several languages, Spanish being one. He knew what the man was saying and he knew why—provocation. Rebecca had just been propositioned as a whore.

Growing up with a father like Roy Payne had at least one advantage—ice water pumped through Rebecca's veins. She said, "Is that how you gentlemen talk to women in Mexico?"

"*Si,* Mexican women love it when we call them whores. So, is your body for sale, *señorita,* or must we take it?"

Delaying further would only allow his attackers the same advantages just afforded him by Rebecca's performance. With lightning speed, Billy Ray shot his right elbow sideways and back, snapping the jaw of Rebecca's insulter. His muscles bunched tight, like twisted steel. Then he unleashed hell. Spinning counterclockwise, he swept a flat left hand across the next man's throat. Momentum transferred through his boot to the head of the group spokesman with a crushing blow. The man's unconscious body cartwheeled off to the side. The crack-o-the-whip came from his right hand balled in an iron fist that he drove into the solar plexus of the last assailant. The man doubled over, out of air, perhaps forever.

The noise of breaking glass had Billy Ray ducking and spinning to face the bar. He was astonished at the scene before him. Atop the bar that Harper had spent so many hours polishing, now lay the unconscious bartender. The man's head rested in a pool of beer and shattered glass. Held skyward like an Olympic torch, Rebecca clutched the broken remains of a longneck bottle of Lone Star beer. The splintered ends glistened in the dim light. She'd smashed the bottle over the head of an attacker he hadn't accounted for.

No time for vainglory. There'd be more attackers. He turned back to see where the next assault would come from. The two Latinos that had been blocking the way to the door now moved toward them, one holding a knife, the other a pool stick.

He swept the crowd for more attackers. All eyes looked his way. Brains registered danger. Some patrons dove under tables while others made a mad dash for the door. One exiting person caught his attention, he was tall with blond hair, and the table being vacated no longer contained the Mexican men or the cigar-smoking Asian, Korean he concluded. They'd all vanished.

Still facing forward, he asked Rebecca, "You all right?"

"Y—yes," she said with a shaky voice.

"See those men coming at us?" He imagined her nodding in the affirmative. "I'll draw them farther from the door. When I do, you run for the car. Watch out for a tall guy with blond hair and a stocky Korean, they're the *real* bad guys. You ready?"

He heard keys rattle behind him, then Rebecca's voice, "I'm ready."

The attackers had slowed their advance after observing the *gringo* and his *chica* destroy their comrades, but now quickened their pace.

Battles were won by those most willing. When outnumbered and fighting from an inferior position with no avenue of escape, it was best to take the fight to the enemy. And that's just what Billy Ray did.

"Go!"

Rebecca took off like a punt returner, zigzagging past tables and chairs, even hurdling one patron ducking to avoid harm. The stampede for the door was on. Billy Ray reached behind and snatched the towel from the unconscious bartender. He wound it around his hand, grabbed the stool, and charged the enemy.

In the pandemonium, the attackers became less sure. They looked for reinforcements. None presented themselves. They turned back just in time to see the bringer of death rushing at them. The man with the pool cue faltered. His partner was a more battle-scarred veteran of such affairs and came at Billy Ray with gritting teeth and waving a knife side to side.

Billy Ray made a tactical move to draw in his attacker by leading with the less menacing towel-wrapped hand, and thus exposing himself. Knifeman took the bait and lunged for a quick kill. Billy Ray pulled back the towel and smashed the stool over Knifeman's head. The body fell to the floor in a heap of snoring flesh.

Stickman charged.

Billy Ray hadn't yet recovered from Knifeman and was out of position to defend himself. Stickman landed one lucky swing on his wrapped hand.

If not for the towel, his bones would be mush. Another swing of the stick nearly found its mark atop his head. Then he lost his balance entirely and fell backwards onto the floor. The breeze of the passing stick lifted his hair.

Stickman made ready for a final strike. As the deathblow descended, Billy Ray managed to hook his foot around the leg of a nearby table and pull it in front of the cascading stick. The room filled with a sound like gunfire and shards of wood shot in every direction. Stickman's arm hung limp.

Time to end this!

Prey became predator. Billy Ray sprang up like a jungle cat and came at the startled Latino. After just two shots Stickman lay flat on his back. The first shot was a punch to the abdomen followed immediately by a second shot, the boot of a really pissed off Billy Ray Jenkins. Foot connected with skull!

Billy Ray dashed out of the tavern.

Sure enough, Rebecca was at the curb revving the car engine.

The car's back door hung open. He sprinted to the car and dove in just as Rebecca stomped on the gas pedal. He managed to right himself and close the door before getting tossed out. He chanced a look back at the Frontier Inn. The black Ford Bronco was gone.

Rebecca laughed excitedly. "What took you?"

Billy Ray snapped his head around. "Huh?"

"You heard me, mister. Don't you know never to keep a gal waiting?" Rebecca threw her head back and laughed all the louder.

He couldn't believe his ears. His heart raced, his hand throbbed, he felt lucky they were still alive. And yet, Rebecca was cackling as though it all was high adventure—spitting in the devil's eye. "I… uh..." He groped for words and finally gave up.

Rebecca said over her shoulder. "You sure know how to treat a lady. I haven't had this much fun on a first date, ever!"

From the back seat of his mother's car, racing away from mortal danger, Billy Ray stared at Rebecca's profile and marveled.

She was the most incredible woman he'd ever met!

27

Wiggins shouted into his cell phone while his driver made haste to return them to their underground command center. “What do you mean they got away? Hold on—Lee, get rid of that damn cigar!”

Lee tossed out a full Cuban Cohiba. For now, Wiggins was in charge of Operation Blood Star. What Wiggins didn’t know was that he’d been secretly tasked with guarding the Dear Leader’s interests and deniability of his country's involvement.

There were more cigars where that came from, and many other advantages to the Mexican cartel his country had contracted with.

Lee was pleased. In a few short days, the Dear Leader would be pleased. Soon, his country would no longer be treated like a dog by America and her allies. Operation Blood Star was just days from bringing riches to his homeland—riches beyond Pyongyang's wildest dreams!

And it would be his name, Lee Dong-moon, on the lips of the People's Armed Forces. Cash from Operation Blood Star would make his country’s military strong, and all due to his efforts. No more amateur kidnappings and printing counterfeit dollars. No more being a laughing stock among the world’s militaries.

Operation Blood Star was going to work. *It had to work,* Lee told himself. The glory of his nation depended on it. His own legacy depended on it, if not his life.

He steered the Bronco to the side of the Texas Waterland security building. He wanted another smoke.

Wiggins ended his call. “I want an emergency meeting of all security teams in thirty minutes.”

Lee fingered a metal tube containing a fresh Cohiba, and then removed his hand from his pocket.

So much for another cigar.

28

There'd been another death in the Big Piney. Too convenient. Agent Lam's intuition said to hurry. The detective handbook for dummies instructed otherwise. The elderly victim had been a witness in the Jenkins case. In turn, the Jenkins family was the only connection to the new drug, Rapture. All other leads ended at the morgue. Analysis of all Rapture victims showed no commonalities, except one—*rigor mortis.*

The action was in Big Sandy. He needed to find out why. He was grasping at straws, but with the kind of bad guys he battled on a daily basis, he didn't like waiting for the action to come to him. If the good folks at the lab were correct, Rapture was a time bomb in the making. And, if Dreyfus' theory was correct, that bomb was ticking and about to explode!

The time was half past ten. Lam was twenty miles from Big Sandy. He switched on the police radio to receive the local channels and pressed a little harder on the accelerator. Just then, his cell phone rang. He touched the button on his Bluetooth headset. It was his boss.

"Hey Chris, how goes it in la-la land?"

"The world's gone mad." Dreyfus had a tired edge to his voice.

"What can you tell me?"

"I can tell you there's one less drug cartel south of the border."

Lam let off the gas. "Is Jesus back scrubbing germs off planet Earth?"

"Maybe so. The Gallina cartel has disappeared, the whole family—wife, kids, bodyguards, everybody—gone!"

"Can you elaborate?"

"Apparently, Gallina gave up…quit the business."

"You mean a truce like the one he issued a few years back?"

"Nope. The real thing this time, white flag and all."

"Sorry, boss, but did you say a drug cartel just up and quit the murder, mayhem, and planetary domination game and there's no trace of them?"

"In a nutshell, Lam, that's exactly what I'm saying. A handwritten letter was taped to the door of the Mexican Attorney General. It bore Angel Gallina's signature."

"So the old man's alive. There'd been rumors of his passing."

"Gallina is very much alive. It's just nobody knows where."

"What did the letter say?" Lam hoped he wasn't acting out of school.

"I happen to have a copy in my tea-stained hands. By now, hundreds more should be in newsrooms around the world." Dreyfus read the letter. It communicated how the Gallina family had had enough of the bloodshed with rival cartels. Orders had been issued for an immediate ceasefire and suppliers and dealers commanded to stop all operations undertaken on behalf of the Gallina family and all weapons turned over to the authorities.

The news was so mind-blowing Lam signaled and turned off to the shoulder of the road. It now made sense why the noise along the border had quieted for the past several months.

Dreyfus had more. "The letter apologizes for any pain the Gallina family may have caused their beloved country, and that they'd ever only had good intentions for Mexico. The family was prepared to make reparations in the form of cash donations to charities. Get this, a hundred million even went to police guilds to help families of dead officers."

"Hey boss, you telling me an entire drug cartel got their pink slips, and that there's no sign of the Gallina family? I've never heard of a disappearing act on that scale."

"Not since Atlantis. Maybe they fell off the end of the earth. We're working round-the-clock here, DEA, Homeland Security, CIA. The intel guys are up to their armpits with North Korean saber-rattling. In fact, you'll be reading about the sinking of another South Korean naval vessel in the morning papers. The Dear Leader has himself a real boner this time. He's threatening to fire nukes on the South if the US doesn't exit the peninsula.

"Add that to the hell still raging in the Middle East, and you got some really busy spooks and diplomats trying to avert war. Take your pick, the two Koreas, Israel and Iran, Democrats and Republicans. Hell…even Dick and Jane got divorced!"

"Then the world *has* gone nuts."

Dreyfus changed the subject. "Where are you now?"

"Halfway to paradise...heading back to our little sleepy hollow in the Piney Woods. Another person just went goodnight."

"You can take the boy out of the country…" Dreyfus said.

"You rather I terminate the trip?"

"Carry on, Agent Lam. We're still in the drug-busting business. Since we can't go to Paris, Bugtussle will have to do. Tell Jed Clampett, *howdy.*"

"Who's that?"

"Geez, Lam, don't you know anything?" Dreyfus hung up.

Five minutes later, Lam's pager sounded. The FBI went to full alert in response to Homeland Security elevating the terror threat to "Imminent."

As yet, no specific information was being released to the public.

29

After escaping the Frontier Inn, they drove east on US Route 80 to the Kilgore turnoff. Rebecca pulled over to let Billy Ray take the wheel. They continued south and then west until reaching Big Sandy. It seemed all roads continually drew him back to this place.

Where death had begun.

He checked the mirrors for the hundredth time. They'd gotten away from the goons who, it was obvious, were acting on orders from Wiggins.

"What are you thinking, Billy Ray?"

"I'm thinking we're getting close."

"Close to what?"

"Close to finding out what happened to my brother."

"And Clarice Richards?"

"Yes. Edward Jones, too."

Rebecca acted hesitant to ask her next question. "Do you think...my father is involved in this mess?"

Billy Ray considered how best to answer. Regardless of what kind of person the sheriff was, he was Rebecca's father. "As much as I'm tempted to say yes, I just don't see it. The man hates me and my family, no doubt. His actions are emotionally motivated. I'm not sure why, exactly—"

"But you have an idea?" Rebecca caught his equivocation.

He didn't know how much Rebecca knew of the history between their families, and didn't think now was the right time to tell her. "I have an idea, but it doesn't involve the matter with Ricky or Clarice, other than his bungling the case."

"Billy Ray?"

"Yes?"

"What about us?" Her voice begged the question.

He stole a glance at Rebecca in the glow of the dashboard. The same question had surfaced a thousand times in his mind since Ricky's funeral.

"Billy Ray...?"

"Hold on."

He spotted a gas station, pulled in, and shut off the motor. He turned and met Rebecca's eyes. Her expression said she'd taken a risk with her question. He felt perched on the edge of forever.

They searched each other's faces, looking ever deeper, seeking places found only in one another's soul, an unspoken language expressed their thoughts and feelings. Was it even right?

He wanted to reach for her, pull her close, touch her skin. He sensed she felt the same. It was but a matter of commanding his body to do so.

He gave the order.

Suddenly, blaring sirens and flashing lights destroyed the night!

The voice of Roy Payne called over a loudspeaker, commanding Billy Ray to remove himself from the vehicle and place his hands on the hood of the car, and for the passenger to remain where she was.

This can't be happening! What had he done to deserve being forever tormented by this man?

Again Payne commanded, "Out of the car, hands in plain sight. My gun is drawn. I'll fire unless you obey my order!"

Billy Ray spotted the lone station attendant pressing his face against the window viewing the commotion at the pumps.

Rebecca's face twisted with worry. "He sounds different. Maybe he thinks there really is something wrong here."

"Perhaps," he conceded. "I'll do my best to control this. I need you to do the same." With that, he exited the car.

"Slowly!" Payne commanded.

Billy Ray did as he was told. He put his hands on the hood in plain sight and then waited for the other shoe to drop. It did. Feet hustled up from behind. He felt rough hands grab his clothing and saw the hood rush up to meet his face. His hands were ripped from their position and yanked behind him. Cold steel clicked around his wrists. Then came Payne's voice, it was filled with hatred.

"You filthy mutt, this is the end for you. You're under arrest!"

"For what?" Billy Ray's mouth pressed against the scorching hood. His answer was a pull of his hair and another slam onto the car.

"You have the right to remain silent."

And so began the reading of his Miranda rights by Roy Payne for the second time in his life.

The universe was repeating itself.

He was yanked backwards from the car and could now see his surroundings—the battlefield. He spotted Rebecca inside the car, craning her neck over the headrest to witness the violent activity.

Dixon joined the fray. The two lawmen picked him up off the ground, nearly dislocating his shoulders. The pain was excruciating, but he didn't panic, he'd had this done to him during SEAL training, plus the extra prison muscles allowed additional resistance.

For Rebecca, the sight proved too much. She threw open the car door and bolted straight at the sheriff swinging her fists. Payne cocked his arm and applied a massive backhand. Rebecca dropped onto the filthy tarmac.

Billy Ray remained calm, not allowing his brain to consider anger or his body to react with unguided reflex. He'd ceased being a civilian. He was now the trained warrior—observing, weighing weakness, seeking advantage, calculating odds, and sorting probabilities, all within fractions of seconds. He allowed the officers to drag him to their vehicle—even allowed them to cram him into the back seat, nearly taking off the top of his head on the door frame. The door slammed shut.

Roy Payne made his way back to his daughter, now lifting herself onto her knees. Payne extended a hand. Rebecca swatted it away like a detestable bug. The sheriff made it obvious there'd be no games between them this night. He reached down, grabbed an arm and pulled up roughly. Rebecca's body followed the path of her arm. She made to swing at her father again, but Payne was having none of it. He caught first one attempt from her and then the other. He held both wrists in his massive hands and applied upward pressure until Rebecca stood on tiptoes.

Billy Ray ached to bust the chains binding him and destroy Roy Payne. It required every fiber in his body to resist doing so. He was forced to witness the struggle between the woman he was falling in love with and the man who was so near to completing the destruction of his family. And yet, he would wait for a time when victory could be fully assured.

Rebecca screamed, "You sick bastard. I hate you!"

"No you don't. You love me," Payne said evenly.

"There's no respecting a man like you!"

"You'll control yourself, if you know what's good for Jenkins."

"Is that a threat?"

"I have a job to do. At the moment, it's taking Jenkins into custody and letting the law decide his fate."

"On what grounds?"

"Assault and destruction of private property at the Frontier Inn. The place is a mess, and there's an unconscious bartender with a nasty gash on his head."

"He didn't do that, I did. We were attacked!"

"That's not what witnesses claim. Besides, Jenkins is a paroled convict. I'm just doing my job." Payne had a way of making even the most unreasonable situation seem commonplace.

Billy Ray wasn't fooled. Payne was sick, delusional in fact. He was sure Rebecca thought so too. It was also clear that she wanted to believe her father's words, that all would be well. Payne played on that fact. He observed the cunning manipulation. Payne ordered Rebecca to return the car to Lela Jenkins. She hesitated, then did as she was told.

How many times in Rebecca's past had the same scene, the same process of manipulation, been replayed? Billy Ray considered how Payne's methods had also been applied to his first love, Brenda Lee, and the horrors she must have felt. Truly, he was witnessing the workings of a psychopath.

All at once, he understood Brenda Lee's death—truth ignited by a single spark. Self-pity had never allowed him to see matters through her eyes, until this moment. For the first time in his life, he met the *real* enemy—himself. He couldn't determine when self-pity came to rule his life, so gradual had been the victory, so subtle the transformation from self-pity to resentment. And finally, so perilously close had resentment come to producing everlasting bitterness.

He'd been wrong. Resentment was not a cause, but an effect—a treacherous wind spawned by self-pity, and bitterness the far horizon, the point of no return. No doubt Roy Payne was an enemy, but one outside the gates—a foe to plan for, one possible to avoid. Whereas, self-pity was the Trojan horse of the soul, inhabiting him—defeating him from within.

He'd been his own worst enemy.

The fog of self-pity vanished in the searing light of revelation. The final layer oppressing him, gone. "I'm sorry, Brenda Lee."

Seated in a police car, hands painfully shackled behind his back, he buried his first love, a funeral so many years in coming.

He never felt so free.

Standing in front of the patrol vehicle, silhouetted against flashing blue and red police lights, was a different man, one feeding his demons. Payne stood six and a half feet tall and carried two hundred and fifty hard pounds. With hands on hips, feet spread, one pant leg tucked into a polished boot, his posture proclaimed defiance. Proud. Jealous. Wanting.

And yet, so small was Roy Payne in the fading tail lights of a daughter leaving him behind.

A barren island in the darkness, reclaimed by the sea at last.

30

The route they took to the county jail was more than just circuitous and a waste of gasoline, it was familiar. Ten years had passed and Billy Ray could still recall every detail of his living nightmare. This time, however, things would be different.

"Here we go again," Billy Ray said from the backseat.

Payne said nothing.

"You'll never leave me alone, will you Payne?"

"That's 'Sheriff ' to you, boy!" Dixon erupted.

Payne shot his deputy a look that said to hold his tongue.

Billy Ray had no intention of letting happen what Payne had in mind. His plan was to provoke both men into making a mistake, to rattle their heads a bit. And he knew just how to do it.

"Brenda Lee was in love with me, but you knew that. Didn't you Payne?" He watched the back of the sheriff's head and neck for any sign of physical response.

There was none.

"We were going to get married and move to Coronado, near my SEAL base. I even had a pretty little house picked out. We were going to be happy." He let the details sink in for a moment. "I always wondered why she begged me to move her so far from home. She once said life in East Texas wasn't worth living anymore."

Still no reaction.

"I didn't understand what she'd meant by that, not until...well, you know, not until she killed herself."

It happened.

The muscles at the back of Payne's neck twitched, his hands tightened on the steering wheel. Even Dixon eyed his boss, awaiting a reaction. Payne remained silent.

"There was one thing I could never figure out, though. Want to know what that was, Payne?"

No response. The silence was thick, palpable even.

Billy Ray didn't wait for an answer. "You charged me with rape. I thought you were just throwing the book at me. I understood all that. I didn't even care by then. Brenda Lee was gone. I could care less if I lived or died." He gave it a moment before continuing. "At my first parole hearing a couple of years back, I was granted access to my file, the court records, and you know what else?" Billy Ray scooted across the seat until he located Payne in the rearview mirror. "I finally read the coroner's report...thought it might be time to bury Brenda Lee, get her off my mind somehow. Aside from the usual medical crap about illicit drugs, the report claimed Brenda Lee was pregnant. You remember that little detail, don't you Roy?"

Payne's knuckles turned white on the steering wheel.

Billy Ray pressed on. "I thought you were playing a cruel joke on me, that you'd ordered one of your lackeys to add that little detail to sweeten your case...a little revenge, perhaps. I thought about that for a long time."

Dixon's agitation loomed. Wagering on the length of time before the deputy disobeyed Payne's order was easy money.

Billy Ray pressed. "It finally dawned on me that you're a psychopath with some real disturbing personality traits, which explains why my mother dumped you—"

Dixon pulled his gun and flew around in the seat. "Shut your filthy mouth or I'll blow your brains out!"

"Tom! Put the gun away. He's messing with us."

"But, boss, you can't just let this punk talk to you like that."

"Don't worry. Let him talk all he wants."

Dixon holstered the gun, but continued staring down Billy Ray.

"As I was saying, you may be one sick dude, but even I don't think you're dumb. How'd you miss it?"

"Miss what?" Payne responded for the first time.

Billy Ray paid the man no mind, just spoke over the top of him. "How'd you miss the fact there's no possible way Brenda Lee could be pregnant with my child?"

Dead silence filled the car.

Time to drive the spike.

"I hadn't made love to my fiancé in months. Aren't you curious to know who the real father was?" Billy Ray sat back, content to let the question fester in Payne's mind.

Payne didn't reply, though it was evident his brain cycled at full speed. Muscles on his neck betrayed the inner turmoil.

They arrived at very familiar territory. Payne turned the vehicle off of State Highway 155 onto an access road to a pecan orchard. It was the very same location as on the night of his first arrest a decade ago. In the light of the lone lamppost marking the entrance to the orchard, Billy Ray caught a fleeting glimpse of his captors. Payne wore an expression he was surprised to see, confusion. Dixon's look was that of an executioner, though mixed with something else, fear? He'd seen such looks on men's faces before.

There'd be no further need for provocation. He was in their heads.

The vehicle came to a stop.

Payne made the first move. He looked down at his watch. Then without emotion said, "Time's up, Jenkins."

Dixon jumped out, eager, like a kid at a carnival. He rounded the vehicle, nearly beating his boss to the back door.

Payne gave a nod.

Dixon tore at the handle. "Outa' the car, punk!" His gun was back in his hand, the safety switched off.

Payne stepped to one side, Dixon the other. As Billy Ray swung his legs out the door, both men grabbed a foot and yanked him from the vehicle. His head slammed on the ground. The sandy soil prevented his losing consciousness from the blow.

The first thing Billy Ray felt after hitting the ground was a boot sinking into his side, narrowly missing a direct hit to his ribs. Payne's kick proved more accurate. A searing pain shot up the trunk of his body and flashed like a bolt of lightning in his brain.

He couldn't sustain the punishing blows for long and still retain the wherewithal to fight back. Better to be battered with fists than stomped by heavy boots. His hands were bound behind his back and pinned beneath him. Only his legs and feet were available for his defense. He was never so thankful for his training in jujitsu as now. Eighty percent of the time in a fight, a person wound up on the ground. Jujitsu was designed to survive an attack from the ground. He'd use his legs to gain leverage and momentum. He hoped to disable one or both of his attackers long enough to gain a standing position. If he failed....

The kicks from both lawmen assumed a rhythm that proved their undoing. Billy Ray timed an incoming blow from Dixon, caught the kick, scissored his legs, and log-rolled in one violent motion. Dixon's momentum betrayed him. He slammed into Payne and lost hold of his gun, which flew through the air and landed a safe distance.

Payne's natural reflex was to catch Dixon, and would have succeeded if not for snagging a heel on a tree root. Both men went down in a heap, Dixon on top of Payne. They struggled in each other's arms to get upright.

Billy Ray wasted no time. He pulled his knees to his chest, kipped outward to a squatting position, and rose to his feet.

Payne lay on his back with his potbellied deputy on top. Seeing no chance to right himself, he grabbed for his gun.

Billy Ray kicked him in the head. Payne went limp.

Dixon untangled himself and get to his knees. He frantically searched for his gun, spotted it, and moved to retrieve it. He failed to reach his goal.

Billy Ray shifted his balance and kneed the despicable deputy in the temple. Dixon let out a groan and fell onto his boss' unconscious body.

The scene of two large men juxtaposed atop one another in a tangle of limbs and brown uniforms, while a third man of lesser size, hands cuffed behind his back, lowered in a semi-crouch, gave testament to the twin powers of martial arts—balance and leverage. On the other hand, youth and prison muscles didn't hurt matters.

He located the keys to the handcuffs and set himself free. Then he disarmed Payne, retrieved Dixon's gun, and dragged both men to the far side of the car and cuffed them to the door.

His side hurt from the effort. He didn't know if his ribs were cracked or if blood would color his urine in the morning. He ignored the pain and got to work safing the area.

Mission accomplished, Billy Ray then did the unthinkable for most arrested convicts. He let himself into the patrol car and radioed for help. Afterward, he reapplied the cuffs, hands in front this time, and moved to the rear seat opposite his oppressors.

Then he waited.

31

Lam turned onto State Highway 155 North to begin the final few miles into Big Sandy. He'd called ahead and secured a room at a motor lodge. Before retiring for the night, he hoped to talk with the duty officer at the Big Sandy station. He wanted access to the police reports dealing with the Jenkins drowning and statements by any and all witnesses. The parents of the missing Richards girl may shed light on the matter. However, there'd been two additional witnesses who saw Ricky Jenkins and the Richards girl together that might provide greater detail and establish time and proximity. One of those witnesses was now dead, Edward Jones. Lam had only a first name for the second witness in his notebook. *Rebecca.* He needed to learn the woman's full name and question her.

The police radio crackled to life. The scanner stopped on a local transmission. He hadn't been paying close attention. The message repeated itself. What he heard snapped his mind back to reality!

"...Chief Harlan or units of the Big Sandy Police Department, I'm calling for backup. My name is Billy Ray Jenkins. I'm currently under arrest by Upshur County Sheriff Roy Payne and his deputy. Our current situation requires immediate assistance as both officers are presently incapable of making this call."

Lam almost hit an armadillo crossing the road. He slammed on his breaks and swerved. He was so shocked by the call that he sat idling in the middle of the highway.

"Our position is approximately four miles from the I-20 turn-off on Texas Route 155 North, near Winona. Look for the service road to a pecan orchard. A lamppost marks the entrance. If no one responds, it'll be a very long night for Payne and Dixon."

Lam checked his odometer. He couldn't have driven more than a mile or two on 155 after turning off the Interstate. He had to be close to the origin of the radio transmission. He put his car in gear and drove slowly for the next two miles.

The lamppost shone like a beacon in the night. He made the turn onto the dirt service road. He didn't get far before seeing the glow of car lights in the distance. He approached the scene with extreme caution and came to a stop several hundred feet from his objective. He pulled the keys, and doused the headlights. Then he unholstered his Glock 22 service pistol, checked the 15-round ammo magazine, and chambered a round. He reached up and switched the overhead cab light to the *off* position.

He exited the vehicle, but allowed the door to stand ajar in case the scene went to hell and he had to beat feet. The darkness was oppressive. The moon had not yet risen and the night sky was cloudy. Lam concentrated his efforts on keeping steady footing over the dirt road as he headed towards the glow in the distance. He topped a hill and looked down onto a truly strange site. It made him think of those shows on television about alien abductions. In this case, the abductees were chained to a police car. In the back of the cruiser was the clear silhouette of a man's head.

He circled the area, careful to avoid the vehicle headlights. He chose a position that allowed a clear line of sight into the back of the vehicle. The Jenkins guy sat still and quiet in the back seat. The hands appeared to be cuffed and folded in Jenkins' lap. On the far side of the vehicle, two slumping bodies in uniforms hung from the door handle. Special Agent Johnny Lam had witnessed his share of weird cases, but nothing like this. What was Jenkins up to?

There was only one way to find out. He unsafed his weapon and crept closer. He took a knee and positioned his pistol.

He commanded, "Identify yourself."

"You know who I am, Agent Lam." Billy Ray turned his head to the voice. "It took you long enough to recon the area."

Lam was impressed. The guy had keen senses and must've been hell in the bush. He'd heard those SEALs were good warfighters. He held his aim. "What gave me away?"

"I'll tell you someday. I admit you did pretty well. Army?"

Jenkins had him on that one, too. Enough banter, he decided. "What's going on here, Jenkins?"

"The sheriff and his deputy arrested me."

"For what?"

"They didn't say."

Lam became testy. "Cut the crap. Why are two officers of the law hanging from the side of the car?"

"Isn't it obvious?"

"Humor me."

"Long story, sir. Let's just say the sheriff had his own agenda. One I couldn't allow. Now how about I ask you a question?"

This Jenkins guy had stone balls.

"Ask away," Lam said.

"Why'd you come back?"

"To learn more about your brother's death, and about what happened to Edward Jones."

"He was hit by a car."

"A little coincidental, don't you think?"

"Kind of what I thought when I found his body."

That statement got Lam's attention. He'd scoured the police reports and didn't remember seeing Jenkins's name.

"What do you mean *you* found Jones? You're nowhere in the reports. How do I know it wasn't you who killed the old man?"

There was stirring on the far side of the sheriff's cruiser and then an audible groan. Both men heard it.

"No need to insult me. Jonesy was long dead when I found him. I can't answer why I don't appear in the reports. Maybe you should ask the sheriff when he wakes up."

Lam didn't know what to make of Jenkins. It was time to approach the car. "Am I going to have any trouble from you?"

"None whatsoever, sir, so long as you exercise your police powers according to the law."

"Keep your hands where I can see them."

Lam made his way to the vehicle and poked his head around the door. Convinced the prisoner was secure, he went to the downed officers. The nametag of the man beginning to stir read "Dixon." The badge and insignias of the other man made it clear who he was, Sheriff Roy Payne.

"Holy cow, Jenkins! What did you do to these guys. You're in handcuffs, for goodness sake!"

"If you want to be really impressed, my hands were cuffed behind me at the time."

Lam was speechless. He located a key for the cuffs in the sheriff's pocket, unlatched the men, and lowered them to the ground. Chatter erupted on the police radio. The dispatcher was calling for verification. As a federal agent, he was far beyond his jurisdiction. But as a sworn officer of the law, it was incumbent upon him to aid and assist law enforcement officers when needed—such as when rendered unconscious by a prisoner, disarmed, and chained to their own vehicle. Jenkins was where he should be, cuffed and back, and had even called for backup to the scene.

Lam wasn't quite ready to call in the cavalry. He wanted to know more. Not just what happened between Jenkins and the two lawmen, but anything Jenkins might know about the death of Edward Jones.

He rounded the vehicle and stood before the open door, pistol hanging at his side.

"You're one strange dude, Jenkins."

Billy Ray smiled. "I'll take that as a compliment, sir."

"And one more thing," Lam said.

"Yes, sir?"

"Stop calling me sir!"

"Yes, s—" Billy Ray caught himself. "What do I call you?"

"*Lam* will do for now."

"Well then, Lam, you'll find both their weapons locked in the trunk."

The police radio sounded. The voice was different this time. Both men stopped their conversation and looked toward the radio.

Billy Ray nodded. "That's the Big Sandy Police Chief, Wesley Harlan. I suggest you answer the call. Harlan's a straight shooter, I trust him to get this mess cleared up. I can also *guaran-damn-tee* you it'll be more pleasant dealing with him than with the sheriff."

"And why should I care, you stuck your own foot in this stink pile. I'm FBI, not a local cop. You don't need me. In fact, I'd say you need a lawyer...or a really good shrink!"

"You should care. I know who killed my brother and Edward Jones."

Lam hesitated. A second groggy voice joined the first on the far side of the car and the radio came to life again. Things were speeding up. Soon the place would be crawling with cops. He made a decision, one he'd been contemplating since first hearing Jenkins' voice over the radio. His gut said something nasty was crawling through the Big Piney. There were bits and pieces of information, he needed a lot more. He was a detective not a clairvoyant.

"Yup…one strange dude." Lam holstered his weapon. He moved to the front door, bent in, and retrieved the handset.

From the other side of the car, a groggy voice said, "What the hell?" It was Dixon, conscious and looking at his fallen comrade.

Lam made the call on the radio to Chief Harlan, informing him how to get to the scene, and requesting an ambulance as well. He managed to avoid Harlan's questions over the radio. He didn't want all hell descending on the area at once. He placed the radio set back in the vehicle and returned to the prisoner. "Here's the deal, Jenkins. You're going to tell me all you know about Jones and your brother. And you're also going to do things my way. Got it?"

"Loud and clear, Lam. Your way."

The word messy didn't begin to describe what happened next, confusion, commotion, cussing, shouting—and all in the middle of a pecan orchard near Winona, Texas, on a dark June night. Along with the wailing sirens of police cars and ambulances there was the chore of keeping two insanely pissed off sheriff personnel from shooting Billy Ray Jenkins full of holes. Just as Lam got Payne corralled, the deputy would rush the car in an attempt to drag the prisoner from the back seat, all the while screaming how he was "gonna kill the bastard" and "I know all your tricks now, you coward!" Lam noted the hollow ring to Dixon's bravado.

Order was finally established when Chief Harlan placed the prisoner in the back of his own police car and locked the doors. Peace was achieved when the sirens went silent. Harmony, however, became forever impossible. It was obvious to all present that the only damage sustained by the two lawmen was to their pride. Both would enjoy headaches come morning, partly from Jenkins' clobbering, but more from all the yelling they'd done. Nothing a few aspirin couldn't cure. Harlan retrieved both men's weapons from the trunk of their vehicle and sent them on their way with a promise that the prisoner would be properly attended to at the Big Sandy station. Only Dixon left with a parting threat. Payne needed no words to convey his intentions. Lam had seen the look before, vengeance mixed with murder.

He shuddered at what Payne had in mind for Billy Ray Jenkins.

* * *

Five minutes after the gathering of law officers had dispersed, headlights from two electric motorbikes punctured the darkness in the orchard. The riders removed compact Heckler and Koch MP7 machine guns from beneath their jackets. Headlights were extinguished. Both men flipped down special visors on their helmets to give them night vision capability. The men scanned the area that only moments ago had been the site of so much chaos. All was quiet. The men stowed their weapons, flipped up their night vision visors, turned on their headlights, and departed.

32

Neither man spoke on the trip to the Big Sandy police station. Billy Ray remained calm in the back of Harlan's patrol car, content in his faith that justice would prevail.

Eventually.

Lam followed behind.

Billy Ray had to admit, it hadn't taken him long to like the guy. Lam was a bit of a prick, but certainly cut from strong cloth. There was character in the man, likely forged in the heat of battle. He sensed a kinship.

Harlan pulled up to the front of the station and turned off the engine. He turned and faced his charge. "Son, you do have a way of calling lightning down on you. What'd you ever do to make Roy Payne hate you so much?"

"I loved his daughter."

"That'd about do it. But if you ask me, it seems to go deeper."

"I can only speak for myself, Chief. I loved Payne's daughter and she killed herself on my watch. It's taken me years to forgive myself."

Harlan grunted and shifted his attention back to police business.

Lam pulled in beside Harlan's patrol car and shut off the motor. All was quiet, for about five seconds.

Harlan extracted his prisoner from the rear of the police cruiser. Lam stood nearby to observe. Just then, another vehicle pulled into the parking lot. It was his mother's car, Gus at the wheel, Lela and Rebecca in the back. Billy Ray was shocked to see his mother. He didn't know she'd been discharged from the hospital.

The two lawmen flanked Billy Ray on either side, and began leading him in cuffs into the station.

Lela's voice called out from behind. "Billy Ray!"

The three stopped their progress and turned to face Lela Jenkins rushing up to meet them.

"Billy Ray…Wesley…what's going on here?" Lela panted, out of breath from her sprint across the parking lot.

Billy Ray looked at Harlan, who took the lead. "Now, Lela—"

"Don't you 'now Lela' me, Wesley Harlan. You know my son hasn't done anything wrong."

"I don't know what's goin' on, I'm just followin' procedure."

Billy Ray and Lam glanced at each other. Both knew a mother's anger could be tough to deal with.

“Well, I know what's going on. Rebecca told me all about it.” Lela placed hands on hips in typical mad-mother fashion.

Gus and Rebecca caught up alongside.

Lam broke the silence. “Rebecca, I presume?”

She looked Lam up and down. “Yes. And who might you be?”

Harlan broke in. “Now folks, how ‘bout moving indoors for howdy-dos. I’d kinda’ like to get to the bottom of this.”

Five heads nodded.

Harlan produced a key. “Billy Ray, if you wouldn't mind.”

He took the hint and lifted his hands. The chief removed the cuffs. Without another word the grizzled old lawman turned on his heel and marched straight to his office. Like spring ducklings the group followed behind.

The office was small with only one available chair. Harlan offered it to Lela. She obliged and sat down.

Harlan remained standing. He looked over at the wall clock and back at the folks assembled before him, ready to wrap the matter up quickly and get back to bed. He leaned forward, placed his palms on his desk, and let out a sigh. “Now, could somebody please tell me what in Betty's bloomers is going on in my town?”

Five heads began talking at once.

Harlan sat down and buried his face in his hands.

* * *

Two men wearing motorcycle helmets stood at attention before Wiggins. Their faces showed worried expressions.

“What do you mean there was no sign of them?”

Neither guard dared an answer.

Wiggins persisted. “Who took the radio call and dispatched your team?” He scanned the room. The twelve faces of his top security team stared back at him in silence.

Yet another lapse in the finely woven security web around Operation Blood Star.

He checked his cheap-looking Casio wristwatch. A tiny symbol blinked constantly beside the digital date readout.

The meeting of his security team had been hastily convened. These dozen men were his most trusted guards. He had fifty more highly-trained men tasked with perimeter security, but none having the operational knowledge of these twelve. They were sworn on their lives to protect the mission. If ever captured, they were to bite down on the fake porcelain molar imbedded in their mouths, bursting a cyanide capsule to end their lives and foiling any attempt by an enemy to extract information—or so the guards were told.

Wiggins had actually made the doctors in Pyongyang implant tiny explosive charges in each man's tooth, instead. A man's willingness to commit suicide was never guaranteed. Nor was his Casio watch what it appeared to be. What was advertised as a cheap timepiece had been vastly altered. With the push of a button, a guard's brain could be rendered a worthless skull of mush. It was for that very purpose the tiny symbol of a cracked egg now blinked.

He studied the faces of the guards, searching their souls as it were. The day would come when all evidence would be erased. But not this day. He pressed another button on the watch and the egg stopped blinking.

Lee Dong-moon hung up the phone he'd been on since the start of the meeting and stepped forward. "It was I who heard the radio call for help by the man named Jenkins. I concluded your plan of deception had failed. I sent the teams to eliminate Jenkins."

Wiggins stepped close to Lee. He took advantage of the height difference to show supremacy. He couldn't allow his number two in charge to erode his control. Furthermore, he suspected Lee of having secret orders from the Dear Leader. All the more reason Wiggins did what came next.

"Did you consider killing the police to eliminate witnesses?"

"Yes. They were to be eliminated as well."

"You fool!" Wiggins shouted down into the shorter man's face.

Lee shouted back. "I assumed your plan had failed. To save the operation, I took matters into my own hands!"

With lightning speed, Wiggins snatched a machine gun from a helmeted guard and brought it to bear against Lee's head. The gun was switched to *full auto*. "Challenging my authority, Mr. Lee?"

Lee didn't move a muscle. He didn't even breathe.

"Cat got your tongue, Mr. Lee?"

Lee knew that further resistance was pointless, and probably lethal. He could wait out this foreigner. At the right time he'd kill Wiggins. But until then, there was a mission to complete.

Ever so slowly, Lee lowered his eyes from looking directly into the face of Wiggins. He exhaled slowly and allowed his shoulders to sag in a show of contrition. "I apologize. Your plan is a good one. I acted impatiently."

"I'll accept that, mate." Wiggins removed the gun from Lee's head and motioned him back into formation. "At ease, men"

Twelve guards relaxed their stance, barely. Lee did not.

"Now listen to me very carefully. I can't afford any more of your mistakes. Failure is not an option."

Twelve heads nodded obligatorily.

"We're fortunate the elimination team arrived too late. A firefight with local law enforcement would've blown our entire operation."

He couldn't allow his father's memory to end in failure.

"Blood Star goes fully operational in three days. Until then, we stick to my plan. If there's to be killing, it comes on my orders only."

He saw twelve faces eager to please.

"Do I make myself understood, mates?"

With the precision of an Irish dance troop, the line of men slapped their heels and shouted, "Yes, sir!"

Wiggins dismissed the men to their posts.

Lee remained. He removed any tone of hatred from his voice. He'd rise above the conflict. The mission came first. "Master Wiggins, what do you propose to do about this man, Jenkins? He's sniffing our trail like a dog."

"I agree, mate. But he's only one man."

"Maybe not. The FBI agent who was in town asking questions has returned. Our source informed me only minutes ago that the agent is even now with Jenkins at the Big Sandy police station."

"Was the agent present during the fiasco in the orchard?"

"Our source indicates he was."

"Then I'd say we've been dealt our first lucky card, mate. Had that elimination team arrived sooner, it would've spelled disaster for Operation Blood Star. One call from a live FBI agent or missed call-in from a dead one would bring the world crashing on our heads."

Wiggins rubbed his chin in thought. A smile spread across his face, as it tended to do whenever he countered the simple forward movement of a pawn with the stealth and misdirection of a knight. "We can't have the FBI snooping around. It's time to have a little chat with an angel."

"You mean Gallina?"

"Right. Angel Gallina."

Wiggins turned and headed into his office.

33

It took a while, but eventually the story came out of how Billy Ray and Rebecca were attacked at the Frontier Inn. Dixon claimed an anonymous caller phoned the sheriff to report a man going berserk and tearing up the joint. No explanation was given as to how the sheriff and deputy ended up in a pecan orchard with the suspected culprit from the tavern, nor was one requested.

Chief Harlan ended the call and hung up the phone. Dixon had only been running interference for the sheriff. If he wanted to know more it'd have to come from Payne himself, which would happen the same day hell froze over.

There was a form of communication between law officers beyond the use of actual words. To keep peace between his station and the Upshur County Sheriff Department, some ass-covering was needed. It'd be granted against future favors owed. The law still needed to be respected. So it was no big surprise to Billy Ray at what came next.

"Here's what we're going to do," Harlan announced. He faced Lam. "It's agreed. Mr. Jenkins will be released into your custody." Harlan then turned his comments toward Billy Ray. "Well son, other than the anonymous call to the sheriff's office, no other complaints have come forth. I had one of my patrol officers run by the Frontier Inn a few minutes ago. He reported all was peaceful. The bartender claimed there'd been no trouble."

Billy Ray interrupted. "Chief, did your patrolman happen to mention the bartender's ethnicity?"

Harlan cast Billy Ray a curious look. "My man's exact words were, 'the Mexican dude behind the bar said, *no problemas.*'"

Billy Ray shot Rebecca a look.

"Now if you don't mind, son, I'd like to finish my little speech."

"Sorry, Chief."

"I sure hope so, as much for your mother's sake as for your own." He looked at Lela sitting to his side. "There'll be no charges filed against you, and you'll file no charges against anyone else...if you get my drift. I just can't keep covering for you and Payne. So whatever set the two of you at each other's throats, you'd better get it solved, and damn quick."

Billy Ray merely nodded.

"I might also suggest something for your health and wellbeing."

Billy Ray formed a curious look. "Sir?"

"Consider moving to Alaska. Or better yet, try Europe. Just get as far away from here as possible."

Rebecca began to say something and stopped.

"Now, if y'all wouldn't mind getting the hell out of my office so an old man can go back to bed."

As she stood with the help of an arm from Lam, Lela spoke up. "Wesley, as I've always said, there's no more fair and honest man in this county than you, except for my son here."

"Thank you, Lela. And I'm sure you're right about your boy, considering the company he keeps." Harlan motioned at the group.

Lela shook hands with Harlan, as did Billy Ray and Rebecca. Lam cast a two-finger salute. Gus held the door.

They all gathered in the parking lot. It was decided they'd all go to Lela's and discuss the evening's events. Gus drove Lela in her car, Billy Ray and Rebecca rode with Lam.

Rebecca was offered the front seat. Billy Ray took the back. "Hey, third time tonight in the back of a cop car."

"Uhh, that's not a good thing," Rebecca said.

"I could cuff you if it'd make you feel more at home," Lam threw in. He turned to Rebecca. "We haven't formally met."

"Where are my manners?" Billy Ray said from the back.

"You never had any!" Lam said over his shoulder.

Billy Ray let that one go. "Agent Johnny Lam, please allow me to introduce a truly wonderful lady, Rebecca Payne."

She batted her eyelashes. "Flattery will get you nowhere."

Outwardly, Lam's face yielded little. Inwardly, he was shocked to hear Rebecca's full name. "Are you—"

"The sheriff's daughter," she interrupted, then offered Lam a pretty smile for his trouble.

"I see. Are you also the Rebecca listed as one of the eyewitness who saw Ricky Jenkins and Clarice Richards together the day of the incident?"

"Yes. I reported what I saw to officer Glover just as soon as I heard about Ricky."

Lam started the car. "You mind telling me your story?"

"Actually, we both have a lot to say, stuff you won't find in any police report—starting with Ricky and Clarice being murdered."

"Ms. Payne, I'm all ears." Lam wasn't actually shocked by Rebecca's statement. After what he'd just been through, nothing with these people would surprise him anymore.

During the twenty-minute drive to Gladewater, Rebecca and Billy Ray gave their accounting of Edward Jones and the old man's story, Billy Ray's suspicions about Joseph Wiggins and his Korean employees, even a short history of him and Sheriff Payne. Rebecca filled in the gaps. It was still a mystery, however, how the Mexican hooligans fit in.

Lam listened without interrupting. He catalogued the bits and pieces of information, assembled a logical outline…if this then that, if that then the other thing, and so on. It wasn't that he doubted Jenkins and Rebecca. It was just that nothing tied together. Crime or not, nothing warranted the involvement of the Bureau. He was getting tangled in the weeds. Only one matter prompted his venturing into the Big Piney—drugs. Even then, only to investigate the new product, Rapture. Nothing else justified being so far off the reservation. Consequently, nothing expressed thus far related to drugs. Dreyfus was expected from D.C. in three days. Lam gave himself two. If nothing turned up, he'd head back to Dallas and partake in some Independence Day celebrating.

They pulled into Lela's driveway, ended their conversation, and made their way into the house. Lela made everyone feel welcome with tea and sandwiches.

"Mom, you're supposed to be in the hospital resting."

Gus took the question. "Billy Ray, uh...that'd be my fault."

"How so, Gus?"

Lela joined in, "Yeah, how so?"

"After Rebecca found me at the hospital saying good night to Lela, and informed us that you'd been taken by her dad, I should've gone straight to my car, retrieved a roll of duct tape, and trussed her up but good!"

"It would've done you no good, Gus. I'd chew through logger chains to get my son back!"

Everyone drank tea and shared a snack. They discussed the night's events, though not all. Billy Ray, Lam, and Rebecca had agreed beforehand on that matter. It was decided to just avoid the sheriff and his deputies. Lam also suggested Billy Ray make the rounds with him in the morning to fulfill Chief Harlan's orders. Rebecca begged to join them. However, her presence in the group would only serve to aggravate matters further with Sheriff Payne. Reluctantly, she agreed to remain behind.

Regarding the last order of business, Lela insisted Lam stay the night. After calling the travel lodge where he'd reserved a room and getting no answer, Lam accepted the invite.

"Okay everyone, sunup is in four hours." Billy Ray turned to Gus. "I know it's late, but would you mind dropping Rebecca off at her apartment?"

Gus waved off the concern. "No problem."

Billy Ray could swear Rebecca was pouting, but doing her best to hide it. He now had a much better understanding of this lovely lady—she preferred being in the middle of the action.

The day had been long and filled with stress. They were all well past tired. Lela showed Lam to his sleeping quarters. Gus headed out to start the car. Billy Ray and Rebecca were left alone, standing face to face in the living room.

They searched each other's eyes. The silence was comfortable and allowed for discovering feelings usually drowned by words.

Billy Ray took Rebecca's hands in his. "I'm sorry for all of this. I'm sorry for being a thorn in your father's side. This can only mean trouble for you."

Rebecca put a finger to Billy Ray's lips. "Let's see where this goes. If it's right, nothing in this world can stop it."

Billy Ray kissed her finger. He escorted her to the waiting car and then watched as Rebecca disappeared into the night. He hadn't heard Lam approach.

"What an extraordinary woman," Lam offered softly.

He considered Lam's words and it came to him. Rebecca was so much more than extraordinary, she was familiar.

He faced Lam. "Thanks for saving my butt tonight."

Lam flashed a smile. "You're welcome, Navy boy."

The two men headed back into the house.

* * *

A gray sedan parked behind a stand of Laurel bushes half a block from Lela's house. A man got out and stood to one side of the vehicle. He wore dark clothing and a black ball cap. He watched the front of Lela Jenkins' house through binoculars. He'd witnessed the Payne girl leave with the old man. Now he watched the FBI agent and Jenkins end their conversation and disappear into the house.

The man got back in his car, stowed the binoculars, and left.

34

The smell of eggs and bacon filled the house. Billy Ray entered the kitchen dressed in Navy-issue sweat clothes and took a seat opposite a fully dressed and spry Johnny Lam.

Lam said, “Mornin’ sweetheart. Enjoy your beauty sleep?”

Billy Ray grunted. “I must’ve missed reveille.”

Lela passed Billy Ray a plate of breakfast. His side hurt from Payne’s boot, but there was nothing wrong with his teeth. He satisfied his hunger on a good, home-cooked meal.

“You missed more than the bugle call, sailor. You lost out on a beautiful sunrise and a two-mile run.”

Billy Ray looked at Lam. “You an Army guy or something?”

“Captain, Green Berets. 7th Special Forces Group, Fort Bragg.”

“That explains it, then.”

“Explains what?”

“Why your mommy broke your plate and burned your picture.”

Lela giggled. “Stick a fork in it, boys. I need the dishes for the next crew.”

It was good seeing his mother back in action. The doctor was right, she’d just needed rest. “Look who’s got her sparkle on.”

“It feels good to cook for hungry men!” The fun stuff out of the way, she turned to the topic troubling them—Roy Payne. “What are we going to do about the sheriff? My bet is he’ll consume every waking minute planning how to destroy Billy Ray.”

“You seem to know his habits pretty well,” Billy Ray probed.

“Payne’s been a rock in my shoe since before you were born.”

“I know, Gus told me.”

“I see. Then you also know Payne ruined your father's life.”

“I thought alcohol ruined his life.”

“It did, later. But I believe someone pushed him over the edge until he was too sick to find his way back.”

“And you think that someone was Payne?”

“I don’t think…I know.”

Sensing it was his turn to talk, Lam offered a solution. “Lela, I gave the matter of Sheriff Payne more thought. I’ve changed my mind. I now think the best way—the only way—to deal with a bully is to go straight at him.”

“How so?” Lela asked.

Maybe Lam had more balls than brains, Billy Ray thought.

Lam answered, “I’m going to take Billy Ray over to Payne’s office and make him apologize.”

Billy Ray nearly gagged on his eggs. “Are you nuts!”

Lam threw up his hands. “Hear me out.”

Billy Ray nodded. Lela took the third seat at the table. Lam spent the next five minutes outlining his idea.

“I thought you FBI guys always play by the book.”

“I am playing by the book,” Lam shot back.

“Then you added a centerfold,” Billy Ray said.

Lam smiled. “I’m betting Payne swallows hook, line, and sinker.”

“What will your boss say?” Lela asked.

“After what I heard last night, he’d be fine with my decision. Besides, we’re kind of fishing for bad guys at the moment.”

Lela gave a curious look. “Fishing?”

Lam’s training said to keep his mouth shut…need-to-know and all. His logic said otherwise. He chose logic. “There’s a new drug coming on the market, and it’s killing people.”

“The one found in my brother’s system?”

“It’s called Rapture. We don’t know where it’s coming from. We only have corpses. Worse yet, our lab guys predict that if Rapture hits the streets, we could see tens of thousands of overdoses.”

Lela and Billy Ray looked at each other.

“I’m also trolling for another big fish. One of the major Mexican drug cartels has just come up missing.”

Billy Ray hadn't heard that one before, it sounded like a joke.

“By the way, this conversation doesn't leave this room.” Lam looked at the others. They nodded. “For now, let’s just concentrate on Sheriff Payne.”

Lela stood and gathered up the breakfast dishes.

“May I help with cleanup?” Lam asked.

Lela began to decline, then changed her mind. “That’d be nice of you.”

Billy Ray handed over his dishes. “I’d better get ready for inspection. Payne might arrest me for having a hair out of place.”

“Go get squared away, Johnny and I will clear the mess deck.”

“I’ll be ready in twenty,” Billy Ray said and headed off to shower, wondering where his mother learned all the Navy lingo.

35

Lam took wash duty, Lela drying and putting away.

"Johnny, can you tell me if Billy Ray is going to get through this? He's a good man, and not deserving of any more prison." She bit her lip. "He wasn't deserving the first time, if you can believe that."

Lam finished the last plate and handed it to Lela. "I do believe that. You once told me that if I was worth my salt, I'd have the skinny on Billy Ray before leaving Dallas. As far as I could determine, your son committed no crime. He was a victim of circumstances and shouldn't have gone to prison, though he could've done more to help his cause."

"I agree. Some of that mess was Billy Ray's own making. He tried so hard to love the Payne girl. He just couldn't forgive himself when she died."

"And neither could Roy Payne, I take it."

"But there's more. It goes back before those kids were born." Lela sat down. "After dating just a week, Payne wanted me to be his wife. I turned him down. He pushed himself on me anyway. As an only child in a rich family, he was used to getting everything he wanted." Lela pulled herself up straight. "This time he didn't get it."

"So you think Payne was jealous of you."

"Yes, to the extreme. He nearly killed Rodney over me." Lela looked out the kitchen window. "It probably would've been better had Payne killed Rodney that night. In many ways my husband died then anyway. Payne busted his leg, and with it, all chances of winning a college scholarship."

"Your husband was an athlete?"

"One of the best in Texas. Payne damaged Rodney's leg on purpose, ruining his chances for college."

"Sounds like Payne has always been a bully."

Lela lowered her voice. "It goes beyond bully…the man's sick. He saw to it that Rodney always got fired from his jobs. We didn't know it until later. By then, the damage was done, nobody would hire my husband. We lost our home and moved into a shack near the highway. Rodney began to drink, but he'd never say where the money came from for the alcohol."

Lam let Lela build the story at her own pace.

"One day I got a callback on a job application, cleaning the courthouse and sheriff's office of all places. I suspected Payne had something to do with it, but the money would help. It didn't. Rodney got worse, much worse."

"And that's what Billy Ray was referring to?"

"Yes. His father became an alcoholic. But here's the part Billy Ray knows nothing about. Rodney began imagining that Payne and I were having an affair."

"Were you?"

"No."

"Sorry, Lela. I had to ask." He was a detective first, a hand-holder second. Being a cop could be difficult at times like this.

"It's your job. Besides, I want this out. It may save my son's life."

It may save his own life. He was about to confront Payne. If the man was dangerous, it'd be nice to know it up front. He proceeded with his questions. "Was there something that made your husband suspicious or was it just the booze talking?"

"I discovered Payne had been pumping my husband with lies and drink all along. He told Rodney that I tried coming on to him at work, and to keep his wife on a leash." Lela's face turned red.

Ouch! Lam had no respect for men who said such things.

"I tried telling Rodney it was a lie. That was the first time he hit me." Lela breathed deep. "It was Payne, he tried to rape me!"

Lam was a man first, cop second. He felt his fists balling up.

"It happened one night during the Christmas holiday. Payne had the holiday shift. He and I were the only people in the building. He cornered me in a storage closet while I was stowing my cleaning materials. He shut the door and barred the way."

Lam could feel his blood beginning to boil.

"It was obvious what he wanted. It's what he'd always wanted from me and never got. Payne didn't bother with words, he just grabbed my blouse and tore it off. I screamed and slapped his face. There was no one to hear my cries. He came at me with all his size. I managed to grab an open bottle of ammonia and throw it in his face. Then it was his turn to scream!"

Outwardly, Lam remained calm. Inside, however, he seethed. He hated brutes who forced themselves on women. "What happened next?"

"Payne let go. I grabbed my blouse and ran. A good Samaritan found me and drove me home. And then Rodney beat me." Lela paused, the pain still obvious after so many years. "I can't say how Payne bewitched my husband, but I can tell you the next dozen years were hell."

Lam wondered where the story was going.

Lela sensed Lam's concern and fast-forwarded. "Rodney came home one night after money that Billy Ray was mailing from his paychecks. He beat me up and even hurt little Ricky, and kept screaming that I was a whore and demanding the money Payne was giving me, and how Ricky was Payne's son, not his."

Lam held still.

"Now I knew where Rodney was getting all those terrible ideas. Payne hadn't been content just ruining Rodney's leg, he wanted my husband's soul. Payne made sure Rodney had nobody to turn to but him. Rodney never told me. He thought I was the enemy."

Lela's eyes grew moist. Her shoulders slumped. Lam felt her agony. What Payne had done was more than criminal—it was evil. He put an arm around Lela. "Does your son know this?"

"Not what I told you. I'm afraid if he finds out there'll be no stopping him. He'll kill Payne and go to prison forever."

"What can I do to help?"

Lela patted Lam's arm. "I appreciate what you've already done. I know you're outside your jurisdiction, but there's more." She poured a glass of water at the sink. She looked at Lam. "I've told you my story in hopes you'll believe me when I say Payne murdered my husband. And now he wants to kill Billy Ray."

That hit Lam between the eyes. From Lela's story, he'd assumed she was divorced. Now he was learning that Rodney Jenkins was dead, and that the Sheriff had killed him.

"Do you have proof?"

"Some. I hope to know more soon."

"What does Billy Ray know?"

"He thinks his father ran off to avoid arrest."

"And you know different?"

"A week after my husband put me in the hospital, he was seen riding in Payne's car onto his family's vacation property."

"Wait, so you're telling me Rodney abused you, linked up with Payne, and was taken to the Gulf, and not heard from again?"

Lela swallowed more water to calm her nerves. "I'm saying Roy Payne found out Billy Ray was sending me money, then manipulated my by-now alcoholic husband into believing his wife was prostituting herself and had the cash and one bastard child to prove it. And I'm saying Roy Payne killed my husband over the course of many years, until getting the opportunity to finally murder him. And now he won't rest until Billy Ray is dead."

"But why, what would make Payne want to hurt your family?"

"He's sick. It's me he's killing. It's me he wants—has always wanted. And if he can't have me, he'll make sure nobody can."

Lam thought hard on Lela's words. If he hadn't been an FBI agent for the past ten years and seen things to boggle the mind, he would've dismissed her story. But evil did exist, he'd seen it.

He'd also seen Payne in action.

The shower turned off. Lam heard the door to the bedroom open and close. Billy Ray would be joining them soon.

"Who else have you told this to?"

"Chief Harlan," Lela said.

"What is Harlan doing to investigate your claims?"

"You'll have to ask him. I gave him all the information."

"I'll keep it in mind, Lela. That's all I can promise."

Billy Ray entered the kitchen and looked around. "Nice job, Lam. And you only claim to be a Green Beret. I'd say you're selling yourself short."

"And I'd say that was one hell of a Hollywood shower, pretty boy." Lam thanked Lela for breakfast and offered a handshake. He got a hug instead.

Billy Ray kissed his mother on the cheek and then turned to Lam. "You ready to get to work, Army?"

"Got no choice. Somebody's gotta' hold your hand, Navy boy."

They walked away engaged in the usual interservice rivalry.

36

Only a double-dose of ibuprofen quelled Dixon's aching head. The next time he ran into Jenkins, only one would walk out alive. Dixon did his duty, or perhaps just the really smart thing. He brought his boss' favorite latte. When he entered the office, he was surprised to see Roy Payne with his feet up on the desk and the morning newspaper spread out in front of him. The sheriff was even whistling an old show tune, as if he hadn't a care in the world. It didn't make sense. Payne had taken one hell of a whack from Jenkins. Dixon expected him to be spitting mad and tossing things around the office. He was forever amazed at Payne's reactions to things. It was as if Payne had other personalities. The latte always did the trick though. "Hey boss, gotcha' a cup of that good joe."

"Just put it on the desk." The whistling continued.

Dixon did so. Maybe Jenkins knocked something loose in Payne's head. He could take the waiting no longer. "Roy, aren't you even mad?"

"Mad about what?" Payne said from behind the newspaper.

"Mad about the Astros moving to the American league. What the hell you think I'm talking about, mad about Billy Ray Jenkins!"

"You're right, Tom." Payne lowered the paper, his eyes peered over the top. "What the hell's ours team doing on the left coast?" The paper lifted, Payne's eyes disappeared behind the newsprint.

Payne's phone buzzed. "Could you get that, Tom?"

Dixon grabbed the receiver. He grinned big and hung up.

"Who was it?"

"Beverly, out in the lobby. She says there's an FBI agent here to see you and that he has another man with him."

"Tell her to send them in."

Dixon delivered the message and then sat back with drink in hand, like a kid fixin' to watch cartoons.

"You can go in now, sir," the receptionist said.

Lam looked at Billy Ray. "Let me do the talking."

"You're a Captain, I'm but a lowly enlisted puke."

"That's right, Skippy. Don't ever forget it."

"Gotcha'."

"That's 'gotcha *sir'* to you, sailor."

"I thought you hated being called sir." Billy Ray shook his head.

Neither of them could have imagined what they'd find inside the sheriff's office. Payne was whistling and reading the paper, his sizefourteens on the desk. Dixon squatted like a service dog beside his master trying to act calm. Hand tremors spoiled that.

For a full minute, Billy Ray and Lam faced a newspaper.

Dixon sipped repeatedly at his coffee, but failed to outlast the quiet spell. "Uh, boss, you have guests."

"No guests of mine," said Payne from behind his paper.

They both knew what Payne was up to. This was his bailiwick and they but common petitioners.

"Sheriff Roy Payne, you may remember me from last night. My name's Lam. I'm an employee of the US Department of Justice, a Special Agent of the Federal Bureau of Investigation, to be precise."

"That's a mouthful," Payne said from behind the paper.

"You may also remember from last night, once you woke up," Lam jabbed, "that substantial evidence exists suggesting you and your deputy were engaged in a crime when I arrived at the scene."

Dixon shot up out of his chair. "Now wait just a minute!"

"Sit down, Tom." Payne lowered the newspaper an inch.

Lam pressed onward. "That'll be a matter for the Texas State Attorney General to decide. I know him well. The AG has very little patience for police who abuse their powers."

Dixon mumbled about it not being his fault, clearly the weak link.

The paper came down, Payne's feet came off the desk. He lifted a hand for Dixon to shut up. "You threatening me, FBI man?"

"No threat."

"How'd you like me to throw your ass outa here?"

"That'd be the day."

Payne stepped around the desk to directly in front of Lam. Billy Ray stood to one side, Dixon the other. It wasn't lost on Billy Ray that their opponents were both larger men, though the saying about being bigger and falling harder had certainly held true the previous night. He and Lam were flappin' in the breeze on this one, however. The room fell silent, the quiet before the trumpet sound. Billy Ray could almost smell Dixon's fear.

Payne went first. "Does your daddy Dreyfus know you're down here playing in my backyard, little FBI boy?"

"So you did your homework. Call him." Lam recited the number.

Billy Ray watched Payne consider the options. If correct that Lam was running rogue in Upshur County, Payne would get the best of the situation, but lose face if wrong. The process was rather like watching ice freeze in the arctic. Dixon, however, acted quite the opposite...clearly melting in the heat. He acted scared, a response incongruent with the circumstances. The guy was probably just a coward. Or was it something else? Billy Ray was past giving benefits of doubt. He was beyond naiveté. The last of his innocence lay in a dirt hole beside Ricky.

"I also have Abbott's number if you need." Payne countered.

"No need. Got Greg right here in my phone," Lam countered.

If Payne was ice, Lam was granite.

"What do you want?" The sound of ice cracking.

"Drop all charges against Mr. Jenkins."

Not one to be upstaged Payne said, "Already did. After further investigation, I learned the call last night was bogus."

"That's not all. I want you to back off, leave Jenkins alone."

For the first time since their arrival, Payne looked at Billy Ray.

If looks could kill.

No one spoke. Dixon appeared to have quit breathing. Lam stood his ground. Billy Ray met the eyes of hatred.

"Why should I ignore the presence of a criminal in my county?"

"Because he's working for me now."

"How so?"

"A confidential informant."

Payne gestured for them to get the hell out of his office and never come back.

Granite wins.

* * *

The pressure mounted. Three days until the pre-grand opening of the Texas Waterland Family Park. The arrival of the FBI agent had been unforeseeable. There was no way anyone could suspect the true function of the park. However, to do nothing might allow the agent to stumble onto their secret. Stopping him could pose even greater risks. The decision to quit the area had to come from the agent.

Wiggins had learned that Lam had a daughter on the East Coast. It was arranged. If Lam drew any closer, Gallina's contacts in the Eastern gangs would kidnap the girl. Lam would drop all to rush back and search for his daughter. As for Jenkins, no worries. Jenkins was just a local punk.

Phase One for the mass release of Rapture was all he needed to achieve his agenda. America, the great whore, would swallow the poison pill. By the time authorities located the source of death it'd be too late. Millions would be poisoned, the country thrown into chaos, people tearing at each other like rabid dogs. Operation Blood Star would meet with success—at least his portion of it.

His father would be avenged.

37

Lam led the way to the car. "I'm proud of you, Jenkins."

Billy Ray buckled the seatbelt and faced Lam. "Why's that?"

"You kept your mouth shut and your finger out of your nose."

"Gee, Lam, do you talk loud and slow to all your employees?"

"Just Navy guys."

Billy Ray conceded one point for Lam. He'd get him back later.

Lam started the car. "What you say we get the hell out of here before Payne actually does call the AG."

"You bullshitter!" Billy Ray laughed out loud.

Lam spun the car tires in a show of one dog kicking dirt in the face of another. They sped away from the Upshur County Sheriff's office as fast as safety would allow.

"Where to, Captain?" Billy Ray asked.

"Let's hit this thing head on...see if you're right about all this."

"Yeah, see if what we think is what we know."

"Huh?"

"Never mind, Lam."

"Right, Jenkins. Best let me do the thinking, too. Your job is to spot chicks and call in food orders."

"I never knew detective work could be so difficult, so…abusive."

"Well it is, Jenkins."

"Hand me your phone."

"I'm not hungry yet."

"Forget restaurants. I'm calling Greg!"

They headed south from the Upshur County Justice Center on US Route 271 toward Gladewater. The plan was for Billy Ray to show Lam the lay of the land, the location of Jonesy's murder, the Texas Waterland Park, even the route taken by Ricky and Clarice to the Loma Reservoir. After turning onto Main Street, Billy Ray spotted a familiar sight. A Ford Bronco pulled out of a deserted Frontier Inn parking lot.

"Lam, slow down." Billy Ray pointed.

Lam saw it too. "Think it's the same vehicle you told me about?"

"Leaving the Frontier Inn? I'd bet my life on it."

"Get a plate number. There's set of binoculars in the glove box."

Billy Ray focused the binoculars. The Bronco's license plate came in crystal clear. "It's the same vehicle."

Lam slowed the car to allow for an effective tail. As they passed by the Frontier Inn, they saw a CLOSED sign in the window.

"Jenkins, look." The Bronco turned east onto US Route 80.

"Same direction we're headed. The spot where I located Jonesy is about a mile this side of the water park. What do you want to do?"

Lam said, "Let's follow the Bronco. We can double back later."

The Bronco drove past the Texas Waterland entrance. After three miles, it signaled and turned.

"Stop here," Billy Ray said.

Lam pulled to the side of the road. Billy Ray pressed the powerful glasses to his eyes and watched the menacing vehicle turn onto a very familiar road, one he'd traveled in a past life. Except for dozens of No Trespassing signs, not much had changed in ten years. Even the white bull still guarded his cows from a hilltop perch at the back of the field.

"Now what?" Lam inquired.

He handed back the glasses and pointed. "Through those woods…."

Lam put the binoculars to his face. "Yeah...?"

"Are where dreams go to die."

Lam shot Billy Ray a quizzical look then returned his attention to the Bronco. A minute later he put the car in gear, turned, and sped off toward Texas Waterland Family Park.

Billy Ray watched the Bronco disappear into the forest.

Dark forces tugged at him.

38

Billy Ray marveled at the size of the entrance to the Texas Waterland Family Park. A massive bronze arch spanned the entrance. It was cast to depict an olive branch on one side and live oak on the other. A silver star the size of a Volkswagen hung beneath the arch, a fitting tribute to Texas, the Lone Star State. The gates were closed. A side entrance passed through a guard station.

He craned his neck as they drove under the arch. "Look at that!"

"Impressive," Lam said. "But aren't I seeing an upside down view of my beloved state seal?"

The actual Texas State Seal was a crescent with a star, not an arch. But leave it to a skeptic like Lam to point it out. "Is it your turn to be stupid? Imagine what'd happen if they flipped it belly down."

"Yeah, they'd get the symbol right."

"But how would cars drive through it?"

"Cut a hole in it."

Billy Ray played along. "It would fill up with rainwater."

Lam rolled his eyes. "Drill some drain holes."

"It would look like Swiss cheese."

"Then move the damn thing to Wisconsin!"

"Good thing you were a bullet-catcher in the Army and not an engineer, our nation's bridges would be a mess!"

They pulled up to the guard shack still busting each other's chops. Lam got a hold of himself and rolled the window down.

"May I help you?" The guard offered in a professional tone.

"You may," Lam said. "I wish to speak with the park manager."

The guard coughed, then recovered and checked his clipboard. "The park manager is unavailable, sir."

Lam made a show of thinking hard on what to ask for next. Billy Ray was convinced it was no act. "Then how about I speak with your head of security?" Lam flashed his FBI badge at the guard.

The guard's eyes widened. He turned into the shack and was back a minute later. "May I see identification for both of you?"

"Tight security. I like that," Lam said.

They presented their IDs—a handsome leather case and shiny badge for Lam, a plastic driver's license for Billy Ray.

The guard scanned the IDs. He pointed in the distance. "Follow that road for one mile. The administrative building is beyond the Black Anaconda. Mr. Wiggins will be awaiting your arrival."

"Thanks. So what's a Black Anaconda?"

"Oh, right. It's the feature ride of Texas Waterland and what sets us apart from all other waterslide parks. You can't miss it."

"How so?"

"It's black."

Billy Ray nearly lost his breakfast. "I was wondering that too!"

Lam mumbled under his breath.

The road led them through exotic foliage, around billowing fountains, past colorful arcades, and across bridges spanning a manmade river. From there, the scenery changed from enchanting rainbow colors to a theme dominated by a menacing sight and what could only be the Black Anaconda. "I bet that's it." Billy Ray pointed at a coiled structure rising ten stories and, of course, black in color.

Lam rolled his eyes. "As far as I'm concerned, everything you've told me is circumstantial. I'm a hard-facts guy." He swept his hand across their view. "Look at this place, it's fairytale land. Besides high colonics and major-league wedgies, what here can hurt you?"

Billy Ray had to admit, Lam was probably right.

* * *

"I want that file. Offer whatever they want. Just get it!"

Lee snapped a salute and hurried away.

Wiggins checked the date readout on his watch for the thousandth time. Three days and all would be well. There'd be no stopping Operation Blood Star once begun—not after his little addition. The end was near.

39

Beyond the make-believe scenery came a welcoming sight to a rational mind, actual brick and mortar, the administration building. Standing tall in front of the door, dressed in a tan African game warden uniform and Danner boots, was Joseph Wiggins.

So much for rational.

"Look, the spawn of Marlin Perkins!" Lam couldn't contain himself.

"Easy now."

"Where's the pith helmet and mosquito netting?"

"Be nice."

"Okay, Boo-Boo, let's see if Ranger Smith has any candy."

As they approached Wiggins, another man joined the gathering. He was short, powerfully built, and had Asian features. Billy Ray recognized him as the man from the Frontier Inn, minus the cigar.

Wiggins addressed Billy Ray first. "So we meet again."

"Yes. Thank you for seeing us."

"I'm always excited to show off our wonderful creation."

Lam shook Wiggins' hand and cast a look at the Asian man. Wiggins made no attempt to introduce his sidekick.

"So what brings an FBI agent to our park?" Wiggins asked.

"I was hoping to get free tickets," Lam said with straight face.

It was just like the guy, Billy Ray thought. In only a couple short days, he'd come to learn Lam's modus operandi—misdirection, obfuscation, and dumb humor. Dressed in a teal-colored sport coat, white shirt unbuttoned to the breastbone, brown slacks and tennis shoes, he appeared anything but menacing. However, the slick black hair, sunglasses, and a telltale bulge under his jacket signaled otherwise to the trained eye. Lam had style, Billy Ray gave him that. Wiggins never flinched. Nor did he comment. Lam allowed another couple ticks off the clock before stating his business.

"Mr. Wiggins, are you aware of the drowning that took place on your property a while back?"

"Most certainly, Agent Lam. It's my job to know everything that takes place on Waterland property."

"Of course. As head of security, you would. Then you're also aware an old man named Edward Jones was found dead just beyond your front gate."

“That happened off of park grounds. I only read about the unfortunate incident in the local newspaper. A shameful end to a war hero. But alas, the matter is outside my purview.”

Lam persisted. “I’m not from around here. What paper are you referring to? I'll pick up a copy.”

“The Gladewater Gazette, yesterday’s edition. I may have a copy in my office. You’re welcome to it.”

“Thanks. Is there a sports section?”

Wiggins ignored the silliness. “Do you have further questions?”

“Oh yeah. I’m just getting started.”

“Then might I suggest we remove ourselves from this heat. I’d be happy to take your questions in my office.”

Lam turned to Billy Ray. “You coming, Chubby?”

Wiggins gave a polite chuckle. The Korean sidekick formed a hairline crack on his face. Billy Ray played the butt of the joke.

“Shall we?” Wiggins gestured to the door. He led them down a short hallway that opened to a room with dozens of cubicles and an entire wall of display panels. Several technicians stood at the displays with clipboards.

Billy Ray spotted a particular bank of monitors that surprised him. They normally had only military application.

Wiggins waved his arm. “We monitor everything taking place in the park, rides, attractions, public activities above ground, as well as equipment, chemicals, and utilities below ground. You must admit,” he pressed, “we offer a tempting target for terrorists. Under the guidance of Homeland Security and the State of Texas, we anticipated such concerns and aim to keep our guests safe.”

“Impressive. What about the reservoir, any recordings of the accident?” Lam asked.

Wiggins shook his head. “No. That area is off-limits to the public. Besides, the expense to monitor the entire eleven square miles of park property would be prohibitive, to say the least.”

“I’d sure like a tour of your facility,” Lam said.

“How about now? The crowds don’t begin for three days.”

“Thank you, but no. My day’s booked. Besides, I’d prefer to witness the operation at full speed.”

“Another time, perhaps.”

Wiggins led them to a large office at the back of the control room. Once everyone was seated, he brought the meeting back on point. “So what can I do for you two?”

“I’m interested in touring a different part of your facilities.”

"Oh? And what might that be?" Wiggins asked.

Billy Ray had kept his mouth shut per *El Capitan's* orders, but decided to jump into the conversation. "The Loma Reservoir. We want permission to scout for clues to my brother's death."

Lam must've felt the need to keep control, because he added what came next. "Mr. Wiggins, I understand that the Loma Reservoir is owned by Texas Waterland, is that correct?"

"Yes. Except for an easement provided to the last remaining tenant of the Ambassador Ranch, we own the land on which the reservoir sits. In time, we'll own the property entirely."

"Why an easement?"

"To allow cattle access to water during the summer months."

"I—" Lam motioned to Billy Ray sitting next him. "We'd like to look around the area."

"Proper authorities already completed their investigation." The word "proper" was a warning to Lam.

"Perhaps the police missed something," Lam said.

"Such as?"

Lam didn't have an answer, but Billy Ray did. "I don't believe the sheriff's report about my brother's death. There must be another explanation, something the *proper* authorities missed."

Wiggins locked eyes on Billy Ray. The Korean assistant remained stoic. Lam let the situation unfold without interruption.

Wiggins blinked. "I assure you both that the sheriff and his deputy performed a thorough inspection of the area. My assistant here," Wiggins brought attention to the man for the first time, "aided the investigation."

"I understand the case was solved and closed," Wiggins said.

Billy Ray countered. "That may be, but—"

Lam jumped in. "We'd merely appreciate the opportunity to look around the area."

"Sorry, gentlemen, I just can't allow it. Our insurance policy imposes strict terms."

"What insurance?"

"Liability insurance."

Wiggins launched into a lengthy explanation of liability, indemnity, and fiduciary obligations to stock holders, cost factors, and more....

Lam played a bored schoolchild waiting for recess. Billy Ray counted ceiling tiles. Wiggins won the battle.

"....And so, if you'd like to come back another day to tour the facilities, please call ahead to make appropriate arrangements."

Lam came back on point. "By arrangements, you mean a federal warrant to inspect the area of Ricky Jenkins' demise?"

"I'm afraid such a document would be required."

A knock at the door interrupted the conversation. An Asian man stood stiffly at attention, a red manila folder tucked under his arm. He too wore the uniform *du jour*, tan khakis and Danner boots. Wiggins waved the man forward and received the folder. After scanning its contents, he scribbled instructions in the file and handed it back. The employee made an about-face and left.

Another Asian, Billy Ray noted, and acting more like a soldier than an employee. After his experience at the Frontier Inn, he assumed these men were Korean. Harper had made a stink about there being no Koreans in town. Jonesy looked to be correct. That meant Harper was lying or dead wrong. But what did it all signify? He was no bigot. He respected the Korean people, had even spent several months in South Korea training their Special Forces.

So who were these guys?

Wiggins returned his attention to the guests. "Agent Lam, Mr. Jenkins, do either of you have further questions?"

"Yes—"

"No." Lam cut Billy Ray off. "As you've stated, without a warrant you're unable to assist us further."

"Correct. Nothing personal." Wiggins made a wry smile to indicate the matter was out of his hands.

They ushered themselves out.

40

They retraced their steps through the security building. Billy Ray wanted a closer look at the wall of monitors. Lam signaled negative. Neither of them spoke until they reached the car.

"That was sure interesting," Lam said, busying himself with starting the car and rolling down the windows. He put the vehicle in gear and drove off—in the wrong direction!

"What the hell you doing, Yogi?"

"Do you even have to ask?"

Billy Ray liked this maverick lawman. "If we get caught you can play dumb, nobody would ever doubt it."

They didn't get far. A uniformed man sat inside a tan-painted ATV not more than thirty yards distance. He was a carbon copy of the two guards they'd just seen in Wiggins' office.

Lam came to a stop. A stare down ensued.

"Do you know what we're looking at, Lam?"

"A Chinese waiter?"

"Be nice."

"Okay, so how about telling your Korean buddy to move ass."

"I meant do you know what kind of equipment that is?"

"Yeah, dune buggy. Rode one in Michigan once."

"When I said for you to play dumb, I didn't mean win an Tony!"

"Enlighten me, Jenkins. What am I looking at, besides one of your Korean pals sitting on an all-terrain vehicle blocking the road?"

"You're looking at a vehicle I used for chasing bad guys in Africa, minus the hood-mounted M-249 Squad Automatic Weapon."

"Still looks like a fancy dune buggy to me."

"Look closer. Those lugs on the hood fit a machine gun."

"Oh really? I thought they were for the beer cooler."

The security guard put a phone to his mouth and spoke.

"Who do you suppose your pal is calling on the phone?"

A glint of light from beyond the tree line caught Billy Ray's attention. He retrieved the binoculars from the glove box.

There it was again. He adjusted the focus and located the source of the reflection. It was no security camera. It was a scope mounted atop a rifle, and it was pointing at Lam!

Billy Ray dropped the binoculars. "Get us out of here!"

"Why?"

"Your thick head is lined up in the crosshairs of a sniper rifle!"

"So much for wedgies in fairytale land." Lam shifted the car into reverse and punched the gas pedal. He made a K turn, and headed for the gate. Both men eyed their surroundings until well clear of the park and back onto US Route 80.

Lam spoke first. "What the hell just happened? Are you sure you spotted a gun pointed at us?"

"Not us. You!"

Lam pulled to the shoulder of the road. "How can you be sure the sniper was Wiggins' man or that he was even on Texas Waterland property?"

"I can't. I'm only certain of seeing a scope mounted on a gun barrel, and almost positive the weapon was a Remington."

"Edward Jones claimed hearing a rifle the morning your brother was killed. He said it was a Remington M-40 sniper rifle."

"I'd say Jonesy was right."

"Well then, that explains a few things—"

"Like high-tech camera equipment, heat and motion detectors, and ground pressure sensors?" Billy Ray said.

"Who are you, Superman?"

That was why Billy Ray had wanted a closer look at the control center. "Several of those monitors are used for military purposes. What's more, I spotted a door at the end of the hallway employing security measures hardly reasonable for an amusement park."

"Not if it's required by Homeland Security."

"....Or his insurance company," Billy Ray added sarcastically. "I think what we saw might only be the tip of the iceberg."

"Let's calm down and review. What's your impression of Wiggins and his band of merry men? And why all Koreans?"

"They're definitely pros, and not all are Koreans—the Mexicans must be somewhere. Plus the gate guard was a SoCal guy."

"How do you know?"

"I was stationed in San Diego for eight years. The surfer tan and long hair was my first clue and I heard it in his voice. I half expected him to say, 'far out dude,' when he saw your fancy badge."

"I'm beginning to think I was wrong to listen to your pet theories last night. You even have me paranoid."

"At least you have police training to fall back on. I'm strictly military with a bit of prison-yard smarts. Paranoia keeps me alive."

"I see your point. Maybe I've gone soft. In the jungle we needed eyes in the back of our head, or we'd be dead men."

"I don't know about soft, maybe you were always a pussy. But I do think you're one hell of a cop."

"Gee thanks, Jenkins. You want a big sloppy kiss now?"

Billy Ray conceded he'd never win. The G-man was relentless and would just wear him down in the end—definitely a good cop. "So what's your take, Sherlock?"

"I think there's an explanation for everything we've seen."

"Not quite." Billy Ray turned serious. "There's no way my brother died the way the sheriff claims. And there's no explanation for Clarice Richards' disappearance."

"Certainly, but just because that Wiggins fellow is a prick doesn't bring us any closer to solving the matter."

"You're probably right. So where does that leave us?"

"I think we've come full circle. You were my lead for locating Rapture. Now that you're scratched off the shit list, I got nothing." Lam's beeper sounded. "I'll be leaving for Dallas in the morning."

"Does this mean we're breaking up?"

"You Navy guys are all alike."

Lam's beeper sounded again. He glanced at it. "That's odd. It's Katie's mother."

Lam dialed the number. A full minute of silence ensued. As he listened, Lam stared at a picture of a young girl pasted on the dashboard. She had dark hair, chocolate brown eyes, and wore a pink Rainbow Brite shirt. His face grew paler by the second. At last he said, "Hold tight. I'm on my way!"

"What is it?"

"My daughter, she's been kidnapped!"

Billy Ray looked at the picture and back at Lam. "Talk to me."

"It happened on her way to school. The police say Katie and a friend were seen getting into a white van. A witness heard screams. My daughter's book bag was found on the sidewalk."

"When?"

"Thirty minutes ago."

They sat in the idling car staring down at Lam's cell phone.

41

Lam recovered—barely. Men and women in his profession were trained to compartmentalize emotional strains when under fire to counter the debilitating effects.

But when it was your own child....

Lam flipped his phone shut, put the car in gear, and punched the gas. "Investigation over, Jenkins."

"What are you going to do?"

"Get to North Carolina and find Katie."

"Aren't the local cops all over it? What will you do?"

Lam cast Billy Ray a stern look. "For starters, I can act like a father and go help my daughter. Then I'll comfort her mother."

Billy Ray knew the pain. "I'll pray for her safe return."

Lam settled a bit. "Thanks."

"What are the facts?"

"I know as much as you. Katie and a friend were abducted by persons unknown in a white van. Screams were heard. Katie's bag was recovered. And there's been no contact by the perps."

"Then I say you'd better get your brown butt home. Drop me off at my mother's and get out of here."

"Thanks, Navy."

"Don't mention it." Billy Ray checked his seatbelt. The powerful V-8 engine pressed him into the seat. "I need to know one thing."

"State your question," Lam said robotically, busy with placing a magnetic police beacon on the roof and plugging it into the cigarette lighter. A blue light began strobing.

"What about Chief Harlan's directive? Aren't I supposed to be in your custody? Maybe I could help."

"Not where I'm going, Jenkins. Promise me you'll stay home with crayons and a color book and I'll grant you early parole."

Lam cut the fifteen minute drive to Lela's house in half.

Billy Ray barely got the passenger door shut before the car tires tossed up a cloud of dust.

He stood in his mother's driveway watching his friend disappear into the distance.

Lam was gone.

* * *

Three days...an eternity...a blink of an eye.

Pressure in the command center neared the bursting point. The stakes were enormous, but Wiggins held all aces. His goals, his dreams, his life, his vengeance—all wagered on the result of the next seventy-two hours. Security patrols were on heightened alert. His chemist was secretly accessorizing the vats of Rapture. Hundreds of men, thousands of hours, a billion dollars invested over many years for a single, solitary outcome.

Wiggins took his position at the head of the table, its surface was papered over with blueprints, maps, and color satellite photos. His twelve trusted men gathered around him to review security protocols. No scenario went unaccounted. Early warning and perimeter defenses were fully operational. Forces large or small couldn't penetrate the park without announcing their presence and getting cut to pieces. Nor could hostile forces breach his laboratory without being vaporized by a thousand pounds of plastic explosives.

His strategy was to bottleneck the enemy into predetermined kill zones. In the unlikely event the enemy overcame those defenses, a half ton of Semtex would demolish the underground facilities, turning all to a smoking pile of toxic rubble. No tangible evidence could survive to link the People's Democratic Republic of Korea, the Gallina cartel, or himself to the Texas Waterland Family Park. Even the one possible entry point to his command center, the water treatment plant, had received added attention with heat and motion sensors, underwater explosives, titanium grating over the intake pipes, and additional patrols. And then there were the piranhas. For himself and the old chieftain, there were secret escape routes. As for all others connected with Operation Blood Star, there was only the cracked egg icon on his watch and a button to erase all human evidence. And yet, he felt unsatisfied, ill-prepared even. How could that be? He'd planned for years for this moment. So why the feeling of inadequacy? Was doubt merely the footstool of perfection? Or might there be something else, Pao's warning perhaps?

Wiggins stared down at the blueprints. Experience had taught him that no facility could ever be hardened one hundred percent. And yet, he couldn't help marveling at his own genius by using an amusement park to produce the thrills American's craved. And also the poison to kill millions!

A waterslide park was the perfect cover for his vast operation. He was wise to build the water treatment plant on the shores of the Loma Reservoir. The area was mostly inaccessible to the public. The reservoir supplied the vast amounts of water needed for the park. Its water required treating to remove bacteria and other impurities, then refrigerated before being piped throughout Texas Waterland for myriad uses.

And the list went on. Dozens more legitimate operations in the park required the use of a wide variety of chemical substances and compounds, all of which could be procured legally and with little or no attention from government regulators. Anhydrous ammonia and iodine refrigerated and purified water during the hot Texas summers. A host of organic substances were needed to fabricate and repair the miles of fiberglass slides. Various cleaning fluids were key contributors in the production of meth. Even the red phosphorus from the nightly firework displays lent more than just visual entertainment. Best of all, the Gallina cartel delivered unlimited quantities of ephedrine from North Korea to his underground lab. Then there were the secret chemicals that would convert Rapture from a wild, euphoric high on super-meth into a hideous, irreversible death sentence for millions of Americans.

Wiggins felt like pinching himself. Soon the great whore would truly know the Rapture!

From a technical standpoint, the treatment plant was the most vital link in Operation Blood Star. And in his experience, any element deemed vital to an operation was also its weakest link, its Achilles' heel. He'd done everything humanly possible to ensure success. There remained only the impossible, from which there was no defense.

Preparations were complete. The time had come.

Destiny was at hand.

He pulled a long breath, released it slowly, and then straightened. "Lieutenant Lee."

Lee ended his scrutiny of the maps and charts. "Yes, comrade?"

"You've done well. Your efforts here will mean great wealth for the homeland. The Dear Leader will be pleased."

Lee expanded his chest in a show of pride. The dozen men at the table snapped to attention. Praise from Wiggins was rare.

"Start the countdown."

Lee saluted. Twelve pairs of boots clicked together in unison sending a sharp report throughout the room.

Wiggins smiled.

He'd dreamed of this day.

42

Billy Ray cast a final look over his shoulder. He whispered a prayer for his new friend and the safe return of Lam's daughter.

Lela looked at him through the screen door. "What is it?"

"Lam just got a phone call. His daughter was kidnapped."

"Oh my!" Lela threw her hands up to her face. "Poor Lam. He's such a nice man. He reminds me of you."

"I wish I could help. I'd be all over it." He came inside.

Lela wrapped her arms around her son. "I know you would."

He enjoyed his mother's warmth. There'd be no making up for lost time, just relishing every moment in the days remaining.

"Will he call?"

"I wouldn't count on it. We're really just a couple of folks he met while doing his duty. But he left his private cell number in case I dig up something new."

"I'll pray for him. Let me know when you hear anything." She ended her embrace. "I almost forgot. There are phone messages for you, two from Rebecca Payne and one from a woman I don't know, someone named Eva."

"Okay, thanks."

Lela returned to the couch and her Bible reading.

His mother was still grieving, and seeking the strength needed to face each new day. He was grieving too, but in his own way by hunting down the truth about Ricky's death.

He made his way to the phone, grabbed a blank tablet and pen from a drawer, and pushed the button for messages. The first two were from Rebecca. One said, "Call me." The other said, "How come you haven't called me?"

He couldn't blame Rebecca. She'd hated being left behind. He placed the call, but only got her recorded voice. He told the recording that he'd try back in a few minutes and then hung up.

He listened to Eva's message next. Her voice was lush, but halting in delivery. "Billy Ray...I have information...about Uncle Edward. He kept a diary. Let me know when we can meet."

A diary?

He felt a jolt of excitement and phoned her. As with Rebecca, he got a recording and hung up without leaving a message.

He tried Rebecca again. She answered on the first ring.

"Where are you?"

"How did you know it was me and not some pervert?"

"Caller ID," she shot back.

"If you have caller ID, then you should know where I am."

"Billy Ray, I know where you're calling from. 'Where are you' means, where are YOU? Where've you BEEN? Why aren't you HERE? And WHEN WILL I SEE YOU!"

Rebecca had accepted Lam's logic to remain behind. She knew her father would use her against them. But that didn't mean she had to like it. The phone was melting in his hand.

"Ohh," he drew out the word. "So how are you, anyway?"

"Billy Ray?"

"Yes?"

"Get over here!"

"Where's here?"

"My apartment." She hung up.

On the way to Rebecca's apartment, he stopped by a store in Gladewater that advertised cell phones. After ten minutes with a salesman, he made his choice and departed the proud owner of a smartphone, and poorer for the bragging rights.

He dialed Eva's number first. Again he got her message machine and hung up. Curiosity won so he drove to her home. The trip would delay arriving at Rebecca's by a few minutes, but he was anxious to learn what Eva had discovered. He turned the corner to approach Eva's house and was surprised to see an Upshur County Sheriff vehicle in front. He decided not to stop.

Rebecca paced back and forth on the sidewalk when he drove up. She pulled open the door and jumped in.

"Hi Rebecca. How—"

"Drive!"

"Where to?"

"Anywhere—just get us out of here!"

Billy Ray stifled further comment and drove off. They needed to talk. Much had happened in the time they'd been apart. He would need her help in the days ahead. For the moment, however, a blind moose could see Rebecca's agitation.

Gus' store was the safest place to talk without interruptions. Mildred was minding the till when they arrived and Jeff had been entrusted with running the place while Gus left to run errands. He guided Rebecca upstairs to the office.

They faced each other in silence.

Rebecca made the first move. She reached across the short distance and put her arms around him. Her body shook.

He pulled her tight to his chest. She sank her face into the small of his neck. Her breath ignited his skin. Her shape molded to his body and her heat warmed him.

They held each other for several minutes until her shaking subsided. Then Rebecca reached up and took his face in her hands and searched in his eyes—past the man, past the years, beyond the abuse, before the history, and through the protective shell. She found what it was she sought and pressed her full moist lips to his.

He pressed his mouth to Rebecca's with the weight of a decade of loneliness. His heart escaped the oppression of love's absence.

He felt his body dissolve.

43

Johnny Lam beat feet to North Carolina. Good luck played—there was a direct flight to Fayetteville. Bad luck trumped—the flight was full. Only after flashing his ID, declaring an emergency, and charging a thousand dollars on his credit card did he gain passage. Four hours after leaving Gladewater, he walked into the Fayetteville police station. It'd been decided for him to go straight there and report to Katie's mom once he knew something. He flashed his ID and asked for the person in charge of kidnappings. The duty officer cocked a brow at the FBI badge. He didn't have long to wait.

A tall, husky man in a gray suit approached. "Agent Lam, I'm Captain Tim Ulrich. I oversee kidnapping cases." Ulrich had thinning brown hair, pale complexion, and small mouth set above an exaggerated chin. The lawman evoked impressions of a hard-nosed football player, a quarterback quite likely, a no-nonsense guy most assuredly. "Let me guess. Last month's kidnapping...our intelligence indicates the missing teen was taken across state lines."

Lam reddened from embarrassment. He had no authorization to be in North Carolina flashing his creds. But he'd crawl through broken glass and bend the rules however necessary to get his daughter back. He was betting on the brotherhood shared by those serving in harm's way. He just wanted Katie back safe in his arms.

"Actually, Captain, I'm here regarding the kidnapping incident that took place this morning. One of the victims is my daughter."

Ulrich released a breath, his shoulders sagged at the news.

"I'm here to help," Lam said. "What can you tell me?"

* * *

They held each other, resisting the end of magic. Rebecca's moist lips and soft caresses were heaven to his soul. He wished the world would go away and leave them forever in each other's arms. But they had to talk, their safety was his first concern.

His instincts shouted danger. Pieces of the puzzle hinted at shape and form, a ghostly outline, but nothing concrete. Information was paramount to survival. Any help from law enforcement was quashed the moment Payne closed Ricky's case. Furthermore, four weeks was plenty for erasing all traces of the truth. With Lam gone, he and Rebecca remained the final obstacles to a perfect crime. He had to act now.

But on what basis, that Wiggins was involved somehow? That wasn't enough. He needed access to the area where Ricky died. He'd seen things at Texas Waterland that made no sense. A plan began forming in his mind.

He pushed Rebecca to arm's length. He liked what he saw. Beauty. Passion. Trust. Elements long absent from his life, and likely hers too—the substance of things hoped for.

"Rebecca?"

Her eyes spoke instead. Indeed, they beckoned.

"We need to talk."

"Last night," she said breathy, still in the dream, "was so long ago. I worried about you."

Billy Ray looked into Rebecca's emerald eyes and time lost all meaning. The span of a single moment, a day, a year, an eternity could not be measured by clocks and calendars, only by revelation. He was torn between passion and risk. His heart relaxed, secure in the warmth of promise...his mind raced, a dozen possible dangers. Was his life to be forever conflicted, forever pulled between heaven and hell...love interrupted? He was finally here, in the moment, in a place he'd dreamed of, ached for. Yet again, enemies gathered at the gate. Would it always be this way, love's Prometheus?

No!

Passion overruled prejudice. Heart won, ignoring mind, pulling him back into the dream...the warm place—the safety in each other's arms.

Last night. Now. Forever.

Love had no boundary.

44

Billy Ray lifted Rebecca to her feet.

He hated breaking the spell between them. What if this was to be their only moment, to have finally discovered the thing long sought, only to be consumed by earthly concerns? Was it enough to have found the thing absent from their lives—trust? Would love grow? Could it survive?

They'd know soon enough.

He quieted his heart.

"We need to talk. I think we're in danger."

Sadly, business replaced passion on Rebecca's face, the temporal dismissing the divine.

"Start at the top. What's happened since yesterday?"

He told Rebecca about the visit to the sheriff's office and the confrontation between Lam and her father. He told her of their trip to Texas Waterland, the high security, their dangerous confrontation in the park, and denial of access to the Loma Reservoir. Lastly, he told her about Lam's daughter.

"Oh my God! Johnny must be worried sick."

"You wouldn't know by looking at him. He's a cool customer."

"Are the police on the case?"

"I assume so. Now Lam is too. If anybody can track down the scum who took those girls, he can. Although…." Billy Ray's voice trailed off.

"What is it?"

"I don't like it."

"Nobody likes kidnapping, darling."

"I mean it stinks. Why Lam, why now?"

"Is there ever a good time?"

He thought a moment. "Nothing adds up these past weeks."

"Why would you expect rhyme or reason from tragedy?"

Rebecca's words showed the civilian perspective of accepted social norms—legal, ethical, moral. However, her question struck a chord. His military mind took control. Through the prism of warfare, coincidence shifted from tragedy to truth, chaos to cunning. Viewed asymmetrically, shadowy anomalies formed ghostly shapes, then ghosts became flesh and bone and blood—men bent on conquest.

"I could expect rhyme and reason if I planned for it."

"What do you mean?"

"Asymmetric warfare," Billy Ray said.

Rebecca placed a hand on a hip and said, "A—what?"

If he read her body language correctly, the motion said, *and you interrupted our love-making for this?*

"Asymmetric warfare. A term referring to conflict between unevenly matched opponents where the smaller or weaker force must exploit geography, timing, surprise, or specific vulnerabilities of a larger and stronger enemy force to achieve victory—"

"Speak English!"

"We're being manipulated. Behind these tragedies and coincidences lies a professional provocateur. Furthermore, I believe I know who the enemy is."

"Who?" Rebecca's posture changed, her interest piqued.

"Wiggins."

"The man from the waterslide park?"

"I suspect he's behind it all, Ricky's death, Clarice's disappearance, Jonesy's murder, our fight at the Frontier Inn, even the kidnapping of Lam's daughter."

"Why would Wiggins want to kill people and kidnap kids? He has a billion-dollar amusement park to run. Murder and kidnapping tend to drive down business."

"I don't know why. But I aim to find out!"

The tension in the room was cut by the sound of footsteps approaching from the stairway. Gus appeared. "Hi guys. Jeff told me you were here. I hope I'm not interrupting."

Rebecca gave Gus a hug. The old shopkeeper blushed.

"You're not interrupting. In fact, I could use your advice."

"Oh?" Gus' curiosity showed.

"I was just saying who I think murdered my brother."

As was his style, Gus held back comment. He sat down and plucked bottles of Cheerwine soda from his ice chest. "Well, unless you two are in a hurry, how about joining me in a little refreshment?"

"I could use a pop," Rebecca said.

"Take a seat, Billy Ray. It's your turn to tell the story."

Gus and Rebecca sipped their drinks. Billy Ray took a moment to put his ducks in a row.

"You ever meet a Joseph Wiggins?" Billy Ray began.

"You mean the man that runs the Texas Waterland Family Park? Tall guy, blond hair?"

"That's him."

"Met him at a Chamber breakfast. Why do you ask?"

"Because I think he knows what really happened to my brother and Clarice, Edward Jones, too. I've had experience with men like him. I believe he's a highly-trained operative."

"Trained in what?" Rebecca said.

"Military training, special ops and the like. He's cut from the same cloth as the SEAL team officers and the Delta Force guys I've served with, or even the CIA spooks." He gave Gus and Rebecca time to digest the information before going on. "I believe Wiggins was behind our dustup at the bar the other night. He had command over the entire lot of attackers."

"Let's say you're right. Why stage such an elaborate incident?"

"Deniability. I also get the impression Wiggins is a bit full of himself, a megalomaniac even. It's clear he's been taking my measure since our first meeting."

"Then I'd say he miscalculated," Gus said.

"Yeah, Billy Ray, you cleaned their clocks!" Rebecca added, reliving her exhilaration from the event.

He didn't share the excitement. He was glad just to come out alive. "There's more. You know I've been asking questions around town about Ricky's death. The more I pursue the matter the more trouble comes of it, and Wiggins' shadow always appears nearby."

"Meaning there's no proof."

"Correct. No proof. But I'm not a cop, shadows are enough."

"What does Agent Lam think?"

Billy Ray and Rebecca looked at each other.

"What?" Gus pleaded. "You look like you saw another shadow."

"Lam's gone. His daughter was kidnapped this morning."

After a moment of shock, Gus put down his soda. "Let's say I do believe in ghosts. You can't just storm into Texas Waterland and punch the guy in the nose. You'd be arrested immediately."

"Gus is right, Billy Ray. My father is looking for any reason to get at you. I don't want anything bad to happen."

Rebecca's eyes moistened—humidity before a downpour. Billy Ray caught the possibility of rain.

But there'd be no going off half-cocked. That wasn't his way or his training. However, unlike civilian law enforcement, constrained to rules of evidence, his role would be gathering intelligence to form a plan. The key difference was *action.* Burden of proof didn't apply to a warfighter, only the worthiness of the mission. If intel showed Wiggins linked to the killings, there'd be no judge or jury.

Only the hangman—him!

"Rebecca, Gus." He softened his tone. "You're both right. I'll proceed with extreme caution."

"*We'll* proceed," Rebecca corrected. "You aren't ditching me again, Billy Ray Jenkins!"

Her eyes cleared. The threat of precipitation evaporated in the heat of glowing resolve. There'd be no keeping her from his side now. Besides, she'd proven herself a worthy maiden in battle, to say the least.

"Now what?" Gus broke the tension.

Billy Ray pulled out the notes he'd written previously, plus satellite photos he'd printed off the library computer, and spread them on the table. After what he'd spied inside the security building at Texas Waterland, witnessed with Lam at the back of the park, and now the kidnapping, shadows and ghosts formed mortal bodies. The enemy materialized.

"I—*we* need intel, proof if we can get it."

Rebecca smiled. She liked what she was hearing.

"Sounds a little backwards," Gus said.

"For police work that's correct. But there'll be no police. We're on our own. Even with proof, law enforcement would likely think twice before moving on a facility like the Texas Waterland. Millions of dollars in tax revenues and a thousand badly needed jobs would be at stake. The incentive would be to sweep things under the rug."

"I see your point, son."

"Me too," said Rebecca.

Billy Ray tapped the satellite photo of the park. "We start here, where Ricky was killed." His finger rested over the Loma Reservoir.

"But that's on park property. I thought lake access was denied. We can't just sneak in there, commando-style."

"No need. We'll get a police escort."

Gus and Rebecca couldn't get their questions out fast enough.

Billy Ray waved his hand. "I know. There's no way Roy Payne or even Chief Harlan is going to agree to that."

"I'm confused," Gus said. "So what do you have in mind?

"Simple." He turned to Rebecca. "Deputy Bell will give us a ride back to the reservoir in a sheriff department vehicle."

Rebecca reassumed the hands-on-hips pose. "Are you crazy? How do we get him to agree to that? Larry would have to report official business to the dispatcher or my father."

"Bell takes the vehicle home with him each night, does he not? It won't be official. We can call it a picnic or something."

"Why would he want to drive that far for a picnic with us?"

"What if there was a fourth person? It can be like a date."

Rebecca caught his drift. "I got it! Larry wants me real bad, he always has. Our double date could be me and Larry and you and Shandi. Plus, I kind of owe Larry for punking him the other day."

As dumb as it was, given their situation, Billy Ray felt a pang of jealousy. But they had work to do, he ignored the feeling.

"I'll call him right now." She took her phone and left the table.

Gus moved close to Billy Ray and whispered, "Is this wise?"

"Pursuing Ricky's killer or involving Rebecca?"

"Both. I see your point about learning what happened to Ricky and the Richards' girl. But how will you keep Rebecca safe?"

He didn't offer a quick answer. There were no guarantees. Battle plans often got flushed after the first shot. "I can only try, Gus. And keeping her nearby should help."

Gus squeezed Billy Ray's shoulder. "Well then, be careful."

Rebecca returned to the desk. "It's all settled. Larry's shift ends in two hours. I told him to meet us at the Piggly Wiggly parking lot."

"In the sheriff department vehicle?"

"You got it."

"How did you get him to agree to that?"

Rebecca struck another pose only women seemed capable of, equal parts pride and indignation. She began explaining.

Billy Ray cut her off. "Never mind." He waved his hands in surrender. "You can tell me later. I say we get going."

Gus nodded at Billy Ray's directive. Billy Ray shook his partner's hand. Rebecca did better with another hug. They exited the Heavenor hardware store not knowing what the future held.

Only that truth lay somewhere ahead.

45

Billy Ray drove Rebecca home. She and Shandi would use the time before meeting Deputy Bell at the Piggly Wiggly to prepare for their picnic. He, on the other hand, had unfinished business.

He phoned Eva and got her answering machine once again. Now he was suspicious and drove to her house. As he rounded the corner, the sheriff vehicle drove away. He pulled to the side of the road and waited until it was gone from sight. Again he dialed Eva's number. He wasn't sure what was going on. Maybe she was dating one of the deputies, or perhaps something had happened to Wilhelmine. If the matter had involved Jonesy, then two hours was a mighty long time for conducting Q and A.

She picked up on the first ring.

"Eva? I saw a sheriff vehicle leave your house just now."

"Dixon, again. The man frightens me."

"Did he hurt you?"

"No."

A single word was all he got. "I'm just down the road from your house. Would you like me to drop in? Is now a good time?"

"Yes, please come."

His knock was answered by Eva. She invited him in. He looked around. No Wilhelmine, but all looked to be in order.

Eva guessed his thoughts. "She's at her weekly bingo game. The church sends around a van to pick up the senior citizens."

Billy Ray looked around again. "I tried calling a couple of times."

Eva smiled. Her full lips formed a perfect crescent. "Come in and make yourself comfortable." She motioned to the living room. "Would you like a refreshment?"

He looked down at his watch. Eva caught the movement.

"If you're in a hurry, I can just go get my uncle's diary."

"Oh, no. I'd love a cold drink."

She gave him a moment to get his story straight. "Ice tea?"

"Do you have anything stronger?"

"I have Guinness. Will that do?"

Billy Ray imagined his jaw dropping. "I'd love a Guinness!"

She directed him to the couch. In a moment, she was back with a platter of frozen mugs and two bottles of beer. She placed her burden on the table and sat down beside him. Also on the platter was a small book. The maroon-colored object resembled a Bible. Then she poured the beers.

Billy Ray took a long draw. "Ahhh...fell in love with Guinness while serving overseas. He raised his mug for a toast. "You pour a great glass."

Eva went first. "Thanks for coming." She pointed at the book. "My uncle was a fascinating man. I don't think anybody around here knew who he really was, or what he was like. I learned a great deal from his diary."

"Jonesy was always a mystery to me."

"Grandpa always said his brother was one of the lucky ones to have survived so much war. Although, I'm sure Uncle Edward would disagree. Perhaps some things should never see the light of day. There are things in Uncle Edward's diary that should probably go to the grave with him."

He paid Eva a curious look before turning to the book. He noticed strips of paper marking places toward the end of the book.

"May I?"

"Certainly."

Billy Ray lifted the diary with a show of reverence. He hadn't known much about Edward Jones, just that he'd served his country in two major wars, and had struggled with the ghosts of combat. He felt for Jonesy. After all, he had nightmares of his own to contend with, all warriors did. "Where do I start?"

"How much time do you have?"

Billy Ray checked his watch again. "Only a few minutes."

"Then you might want to go to the back. I marked places I thought had relevance to your brother and Clarice Richards."

Billy Ray noticed the neat penmanship. He remembered how Jonesy's hands shook at the Frontier Inn.

"Your uncle had nice handwriting."

"I agree. Although, over the last few years his medications made him increasingly unsteady."

"Please forgive me, Eva. Like the rest of the town, I just assumed his wobbly walk and shaky hands came from his drinking." He looked down. "I always thought Jonesy was an alcoholic."

Eva touched his arm. "Everyone thought my uncle was a drunk. Maybe he was by the end, just not in the way people thought. His problem had been mixing alcohol with medications. I'm not looking to justify his habits, by any means, only clarify them."

"I appreciate that. If it means anything, I never looked down on him. He was respectful to me and always seemed to know who I was. I'm glad to learn I was wrong the whole time."

"He mentions you in the diary."

Billy Ray didn't know what to say.

Eva changed the subject. "Was your father named Rodney?"

"Yes. He disappeared years ago to who-knows-where. Why?"

"Well..." Eva hesitated. "Maybe somebody knows."

Billy Ray looked at Eva. "Knows what?"

She left the question unanswered. "My uncle makes some shocking claims in his book that could cause problems for some people."

Billy Ray could hardly believe his ears. "What claims?"

"I'd rather you read the diary to draw your own conclusions."

He wondered what Jonesy could've recorded about his father. It was then he remembered back to his childhood. He'd seen his father occasionally sitting next to Jonesy at the bar. He never paid it any mind. Jonesy had known his father.

"Are you suggesting I take your uncle's diary home with me?"

"If you'd like. You can give it back to me before the funeral."

Jonesy's funeral! In all his running around the past couple of days, he'd completely forgotten about the funeral. "When is it?"

"It was going to be tomorrow. Then I received a phone call this morning from an official with the Veteran's Administration asking if I wouldn't mind pushing the date back a week."

"A week? That's strange."

"I thought so, too, but the man indicated my uncle had been an important figure in the wars and that the country wished to pay a fallen hero proper respect. The man said it would take several days to complete the necessary arrangements."

"What arrangements?"

"He didn't say. He sounded so official, and even put me on with his secretary afterward to exchange information. Do you want me to go get my notes and read you the man's name?"

"I'm sure it's legit. Besides, I wouldn't know the guy from Adam." He downed the beer and checked his watch. It was time to leave.

Eva took the queue. She gathered up the platter and delivered it to the kitchen. She returned carrying a small box. "Here," she handed the box to Billy Ray, "my uncle kept the diary in this."

"Thank you, Eva. A week from tomorrow you say?"

"Yes. Oak Hills Cemetery, in the evening."

"That's where we buried Ricky." Billy Ray felt a prick of anguish, the wound still raw. "There was an old tree up in back perfect for his final resting place. I'm sure he and Edward Jones will get along wonderfully."

He took the diary and left. There was much to prepare for.

Hopefully not a tree of his own at the cemetery.

46

The Piggly Wiggly was packed with local shoppers preparing for the Independence Day weekend. Excited teenagers surrounded a fireworks booth. The rest of the commotion in the lot had a different source. Standing in all her glory, sunrays reflecting off her auburn hair and into the eyes of mortals, was Rebecca. She wore a pair of white cotton shorts, a teal-colored sleeveless blouse, and leather sandals. Shandi was equally stunning in a pink one-piece summer jumpsuit, and only slightly shorter than Rebecca. Together, they stopped traffic.

Billy Ray was fairly certain two pairs of tanned shapely legs added up to four. He noticed most of the fellas in the parking lot double-checking their math. Deputy Bell didn't stand a chance!

It took him a moment to realize Rebecca and Shandi were guarding an open parking space. They made eye contact and waived him over. Billy Ray was thankful to have a place to park, and just hoped he didn't get beat up by a mob of jealous men. Taking the only parking spot and both pretty ladies, how dare he? He imagined pitchforks and torches heading his way.

Before Billy Ray could exit his car, an Upshur County Sheriff vehicle pulled up behind. It was one of the Department's Chevy Suburbans. Bell rolled down his window and called the ladies over. Billy Ray joined them.

"Hi Rebecca, Shandi." Bell made a motion of tipping an imaginary hat. "You ladies sure look pretty!"

Two voices thanked him in unison.

"Hey there, Jenkins."

"Hey ya, Deputy."

"Better call me Larry. Rebecca insists on us being friends."

Billy Ray chuckled, remembering their first meeting.

Bell got out of the vehicle. All eyes in the lot stared at them. Billy Ray could almost read people's thoughts—the women all glad the law finally arrived to chase off the young female exhibitionists, and the men hoping the big guy with the cleft chin got beat senseless and dragged off in chains. Everyone would've been wrong. One look at Bell's smiling face told the tale!

"How about you and Shandi hop in the back. I'll put Rebecca up front with me," Bell said, overflowing with joy.

He was impressed by Bell taking charge. He liked that—just not with his gal, but kept clam on the matter.

"Fine by me, if Shandi agrees."

“I do.” Shandi hopped in and buckled her seatbelt.

Billy Ray put the cooler in the Suburban, then made a quick trip to his mother’s car and retrieved a large rubberized bag and small duffle from the trunk. The large bag went in the back, the duffle stayed with him. He buckled in and awaited Bell’s next directive.

The passengers in front smiled at each other. Billy Ray played his part and did the same in back.

“Shall we be off?” Bell asked.

“Thought you’d never ask,” Rebecca said.

Bell put his hand to the shifter. “Okay, gang, where to?”

Billy Ray almost choked. Rebecca hadn’t told Bell about picnicking on the *Bonny Banks o’ Loch Loma.*

“Just drive, Larry. It’s a surprise.”

That confirmed it, Rebecca was making it up as they went.

Not unlike himself.

They turned east onto US Route 80 toward Big Sandy. Bell asked again where they were going. Billy Ray kept silent. He was content to let Rebecca take the lead. She knew what needed to be done, and her skills at getting what she wanted were proving remarkable. It would take stronger men than the two currently in the Suburban to withstand her charms.

“Keep going, Larry. It’s just a little farther.”

“But I don’t like surprises.”

“You like me, don’t you?”

If not for knowing Rebecca and Larry were friends, Billy Ray would’ve taken a different view of her treatment of the poor defenseless deputy. Men were suckers. That included himself.

“Yes, but—”

Rebecca reached across the console and placed a reassuring hand on Bell’s arm. “Trust me, Larry. You’re heading in the right direction.”

Bell looked at her with puppy dog eyes and smiled.

Suckers indeed!

Billy Ray turned to Shandi. “I understand you just graduated.”

“I did,” she said excitedly. “A Bachelor’s degree in political science. I’m going to be governor some day.”

“Well, you got my vote. Make it president!”

Shandi had a pleasing figure. Her brown hair and soft curls perfectly framed her round eyes and genuine smile. The man who ended up on her ticket would be one lucky running mate.

“Rebecca says you got your degree, too. Theology, was it?”

Rebecca had discussed him with others, he liked that. “Yes, theology.”

“My father was a church pastor.”

“Was?”

“He passed away my second year at the university.”

“I’m sorry to hear that, Shandi.”

“He would’ve liked you.”

He would’ve blushed if not for spotting a twitch in the back of Rebecca’s neck. Perhaps he wasn’t the only one feeling jealous.

The Texas Waterland Family Park entrance appeared on the right. Heads turned to see the imposing site as they drove past.

“The park opens to the public on Sunday,” Bell announced. “A few of us deputies will be moonlighting as park security.”

Billy Ray spoke for the first time. “I understand there’s a pre-grand opening scheduled. Are you working that?”

“Funny you ask. None of us are working that event.”

Billy Ray thought that a bit odd.

So did Rebecca. “Why’s that, Larry?”

“Not sure. One of the guys phoned their security office and was told arrangements had already been made.” Larry added, “They’re a secretive bunch over there.”

Rebecca pointed. “There. Turn onto that dirt road.”

Bell shot Rebecca a look. Confusion spread across his face. Billy Ray was surprised that Bell offered no comment, just made the turn. Signs clearly indicated they were entering onto private property. He began counting backwards from five, predicting the time it would take before Bell stopped the car and demanded answers. He only made four.

The Suburban skidded to a halt. “What’s going on?”

“We’re going to the area where Ricky was killed,” Rebecca said.

Silence filled the car.

Rebecca’s charade had worked. Although, proving she was no conniving manipulator, she’d confessed immediately. Before Bell’s face completed its transformation to red, Rebecca said, “We’re going to find out what really happened at the Loma Reservoir, and you’re going to help us.”

Bell protested, “But—”

“Larry, you know that investigation was botched. You’re too good a cop not to. The only way we can get back there to look for clues is if you take us in this vehicle. It has to look official.”

What she failed to add, was that even with Bell’s help, success was a long shot. They were gambling and both knew it. Life had dealt them lousy cards in a high-stakes game and their chips were all in. Rebecca was selling the hand.

Bell persisted, "What about your father, I mean, Sheriff Payne?"

"Did he ever order you not to go to the Loma Reservoir or not to ask questions about Ricky Jenkins' death? Did he command you to ignore the disappearance of Clarice Richards?"

"Of course not. It's just understood to stay away from the case, and to stay away from Texas Waterland property, too. Besides, I'm only a deputy."

"Not in my eyes, Larry."

Bell blushed.

"What gives them the right to avoid justice?" Rebecca argued.

"Look at those signs. NO TRESSPASSING means what it says. I need a warrant to conduct a search."

"You don't need a warrant," Rebecca countered. "Because you won't be doing any searching."

"What about the signs?"

"We'll think of something if anyone asks. Besides, a sheriff vehicle and uniformed deputy must count for something."

"I don't know...." Bell blinked. "What will I be doing?"

"Having a picnic."

Bell scanned the faces of his passengers. He looked trapped, searching for a lifeline.

"Come on, Larry, let's go. The beer's getting warm."

Bell stared into Rebecca's eyes for a long moment. She smiled big—the kind of smile that lit up a man's world. He folded.

Bell shifted the Suburban and drove into the Big Piney.

Billy Ray marveled at Rebecca's charm. He made a mental note never to challenge her in poker. He also reminded himself.

Their next opponent held all aces.

47

A North Carolina Trooper spotted the van while driving home after a twelve-hour shift. If not for a perfect description and all but one digit of the plate number provided by the lone witness, the tired officer may have missed it. Unfortunately, the only evidence found inside was a girl's hair band. The vehicle proved a dry hole.

They completed their questioning at the car lot from where the van had been stolen. The high school boy hired to wash the day's front line vehicles had discovered the theft, but delayed reporting the van's absence for fear that the lot owner would suspect him of foul play and issue a pink slip. Then upon further consideration, the teen worried he may be in worse trouble for his silence. As a result, the crime went unreported until noon. The lot owner was at a loss to shed further light on the matter, saying only that the vehicle had been present among the previous day's inventory, and proclaiming his lot barely made payroll and couldn't afford surveillance cameras.

Lam wasn't so sure, but admitted he was probably just being overly suspicious. He wanted Katie back. Time was critical. The clock was the enemy and it was ticking louder, faster. Each hour that passed with no word of her whereabouts, or clues to her abductors, sent the odds of finding her toward zero.

"I'm sorry, Agent Lam. Something will turn up to help us get your daughter back," Ulrich said after getting out of the earshot of others.

"I don't blame you, Captain. You run a good shop. Too bad the witness couldn't provide better descriptions of the perps."

"We're lucky we got what we did. Maybe the crime scene guys can find something...a fingerprint, DNA, something."

"Hope springs eternal." Lam tried sounding positive.

What now? At the very least, he hoped the kidnappers would call to establish their demands. Frighteningly, there'd been no contact, no notes, and no evidence of any kind.

Something had to turn up soon.

He was facing the stark reality that the scum who took his daughter were sophisticated, and probably had other designs for the girls.

The witness had reported seeing three suspects, all wearing hoodies, but only managed to catch a fleeting glimpse of one man's face. The witness swore the man was brown—not black, not white—and had a mustache.

The M.O. excluded local perverts. The girls' abduction had all the hallmarks of planning and coordination by an organized gang.

Lam forced himself to consider the obvious, something Captain Ulrich had the class not to mention. Katie and her friend may have been taken by human sex traffickers.

He shuddered at the thought.

* * *

Lela carried the groceries into the house from the Dahlgren's car and set them on the kitchen table. A maroon book next to the phone caught her attention. Billy Ray's Bible, she supposed. She was proud of him for having converted to Christianity, and even getting a college degree in Bible Studies.

She brushed her hand along the book and smiled. On a whim, she wrote a loving message on a slip of paper and moved to place it inside Billy Ray's Bible. She was surprised to discover the book wasn't a Bible at all, but a diary. She turned to the front and read the name, Edward Jones.

Curiosity got the better of her and she began reading.

48

Billy Ray spotted another hidden camera in a tree along the route to the reservoir. He opened the duffle and retrieved a set of binoculars barrowed from Gus' store. He scanned the area ahead and spotted another well-disguised camera. "Slow to a crawl, Larry. Act as if you're struggling with the road or something. Everybody keep your eyes forward."

Rebecca was alarmed. "What is it, Billy Ray?"

"We're being watched."

"Watched? By who?" Shandi turned to look out the window.

"Keep looking forward, it's better we don't act suspicious."

Spotting cameras was a chore, but one he'd had considerable practice with during his many SEAL team assignments. Locating the enemy's eyes and ears were critical to mission success. More importantly, anticipating enemy booby traps and ambushes were critical for continued good health. He was limited to just the field glasses and his instincts. He was certain to miss a camera or two, and probably other sensors as well. However, what he had discovered spoke volumes about the park and about Joseph Wiggins. Namely, that the man was a liar. Wiggins had claimed no security cameras were employed around the reservoir. Why lie?

Where there's smoke, there's fire.

He could think of only one reason to place cameras in the area—to protect something. That meant this and their destination at the reservoir held high importance. Wiggins claimed the reason to be the water treatment plant. Lam had argued on behalf of anti-terror measures for a venture the size and scope of Texas Waterland. Fine, but why be blatantly untruthful? Perhaps Wiggins lied just to mess with them, to show who had a bigger dog, or maybe just to get even with Lam for being a smartass. Doubt grows quickly in the minds of the desperate. He felt his theories fading in the light of alternate choices. Maybe he was chasing zebras. Then he spotted something through the binoculars that forever changed his thinking. It was a miracle he'd made the discovery at all. Straddling the seat of a woodland-patterned motorcycle, dressed in matching camouflage uniform, helmet, and accessories, was a person observing every inch of their progress through the scope of a Heckler & Koch MP7A1 Personal Defense Weapon, or PDW. A suppressor attached to the gun made its barrel long and menacing.

Billy Ray's blood went cold. He knew this weapon. The highly-advanced gun had come into production shortly before his troubles began with Brenda Lee's death. He'd been among several men from his SEAL team tasked with putting the weapon through trials on the gun range. Its 4.6×30mm ammunition was lighter in weight than other automatic weapons, allowing soldiers to transport more bullets to the battlefield. The rounds had no trouble penetrating armor, and could make a complete mess of the human body.

The gunman tracked them through a telescopic sight, a logical choice for a security force needing to repel potential threats. The game-changer was the suppressor. Silenced weapons had no legitimate use among civilians. The presence of an armed man at a waterslide park, outfitted with high-tech military equipment, and a weapon unavailable to civilians fixed with a suppressor, meant but one thing. The mission was offensive.

He reviewed his findings. On his first visit, there was the high-tech control center, advanced monitoring equipment, snipers, and military ATVs. Now here was a camouflaged man on a stealthy electric motorbike wielding a weapon used by military Special Forces. What was going on?

"Speak up, Jenkins," Bell demanded. "Who's watching us?"

Billy Ray was careful to answer. They were in potential danger. The safest thing would be to order Bell to get them the hell out of there. But here was smoke. Now he knew there had to be fire. "Park security, Larry. They have video monitors mounted in the trees," he said matter-of-factly.

"Why would they put cameras here? It's a long ways from the park."

"The head of park security told me earlier today it's because of the water treatment plant." Billy Ray offered a half-truth.

He felt terrible doing so. It wasn't right involving the young deputy without the man's knowledge. Defending his friends against snipers and fighting off men on motorbikes with high-powered machine guns was impossible. He could be risking their lives by going forward, involving his friends in a deadly game of chess, using them as pawns. Nevertheless, he had to know more. He needed to know what really happened on the shores of the Loma Reservoir. The dark waters had already claimed two people he loved. He couldn't allow this place to claim more lives. He sensed they were being monitored only, and that if Wiggins had meant them harm, it would've happened within the depths of the forest. Now they were nearly to their destination. Using a sheriff department vehicle and a uniformed deputy had proven a wise choice. Yet, he was no fool. He needed to be ready for anything. There was smoke. Now he would locate the fire and stomp it out.

"You can speed up, Larry."

49

The lead chemist ended his report. Rapture was now a weapon of mass destruction. Forty thousand gallons of highly-advanced meth, capable of producing a billion doses, had just switched from a pleasure drug for hooking gluttonous Americans to killing any fool who stuck the poison in their bodies. Thanks to gangs controlled by the Gallina cartel, the masses were already lining up. Word on the street was spreading fast of a mysterious new meth, said to last six times longer and safer than the scads of designer "bath salts." News media had fueled interest by describing the effects, deaths seemed not to matter. However, that was the first Rapture. The second coming would be his getting revenge on America—a drug to drive users insane, transforming humans into ravenous animals—clawing, tearing, killing! The one test case in Miami had produced horrific results, leaving one user's naked body shot full of holes by police and his victim half-eaten. Operation Blood Star now had a new mission, one only he and the chemist knew about—kill Americans!

Wiggins applauded his genius. The deaths from Rapture had served a double purpose of advertising the product while ridding potential threats to Operation Blood Star, such as the Jenkins kid. At the thought of the Jenkins boy, he felt sudden dread, a sensation he'd never experienced throughout his professional years. He dismissed it immediately. Nothing could stop him now. A fleet of tanker trucks would roll from the gates of Texas Waterland delivering Rapture to American cities strategically chosen for their population, gang activity, drug use, and one additional factor, saturation of firearms.

Each tanker would be accompanied by a ten-man security team from the Gallina cartel. Eighty Gallina soldiers would gather during the Texas Waterland pre-grand opening disguised as legitimate contractors, VIPs, and park employees to take possession of the shipments. When Americans gathered for their Independence Day celebrations the following night, Operation Blood Star would burst upon the nation and the real fireworks would begin—the downfall of the great whore, America!

Wiggins' phone rang. "Speak." He listened for nearly a minute. "Tell them to cover and pursue only." He gathered his security team five minutes later and had Lee repeat the course of events. A kill squad awaited further orders.

Wiggins cursed. His single failure had been the inability to acquire the entirety of the ranch property bordering the Loma Reservoir. The owner would only agree to the forested lands between the north section of pasture and the shore of the reservoir, and then only under a forty-nine-year lease. Furthermore, the lease was contingent upon the rancher having easement to the lake once each week to water his cows. That had been the best deal he could negotiate. No amount of money could persuade the landowner, who claimed the property had been in his family "since the days of Sam Houston." He'd considered killing the rancher, but that would've led to further complications of having to deal with the man's heirs or a probate court. So he'd granted the stubborn Texan his price.

"Who's in the sheriff vehicle?" Wiggins asked.

"Four people. The driver appears to be a sheriff deputy. Yes," a hushed voice crackled over the radio, "the young deputy often seen accompanying Sheriff Payne. There are two females. I recognize the one in the front as Payne's daughter. I'm unable to identify the second female. There is one male in the back seat. Hold—" the radio went silent a moment. "Comrade Wiggins, it's the same man who visited you this morning, the one I was dispatched to eliminate in the pecan orchard."

"Jenkins!"

"Perhaps we've underestimated this man," Lee said.

Wiggins shot Lee a murderous look, but he was correct.

"Eliminate them?" asked the voice.

Wiggins grabbed the radio from Lee's hand. "No! Copy that."

"Copy, 'negative,'" returned the voice.

"Do not approach. Pull back to a safe distance and stay hidden."

He'd underestimated Jenkins. He'd read the man's file, a US Navy SEAL. However, SEALS operated in teams with heavy firepower and sophisticated equipment. A single man could hardly get far against his security forces. And judging by what Jenkins considered his present team, a young deputy and a couple of the local women, there was hardly reason for alarm. If not for other considerations, he'd kill Jenkins and be done with it. However, he was too close to victory to take chances. Operation Blood Star would begin in two days. A more crafty approach made better sense, and he had the perfect idea. Jenkins would get a dose of what the FBI agent was experiencing albeit with a major twist. At the moment, he just needed to get the guy off his property.

"All of you, back to your assigned duties. Lee, follow me."

They headed back to the drug labs. Wiggins pulled out his cell phone and touched a single digit. A man's voice answered on the first ring. He gave the man his orders, to be executed immediately, if not sooner.

50

They hadn't been attacked. That meant the guard had orders not to shoot. He made a final sweep of the area along the lakeshore and put away the field glasses. All looked peaceful and the water inviting, as it always had for him at this spot on the Loma Reservoir. There was sadness, too.

The Texas Waterland's water treatment plant stood silent on the far shore. There was no activity anywhere in sight, not even the stirring of birds or squirrels. The air was hot and muggy from a Texas toad-choker making its way up from the Gulf, pushing moist air ahead of it. The group waited on Billy Ray's announcement that it was safe to exit the vehicle. Bell showed distress and kept looking down at his watch. The girls remained quiet and looked out the windows at the surrounding area. He couldn't imagine Wiggins letting them roam for long. Best they got on with scouting for clues.

"Okay, let's set up our picnic. I could really use a sandwich."

Rebecca needed no prodding. She opened her door and leapt to the ground like a bull rider making the eight-second horn. Shandi wasn't far behind. They fetched the supplies from the back of the Suburban. Bell, on the other hand, moved with reluctance.

Billy Ray headed to the water's edge, careful of any tracks in the sand or other physical sign that might shed light on what took place on this spot of ground a month ago. There'd been rain since the day of Ricky's death. Finding tracks was probably too much to ask.

Bell came alongside. "What have you gotten me into?"

Billy Ray felt for the man. Days earlier, Bell had endured Rebecca's hazing and then humiliation by his boss in front of his peers. And now he was way off home turf, probably anticipating disciplinary action. However, Bell was a secondary concern. The first priority was finding clues. Warnings of trespass and forbidding orders to young deputies be damned.

He looked Bell straight in the eye, one man's respect for another. "I have to know what really killed my brother."

"So you don't buy the official report?"

"Not for a second."

"I have to admit, I didn't like how the investigation went down, either. Too fast and too neat."

Billy Ray put it straight. "My brother hated drugs and loved Clarice. Something awful happened to those kids. I just know it."

"But it is a fact drugs were found in his system. I saw the tox report, and those guys don't lie. The lab tech even told me the drug was some new designer crap, like meth only way worse."

"I don't doubt the presence of drugs, just how they got there."

"What do you mean?" Bell's curiosity showed.

"You ever hear of waterboarding?"

"Enhanced interrogation...sure. Who hasn't?"

"A lot of water ends up in the lungs and gut. I know, it's been done to me. And there are worse methods, like jamming a hose in a man's throat."

Bell stared in awe at Billy Ray. "You suggesting somebody purposefully drowned your brother?"

"Yes, and drugged him in the process."

"Possible, no doubt. He did have a lot of water in his body."

"Can you tell me more about his corpse? Were there any bruises or marks to indicate torture?"

"I wish I could help you, Jenkins, but I'm low on the totem pole. I fetch coffee and donuts for Payne. I only saw the body for a moment."

Billy Ray laid a firm hand on Bell's shoulder. "Don't sell yourself short. You're a good man and a good cop. You have what it takes."

"Yeah? And what's that?"

"Instinct. You can't get that from a book." He offered no assurances to Bell. How could he? There was no way of knowing how things would end.

He left Bell and retrieved the large rubber bag and duffle, then stepped out of view of the others to change into swim trunks. He walked to the water's edge. The scene up and down the shore hadn't changed in ten years. Only the treatment plant was new. He set the equipment bag on the warm sand and removed the items borrowed from Gus—a mask, snorkel, fins, and flashlight. He also removed a treasured memento from his days at the tip of the spear. It was an MPK dive knife, made of non-conductive titanium for use around explosive ordinance. Only by a fluke had he managed to keep the knife. He'd asked a fellow team-member to sharpen it for him while he was home on leave from the Navy. The buddy agreed to the chore as a wedding present. Months later after his incarceration, a box arrived at his mother's house. It was his knife, honed to a razor's edge. A card inside read "No matter what—Sea, Air or Land—just call." It was signed "Dolittle" and followed by a phone number.

He stared at the water. A snake appeared, looked at him, and swam off. Demons tugged at the corners of his mind, struggling to gain purchase. He belted on his knife, tugged on the flippers, and pulled down the mask.

Black waters awaited him.

51

Before issuing an all-clear, Billy Ray had instructed the group how to look for evidence to Ricky's death. If they found something, they were to photograph the item using their cell phone cameras and poke a stick in the ground to mark the location. While the others scouted clues on land, he searched underwater. He'd begun along the lake bottom where Bell indicated Ricky's body was found. The water was dark, visibility poor, a few feet at best using the flashlight. He was especially careful not to disturb the silty bottom. He completed searching the area that held the best promise for clues, but came up empty. His internal clock said they were out of time. No doubt the ruse of a picnic had long since lost validity, if it ever had any. Surely, Wiggins had a plan in action by now. He just hoped it wouldn't be of a lethal variety. He hated putting his friends at risk. Rebecca made it clear there'd be no ditching her. However, Bell and Shandi had no stake in the matter, except their lives.

His lungs hurt. He should've surfaced, checked on the progress of the others, and called it a day. Thirty minutes of snorkeling was all it had taken to prove he was a sorry shadow of a Navy SEAL....Snorkeling, for goodness sake! Kids' play compared to drown-proofing at NAB Coronado. A voice in his brain said to give up. He ignored the message. Only once during the grueling six-month Basic Underwater Demolition/SEAL course had he been tempted to quit, go check into a local hotel with a gallon of tequila, and sleep for a week. He'd witnessed men far stronger and smarter than him take up a taunting drill instructor's invitation to walk to the center of camp and ring the brass bell. He'd had just one issue with ringing that bell, the same as now. His mind wouldn't let him quit! Deep in his soul a different voice screamed at him, louder than any drill instructor. A voice that had gone silent ten years ago, but was now back, louder than ever, urging him onward.

He would never ring the bell. Not now...not ever again!

He began one last circuit around the area of Ricky's death. He surfaced, exhaled spent air, sucked in a lungful, and submerged. Something half-buried in the silt reflected the flashlight. He opted not to surface for another breath, afraid he'd lose the source. Without GPS equipment, reacquiring a tiny object in the brown water would be like finding a needle in a haystack, twice. He was able to hold his breath for six minutes, double that when sedentary. At least that much had been possible to practice in a tiny prison cell. The source of the reflection might just be the tip of a beer can. Then again, he was out of time and nearly out of energy.

He went to the object and brought his mask to within inches of the bottom, careful not to disturb sediment. His muscles screamed as he struggled to maintain neutral buoyancy. What he saw poking out of the mud nearly robbed the last of his breath—a human finger, flesh gone, bone gleaming brightly under the flashlight! He craned his neck slowly from side to side and spotted more bones, white against the dark mud. He retrieved the finger. The dark silt lifted from the bottom and began spreading in the water.

He managed to grab an additional group of bones before visibility ceased entirely. It'd be hours before the silt settled and the water cleared sufficiently to locate and recover more evidence. He had neither the time nor the proper equipment and the oxygen in his body's tissues was spent. White stars began popping like champagne bubbles in his brain. He held tight to the precious objects and surfaced.

Oxygen replaced carbon dioxide, clearing his mind of the ill effects. He looked around to gather his bearings. Bell and the ladies stood at the water's edge ninety feet away, looking in his direction. At once, they began waving their arms, signaling frantically for him to return to shore. It was then his senses cleared sufficiently to hear the shrill sound of a siren growing louder by the second. A police vehicle was speeding their way.

Just as he'd expected—the action.

52

Wiggins watched the scene at the reservoir on one of the closed circuit monitors. With revenge against America so near, he couldn't afford any mistakes. His every move required precision.

"Lee, full resolution on those cameras. Move Sniper One into position. Fire only on my command."

"What about the ATV's?"

"Maintain current positions."

Lee spoke into a hand radio. "Cameras coming up now. Sniper One will report from his new position in five minutes."

"Tell him to make it two!"

* * *

Billy Ray came ashore as a sheriff vehicle stopped beside the suburban. They waited for what was to come next—Sheriff Payne.

To everyone's surprise, or relief, Tom Dixon exited the car, clambered down the sandy bank, and stopped in front of them. He said to Bell. "What in hell is going on here?".

Billy Ray sat down to remove his snorkeling equipment. Bell looked around for someone to come to his rescue. Rebecca and Shandi didn't say a word.

"A picnic," Bell said.

"Bullshit!" Dixon pointed at Billy Ray. "You can't eat underwater!"

"Now, Tom—"

"Don't you *Tom* me, boy, I'm the Deputy Sheriff. So in case you can't count, that makes me the number two guy in the department and your superior!"

Bell may have bristled, but hid it well. As for himself, men far more brutal than Dixon had worked to ruin his day. SEALs learned to endure pain and discomfort. Only then was a man granted his Budweiser pin and allowed on missions to where true evil lurked in the shadows. He'd won the right to fight beside the world's finest warriors, battling the worst humanity or Mother Nature offered. He'd tasted blood, his own and others. Dixon didn't begin to compare.

Dixon turned on Rebecca. "Does your father know you're here with this scum?" Again indicating Billy Ray.

"What business is that of yours, Dicksock?"

"How dare you sass me!"

Dixon cocked a hand to strike Rebecca. Billy Ray came off the sand with lightning speed, sore muscles forgotten. His vice-like grip froze the fat deputy's arm. Dixon pushed harder, too dumb to sense his disadvantage, too proud to realize a smaller man in swim trunks, all wet and sandy, had the nerve to defy an officer of the law. And lastly, too angry to adjust his tactics.

"Stow it, Dixon," Billy Ray said through clenched teeth.

"How dare you interfere!" Dixon went for his gun.

Without loosening his grip on Dixon's wrist, Billy Ray pulled his dive knife and stuck it against the man's spleen. One thing the mind of a bully can register with warp speed is seven inches of razor-sharp titanium poking into his bowels. The struggle ended faster than it took the others to realize what'd happened.

The ladies gasped. Bell froze.

"You listen to me, Dixon. You'll not lay a hand on Rebecca. You'll conduct your business professionally. Is that clear?"

Dixon looked near to messing his pants.

Billy Ray applied pressure to the knife. Dixon's eyes widened. "I'm going to remove my knife. We'll listen to your directives and attempt with all due respect to oblige. Agreed?"

More nodding.

* * *

"Comrade, Jenkins just pulled a knife on the deputy sheriff."

"I see that, Lee. Most impressive. It appears the man's service record accurately stated his abilities."

"Do I order the men to shoot?"

Wiggins watched on the monitor. Four monitors, actually. Each screen broadcasted a different angle of the action on the shores of the Loma Reservoir. He was impressed with Jenkins' skill at close quarters combat. The deputy was larger, but no match for Jenkins.

What worried him wasn't the ability of a former Navy SEAL to react in such an impressive fashion. After all, he himself had been a champion fighter in the KGB and had never been bested, not when young and in training, nor later on assignments around the globe. He'd beaten them all. Ultimately, he was not even worried about whether he could stop Jenkins. After all, he was just one man. Rather, his concern was not knowing what Jenkins had been doing underwater, where no cameras could penetrate. His spotters in the field indicated Jenkins had remained close to shore and showed no interest in the water treatment plant. He'd been tempted to let loose the piranhas on Jenkins, but dismissed the idea. The matter was under control. Better to just get the people off the grounds peacefully and then deal with them individually at a time and manner of his own choosing.

Lee repeated the question. “Take them out, comrade?”

“No. I have a better idea.”

* * *

Dixon lost his bluster. He simply ordered them off Texas Waterland property on account of the land being posted and complaints by the owners. Next he informed Billy Ray that a local judge had issued a temporary restraining order for him to stay clear of all Waterland properties and personnel. Lastly, the deputy ordered Bell back to the station, even said “please.” Then he drove off in a cloud of dust, but no siren.

The ride to town lacked conversation. Worry carved deep lines on Bell’s face. Rebecca’s thoughts went unspoken. Shandi wore a polite smile and watched the view from the window. Billy Ray could think of only one thing—the bones in his pocket. He hadn’t told the others about the discovery. He wanted to know more before deciding who to share it with.

Bell delivered them back to the Piggly Wiggly. Rebecca offered encouragement to her friend, but her words fell on deaf ears. Bell drove off without saying goodbye. Shandi excused herself and headed to her apartment across the street.

Billy Ray stowed his gear in the trunk of his mother’s car.

Rebecca came up beside him. “I’m worried about Larry. Are you sure we did the right thing? I mean, what did we accomplish by our little stunt?”

He wanted to show her the hard evidence that proved a terrible thing had happened at the Loma Reservoir, but held off. “Yes, we did the right thing. I’m not sure what will happen to Larry. Maybe just a chewing out, maybe more. He’s a good man and good cop. He’ll be fine in the long run.”

“I hope you’re right.”

“Trust me. We did the right thing. Larry will get the credit he deserves and we’ll have solved what happened to Ricky and Clarice.”

Rebecca made a suspicious look. “What do you mean?”

“I can’t tell you. There’s something I have to check on first.”

“What?”

“Rebecca—”

“Okay. But you’d better not be trying to cut me out again.”

“I’m not,” Billy Ray said. “I’ll call you tomorrow, when I know more.”

“Okay, I’ll be at the store so come there.”

She stepped close. Her soft breasts pressed against his chest. She wrapped her arms around him. His knees nearly buckled.

Billy Ray pulled Rebecca in tight wanting to kiss her, but a horn honked and he became self-conscious. Before releasing her warm body he asked, "What's with you and Dixon?"

"What do you mean?"

"You're quick on the draw with him. You must not like him."

"What's to like," Rebecca said. "He acts like an uncle just because he goes so far back with my father."

"Is he married?"

"Divorced."

"What about kids of his own?"

Rebecca was slow to answer. "No," she finally said.

Strange, he thought, but let it go. "It just seems by the way you dig at him that there's some bad history."

Rebecca looked at him strangely, like someone whose secret just got discovered. "I hate Dixon."

He should've let the matter drop, but he'd fallen for her and felt the need to probe. Besides, Dixon was proving dangerous. If he was to protect them, then he needed to know all he could of a potential enemy.

"Why do you hate him?"

"I have my reasons."

"Anything I should know? He's determined to nail my hide to a tree."

Rebecca reined him in close. She rose up on her tiptoes and whispered in his ear, "Now it's your turn to trust *me*." She brushed her lips across his and walked away.

What wasn't she telling him, and why? Finding Ricky's killer was important. But most concerning to him was keeping them safe. Certainly, Rebecca knew better than to jeopardize that.

He decided not to pressure her on the matter.

53

Night had fallen by the time Billy Ray entered the house. There was no sign of his mother. He checked the house phone for messages. There were two. One was a recorded plug to join a politician on the steps of city hall on Independence Day. The other was from Eva, asking if he'd read the diary. Specifically, her uncle's claims that North Korean operatives were behind the construction of Texas Waterland, and that an unholy alliance had formed between them and a Mexican drug gang.

Billy Ray was stumped. He listened to Eva's message twice more. He hadn't yet read the diary, but didn't think his opinion would change much. He believed Jonesy about witnessing Ricky and Clarice together, and observing Koreans working with Wiggins. He even accepted Jonesy having guessed the make and model of the sniper rifle pointed at Lam. However, those matters all had one thing in common, proximity. Jonesy could've deduced those facts by simply being near them or overhearing things at the tavern. Claims as large as those mentioned in Eva's message seemed far beyond an elderly man's ability to acquire, especially one crippled, over-medicated, and known to imbibe on regular occasion. It sounded like fantasy. So he decided it'd be imprudent to phone Eva with his true feelings. He could skip to hard evidence. He retrieved the phone book and looked up a number he hadn't used in a decade, Doc Hastings.

It was well past closing time for a doctor's office. He tried the number anyway, hoping to leave a message on a machine or with a call center operator. He hoped to have the old physician take a look at the bones he'd found.

The phone rang half a dozen times before the voice of an elderly man answered. "Hastings Clinic."

Billy Ray was shocked to hear a live person at such an hour. "I want to leave a message for Doctor Hastings."

"Why do that? Just speak your piece...this is Hastings."

"You may not remember me—"

"Sure I do, Billy Ray. How could I ever forget?"

"How'd you know who I was?"

"I'd like to claim we country docs know all, but I'd be yanking your chain. I have caller ID, in case a patient gets cut off during an emergency phone call. What planet you been on?"

"Houston."

"That explains it."

"Incredible...I haven't talked to you in years."

"I must confess. I've been attending your mother. She told me of your coming home. So when her number showed, and with Ricky gone, well, that leaves you," Doc said with some sadness.

"So what you doing answering your clinic phone after hours?"

"Paperwork. Uncle Sam has us doing their work for them. Damn bean counters want to know every detail of our lives."

Now that was the Doc he remembered. The voice sounded fit for a man slamming into eighty. His wit was as sharp as ever.

"What can I do for you, Billy Ray?"

"It's kind of hard to explain over the phone. Is there any way I can meet with you in the next day or two?"

"Sure. But if you want to beat the crowds and save an old man from the tedium of endless government paperwork, then grab some cold beers and come see me now."

"Did you say now?"

"Is it a hearing problem?"

"Actually Doc, it's a bone problem."

"Well then, come on over. You remember how to get here?"

"Big Sandy, next to Annie's Attic. See you in twenty."

Billy Ray hung up and scribbled a quick note for his mother.

He wondered where she was.

54

Bell took his lumps. He should've known better, Rebecca had tricked him before. But this time was different. She'd come clean immediately. He could've turned the vehicle around, probably should have. He had nobody to blame but himself. Now he was suspended without pay. Furthermore, he'd lied and kept his mouth shut about the incident involving Jenkins and Dixon. Actually, Dixon himself had been the first to omit the matter of Jenkins putting a knife to his gut. He didn't know what game Dixon was playing. The Deputy Sheriff had concentrated on ratting him out for using department equipment for personal pleasure—and doing so with a known felon and the sheriff's daughter. He knew the later charge was worse than the first. In Payne's mind, it was a matter of aiding and abetting.

He left wondering what to do next...and how to pay his bills.

Payne waited for his young deputy to depart before turning on Dixon. "Tell me again how you learned of the trespass."

"I received a call on my cell phone."

"From who?"

"A man. He refused to give a name, claimed Jenkins was headed to the old reservoir with your daughter, and she seemed in distress."

"And you didn't see fit to inform me?"

"Sorry, boss." His shoulders slumped. "I kinda lost my head, what with it involving Rebecca and all."

Payne rounded the desk. "Let me make something clear." He pointed in Dixon's face. "Don't ever respond to a call involving my daughter without informing me. You got that?"

"Yes sir, Roy, loud and clear."

Payne lowered his finger. He returned to his seat and put his feet up on the desk. "So what was my daughter doing with Jenkins back at the reservoir, and why was Bell helping them? Was she in trouble or not?"

"I can't say. She told me the same thing Bell, about having a picnic."

"Where we pulled Ricky Jenkins' worthless body out of the water?"

"Yup. And also the same spot where Brenda Lee died. It's like Billy Ray Jenkins has a hard-on for your daughters. "

When Payne spoke it was with a chill to freeze hell. "You get on Jenkins like stink. Find us a reason to throw his sorry ass in a cage."

"Yes, sir. By the way, I had Judge Johnson issue a restraining order on Jenkins for Texas Waterland and all company personnel."

"Good thinking, Tom." Payne paused and looked hard at Dixon. "You trying to get my job in the upcoming election?"

"No sir! You're the best sheriff this county's ever had."

"That's right. So don't even think about it. Not now, not ever. You help me win this next election, and I'll make sure you're taken care of. Haven't I always taken care of you, Tom?"

"You sure have. You've been there for me since we were kids." Dixon stiffened his posture. "You can count on me, Roy."

"Good. Go after Jenkins. Let me know what that dog's up to."

Dixon grabbed his hat and made ready to leave.

"Another thing. How'd the man get your personal cell phone number?"

"I have no idea, boss."

Payne stared at his deputy for a long moment. "Dismissed." He waited for the door to close and then dialed the phone.

A man answered. "Yeah?"

"Anything?"

"Nothing."

"Where are they now?"

"Out back, looking around."

"Let me know if anything happens." Payne hung up.

He pulled a political flyer from a stack just back from the printers and tilted the glossy print to capture better light. In his sixties, and yet, with airbrushing, years dissolved like magic. He loved being the sheriff, the power, cutting through the bullshit. Nobody had even filed to run against him. The Jenkins/Richards case should've put him over the top. Instead there were rumors of disgruntled voters. If only the Richards girl had turned up, he would've solved a big crime *and* stabbed the heart of the woman he loved one more time. What was wrong with voters, hadn't he always kept Upshur County clean from riff raff, druggies, saggy pants punks, and the like? He needed one more high-profile case. Then nobody would dare campaign against him. And he knew just what that case should be. There was one more thing that needed cleaning up in his county, one last piece of human garbage taken out. That'd show his mettle and shut the mouths of those voters.

He would get his revenge and his votes in a single stroke. Billy Ray Jenkins would be eliminated and Lela Jenkins would be destroyed. He would never let anyone reject him without coming to regret it...no matter what it took...no matter how long.

Payne leaned back, put his feet on the desk, and crossed his arms. A smile played across his face.

55

They were gathered in the lab at the back of the clinic. Doc Hastings pulled away from an old Zeiss compound microscope and returned the objectives wheel to a neutral position. He slid his roller chair back and looked up at Billy Ray. His face showed a mix of curiosity and concern.

"Where'd you get these samples?"

"I'd rather not say just yet."

"I see. Is this going to involve Sheriff Payne again?"

Billy Ray couldn't blame Doc for his concern. Even after ten years, the sight of a dead woman on his clinic doorstep was something impossible to forget. "It's bigger than Payne this time. So what can you tell me?"

Doc cocked an eyebrow at that and then provided an answer. "I can tell you the sample we're looking at is the *digitus annularis* from a human subject, most likely that of an adult female, and comprises both middle and proximal phalanx joined by soft cartilage. Furthermore, the sample appears to have been detached from the first metacarpal bone in a most peculiar manner."

"Is that fancy talk for the ring finger of the left hand?"

Hastings shot Billy Ray a look. "Yes. How'd you know?"

He removed a ziploc bag from his duffle that contained the skeletal hand. He placed the bag of bones on the lab table.

The Doctor's eyes went wide. "Are there more?"

"Yes. But not with me."

"These are human remains. What's more they're fresh—unindicative of their condition, I might add. A body takes a good deal more time to arrive at this state of decomposition. This one had help." Doc looked hard at Billy Ray. "I think you'd better start explaining yourself."

"I believe these to be the remains of Clarice Richards."

"DNA can confirm that." Doc folded his arms on his chest. "Suppose you tell me what's going on here. What makes you suggest such a thing?"

"Because these bones were found where my brother's body was pulled from the Loma Reservoir. I know where Clarice Richards is, or what's left of her, just not how she got there."

"I do."

That got Billy Ray's attention. "How?"

Doc turned back to the microscope. He chose the appropriate lens, adjusted the coarse and fine focus knobs until satisfied with the image, and then motioned for Billy Ray to take a look.

At first he wasn't sure what he was looking at. Deep lines and gashes scored the sample. Near the tip of the middle phalanx, one long cut appeared to slice clean through. The bones were stripped clean. Suddenly, the cuts made sense. He pulled back.

"Am I looking at teeth marks?"

"Brilliant deduction, Watson."

"What creature in Texas can strip a bone like that?"

"Not Texas, Billy Ray. Brazil."

"Huh?"

"*Pygocentrus nattereri.*"

"In English, Doc."

"Red-bellied piranha."

Billy Ray couldn't believe his ears. Maybe he did have a hearing problem. "How the hell did piranha get into the Loma Reservoir?"

"Not through evolution, I can assure you." Doc turned off the microscope and faced Billy Ray. "I catch a story in the press occasionally of a fisherman catching one. But I'm sure those cases can be attributed to some idiot growing the thing in a tank and then releasing it. I hasten to add, one piranha cannot strip a small animal, let alone a human. It would take many hundreds of them."

Billy Ray stared at Doc Hastings in disbelief.

"So now do we call the sheriff?" Doc asked.

"Not this time. In fact, we better open those beers. I have a long story."

"Billy Ray, you sure know how to cure boredom."

He had to disagree with Doc. Boredom would be welcome. The cure he had in mind could end up killing them!

* * *

Nearly two days and still no word—no word and no clues. It was as if Katie had dropped off the face of the earth. The thought pained Lam to his core. His usually steady hands trembled from worry and lack of sleep. He had to keep it together. He couldn't afford to fall to pieces, not if he wanted any chance at getting his daughter back.

"I'm sorry any of this happened, and in my town!"

"Not your fault, Captain. If we knew where the bad guys would strike next, there wouldn't be any bad guys."

"Keep the faith, Lam. I just know something'll turn up soon."

"I hope you're right."

Lam turned away. He didn't want Ulrich to see tears.

* * *

Billy Ray's phone rang as he walked into his mother's house. He fully expected Rebecca to be calling. It wasn't.

"Hello?"

"This is Wes Harlan. Your mother wishes to speak to you."

There was the noise of a phone being shuffled. "Billy Ray?"

"Mom! Where are you? Are you okay?"

"I'm fine. I can't tell you where I am right now."

"Why?" Billy Ray thought that strange.

"I just can't, but I will soon. I wanted to call to say not to worry. I'm safe. I'm with Wesley."

"Okay. When will I see you?"

"Tomorrow or the next day. I can't be sure."

"Are you sure you're okay?"

"Absolutely. I'll tell you all about it when I get back to town. I love you, son. Goodbye." Lela ended the call.

So she was with the Chief. He didn't know what to make of that. Maybe they were dating. Just as well though, there was lots of work to do, possibly dangerous work. He was glad to have her out of harm's way.

He finally grabbed a sandwich and decided to read Jonesy's diary while he ate. Eva's message referred to several outrageous claims by her uncle.

Two hours later, he laid the diary on the table. He couldn't determine whether he was stunned or confused. His head swam with a million thoughts. His heart wrestled with troublesome feelings and emotions. Was any of this true?

On the matter of Texas Waterland, he was stunned. Jonesy claimed to have spent hundreds of hours observing activities on the property formerly owned by a Bible college and which now formed the site of the Texas Waterland Family Park. If what Jonesy recorded was true, then he was up against an enemy he had no chance against fighting on his own. Yet, where could he turn? Who'd believe an old drunk and a convicted felon?

Regarding his father and Roy Payne, he was confused. According to the diary, Payne had contributed heavily to Rodney's alcoholism and directly influenced the drunken rages. Payne had manipulated Rodney from the start. Did his mother know this? If Jonesy's story was true, then he'd vastly underestimated Payne. Could it be Roy Payne was so evil he'd conspired to ruin Rodney using any means possible—lies, alcohol, sex, money?

Rebecca had said her father was sick and always had been. He now realized what that meant.

Nothing was beyond Roy Payne.

He thought of his first love, Brenda Lee and the agony she'd felt from an abusive father. Then anger overwhelmed him. Suddenly, without warning, tormentors rose from the underworld of grief in their familiar forms, sadness and guilt….

Brenda Lee's smiling face appeared for a fleeting moment. He felt her anguish, her weakness to fight on, her softness against the brutality of emotional abuse.

He heard her cries—begging to be loved.

He saw her spirit—trapped, grasping for acceptance.

He sensed her welcome surrender—death.

And he had loved her so….

Billy Ray shook his head to clear his mind. He had to end this vicious cycle—to be free at last. Free from history. Free from the pull of the grave. Free from blaming himself.

Things had changed, he'd changed.

New voices carried on the wind. Truth beckoned. Justice called out. It was time for stopping a killer, for avenging the deaths of the innocent. But to do so demanded he rise up, bend plowshare into sword, become the warrior once again. Going forward also meant sliding back—back to a person he'd buried with Reverend Greer's help. He'd been warned.

Billy Ray made his decision.

He would backslide.

56

How long he sat in his mother's kitchen, head held in shaking hands, praying, whispering, deciding, Billy Ray hadn't a clue. It could've been a minute or a million years. He only knew that a path forward now appeared. Answers surfaced. What had to be done became evident at last.

God was his ally above, most certainly. He needed more...he needed allies on earth. If he was to survive against professional killers, he could no longer be the loner. He needed boots on the ground.

He'd seen the enemy, their weapons, their capabilities, and their vast facilities. If the reports in Jonesy's diary were correct, he'd need an entire army to root them out. He didn't have an army, only himself. He couldn't seek help from authorities. They'd think him insane and send him back to Eastham. Lam might believe him, but that was no guarantee, either. Lam hadn't been overly-moved by what they'd witnessed at Texas Waterland, justifying the high level of security and weapons as that needed to defend against potential terror threats. Plus Lam had his own hell dealing with his daughter's kidnapping. That left only one man who might help—Dolittle.

He had no idea where his old friend was or whether Dolittle was even alive. He'd lost contact with his SEAL Team years ago. Doolittle owed him a favor for saving his life, not once, but twice. Of course, anyone on his team would've done the same for him. They'd all pledged their lives to one another.

He lifted his head from prayer. His hands held steady and strong. A high tide of resolve flooded him with strength.

The arrows on the wall clock pointed north, the passing of one day, the birth of another.

What would the new day be like?

Harder! The only easy day was yesterday.

He went to the bedroom and retrieved the box that had contained his dive knife. The small card that accompanied the gift a decade ago lay in the bottom. He pulled it out and carried it back to the kitchen. The thing he sought was scribbled at the bottom, a phone number.

Another check of the clock made him consider it too late to dial the number. He dismissed the thought, knowing the man he was about to call was trained as he'd been. Theirs was a brotherhood, an unbreakable bond. Any time, any place—sea, air, or land.

The man would be ready or dead, nothing in between.

Billy Ray used his cell phone instead of the landline. He turned off the caller ID function and placed the call. A computerized voice came on after ten rings, it said to leave a message. He spoke a single word, the nickname given him by fellow SEALs. He pressed "end call" and waited. If the number was no longer valid, the new owner would simply dismiss the message as a prank call. If the number was correct—

The phone rang!

No return number, just the word "Unknown."

"Speak," Billy Ray said.

"Dolittle," a male voice responded.

"Wolverine." Billy Ray repeated his call sign.

"Jenkins! How the hell are you?"

"Still among the breathing, Mr. Dodd. And you?"

"Likewise, although I'm no longer among the walking. Lost both legs seven years back. Some new kind of underwater mine developed by the Iranians, those tricky bastards!"

"Why were you performing the extraction? Where were your babies, Flipper and Skipper?"

"Damn animal rights activists…the program got canceled. Regardless, I wouldn't have let my darlings do dirty work on anything new, anyway. Far too risky. The enemy caught on to some of our little tricks, sorta turned the cards against us. It makes me sick to think somebody would train dolphins and sea lions to attack their own kind. Maybe the animal rights kooks had it right, after all."

"But the Navy Marine Mammal Program still exists, I read about it in a magazine."

Dodd laughed. "You know better than that. If you're reading about black-budget programs in Playboy, they can't be too secret."

"Guess not, buddy. Sorry to hear that. You always had a knack for talking with the animals."

"Just like dad..." Dodd's voice trailed off.

John P. Dodd, aka Dolittle, was a second-generation trainer for the U.S. NMMP. He was the best animal trainer the government had for Dolphins and California Sea Lions, or had been. Not only a genius, Dodd was also one hell of a SEAL. Dodd's father had been one of the original scientists who developed the use of marine mammals to assist with ship and harbor protection, mine detection and clearance, and equipment recovery. The elder Dodd had also been among the first SEAL members. Like his father, the younger Dodd also possessed the uncanny ability to speak with the animals. After his father's untimely death in a diving accident, John P. took his dad's call sign, Dolittle.

"So what's up, Jenkins? You still hiding out in Eastham?"

"Been out a month."

"About time. I did a little checking on your case after I heard what happened. What a load of crap!"

"Thanks, ol' buddy. I know that now. Back then, I guess I just threw in the towel."

"So what's up, Jenkins?"

"I need help, Dolittle." He used the call sign to signify business.

"Name it, Wolverine. What you got?"

"Some really bad customers moved into the neighborhood."

Spec-Ops guys didn't trifle with bar fights or local beefs. They kept low profiles. The code he used referenced something big. It also told Dolittle to go light on details, in case the walls had ears.

"How about we get together over a coffee and discuss your neighbors. Can you be in Shreveport inside of four hours?"

"Louisiana? Sure. Sooner than that, even."

"Okay. Call me when you get to town. I'll guide you in."

"See you soon." Billy Ray was glad to know Dodd still took necessary precautions.

Once an operative, always an operative.

This would be interesting, he thought as he hung up the phone. John P. Dodd was a man of extreme talents, with or without legs.

* * *

Pulling the short straw won Rebecca the privilege of opening the store. Independence Day was upon them and customers would be eager to get their shopping out of the way early. This meant her arriving at four in the morning, turning on the lights, checking temperatures in the freezers and coolers, and erecting the outdoor display signs...all prior to arrival of the morning shift employees.

She never made it.

57

As he approached the Shreveport Regional Airport, Billy Ray spotted a service station. He pulled in and phoned Dodd.

"That was quick," Dodd said without preamble.

"You know me, Dolittle. I don't like wasting time."

"Just the last decade, right?"

From anyone else, that might've stung. However, buddies who've seen the elephant and heard the owl earned the right to bust each other's balls. "Where to, Mr. Dodd?"

"Get on US Route 71 going north. After you cross the Arkansas border, call again." Dodd hung up.

Billy Ray wondered if Dodd was playing a joke on him.

* * *

One Upshur County Sheriff Department vehicle and one Gladewater Police vehicle sat outside of the Piggly Wiggly store with their lights flashing. The Gladewater cop held position in the store parking lot. Roy Payne and Tom Dixon took the opposite side of the road, next to the bookstore.

"Wait here, Tom." Payne exited the cruiser and climbed the steps to Rebecca's apartment two at a time. He pounded on the door.

A groggy-eyed Shandi answered in her bathrobe and bare feet. She saw the whirling lights of the police vehicles and came fully awake. "Sheriff Payne, what's happened?"

"Where's Rebecca!" Payne demanded gruffly.

Shandi pointed at the Piggly Wiggly. "There—"

"She never showed. Now listen to me, young lady, I know you were part of that little joyride to the Loma Reservoir with my idiot deputy. You'd better tell me the truth. Did something happen between my daughter and Billy Ray Jenkins?"

"Happen? Like what?"

Payne looked ready to launch. "Like he wanted to hurt her."

Shandi's eyes got big, as if realizing having awakened to a nightmare.

Payne grabbed her arm. "Come on, answer me!"

Shandi yelped. "No, nothing like that. Billy Ray was my date for the picnic. Rebecca was with Larry."

"Are you sure?" Payne squeezed harder.

"Yes! Please, you're hurting me!"

Payne released his grip. "Tell me where she is."

Shandi rubbed her arm. "I told you. She left for the store. I heard her alarm and then she showered and left." Shandi had tears. "What's happened to Rebecca?"

"Jenkins took her!"

Payne stormed back to the cruiser.

"So what do you think happened, Roy?" Dixon asked once Payne closed the door.

"A jealous dog, that's what. Rebecca was dating Bell at the reservoir." Payne gathered his thoughts. "Jenkins couldn't have her sister, I wouldn't let him. When he saw Rebecca choosing somebody besides his sorry ass, he kidnapped her!"

"How can you be so sure, Roy?"

"You heard the 911 recording. 'Billy Ray... Don't... Father... Help!'" Payne's face turned beet red. "Dixon, I'm going to kill that mutt for sure this time, and don't you try to stop me!"

"Fill the worthless bastard full of holes for all I care," Dixon said.

Payne radioed an all-points bulletin for the capture of Billy Ray Jenkins...wanted for the forced abduction of Rebecca Payne of Gladewater. Suspect presumed armed and dangerous.

Payne then had orders for Dixon. "Contact all agencies—state, county, and local. Send fliers, too. Post a description of that car he drives. And wake up that gadfly, Ballerd, over at the Gazette. I want his skinny ass on this. The man owes me favors. Then I want pictures of Jenkins' ugly mug tacked on every wall, every telephone pole, and every television in this state. Blast his description over the radio. And call all the other sheriffs, I know my brothers in arms will be pissed!"

* * *

"Where to now?" Dodd had better not be punking him.

"US Route 30 East. When you see the 'Leaving Texarkana' sign, count thirteen miles. You'll come to the juncture of a county road, or what the good folks of Arkansas call a road. Turn right and go seven-point-two miles, then stop. A red station wagon will be waiting for you. Follow them."

"Where are you sending me, Dolittle?"

"You'll see. One more thing, this will be the final transmission available to you from your phone. You're about to go off the grid."

"Oh great. Just where on God's blue marble do you live?"

"Someplace where nobody'll hear you scream." Dodd signed off.

Billy Ray could swear hearing laughter as the phone went dead.

* * *

Gus Heavenor had always been an early-riser. His habit was to catch the early news and weather on the radio. He'd benefited often by offering special sales after hearing a weather report or other news that got people stirred up. That's how he happened to be listening when, right in the middle of the sports scores, regular programming was interrupted and the excited voice of the station manager came on to say, "Upshur County Sheriff Roy Payne has just issued an all-points bulletin for the immediate apprehension of an alleged kidnapper, presumed to be armed and dangerous. The victim is identified as Rebecca Payne of Gladewater...

What was that? Gus sat up in bed. Did he hear that correctly?

The radio voice continued, "...the suspect is described as a white male, six feet, two hundred pounds, named Billy Ray Jenkins...."

Gus about shot through the roof! He stumbled out of bed, nearly taking a header into the wall. He managed to hear the last of the announcement. "I repeat. Suspect is a convicted felon and is to be considered armed and dangerous. Frantic calls were received by the Upshur County 911 emergency operator from the victim's phone. The following is an actual recording of the victim's plea for help. 'Billy Ray... Don't... Father... Help!' As our listening audience can tell, the victim's call cut off before she was able to provide her whereabouts. If anyone has information...."

Gus bolted into the living room to the telephone. He steadied his hand and dialed Lela's house. He got the answering machine. Perhaps Lela was sleeping. Another try yielded the same result. He hurried back to the bedroom, grabbed his wallet off the dresser, and fished through its contents. There it was, the small slip of paper with Billy Ray's new cell number. He ran back to the phone and dialed. No luck. He finally left a message, warning Billy Ray. Then he collapsed on the sofa.

He'd done all he could think of to warn Billy Ray.

The war had begun. Now Payne and countless more police would be gunning for Billy Ray Jenkins.

Gus prayed Lela's child would survive.

58

There, in the light of his high beams, a red station wagon just as Dodd had said. The car flashed its lights and sped off.

Billy Ray gave chase.

After fifteen teeth-clacking minutes, and a thermos of coffee spilled on the seat of his mother's car, the station wagon skidded to a halt and extinguished its lights. He nearly rear-ended the lead car. He turned off the motor, doused the lights, and waited.

An additional ten minutes elapsed. Finally, a knock on the far-side passenger window startled Billy Ray. He heard a muffled voice saying to follow. He was careful to reach up and switch the overhead light to the off position. A great deal of precaution had been displayed, he followed suit.

A clapboard farmhouse materialized in the distance, a gray weathered ghost in the night. No lights shone from inside. Billy Ray followed after the human shadow, careful to mind his footing in the darkness. He had no idea who the person was, or if the shadow was man or woman. It couldn't have been Dodd, he had no legs. And the shape leading the way set far too quick a pace to indicate prosthetic limbs, at least none he was aware existed.

The shadow stopped at a set of porch steps. A man's voice said, "Hands high, feet apart."

Billy Ray did so. He felt expert hands frisk his clothing and the usual places for concealing weapons and recording devices.

"Come."

They continued up the steps to the door. Shadowman stopped and waited, not bothering to knock. After a full minute the door opened from the inside. Billy Ray could barely make out a figure seated in a wheelchair. Then a flashlight came on and shined up into his face.

"You're still one ugly powder monkey," said his old battle buddy.

The light went off.

"And you're shorter, Dolittle."

"True that, Wolverine. Come, I'll hit the lights once you're in."

Dodd wheeled back and Billy Ray stepped across the threshold. The door was pulled shut behind them. Shadowman remained outdoors. Dodd used the flashlight to shine the way down a hall and through a set of double doors.

"Close those behind you."

Billy Ray did, and then came light.

Dodd held a device similar to a TV remote. He pressed a button and a fire lit in the fireplace. Another button brought forth soft music. Yet another made the back wall slide open to reveal a well-stocked bar.

Billy Ray marveled. It was a house built inside another house. The room they stood in reminded him of a ballroom, though not as barren and perfect for wheelchair accessibility.

Arranged along the back wall to the left side of the bar, were beautifully hand-carved furniture pieces, like the kinds one might see in a log home. Along the wall to the right was a splendid table already spread with food in anticipation of the guest. The most impressive feature was an entire wall dedicated to high-tech equipment—computers, monitors, and various electronic displays. Dodd's equipment wall nearly rivaled the one he and Lam had visited at the Texas Waterland security building.

"Holy cow, Dolittle. You work for NASA or something?"

"Or something..." Dodd said, and left it at that.

"You sure took pains guiding me here, wherever here is. And what's up with the guy I followed, he afraid of the light?"

"He's cautious. I'm sure you remember one can never be too careful."

"Depends on what *one* does," Billy Ray suggested. "I haven't seen this kind of careful since our days at the tip of the spear. In fact, it looks a bit paranoid."

"Paranoid keeps me alive," Dodd said. Let me simply suggest there could be competing interests in America today. A lot has changed since last we met, Wolverine."

"Can't argue with you there, old friend. Life's a bigger gamble now than I ever remember it."

"Let's just see how right you are, sucker!" Dodd reached behind himself and pulled out a dark leather case, opened it, and removed a dollar bill.

Billy Ray did the same, folding his bill twice over until only the row of eight serial numbers showed.

Liar's Poker, their traditional challenge.

Dodd said, "Anytime, anywhere, I'll take your money. Four tens...."

The object of the game was to claim as many numbers as you could get away with, twos being the lowest, zeros acting as tens, ones playing the role of aces, and the remaining numbers keeping face value. No straights or full houses, just how many of a number you could bid without getting called down.

Billy Ray switched the bid. "Five aces."

"Looks like you're up to the challenge, Jenkins. Eight aces."

"Eight aces...in a two-man game?"

"I only need four ones to go with your four ones to make eight."

"Thanks for reminding me how to add. But if I don't have four aces, you're screwed. I better just call you down. Show me what you got."

Dodd ignored the call. "Nine aces."

"Did you forget how to play, Dolittle? You don't need to bet. But, if you insist—"

"I insist."

Billy Ray smelled a rat. "I went down on your eight aces, you liar, I'm definitely down on nine of them." He showed his dollar bill. "I only have one ace. You're slipping, Dolittle. Unless all those numbers are ones, then you be da' sucker. Now hand it over."

Liar's Poker, cold beer, and ball-busting had been his SEAL team's main entertainment during downtime and long tours to the far sides of the globe. He missed his Navy family.

Dodd didn't move at first, just stared down at his bill.

"I've never beaten you, Dolittle. My luck has finally changed."

"Not today it hasn't." Dodd turned over his bill.

Billy Ray stared in awe. All eight serial numbers on Dodd's bill read ones. With his ace, that made a total of nine!

Dodd extended his hand. "Just like old times."

Billy Ray handed over the money. "Maybe I'll get lucky in love."

Just then, the double doors burst open. Shadowman walked straight to a consul on the wall and turned a few knobs. The speakers went from soft music to a news station. A man's shrill voice proclaimed an important public announcement—a kidnapping in East Texas. When the radio announcer mentioned the name Rebecca Payne, Billy Ray's heart stopped. When his own name issued from the radio, his brain froze.

The world went black.

When his vision cleared, Dodd was staring at him, mouth drawn tight, and Shadowman held a gun.

It was pointed at his forehead.

59

The radio repeated the public announcement. Rebecca's voice came through as though she stood among them. The sound of her pleading, the anguish, the fear. It shook Billy Ray to his core.

Think!

He was shocked back to reality by the sound of the safety releasing on Shadowman's gun.

"You have five seconds to explain, Jenkins."

Billy Ray's head swam with countless thoughts and emotions.

Pull yourself together!

"It's a mistake. You can see I'm here. I'm not a kidnapper."

"And the girl? Who is Rebecca Payne?" asked Shadowman.

"She's...my friend. I think I'm in love with her."

Dodd and Shadowman looked at each other.

"You just bought more time. Use it wisely," Dodd ordered.

Billy Ray didn't know if Dodd would order his partner to shoot and he certainly didn't care to find out. Dodd had some kind of operation in play. So yeah, maybe he was a dead man. And Dodd's partner was making it clear no friendship stood in the way of blowing his head off. He could try making a break for it, but decided against the idea for a number of reasons, not the least of which he hadn't done anything wrong.

"Rebecca Payne is the daughter of the Upshur County Sheriff. We've been seeing each other. Her father doesn't approve."

"He got something against ex-Navy guys?"

"No, ex-cons. And then there's the matter of Rebecca being the sister of my dead fiancé. Payne blames me for her death. I didn't resist and spent ten years in Eastham for my silence. I didn't know what to do when Brenda Lee died. It was nothing like combat—"

"So you rang the bell."

"After having time to sort things out, I came to see I'd given up. Quit on myself and everybody else. I'd done nothing wrong, and yet I let the sheriff railroad me. Terrible thing is, I lost a decade of my life and it didn't get my woman back."

Shadowman's gun held steady. The man's icy stare hadn't thawed a single degree at hearing Billy Ray's admission.

"I'm not guilty now either, except for falling for Brenda Lee's sister."

And that was all Billy Ray cared to say on the matter. If that wasn't enough, then so be it. He wasn't about to beg for his life, especially from a man supposed to be his friend.

Silence hung over the room. Nobody moved.

"Egolf, stow the weapon. I believe him," Dodd said.

Shadowman had a name, *Egolf.* The man holstered the gun.

Billy Ray lowered his hands.

"I've never known you to lie, Wolverine. Hell, you can't even win at Liar's Poker. I caught your look during that radio announcement."

Billy Ray didn't allow himself relief as yet. "What now, Dolittle?"

John P. Dodd took charge. "We figure out what this kidnapping thing is about. You're a marked man, Jenkins. Every hillbilly cop here to the Gulf will be looking to notch his gun on your account. By the way, might this manhunt have anything to do with your neighbor problem? I really can't buy a sheriff kidnapping his own daughter."

The lights came on. Bells and whistles sounded. There hadn't been time to think. There was the radio announcement and Rebecca's frantic cries for help, then the immediate standoff with Dodd and Egolf. If Wiggins was the person behind Rebecca's abduction and all the mayhem, then the man had shown extraordinary skill creating asymmetry and misdirection. Such an enemy required his undivided attention.

"Mind if I sit, Dolittle? I have much to tell you and very little time. I could use your particular expertise on a matter."

Billy Ray felt rage rise up from his soul like magma, then cool and harden.

He was ready for battle.

60

The hood over Rebecca's head turned the world black. The gag in her mouth made it hopeless to scream and nearly impossible to breathe. Her body's fight-or-flight response was now the enemy, discharging massive amounts of adrenaline into her blood, speeding her heart rate. Her only chance to survive was to cease struggling. If she failed to subdue her body, suffocation awaited. She concentrated on ridding her mind of panic.

Wiggins had tricked her with the phone, making her think she was calling out for help. He'd then forced her to shout statements written on paper. Afterward, a powerful Asian man jammed a rag into her mouth, stretched tape across her face, and trussed her hands and feet. Then a dark hood was pulled over her head. The rough treatment came after she'd fought her abductors tooth and nail, managing to gouge one soldier's eye and connect with a foot to the groin of another. Regardless, she now lay helpless on a hard, damp floor, unable to move or determine her whereabouts. Added to her troubles, Wiggins had ordered her shoes removed.

Her feet were cold.

Information—dampness, cold, concrete…underground?

She'd heard a metal door close after being dropped to the floor and the muffled sounds of men beyond the door. She'd heard the singsong of high-pitched voices...foreign? She assumed they were Asian, as were the men that grabbed her outside the Piggly Wiggly—Koreans, considering Edward Jones' story and the incident at the Frontier Inn.

She focused on every detail, any bit of sensory data that might help save her life and aid her escape. Billy Ray's face appeared in her mind. She wondered where he was and if he was walking into a trap. If only he knew how correct his suspicions proved to be. She had to warn him.

Rebecca beat back the tears by squeezing her eyelids until stars burst in the darkness. To struggle was to die. Her fight now was to deny emotion. To rule the monster of fear. To get free.

To save Billy Ray.

* * *

"Comrade Wiggins, Master Pao requests your presence," the young interpreter said.

Wiggins straightened from looking down at the maps on the table where he and Lee were reviewing perimeter defenses. Everything was in place. Rapture was ready. The tanker trucks were en route to receive their precious loads. Gallina's troops were sequestered below ground, and the rest of the cartel was spread throughout the target cities. There was little to do now but review park security and wait.

The Jenkins matter was out of his hands now. In fact, it'd be a miracle if the man made it to a jail cell at all. The level of moral outrage by the citizens of Texas and surrounding states couldn't have been greater if the APB had been for Adolf Hitler. Wiggins laughed at how gullible people were. What suckers. The bigger the fish, the easier it proved for working his plan. The sheriff and a thousand other yahoos with guns scoured the roads and highways, while countless Southern fathers with shotguns combed the countryside looking for a dangerous kidnapper. If Jenkins' ability to evade the enemy and fight when cornered proved correct, the chase and capture should take a good deal of time and divert attention away from his trucks.

"Excuse me, your attendance please?" the attorney repeated.

Wiggins faced the annoying whelp. "Tell Pao, it'll have to wait."

"That's not acceptable. Master Pao wishes your explanation regarding the recent kidnappings."

Wiggins felt his brain about to explode. He wanted to slap the young man, but reminded himself to keep calm. In thirty-six hours his plan would be complete, then he could slap away. For now, it would be appeasement. "What's done is done," Wiggins answered. "I'll explain my actions tomorrow. Right now I'm busy with security concerns. So unless Pao wishes the ruin of Operation Blood Star, I suggest leaving me to my work."

The interpreter nodded curtly and walked off.

Wiggins turned back to Lee. "Where were we, mate?"

* * *

Sheriff Roy Payne paced back and forth at the front of the briefing room, chastising his deputies. "Nothing? Nothing at all...?"

Bell stood among them. He'd rushed to the office the moment he heard the news and volunteered for the hunt. Payne had waived his punishment, but with the notation to remain in his service record. He could care less. Rebecca was one of his dearest friends. The thought of her being harmed made his blood freeze.

He felt confused, too. Kidnapping? He couldn't picture Jenkins doing such a thing. Could Jenkins actually do harm to Rebecca, even kidnap her? And what would make him do such a thing?

There could be several possibilities. First was Jenkins' role in the death of Brenda Lee Payne and his being sent to prison. Or it could be Jenkins resenting the sheriff for botching the investigation into his brother's death. It could also just be the many years of bad blood between Jenkins and Sheriff Payne finally coming to a head. Lastly, there was the fact of Jenkins' spooky past.

All possibilities, but nothing concrete. He didn't know what to believe. He'd just have to rely on his training and see where the case led. He hoped it didn't involve using deadly force. Pulling the trigger on Jenkins would be difficult.

"....Come on, deputies, that Jenkins scum can't just disappear with my daughter!"

Nobody made a sound, not even Dixon.

Payne didn't seem to be getting through. "If you all value your jobs, I suggest getting your asses busy finding my daughter. Shoot to kill if you have to, just get her back. Now get out of here!"

61

After settling the matter of Billy Ray's innocence, Egolf secured his pistol and left. Focus switched to solving the mystery of Rebecca's cries on the radio. The public announcement was being repeated every five minutes. Dodd recorded the message on his computer and went to work.

"That was easy. Your girlfriend was duped. Her captors recorded her actual voice, complete with emotion. The bastards then edited the message, dialed the emergency operator using her own cell phone, and hit the play button."

"That simple?"

"Yes. What's more, this Wiggins already knew the reaction he'd get. With what you've told me, I'd say he's a trained operative—CIA, Israeli intelligence, ex-KGB…who knows. The fact he's using Korean personnel suggests the latter, assuming you're correct about the ethnicity."

"I'm correct about them being Korean."

"He's probably ex-KGB and now works for Yuri Irsenovich Kim, better known as Kim Jong-il, the Dear Leader of the Democratic People's Republic of Korea."

"Incredible. How the hell did soldiers of the DPRK get here?"

"Is that a rhetorical question? They entered the country the same way you and I got into Bosnia, they walked."

"But we had disguises and good papers."

"Hardly needed here. Aside from our nation's borders being so porous, America has a suicidal fixation against profiling. You can get into America wearing a Black Panther tee shirt, pink tutu, and Groucho Marx glasses. The bad guys have turned our own morals against us."

"It can't be that easy."

"Oh yeah? In addition to several unmanned border crossings with Canada, there's four thousand miles of mostly unguarded wilderness, mountains, and water between our two countries...to say nothing of our southern border with Mexico and two lengthy coasts on the Atlantic and Pacific Oceans. If somebody wants into America, and possesses even a modicum of smarts, there's very little to prevent them from doing so. Once in, an enemy can exploit our freedoms and lackadaisical attitudes about national security."

"Good point," Billy Ray said.

"What's more, citizens don't want a police state. To a degree, our nation's Department of Homeland Security offers the masses false hope. We've been more lucky than good foiling terror plots since 9/11. Terrorists only have to be successful once. It's only a matter of time."

"My gut's telling me time's up. Remember Edward Jones' story about an alliance between Wiggins, the DPRK, and a Mexican drug cartel."

"I doubt an elderly man possesses the ability to gather such intelligence," Dodd said. "Although anything's possible, I guess. You could do it, if you ever reach old age. And you did say the old man was a Naval Academy grad. That counts for something. Anyway, we'll know soon what's true or not."

"How so?"

"We're packing up and moving to scenic Big Sandy. It's time for some special reconnaissance."

"You sure about this, Dolittle?"

"I owe you, Wolverine. You said you needed help. So unless you have other ideas, I say we take this show on the road."

* * *

The police bulletin shocked Gus. It'd taken more than an hour for him to finally rise up from the couch where he'd collapsed. He got himself dressed and fixed a little breakfast.

He concentrated on what to do next. How could he help Billy Ray, and how was Lela going to take the situation?

The phone rang.

Gus nearly spilled his coffee in the effort to answer. "Hello?"

"Gus Heavenor...of Heavenor's Hardware and Sports?"

"Speaking."

"I'd like to place a sizeable order with your store."

"You've called the wrong phone number, this is my home."

"I'm aware of that."

Gus looked at the grandfather clock in the corner. "It's five o'clock in the morning. Could you please call the store number instead? We open at seven on weekdays."

Gus heard the sound of the phone handed to another caller.

* * *

Dodd held an unusual-looking phone to his ear while simultaneously adjusting dials on one of the electronic consoles along the wall. A bar graph indicator fluctuated, slowed, and finally settled on a reading that satisfied him. Then he handed the fancy gadget to Billy Ray.

"Gus, don't say my name. We don't have time, so just listen."

"But the police—"

"It's a setup, orchestrated by a certain curator you met at a Chamber breakfast—"

Gus cut in. "Then where's Reb—the girl?"

"I don't know, but I aim to find out. And when I do...." Billy Ray let the sentence hang. "I need your help. Can you keep the store closed today? Claim it's due to Independence Day."

"Wouldn't make much sense, but I suppose it could be done. What do you have in mind?"

"I'll tell you when I get there. But first, I have a list of supplies I need you to get for me."

"Okay, shoot."

Billy Ray read the list, items for the coming hours to improve the odds against Wiggins, if such was even possible. He ended the call and handed the gadget to Dodd. "Quite a phone. I thought we were in the no-man's land of cell signals."

"It's not a cell phone, and you never saw that thing. Got it?"

No doubts. Dodd was running an operation.

And it had the smell of connections in very high places.

62

Rebecca brought her mind to bear on her troubling circumstances, viewing matters scientifically and not emotionally—mind over matter. She achieved steady, shallow breaths. Calm replaced panic.

Her concentration was broken by a metal door opening and then footsteps. Whoever it was stopped shy of her crumpled form. She felt eyes staring and heard heavy breathing. She assumed a man, but avoided imagining his thoughts.

"Promise not to resist and I'll loosen the ropes."

An Australian accent! She had to know more about her surroundings, about her captors. Information meant survival.

Resist? That was a no-brainer.

The hood was ripped off. Her eyes squinted at the light. When her vision normalized, a powerfully built man stood before her in Danner boots and khaki outfit. He had blond hair and cold gray eyes.

Wiggins held a large knife, the edge glistened. "Know who I am?"

She shook her head.

"I think you do." He twisted the blade.

Rebecca kept still, if only to sow doubt in Wiggins' mind.

Wiggins moved with the speed of a viper. Before she could react at the sudden horror of a plunging knife, the rope connecting her wrists and ankles gave way. Like memory metal, she sprang back to a straitened position. Nothing ever felt so comforting as the new position. Again, she struggled to tame her emotions. She reminded herself pain and discomfort were good—it meant she was alive, that she had a chance at freedom.

"There now...that feels better, I'm sure," Wiggins said with an odd mixture of empathy and cruelty. "I'll remove the gag. You be a good little *sheila.* If you play the bitch again with fang and claw, I'll shove that filthy rag down your throat. I don't wish to hurt you. Do I make myself clear?"

Rebecca acted terrified, an easy task. Wiggins grabbed the duct tape covering her mouth, gave a mighty yank. The tape made a ripping sound. The rag was removed. She sucked in a lungful of air. Her face felt on fire.

"Let's have a chat. Where's your boyfriend, Billy Ray Jenkins?"

"I have no idea. Besides, he's not my boyfriend."

Wiggins slapped Rebecca across the face. "I don't like liars!"

Pain shot through her violated skin. It took every fiber in her body to keep from crying out. "I'm not lying. I don't know where he is!"

"I thought that love tap might help. So he is your mate."

Rebecca fought back the tears. "How would you know?"

"Eyes and ears, *sheila.* Besides, you're a luscious *bluey.* I'm sure that red hair gets Jenkins a bit randy. No way he'd let you wander off." Wiggins stared at her, then said, "Yes, I think you'll make a fine little honey pot, should the bee get past my trap. "

She was tempted to spit in Wiggins' face. She didn't know what a *bluey* was, but assumed it referred to her hair. The man was Australian from his speech. What's more, he was a sociopath or psychopath, or both. One driven by desire, genius turned on its head. The other hardwired, cruel by design...like her father. Both were two sides of the devil's coin.

"I'll ask you once more. Where's your mate?"

"Where is he?"

"I don't stutter."

"I know where he isn't. He's not here or you'd be dead."

She was rewarded with another slap. She ignored the pain by embracing anger. The weak point for men like Wiggins was their egos, and she'd just gotten him to react on her terms. A first step to freedom, or her grave.

"Where is he, you *bluey* bitch!" Wiggins reared back his hand.

"I only know where he's going to be. He's coming for me. And he'll kill you for what you've done!"

The hand struck. The room went black.

* * *

They pulled away from the fake farmhouse. Billy Ray was forced to leave his mother's car in a barn on Dodd's property. He was tucked inside a panel van with colorful logos advertising a pet grooming service. Dodd's van was designed to allow paraplegics and amputees to drive using a special steering wheel for hands-only operation. Viewed through the front window, a passerby would see cupboards with tools and supplies for pet grooming, a hoist apparatus, and just enough space to maneuver a wheelchair. However, the shelving concealed a secret command and control center. Every inch housed high-tech gadgets—monitors, computers, and other electronic equipment. One panel slid up to reveal a cache of lethal weapons, some of which Billy Ray had never seen before. Lastly, two additional passengers had taken up residence on Billy Ray's lap. They were two adorable Jack Russell terriers named Pedro and Lola. He no longer suspected his friend of working for NASA.

He now thought Dodd was an alien from outer space!

63

After passing the Louisiana boarder into Texas, Dodd pulled into a public rest area and remained forward.

Egolf announced it was time to "prep the scouts." He summoned Pedro and Lola and placed tiny earbuds inside each dog. Next, he attached leather dog collars decorated with hardened plastic jewels of varying sizes and colors.

Billy Ray was left wondering what was happening. Egolf explained the dog collars were imbedded with two-way transmitters. Each colorful jewel was a miniature sensor. The collars relayed audio, video, voice, and a host of other data to the onboard computer. Then Egolf put the white and tan-spotted dogs out for a potty break, reclaimed his seat, donned a headset, and powered up the computer and monitors. Live video streamed across two of the screens.

Egolf turned to Billy Ray and said, "Watch this."

After the dogs finished toileting, Egolf issued each a command. Billy Ray was amazed by what came next. Every vocal instruction spoken into the headset mic resulted in perfectly executed reactions by the dogs. The monitor in front of Egolf showed a split screen with blue indicator light for Pedro and pink light for Lola. Each dog's movement tracked on their respective screens. Additionally, the dog collar cameras produced real-time video filtered through a processor to smooth the normally herky-jerky movements of the energetic canines. Camera angles were selected by commanding the dogs to sit, turn, stand, roll, and pirouette.

A doggy ballet.

To prove a point, Egolf directed the dogs to face the spots where they'd just defecated. He switched the monitor to infrared and the heat signatures of two steaming piles suddenly appeared on the screen. Egolf also pointed out additional functions for detecting a smorgasbord of explosives. Billy Ray was relieved when Egolf chose not to demonstrate those, too, and the dogs were called back.

The drive from Arkansas had gone without incident. However, the closer they got to Big Sandy the greater the police presence became. A commercial vehicle with a pet grooming logo offered legitimacy. The downside was the distinctiveness, making it unforgettable. As time passed and desperation mounted in the search for Rebecca, the vehicle would become suspect. Their window of opportunity to recon the Texas Waterland Family Park was closing fast.

Dodd pulled up to the Ambassador Ranch road. He waited a minute to ensure they hadn't been followed. Satisfied, he announced, "Show time, folks. Let the dogs out."

* * *

The first forty-eight hours after a kidnapping are the most critical. Agent Johnny Lam's wristwatch chimed.

The nationwide AMBER Alert had failed to produce any tangible clues. There'd been calls to local police stations from as far away as Oregon, none of which bore fruit. One lady near the nation's capitol called the hotline to report seeing two young girls pounding against the windows of a white limousine as it drove past. When asked to identify herself, the woman hung up. The call was disregarded because Washington, DC, was three hundred miles from the scene of the crime and didn't fit the M.O.

Lam was beside himself. His nerves were frazzled. He'd only managed a catnap in the cold leather chair in Captain Ulrich's office. His clothes were crumpled, he needed a bath, and his stomach felt full of battery acid. And now it was time to go see Katie's mother.

It was also time to pray.

64

After providing Pedro and Lola with a final drink from the water bowl and some loving affection, Egolf moved aside the false cupboard and opened the back door. Pedro and Lola jumped to the ground. They bounced around, sniffed at the ground, and urinated to mark their territory. Billy Ray was amused.

Such was the way with dogs and men!

Egolf closed the door and returned to the computer monitor. He pulled on the wireless headset mic and hit the record button. Then he gave the dogs a command and off they ran, across the cattle guard, down the dirt road, past the white bull, and toward the forest and the Loma Reservoir beyond.

"Get us out of here," Egolf said aloud for Dodd.

Billy Ray felt the big vehicle power up and turn back onto US Route 80. "We're leaving them behind?" He wondered aloud.

Dodd spoke over the noise of the engine. "They have a ten mile range and the batteries last three hours on the collar. So we can drive around or go park. You'll be surprised by how much ground Jack Russells can cover, especially guided by voice command."

"So Pedro and Lola are land versions of Flipper and Skipper."

"Yes, but dogs do have a few more advantages."

Billy Ray heard Egolf's voice in the background giving instructions. "And you guys literally talk to the animals."

"We both do. The dogs can have more than one handler."

"Just dogs?"

Dodd hesitated before saying, "Raccoons and monkeys, too. And Jenkins, if you breathe one word of any of this we're both dead men. *Comprende amigo?*"

"Loud and clear, Dolittle. What could be more dangerous than a monkey with a gun?"

"Humans."

Touche!

Dodd told his story. "After my accident, I couldn't chase bad guys anymore, literally. While recovering at the hospital a nurse brought her pet to work, thinking it might cheer me up. It did far more than that, it inspired me—put me back in the game. That dog was a Jack Russell terrier, one of the smartest creatures I've ever worked with, the same breed as Pedro and Lola. My concept is to replace some duties performed by humans on the field of battle with remote-guided dogs. Drones rule the air, but you still need boots on the ground in battle. So why not make that paws?

"Depending on the breed, dogs can provide a number of extremely valuable assets. You already know about sniffing for bombs, drugs, humans, cadavers, and use for personal protection. I've taken canine utilization to a whole new level, into special reconnaissance. Furthermore, it currently takes only a year and nine weeks to create a dog-soldier, and the restrictions against females in combat don't apply."

"Somehow I think a few animal organizations may take exception to your way of thinking," Billy Ray said.

"Don't misunderstand, Wolverine. I love my pets like my own children. Mothers love their sons, too, and some of them get killed in battle. My opinion is that when it comes to winning wars, it's all hands and paws on deck. I'm sure if our nation ever faced the possibility of defeat, tree huggers and animal rights activists would change their tune. Those kooks seem to forget dogs are a delicacy on menus in many cultures."

Billy Ray ignored the last point. "Dogs are already used in battle."

"Not like my pets. I wasn't the first to strap a camera to the head of a dog and send it into an urban nightmare like Iraq or Afghanistan. But I'm the first to pioneer a complete vocal language and training regimen, along with highly-specialized equipment not yet available even to Special Forces."

"What do you mean by pioneer? Aren't you done yet?"

"My project reached completion just before you called. I couldn't help suspecting you were out to steal my work."

"Do you still think that?"

"No. You live in a whole other world."

Billy Ray was relieved to hear that, sort of. "So when's graduation for Pedro and Lola?"

"Today. They've never been fully tested, until now."

"How do we know your pooches won't go off chasing rabbits or get eaten by bears?"

"Because I trained them and because Egolf monitors their every move. He can steer them away from trouble. Plus their speed and ability to tunnel are helpful genetic traits to aide in their defense. They truly are marvelous creatures, better in some ways than humans."

"No argument there. I know a few knuckleheads I'd gladly move to the backyard to make room for Pedro and Lola."

"Admiral, we have contact," Egolf announced.

"Admiral...?" Billy Ray questioned.

Dodd nodded.

"You were an O-3 the last I saw you. How did you go from lieutenant to flag in ten years?"

"Another story for later. Let's just say it has to do with a little advanced research agency I direct." Dodd ended their conversation. He called out to Egolf, "Report."

Egolf consulted his monitors. "Motorcycle, Zero DS, electric, military rigging, one rider. Hold—" He issued a command to Pedro to adjust the camera angle. "This guy has good taste...H&K PDW, scope and suppressor." Egolf turned to Billy Ray and said, "Ammo's a bit lightweight for my tastes, but it spits lots of lead. This guy's serious."

"Actually," Billy Ray replied, "Evel Knievel is just a lackey. His boss does all the thinking."

Egolf turned back to the monitor. The picture under the blue indicator light held steady, meaning Pedro hadn't moved a muscle without being ordered to do so.

Billy Ray was impressed. Monitors beeped and tweeted as the dogs sped past listening devices, video cameras, and other remote sensing equipment. The location of each was logged by GPS coordinates. Another monitor recorded topographical information. A comprehensive map began taking shape. The Jack Russells worked fast and extremely efficient under Egolf's remote guidance. He was witnessing forward reconnaissance and intelligence-gathering by humans rendered obsolete. The days of men crawling on their bellies at a snail's pace through mud and vermin were greatly outmatched by the likes of Pedro and Lola.

"Hit," said Egolf.

This time the monitor with the pink light showed a picture that could only be coming from Lola pointing skyward. Amazingly, the picture held steady for one coming from a fifteen-inch tall dog standing upright on its hind legs.

"Sniper." Egolf announced. "Good girl, Lola. Forward."

"Wolverine, you were the best special recon man I ever commanded. You were relentless. So what do you think of my little scouts?"

"I think I'm out of a job!"

Both men laughed. Dodd was proud of his "children." And so it went for another forty-five minutes. Pedro and Lola mapped the route along the two-track to the Loma Reservoir as fast as their sensor-laden bodies could travel. According to Egolf, they weren't missing anything. After ninety minutes, they'd discovered two armed motorcyclists, six foot patrols, and one very well-camouflaged sniper. Additionally, two dozen remote cameras, motion detectors, and listening devices were now accounted for.

"What next, Wolverine?" Dodd asked.

"There must be more snipers besides the one Lola identified and the one I spotted the other day. I'd say that gunman was treed right about here." Billy Ray tapped the computer screen displaying a satellite image of the area. "If I was commanding placement of bees in the trees, I'd station at least two more, about here and here." He poked at the monitor.

"We got the backyard pretty well mapped," Egolf said.

"I agree." Billy Ray swiveled to face Dodd. "Is there enough time on the batteries to drop our friends off at the front gate?"

Dodd had parked them on a side road several miles from the Ambassador Ranch access road. Accounting for the time it'd take to retrieve Pedro and Lola from the reservoir, and the return trip, about forty minutes would remain of the batteries.

"If you have something specific in mind, then yes," Dodd responded. "Even then we'd be cutting it close."

"That'll have to do," said Billy Ray. "Bring them back. We'll send them through the front door."

* * *

The sound of a drumbeat played over and over in her head. Then light returned...a single fluorescent bulb from overhead.

It was no drum. Rebecca's skull throbbed. With every beat of her heart came bolts of pain. She struggled to right herself. Her memories came flooding back—the questions, the answers, the beating.

Wiggins was gone.

"Billy Ray…" she whispered through bleeding lips. "Hurry!"

65

The transfer needed to be quick. It was assumed electronic eyes monitored movement along the front of the property. And there was the concern for Pedro and Lola getting run over crossing US Route 80. Dodd timed it perfectly, adjusting speed against the distance of on-coming vehicles and letting the traffic pass. Billy Ray manned the door while Egolf gently tossed the dogs onto the pavement. The entire movement lasted only five seconds. Egolf hurried back to the monitor and began guiding Pedro and Lola to their target.

Billy Ray watched Egolf guide the dogs through the massive gates. They dashed past the Surferdude guard, who waved his arms and whistled for them to heel, then scampered away in the direction of the Black Anaconda, past the security building and Wiggins' domain, and to the rear of the property before doubling back. If not for the deadly nature of the mission, it would've been amusing seeing park staff and black-uniformed soldiers chasing the tiny trespassers.

"Hit," Egolf announced.

Whether from sight, sound, scent, or something subliminal, Lola's ability to sense the presence of well-hidden humans was uncanny. It was the sniper Billy Ray had discovered before. Then Pedro stopped, lifted a front leg and pointed a stubbed tail. Three vehicles appeared. Two quad ATV's, the riders outfitted with more of the H&K MP7s, and the prowler vehicle he and Lam had confronted. Only this time the prowler's mounting lugs held an M-249 machine gun.

"Three soldiers, Admiral…all Korean. That makes eleven by my count, and they're loaded for bear."

"Better than dog," Dodd joked.

"Uh oh, spoken too soon," Egolf said and launched a series of commands to maneuver Pedro away from his current position.

Billy Ray watched over Egolf's shoulder, observing him shift Lola's camera to pick up the action. Voices came through Pedro's collar indicating a capture in progress. Lola's camera confirmed it. A park employee crept up behind Pedro while the soldiers in front provided a distraction. The ploy worked.

A net came down over Pedro. Before Egolf could issue commands to Lola, she reacted out of instinct for her mate and attacked the man with the net, grabbing a mouthful of ankle with her teeth. The man cried out.

Two soldiers came into focus and rushed in and grabbed the dogs. One soldier received a bite for his trouble.

"Shut 'em down, before they upset the soldiers." Dodd said.

Both dogs became docile. The looks on the soldiers' faces turned from anger to something more friendly. What happened next suggested there may actually be a guiding hand of Providence.

The park employee was dismissed, taking away his net. With the dogs now calm in the arms of the two soldiers the cameras and listening devices recorded their journey to the security building. Joseph Wiggins stood tall at the door, a look of annoyance on his face. At the very same moment the soldiers approached their commander a white limousine pulled up, cutting off their approach. The view from the dog collars couldn't have been clearer. Two well-dressed Latinos raced to open the door of the limo and stand guard as a short elderly man stepped from the vehicle. He had white hair, a bulbous nose, and was impeccably dressed in a white tailored suit. The man leaned inside the limousine and grabbed something not at first visible, though the sound through the dog collars was unmistakable—a young girl's scream. The old man pulled the girl from the vehicle. She had dark hair, chocolate brown eyes, and wore a pink Rainbow Brite shirt.

"Lam's daughter!"

"Oh shit!" Dodd cursed. "You know who the old rich guy is?"

Billy Ray turned. "Who?"

"Angel Gallina, head of the Gallina drug cartel in Mexico."

"Formerly of Mexico," Egolf added. "He quit the business three days ago...according to his resignation letter, anyway."

Billy Ray's jaw felt unhinged.

Dodd spoke, "Egolf, can we get the dogs back?"

"We'll have to wait now. The group just went indoors."

Immediately, several displays on the control console came to life. Egolf minded the dog's sensors. "Admiral...Semtex. The needle just pegged. Somebody means business. Three pounds of the stuff can raze a two-story building. There must be a thousand pounds down there...M-112 demolition charges, too. Wow, here's an odd reading. It's coming from the men carrying the dogs."

"Grenades?"

"Not unless they're chewing on them. They have plastic explosives in their teeth. Either those Koreans have terrible dental insurance or somebody plans to blow their heads off."

"You recording the locations of the Semtex?" Billy Ray asked.

"Instruments say it's everywhere, the place is rigged to blow."

"And the conversations...you getting those?"

"Those, too. But I don't speak Korean," Egolf said.

"I do. Well enough to take a first pass, anyway."

"Egolf, how much time left on the batteries?" Dodd asked.

"Just went under the ten minute mark, Admiral."

"Can you get them out?"

Egolf watched the monitor. The pink indicator light went out. "Lola just went off-line. The soldier must've switched off her collar by accident."

Pedro's video was spotty, but showed Lam's daughter and friend, Gallina, the soldier, and Lola waiting at one end of a hall as Wiggins walked a zig-zag pattern to a set of elevator doors.

"The floor's rigged," declared Egolf.

"Yet another thing you don't see at Disneyland," Dodd said.

Wiggins stopped in front of the elevator and performed the required security measures, including a palm print reader and retinal scan. The doors opened. He beckoned the group forward. When the elevator reached its destination, the view wasn't what Billy Ray expected to see at a waterslide park. Wiggins' underground lair was a giant laboratory—white paint, bright lights, stainless steel, and men in lab coats. But a laboratory producing what? He gave himself one guess—drugs!

In stark contrast to lab coats, the group passed Asian soldiers in black uniforms carrying machine guns. They halted in front of a room having scores of monitors manned by white-jacketed technicians and a table overlaid with maps and satellite photos. Wiggins blocked the doorway, but Billy Ray saw enough to confirm Texas Waterland hid a terrible secret. It was a combat information center—a war room!

"We've lost the dogs," Egolf reported. "The white guy ordered them put in the cells with the others, whatever that means."

Billy Ray learned the meaning a moment later. He also learned there were no "maybes" about the hand of Providence. Pedro's captor opened a metal door and tossed him into a bare concrete room lit by a single overhead bulb. The last thing he saw before the door closed and Pedro's camera dying was a female form slumped forward, arms pulled behind her back, auburn hair a wild mess.

Rebecca!

66

Wiggins dismissed his men. Gallina did the same. The war room door closed. One Korean and one Mexican posted outside, Lee and Gallina's personal bodyguard. They stood opposite each other at the map table. Wiggins requested the private meeting for a simple reason. He wanted to rip the old man's head off and piss down his neck! Only madness would cause the most wanted man on the planet to come driving onto Texas Waterland property unannounced, in a vehicle visible from outer space, and with two kidnapped girls, one of which being the daughter of an FBI agent!

"Are you insane, Gallina?"

"Pardon?"

"With due respect, your presence jeopardizes our operation."

"Due respect? My money buys me respect and keeps me safe. I hide in plain sight, surrounded by my army. Perhaps you failed to note the two spotter planes shadowing my entourage. We even carry our own fuel and food. And you think me the fool, comrade Wiggins? Yes, I said *comrade*. I know who you really are. My money also affords me privileges in other countries as well, places like Russia."

Wiggins considered snapping the old man's neck. He'd been careful not to allow anybody to learn his true identity. Gallina could only know of his KGB history. His family was all deceased. No written files existed to attest to his true origins.

"Need I remind you about getting paid your money up front?"

"My honor makes me rich. Money serves only as a signature of good faith, not an enticement. What does a billionaire need with more money?"

"Then what does appeal to you? Why take such a foolish chance coming here unannounced?"

Gallina had never been spoken to in such a manner. *Insane...? Foolish chances...?* His reddening face proved the point. However, a man like him—a Gallina—hadn't ascended his throne by acting out of emotion. So like any successful thief, first get the loot. He'd get what he came for, the reason he agreed to the scheme in the first place. "I'm here because I don't trust you or anyone else. This operation will give me sole power in America. And from here, I'll squash all other cartels. I'm taking direct control of the cities and you're going to help. I will own America!"

Wiggins almost laughed in the old man's face. The king had no clothes. America's doom would begin on the morrow with the departure of thousands of gallons of Rapture, aided by the very man who would be king. In only days, millions of doses of the most debilitating drug the world had ever known would be gobbled like candy by lusting Americans. Gallina would rule over an insane asylum of ten million zombies!

"Please accept my apology, Señor. I showed disrespect."

"Apology accepted." Gallina pointed a wrinkled brown finger. "Don't ever speak to me with such words again."

Wiggins took the hit. He was too close to let anything stop him now. The time for putting a bullet in Gallina's head could wait. He nodded at the old man's warning and played the good host instead.

"Please instruct your troops that the park is theirs to enjoy tonight. I've arranged for female companions to provide the appearance of legitimacy. A bus full of pretty maidens will arrive soon. There's plenty of food and alcohol to be had in the park. Later on, we'll all be treated to a world-class fireworks display. Everyone has earned a few hours of fun, so enjoy."

"My men will be pleased," Gallina said.

Wiggins and Gallina summoned their lieutenants.

* * *

The intel gathered by the dogs was astounding. Aided by Egolf, more had been learned in two hours than would take a Spec Ops team a week to acquire. Billy Ray wouldn't have believed it had he not seen it. Now came collating the data into a coherent picture. Even so, three facts were already evident—they were outmanned, outgunned, and out of time.

Problems mounted as Egolf announced each detail from the recon data. Foremost being that any involvement by police would only end in disaster. The park was so thoroughly hardened that SWAT and FBI hostage rescue teams could not survive an assault without getting cut to pieces. The worst was that the entire facility was wired to blow. Even if Wiggins' defenses could be breached, hostages and rescuers alike would get blown to bits.

Billy Ray knew the mindset of the local cops, especially Payne. They'd all get boners and scramble to be on top. Fewer people were needed, not more. Only one man had the right to fight on—Johnny Lam. And if Lam couldn't be relied upon, then he'd go it alone.

Alone...?

Billy Ray cursed the thought.

His mother might finally get that knock on the door by a man with a hat in hand.

67

After rounding the block again, Dodd announced the all-clear. Just as he did so, a police siren screamed to life. “Belay my last. Batten the hatches, we're being pulled over.”

Billy Ray rotated the false cupboards. The van reverted to a legitimate-appearing vehicle. Dodd needed a good performance. If the cops searched inside the van, game over.

“Hello, officer,” Billy Ray heard Dodd say. “What seems to be the problem? I'm positive I was going the correct speed.”

“No problem with your speed,” said the officer.

Billy Ray recognized the voice. It was Bell. He hadn’t been wrong, Bell was showing good instincts. They’d passed by several police vehicles, none paying them any attention until now.

“You’re circling town. I've seen you twice now.” Bell pressed.

“Is there a crime in that?”

“No crime, but I don't recall your company advertised around here. Are you lost or something?”

“Ahhh,” Dodd made it sound like he guessed the music was Bach. “As you can tell from my plates, I'm down here from Arkansas. I am a bit lost. Would you mind directing me to the Heavenor Hardware and Sports store?”

Bell persisted. “What would Gus Heavenor need with a dog grooming service, especially one from Arkansas?”

Billy Ray's respect for the young deputy grew by the minute. The guy was a darn good cop. Nevertheless, he hoped it wouldn't be necessary to clobber his new friend over the head.

“Hunting dogs,” Dodd replied. “Mr. Heavenor has suggested we go into business breeding and selling hunting dogs.” Dodd changed the subject. “I've never been stopped to be asked about my business. I noticed a sizable police presence in the area. Is there something I should be aware of? Is my safety in question?”

“There's been a kidnapping. It's on the radio. I'm surprised you haven't heard.”

“I listen to self-help recordings, not the radio.”

“Self-help?”

Dodd sounded worried. “I'm dealing with the loss of my legs.”

Billy Ray imagined the silence following Dodd’s admission meant Bell was on tiptoes, looking through Dodd's window.

"My apologies." Bell sounded embarrassed. "I'll still need to see your license and registration. It'll just take a minute."

Billy Ray and Egolf used hand signals, Billy Ray indicating he'd handle the officer if need be.

After a few minutes, Bell was back. "Again, my apologies, Mr. Dodd. Also, please let me compliment you on your courage."

"Thank you, officer."

"If you see any suspicious vehicles, or have any information to help us catch the kidnapper and recover the victim, please call 9-1-1, immediately." Bell gave the names and descriptions of the perpetrator and the victim, and then offered directions to Gus' store before bidding Dodd farewell.

"That was close," Dodd said once they were on their way.

They drove straight to Gus' store. When they came to a stop, Dodd let the motor run for several minutes—waiting, watching.

Billy Ray phoned the store. Mildred put him on hold.

The phone picked up. "Gus Heavenor."

"It's me. I'm at the loading dock."

"The van with a dog grooming logo?"

"Yes. Why's Mildred there?"

"She's just collecting our receipts for deposit."

"Okay. Come to the loading dock when the coast is clear."

Ten minutes later, they all gathered in the back of the store, now locked and displaying a "Closed for the Holidays" sign. Billy Ray announced there'd be no introductions and then provided Gus a quick version of the situation.

"What can I do to help?" Gus asked.

Dodd said, "If you don't mind, Jenkins needs to put his special skills to work. Did you acquire the items we requested?"

"It's all here." Gus turned to Billy Ray. "Special skills?"

"I need to weaponize a few ingredients to use against Wiggins. We've no time to gather military equipment."

"But I only sell shotguns and archery equipment. Surely those aren't enough to fight a whole army."

"No, but they'll help," Billy Ray pointed at the hardware section of the store, "along with a few items from your shelves?"

"Sure. What can you do with any of that stuff?" Gus asked.

"You'd be surprised. Ever hear of Mother of Satan?"

"Isn't that what terrorists use against our boys overseas?"

"Yes. It's made using common ingredients, like acetone peroxide," Billy Ray explained.

"I read that it's tricky stuff, the reason those murdering nuts named it the way they did."

"You're correct, Gus. Mixed improperly or under wrong temperatures and humidity, the cook could become part of the soup. But I don't have a choice, unless you sell TNT."

"I don't sell explosives. I don't think blasting tree stumps is legal anymore." Gus nodded toward the sporting goods. "There's only shotgun shells and small caliber ammunition for killing varmints."

"Those help as primers. If you'll allow me to do compounding in the walk-in cooler, I'm sure I can produce what I need safely. The dry ice you brought will stabilize my package."

Gus waved. "Anything you need, just stop that madman and save Rebecca and the kids."

Dodd chimed in. "I can assure you, sir, Wolverine knows his business. He's a real Angus MacGyver."

"Who?"

"Never mind, Gus. Let's get to work."

He had a lot to do.

68

Egolf left to retrieve equipment he'd need for setting up a temporary command post in the store. The plan was to link with the van plus other sources, which he purposely failed to identify.

Dodd turned to Billy Ray. "Wolverine, we have a good deal of planning to do and very little time. Nightfall is in eight hours. You mentioned a plan for infiltrating Wiggins' operation. I hope you're right, because that's one hardened facility."

Billy Ray looked down at the ground. "I hope I'm right, too."

Dodd pressed his case. "This Wiggins is a pro. Egolf just received a report from Langley. We guessed it, Wiggins is former KGB. There's no record of what he is now, but it can't be good. He has an entire company of trained soldiers backing him and one hell of a head start. And that amusement park is more than a playground, it's a killing field with snipers, explosives, dozens of sensors, and who knows what kinds of booby traps. It's his turf and he's ready for the enemy. I'm afraid an entire Spec Ops team would get picked apart before making it to the hostages.

"So I sure as hell can't imagine how one man with a couple of guns and some homemade bombs can overcome such odds. Irregular wouldn't begin to describe you."

Doubt wanted in, Billy Ray barred the door. It was time for war, no matter the methods. "I have to try...and Lam will want to help."

"You don't know that for sure," Dodd countered. "Even so, I don't want him calling in the feds any more than you do." Dodd adjusted his weight in the chair and rolled closer. "Listen, my friend, I'll never question your skills or the fire in your belly. You're one of the best warfighters I've ever known. Nobody's more resourceful than you on the battlefield. But my involvement here changed the minute you translated those audio signals from Korean into English.

"Added to the video data from my dogs, I'm convinced what's going on at that waterslide park is a matter of national security. Wiggins looks to have the backing of one of America's worst enemies, North Korea. Not to mention an alliance with a ruthless drug cartel." Dodd lowered the boom. "The nation must be defended."

Billy Ray stared at Dodd. "I don't even know who you work for."

Dodd's silence indicated an internal debate—duty versus friendship. At last he said, "POTUS. I work for the President of the United States. That's all I can say. I've shared too much already."

Billy Ray felt incensed. "Then you must already consider me dead. Nobody sworn to your level of secrecy gives away so much unless you think I've already failed. What's your choice, kill me now? Or am I the bait, just a pawn in all this?"

"We're all pawns on the side of justice." Dodd stared back.

He gave that deep thought. John P. Dodd, his friend, his brother-in-arms, and old drinking buddy, had been honest. Honesty was a rare coin, best valued on the high side. "Listen here, Dodd. Rebecca and the two hostages must be saved, your dogs too!"

After a moment Dodd looked down. "I know."

Billy Ray stepped in close and lowered his voice. "You have an elimination team on the way, don't you?"

"Yes," Dodd admitted.

"And I'm merely the backdoor distraction to aid your men."

Dodd looked up, this time without the warm glow of friendship. "They'll destroy everyone inside the kill zone.""

"Dammit, Dolittle!"

"Listen, Wolverine, I'm not even supposed to be here. I agreed to help you because I owe you. And with what's going on at that park, I'm more indebted to you than ever, the whole country is. It's just that I have..." Dodd searched for words, "other priorities that supersede the lives of a few people, including ours. The nation comes first. We're collateral damage."

Billy Ray looked hard at Dodd. He felt socked in the gut. He couldn't believe Dodd would just let the girls die. That wasn't like his friend. Facts could be so cold, so biting. He had to reach Rebecca and the kids. He had to save them. He was their only hope. And now Dodd blocked his way as much as Wiggins. What could he do?

An idea came to mind. "When?"

"When, what?"

"The raid, Dolittle. When?"

"They're on their way now."

"Delay them."

"I can't do that."

"Yes you can, you're the Admiral. Of what, I don't know."

"The enemy must be stopped."

"Stall your men. Give me time to get the hostages out. You said it yourself, that park's a killing field. Let me find a way in. It could even save the lives of your men. You saw how the place is rigged to blow. I'll get in and throw open the gates for your team before Wiggins can push the plunger."

Dodd wore a look of someone knowing things others did not. Finally, he lifted his fancy phone and touched a button. A series of beeps and chirps sounded. A male voice answered. Dodd identified himself with the appropriate code. Then came another voice, one with a forceful tone of command speaking over a strange humming noise. Dodd issued new orders. They were acknowledged without question. "Midnight, Wolverine, If I haven't heard back from you by then, they're coming in, guns blazing."

Billy Ray felt exhilaration, like a death sentence commuted in the final hour and charges dropped. He checked his emotions, death lurked ahead.

But so did hope.

The two men were in close proximity. Gus hadn't caught any of their conversation. Billy Ray reached forth a hand and placed it on Dodd's shoulder. "You'll hear from me…or I'll be dead."

Dodd placed his hand atop Billy Ray's. "Let's hope you can perform miracles, my friend."

"Only God can do that."

"Indeed. But I have some gadgets to make it appear otherwise."

They got down to business. Nothing had changed except the time Dodd's team would storm the park.

"After Egolf gets me set up with the computers, he'll scout an eagle's nest. He has quite a surprise for Wiggins in the way of sniper technology."

"Oh?" Billy Ray was intrigued.

"A long-range laser. The beam can cut through any solid material. Depending on range and pulse duration, the battery is good for a dozen shots from far beyond current sniper range."

Billy Ray was speechless.

"Furthermore," Dodd said, "if I suspect you're a goner before the deadline, I blow the whistle to start the big game. Do I make myself clear?"

Billy Ray came to attention. "Aye aye, Admiral."

Dodd smiled big. "That's the Wolverine I remember. Now, how do you plan to get into that house of horrors?"

"I'll take a page from your book, Dolittle. I'll talk to the animals."

Dodd didn't press. He saluted instead. "Dismissed sailor."

"I'll start by calling a dad who's worried sick over his daughter."

"Use my phone." Dodd handed Billy Ray the device. "It has a few features you don't get with your local service provider. You only have one minute before the call gets intercepted. I suggest you don't let that happen."

69

It had been two days and still no word of Katie. Nothing. Zip. Lam felt exhausted as he left Captain Ulrich's office to make the painful drive to deliver the bad news about Katie.

The case would now shift somewhat in procedure. The fact two girls were missing, and not just one, suggested very bad things—things he fought hard not to think about. Now it was time to face facts. His mission would switch to encouraging everyone to stay strong, hope for the best, and have faith that God could provide miracles. Harder yet would be accomplishing that mission without completely falling to pieces.

He approached Katie's house and pulled in front along the curb. He had no good news for her mother. He needed a few moments undisturbed to come up with words he knew would only sound hollow, explaining why he'd come home empty-handed. The idling engine provided the only sound. He reached to turn off the motor. His phone rang!

The sudden interruption shocked him. He pulled his hand back from the ignition, leaving the car to idle. A ringing cell phone didn't provide the surprise, hoping against hope to receive good news. Rather, it was the fact his Bureau-issued phone was turned off! He'd powered off the moment he arrived, not wanting to be disturbed while sorting his thoughts.

So how could this be?

Lam picked up the phone. It rang and vibrated in his hand. There were no indicator lights, the message window was dark, the power still off. It rang once more. He flipped it open. "Hello?"

"Don't speak, just listen."

He knew the voice. "Jenkins?"

"There's no time for questions. Let me talk. "

Fifty-eight seconds later, Lam stomped on the gas and sped off.

* * *

"Wolverine, we must be off. The sun sets in thirty minutes. Egolf's in position and reports four enemy snipers entered in the ballistics computer. It'll be hell reacquiring them if they move."

"Can I try calling Lam again?"

"Only if you want the cavalry to come flying over the hill."

"I'd sure like to know who you work for."

"No, you wouldn't."

They'd spent all afternoon reviewing the recon data, cataloging and marking scores of hidden sensors and explosive devices and traps, and marking everything on a computer map. They pieced together what they could of the underground facilities.

Several dozen printouts plastered the wall at the back of Gus' store. Colored pins marked the varying instruments of detection and booby traps. Close-up satellite photos provided a bird's-eye view of the area, enough so that Billy Ray was able to memorize the route to the reservoir.

Furthermore, he'd finished creating all the nasty little surprises needed for spoiling the party in the park. A hardware store was a cornucopia of materials that when formulated properly could become a person's worst nightmare—precisely what he had in mind for Wiggins.

All was loaded into the van and Gus had returned from delivering Egolf beyond the borders of the park to a grain silo at the edge of a farmer's property. A perfect perch from which to rid the land of human varmints two miles away.

But where was Lam?

Billy Ray had explained in forceful terms to Lam that unless he wanted to see his daughter blown to bits, do not call in the troops, at least not yet. Get here and get all the facts first. He had no doubt Lam was moving heaven and hell to get to East Texas, but to wait any longer could result in the deaths of three innocent people and Dodd's two dogs.

He slipped Gus a folded note with a single word scribed on the front—*Mother.* Then he instructed Gus what to do if there was no word from him by morning.

Billy Ray turned to his fellow warrior. "Time's up, Mr. Dodd. May God have mercy on our souls."

70

Laughter and music from the Texas Waterland Family Park carried on the moist nighttime air. From farther off in the distance, sounds of thunder rolled across the countryside. The National Weather Service was predicting heavy rain to move through the area. Both men checked their wristwatches. They'd waited twenty additional minutes for Lam's arrival. Egolf reported enemy snipers painted and ready to meet their maker.

Dodd had spelled it out. He and Egolf would vacate the premises at midnight and call in the pros. Billy Ray took that to mean a Delta team or a special activity squad from the CIA, maybe SEAL Team Six. He had no way of knowing and Dodd was tight-lipped on the matter. There'd been rumors of an even more elite squadron than Delta and Team Six, but only rumors. If the weapon Egolf had targeted on Wiggins' snipers was any indication, such rumors were likely true. Dodd claimed to have other priorities. Trapped between the perils of national defense and the world of geo-politics, the lives of three civilians and a couple of Jack Russell terriers didn't amount to much. So truly Dodd was doing him a favor.

Billy Ray turned his focus to a matter puzzling him since the battle at the Frontier Inn. Where were all the Mexican men who'd attacked them? He cycled through the recon video, but came up empty. The recording showed dozens of Koreans within the bowels of the Texas Waterland security building, but no Latinos.

They had to be somewhere. He wanted to account for all the enemy before commencing direct action. And then there it was…the answer. Just prior to the dogs reaching the security building, one of the cameras caught a familiar glimpse. A man stood beside a black door, smoking. He had bandages on his head and a cast on one arm. Stickman.

A black door...?

The Black Anaconda!

Billy Ray thought back to the guard at the gate and Lam's numbskull question to Surferdude, *You can't miss it ... WHY? ... Because it's black!*

He rewound the video and froze the frame. Stickman's face came into perfect focus. The man had nearly scored a direct hit on his head with a pool stick. Behind Stickman, the black door stood open with other heads visible, raven hair and some with mustaches. The reason the Mexican contingent hadn't been seen in town before the incident at the Frontier Inn, nor since, was they were hiding belowground at Texas Waterland.

With the appearance of Angel Gallina, Billy Ray was ready to bet the farm that the Mexicans were cartel members.

A larger mystery remained, however. How did Jonesy know they were there? That mystery might never be solved. The "how" was not recorded in Jonesy's diary, only the "what."

Dodd rolled into the tiny command center. He peered over Billy Ray's shoulder. "What you got, Wolverine?"

"The rest of the bad guys. I found the Mexicans who attacked Rebecca and me."

"So when's showtime?"

"Now. That was the last piece of the puzzle."

"What about your FBI buddy?"

"Can't wait any longer."

Dodd pointed. "Hit the square green button to your left."

Billy Ray did so. A panel slid up, exposing the cache of weapons he'd seen earlier. Two spaces lay empty, the space-age sniper gun and the PDW now in use by Egolf. Remaining were two pistols, both Heckler & Koch Mark 23 .45-caliber Special Operations Command, or SOCOM. Both were tricked out with suppressors and laser aiming modules. Also present was the weird boxy-looking gun he'd spied earlier. It had a snub barrel resembling the tip of an elephant trunk and was much bulkier than the bullpup configuration of the PDW.

"Take a pistol and leave one for me. There's ammo in the drawer below. You'll find Egolf's dive equipment in the aft storage. Take a minute to acquaint yourself with the rebreather and HUD dive mask, they're nothing like what you're used to."

"HUD?"

"Heads Up Display. The dive computer is built into the mask. Data is displayed in front of your eyes for hands-free movement and is interfaced with my computer here."

"Sounds like the SEAL teams have some new equipment."

"They have the masks, but not the rebreathers."

"Am I the guinea pig?"

"No, I was. Trust me, Wolverine, I think you'll approve."

Dodd was more fish than human, or had been. So when a legend like Dolittle claimed an underwater device worked, you banked on it.

Billy Ray retrieved a pistol, hefted it, pulled back the slide, and inspected the chamber. It was clean and well-oiled. A single handgun against a hundred heavily armed men was a joke, but it would help in close quarters. And when suppressed, the MK23 was the quietest gun in the business. Besides, just having one strapped to his leg offered a level of comfort.

Dodd pointed. “See that boxy gun there in the middle?”

“Yeah, what is it?”

“Another Laser. I have a hunch your idea for breaching the enemy's command center by infiltrating the water treatment plant could run aground.”

“How so?”

“If I were Wiggins, I'd pack the area with sensors and booby traps. Then I'd employ metal grating that couldn't be cut using conventional means. The sensors we can foil, if Mother Nature doesn't beat us to it. Using explosives to blow your way past would only announce your presence, plus risk triggering enemy mines. And super-cooling the metal bars to make them brittle only works for MacGyver. You'll get but one chance at breaking through. So save the dry ice for something else.”

Billy Ray removed the weird-looking gun from the padded wall and hefted it. The laser weapon was heavier than expected, but surprisingly well-balanced. “And you think this thing can do something a good cutting torch cannot?”

“I know so. I invented it. It's a high-energy underwater laser. It can cut a donut hole in the bottom of an aircraft carrier.”

“This thing?”

“From a mile away...beyond that and the beam capacity decreases rapidly due to crystalline structures in seawater. A problem I intend to overcome.” Dodd began mumbling something about light speed.

“Lasers can't do that,” Billy Ray said.

“This one can. My team has been working on lasers for years, several showed promising results—solid state, chemical, gas, free-electron, bio, and others. All had inherent limitations with power source or gain medium...”

Billy Ray had guessed right, Dodd was from Mars!

“...and then a new species of jellyfish was discovered living near hydrothermal vents, thousands of feet below the ocean surface off the coast of Oregon. These creatures do more than merely produce and emit their own light, they actually zap their prey from a distance with special filaments using green fluorescent proteins as the gain medium—”

Billy Ray held up his hand. “You lost me at hello.”

“Sorry. It's a passion of mine, along with all God's creatures.”

“Is this thing alive? Are there jelly fish in here?” Billy Ray hefted the gun.

"How about I just show you how to fire the damn thing and leave it at that?" Dodd went on with the instructions.

Billy Ray got out of the van. Dodd had parked in a tractor pullout a half-mile beyond the entrance to the Ambassador Ranch. It wasn't much. The van stuck out like a sore thumb once motorists got close, but it'd have to do. He'd hoof back to the ranch road carrying all of the gear, almost two hundred pounds, the weight of a grown man. Then there'd be the long infiltration into the park by way of the Loma Reservoir. Humping all that weight over a course of nearly three miles would push him to the limits of his physical capabilities. He'd done similar missions in the past, and there was the time he carried Dodd's unconscious bleeding body to safety through several miles of steamy jungle while avoiding an enemy in hot pursuit. But he was older now. He prayed his body had enough in the tank to complete the trip.

"Car...oncoming," Dodd announced.

Billy Ray ducked behind the van and waited for the vehicle to pass. He retrieved the last of his gear. He was outfitted far better than he could've imagined. He implanted one of the tiny ear buds used for the dogs, and even strapped on one of the sensor collars. Dodd could guide him as he would Pedro or Lola.

"Wish me luck," Billy Ray said and jumped out of the van.

"Good hunting, Wolverine."

As Billy Ray rounded the back of the van, bright lights switched on, fully illuminating his camouflaged body and grease-painted face against the stark contrast of the white van. A car door opened and a voice shouted, "Don't move or I'll shoot!"

He froze.

It was Larry Bell. Once again, the young deputy had shown his salt. It'd been Bell's personal car that drove past. He'd recognized Dodd's van and doubled back, lights off. "Raise your hands in the air, now!"

Billy Ray did so. The thought came to him that if Bell had radioed his stop, the entire mission was screwed. Furthermore, he had an idea that Dodd would take matters into his own hands and kill Bell. He had to act fast. "Don't shoot. Let me speak—"

"Jenkins!" Bell recovered quickly. "Where's Rebecca?"

"In the park. Wiggins took her. I'm going in after her."

"No way, you took her. It's all over the radio. There's a thousand cops bearing down on us right now, closing off the town. They've come to get you. Is she in the van?"

"No, Larry. I told you, Wiggins has her."

"I don't believe you."

Before he could reply, a whirling blue police strobe lit up the night from a vehicle bearing down hard. Billy Ray cursed his luck. The mission was a scrub before it even got started!

An unmarked vehicle pulled up beside Bell's car. Out jumped Agent Johnny Lam with his wallet opened and badge in full view. "Officer, stow that weapon, now!" Lam didn't wait to confirm Bell's next move and kept walking straight up to Billy Ray. "Where is she, Jenkins?"

Hands reaching for the sky, Billy Ray twisted one wrist and pointed a finger in the direction of the Texas Waterland Family Park. "Over there."

Lam took control and ordered Bell to stay off the radios. Bell said he hadn't reported the stop. He then had Bell remove the agency car from the road. Bell did and then rejoined them.

Billy Ray was certain more cops would stumble upon them soon. He hastily revised the mission to include Bell, whose job would be to create a lengthy distraction at the Park's front gate. He and Lam would have fifty minutes to reach the Loma Reservoir, traverse the lake underwater, melt a big hole at the intake pipes, and breach the water treatment plant. After that, it'd be all about infiltrating Wiggins' underground control center. If all went well, they'd find a way in.

Billy Ray reminded himself of one immutable fact.

War never went well.

71

The White House Situation Room is a 5,000-square-foot conference room and intelligence management center in the basement of the West Wing of the White House. It is for the use of the President of the United States, POTUS. From there, the President can maintain command and control and respond to national crises. More delicate matters of national security could be addressed in any of several side rooms. Seating in these lead-lined rooms was limited, so too was access.

Special Agent Chris Dreyfus couldn't get comfortable in the plush leather chair for two reasons. The first being that he was sitting opposite the President of the United States!

Five others owned seats at the small conference table—the President's National Security Advisor, the Director of the National Security Agency in charge of Signal Intelligence, the Secretary of Defense who commanded the nation's armed forces, and the Director of the Central Intelligence Agency. The fifth and final person sat closest to the President. Her badge bore the symbol of a downward-facing trident and the words K-KEY Group. In the name space below the agency identifier was a single letter, "V." Curiously, no last name was provided. The Vice President was the final attendee, but remained standing in the back of the room. The most glaring omission among the group was the absence of the FBI or other domestic law enforcement representatives.

The second matter preventing his comfort was the topic of discussion, which had nearly blown his mind.

"So you see, Agent Dreyfus," the President began his closing remarks, "that's why your man was forbidden to contact you. Agent Lam will remain under my command until we bring this matter to a close, which should be in," POTUS consulted his gold wristwatch, "eighty-nine minutes."

Dreyfus had never met the President, hadn't even voted for the guy, but might now be willing to reconsider. The first word of his being summoned to the White House had come from his boss. The FBI Director had insisted *him and only him.* Furthermore, the Director added that no explanation as to the nature of the request had accompanied the summons. The Director also told him not to worry, that all would go well so long as he didn't wet himself.

Here he was, among the most powerful group of people on the planet, temporarily reassigned to the President, dry pants and all.

"You're going back to Texas. You will secure the perimeter of the park. If anyone refuses to cooperate, show them that." The President pointed at a leather case on the table. It contained an ID bearing a government insignia Dreyfus didn't recognize and a picture of the President. "Arrest them on my orders if necessary, just make sure nobody ventures inside the borders we outlined. The park is extensive. However, it appears you'll have plenty of deputized helpers. At this moment, hundreds of police are descending on East Texas to rescue the local sheriff's daughter and capture her abductor. Only you will know the real story, Agent Dreyfus."

"Yes, Mr. President. What will take place inside the perimeter?"

"That shall remain classified." The President eyed the K-KEY woman. Her face remained as unreadable as stone. "The Secretary of Defense has arranged for one of his go-fast machines to deliver you on-sight in," POTUS went to his watch again, "forty-one minutes. You will have very little time to assume command and move all civilians to safety."

Dreyfus possessed a pilot license and knew a little about flight times. Big Sandy was twelve-hundred miles away. He calculated that a plane would need to fly at better than Mach-4, or about 3,000-mph, to make the trip in the time mentioned. That ruled out every flying machine he knew of in the government's arsenal.

The President looked around the table and closed the meeting. "Okay, folks, let's stop these bastards in their tracks."

The weight of knowing what was going on in East Texas, and the ominous threat it posed to the nation, crushed down on Dreyfus' shoulders. How had he not known? How could the enemy have gotten such a foothold, and in his jurisdiction?

Forty-three minutes later, an unidentified flying object hovered over the Big Sandy High School football field, mere inches above the Wildcat logo. A platform lowered and Dreyfus stepped onto the turf. He remembered reading that the former coach of the Chicago Bears football team, Lovie Smith, had played on this field. He half-expected coach Smith to yell at him to get off the grass!

Dreyfus checked his watch. Only two minutes late. POTUS hadn't been off by much. The door closed behind him with barely a whisper. Then the circular craft produced a deep humming sound, lifted into the air, and shot off. He marveled as he stood at mid-field watching the speck of light disappear into the night sky.

The lights of an FBI vehicle appeared. Dreyfus got in and drove off. So much for invaders from outer space.

He had met the aliens and the aliens are us.

72

Billy Ray left to load equipment into Bell's car for the lift to the ranch access road. Lam completed his preparations and made to depart the van when Dodd stopped him.

"Agent Lam, I request you not call the FBI unless I command it."

Lam turned. "Who do you think you are? I need to contact my superior about what's happening in the park. He's awaiting my call."

"Actually, he's not and you will not."

"By what authority can you say that?"

From an overhead compartment, Dodd removed an oblong leather case slightly larger than a checkbook. He handed it to Lam. "By this authority."

Lam opened the case. The first thing to get his attention was a photo of the President of the United States above an official seal he'd never seen before and the words "Full Authority Over All" written below. He'd heard rumors such a group existed, created by secret Executive Order, ostensibly to counter layers of often competing agencies and allow the Commander-in-Chief direct and forceful response to 'enemies foreign and domestic.' But he'd assumed the rumors emanated from the imaginations of sci-fi buffs and conspiracy nuts.

Strange...he'd taken an oath as an Army officer to do the very same, but it pertained to upholding the Constitution.

He wasn't too sure he agreed with the direction the government was taking.

"And another thing, Agent Lam."

He looked up from Dodd's credentials.

"You'll reveal neither my name nor my agency to anyone." Dodd gestured at the leather case. "You never saw that. Understood?"

"Yes, Admiral. But my superior knows I'm here. I phoned him on my way from North Carolina."

"I can assure you he's been apprised of the situation. Forces are standing by on my command."

"A kill squad, no doubt."

"Much more than that, but I've neither the time nor authorization to explain further. We could have a serious *friendly-fire* incident if you choose to disobey my orders. The blood of good men and women would be on your hands. I'm sure you don't wish that."

Lam wanted no such thing. "What about my daughter?"

Dodd pressed a hard fact. “My men are not hostage rescue teams.”

The threat was clear to Lam. “Does Jenkins know this?”

“To a degree. I’ve given him until midnight.”

“That’s less than three hours to free the hostages!”

“Be thankful you have that much time. I assure you, it wasn’t the first choice. I owed Jenkins for saving my life. Regardless, it’s his abilities I trust. Otherwise, this matter would already have received the nuclear option, which is to say everyone inside that park would already be dead. Be glad you have Wolverine—he’s relentless.”

“So I’ve noticed.”

“I’ve done all I can, and all I’m willing to do. Personal debts only go so far. I’m sworn to protect the security of our nation, and that trumps all.”

Lam strained to keep from throttling Dodd around the neck. Truth could be harsh. He exited the vehicle.

The pet grooming van started up and drove off.

“There you are, Lam. Thought you’d changed your mind.”

“Not in a million years, Jenkins. I want my daughter back. You think you can manage that?”

Billy Ray placed the equipment bag and laser in Bell’s trunk. He turned to Lam and said, “I can only guarantee that I’ll try.”

Lam stared at Billy Ray, searching for weakness. None existed. “That’s all I can ask.”

Dodd turned the van in the direction of Heavenor Hardware & Sports, from where he would conduct the battle. He called out as he passed by, “You haven’t said how you’ll get to the lake undetected. You’ll stand out like a herd of cows on Wiggins' sensors.”

Billy Ray smiled. “That's exactly what I intend.”

Dodd drove away.

Bell transported Billy Ray and Lam to the Ambassador Ranch access road, thus making up time lost by Bell’s interference and Lam's arrival. Each man marked time on their watches. Bell left for the main gate.

Data from Dodd's canine recon team showed no evidence of sensors until after the cattle yard. If any had been missed by Pedro and Lola, Billy Ray hoped the dog collar around his own neck would catch it. He handed Lam an earbud and mic and then headed straight for the cattle yard. He had an appointment with a white bull. As they walked, he caught Lam up on the details they hadn't had time for back at Dodd’s van, including his plan for getting to the reservoir undetected.

“Are you nuts, Jenkins? In case you were dropped on your head as a baby, let me remind you. This is not Pamplona!”

"It will be soon. Get ready to run with the bulls. By the way, my operational name is Wolverine. What's yours?"

Lam went quiet.

"Come on soldier, you were in SpecOps, you must have one."

"I don't wish to divulge it," Lam remarked pompously.

"Why not?"

"Because you'll laugh."

"I will not. We're on a mission here."

"Loverboy."

"What?"

"You heard me...*Loverboy*."

Billy Ray busted out laughing!

"I knew I couldn't trust you Navy guys."

They arrived at the gate. It was chained and padlocked, but with no ordinary equipment. Cattle rustlers still existed. This wary rancher had chosen hardened steel chain and vandal-proof lock.

"What now, cowboy?"

Billy Ray felt stupid. He'd planned for everything, or nearly so. He and Lam each carried pistols. His was suppressed, Lam's was not. Shooting off a lock with a single bullet only worked in the movies. It could take an entire magazine of .45 caliber rounds with no guarantee of success against the hardened steel, plus ricochets would be a nasty problem. Furthermore, gunfire would alert the entire countryside the Russians were coming.

He spoke into the mic. "Dolittle, you in place yet?"

"In place and on the computer. What's the problem?"

"You didn't happen to slip a giant set of bolt cutters into my bag before I left did you?"

"Hardly, Wolverine. Why?"

"I'm looking at a hefty chain and padlock—"

"I know what you're thinking. A very quick pulse should suffice, about a normal trigger pull. Mind what's behind the target though, unless you like your steaks well done."

Billy Ray removed the strange gun from its protective case.

Lam's eyes went big. "What the hell is that?"

"Stand behind me and avert your eyes."

Lam did as he was told.

Billy Ray "turned on" the gun and narrowed the aperture per Dodd's instructions. He quick-triggered a single pulse at the chain. An intense beam of green light the width of a pencil shot out. The beam appeared and disappeared in less time than it took to blink. The molten chain dropped away from the padlock and fell to the ground. The hot metal ignited the grass. He stamped out the flame, careful not to burn holes in the bottom of his boot.

"Wow!" Lam said. "You get that from a Martian?"

"Yes." Billy Ray noticed they thought alike.

"What now?" Lam asked.

Billy Ray stowed the laser and hoisted the rubberized equipment bag over his shoulder. "Follow me." He pointed toward the massive bull on the hill in the distance. The old bovine had sensed their presence and was lifting itself to its feet. "We need to get that big boy through the gate and headed toward the reservoir. Then all the cows will follow."

"You mean a stampede?" There was dread in Lam's voice.

"Let's hope for a *controlled* stampede. The cattle are driven to water weekly. I'm betting it's become routine for them. You and I will run amongst the herd." Billy Ray headed off towards the bull. He called over his shoulder to Lam. "And another thing, Loverboy...."

"What?"

"Watch for landmines."

Lam looked down. Mounds of cow droppings littered the ground. He was still dressed in a business suit and his best wingtip shoes. He shouted at Billy Ray's back. "You could've warned me to dress down for this party!"

73

The meeting ended. The Korean technicians took their places in the control center. Lee excused himself from the room. Gallina accompanied his lieutenant to the Black Anaconda to issue orders to his men. Tonight would be their time to play, then tomorrow and the days ahead would be all work. Wiggins considered the vats of Rapture to be pumped into the last five tanker trucks and shipped the following day to processing labs in the target cities. The drug would be broken down into millions of doses of death. Only hours remained for countless Americans.

He was pleased.

"Comrade," a technician called from his monitoring station. "The cattle. They're on the move toward the reservoir."

"Is there a problem?"

"The farmer is a day early on the agreed watering schedule."

"What about notification?"

"None, Comrade. I placed a call, but received no answer."

"Perhaps the farmer is with the herd."

"Negative. I detect only cattle on the infrared cameras, and nothing on the sound sensors except hooves. The farmer usually rides along on an all-terrain vehicle."

"And you're positive all sensors and monitors are working properly?"

"Affirmative."

Wiggins considered the matter. "Perhaps our neighbor is watering early for the holiday. Actually, I'm glad he's doing so. It'll keep the smell of manure from drifting into the park during tomorrow's pre-grand opening."

The technician stared at Wiggins, awaiting further orders.

"Carry on." Wiggins withdrew his cell phone and keyed a number.

"Unit 4, What do you see?"

"Nothing but cattle. They're approaching the water now."

It was always something, Wiggins thought. No plan was ever perfect.

* * *

Firing shots to start the stampede was unnecessary once the old bull's attack instincts shifted into overdrive. Billy Ray then informed Lam that if life atop *terra firma* meant anything he'd better bolt like a Walmart shopper on Black Friday. Lam complied with all haste and dove out of the corral just as one ton of white bull and a hundred head of cattle thundered past. Lam was a mess and smelled like manure, but alive and cussing mad!

Jogging among the cattle soon proved impossible. Not only was the uneven ground treacherous in the darkness, but getting bumper-carred by thousand-pound bovines while jostling improvised explosive devices was downright suicidal. So like any battle plan gone to hell the moment the action began, tactics changed. They hitched rides atop the cows instead.

They made it to the water's edge and slid off the backs of their four-legged taxis, then stripped out of their clothing and readied their fins and masks.

Before depositing his phone, Lam texted Katie's mom. Then he held his Bostonians at arm's length. "What about these?"

"Bury 'em. They'll make good fertilizer." Billy Ray dragged a finger across his throat to indicate the need for silence.

Before placing the snorkel in his mouth Lam crossed himself and whispered, "I'm coming, Katie."

Billy Ray was thankful to have Lam at his side. He had no doubt that when bullets began flying, cop would become Green Beret. He needed every bit of help he could get. With Lam, Dodd, Egolf, and Bell, he had more help than he'd ever imagined. And yet, knowing the incredible challenge he faced against a well-armed enemy on its own killing ground, the odds were stacked against him. If he was to rescue Rebecca and the girls and live to see another day, he'd also need help not of this world. It would take as many miracles as bullets.

He followed Lam's example and said a prayer of his own.

A bolt of lightning lit the sky, then another. The predicted squall let loose its liquid burden. Billy Ray welcomed nature's hand. Lightning killed night vision optics and the noise of splashing rain and rumbling thunder punked sound-sensing devices. Thermal imaging could still be a problem, but only on land, and an entire herd of cattle had just trampled that capability.

Mission perspective replaced dread and worry for the hostages. But there was no blocking the rage in Billy Ray's heart. That's what had always made him a lethal weapon. His was a mind focused on facts, a heart filled with righteous anger—the cold encountering the hot—the tempest and then the tumult of war.

He pulled down the mask and slipped beneath the black waters.

Men would die tonight. Bad men would go to their graves for what they'd done.

74

Egolf's dive mask was incredible. The low-light enhancement feature converted the blackness of night diving into the brightness of a backyard swimming pool. Much better than the goggle-type light enhancers that constricted view through green peepholes. A heads-up display posted dive data on the mask lens, thus leaving hands free to attend other matters. Additionally, the experimental rebreather had advantages over the Draeger equipment he'd used as a SEAL. The device was smaller, allowing for greater ease of movement and more cargo capacity. The mouthpiece incorporated a microphone. Coupled with the earbuds he and Lam wore, they were wired for two-way communication.

Dodd could monitor the data from the mask's dive computer in real-time and then advise and assist by posting text on the display or through audio communication. Because of the helpful rain, they chose audio.

"Two fish, blue fish," Billy Ray used code to indicate he and Lam were commencing the water leg of the mission.

"No need for code, Wolverine. Our coms are encrypted."

"Old habits."

"Then here's to old habits and old friends—"

"What about new friends?" Lam threw in.

"To new ones, also," Dodd added.

"Second that," said Billy Ray.

Dodd gave praise. "Wolverine, you improvised nicely with the cattle."

"Yeah, well…I'll leave talking to the animals to you from now on, Dolittle. Plus, I'm a bit saddle sore."

"What saddle," Lam said.

Dodd came back on task. "Check in when you get to the water intake. I want a look around before you blast."

The tension on the tether linking him to Lam was good. Billy Ray craned his head around anyway just to make sure. Unlike himself, Lam was diving blind. He could hear and speak, but didn't have the benefit of the space-age mask. His respect for the Army guy went up another notch. Lam was turning out better underwater than he'd imagined, and doing so in total darkness.

Billy Ray concentrated on the remainder of the dive.

* * *

Deputy Bell rolled it over in his mind for the hundredth time. He was a traitor, working at cross-purposes with Sheriff Payne and a thousand other law officers now closing off Big Sandy.

But he'd seen the evidence. Rebecca was a prisoner inside the park. Furthermore, two children were also hostage. Jenkins and the legless guy showed him video of the terrible things taking place underground. He'd wanted to call Sheriff Payne immediately. A part of him still did. But he also believed Jenkins, that if he involved the police in any way, the hostages would die.

Before taking position at the gate of Texas Waterland, Bell switched his private car for a department vehicle. He now spent time before his scheduled diversion monitoring the police radio. An anonymous caller had phoned into the 911 dispatcher saying Billy Ray Jenkins had been spotted in the area. Payne had jumped on the call and ordered all hands to surround the town.

Soon all roads leading in and out of Big Sandy would be blocked, citizens requested to stay indoors, traffic diverted through checkpoints, and all because of him. It had been his call to the dispatcher. And that also made him feel like a traitor—this time to Jenkins. However, trust only went so far. Knowing what was truly happening inside the park, Bell wanted a backup plan of his own.

It was nearly time to create a scene at the gate, one large enough to draw the attention of Wiggins and his goons, which was the other reason he'd placed the call to the emergency operator. He knew who else would come rushing to the park besides cops.

A yellow Jeep Cherokee caught Bell's attention. The logo on the side advertised the Gladewater News in bold letters. Bell's idea was to get help with the diversion. His unsuspecting accomplice, Clive Ballerd, rode inside the news vehicle. Bell had no doubt Ballerd would take the bait and then afterward nothing would stop the pesky gadfly. His presence and the sheriff vehicle provided all the authenticity needed.

75

They came to the intake pipes. Just as Dodd predicted, the grating was a special steel alloy, titanium most likely. Billy Ray could see clearly through the hi-tech dive mask. Lam didn't share the luxury so he made sure he understood to maintain neutral buoyancy and not touch anything, such as trip wires. Next he had Dodd foil all sound and infrared sensors. That little trick was accomplished by Dodd activating two of the colored stones on the dog collar. He was aware of noise-cancelling technology, but cancelling infrared signals was a mystery.

Billy Ray focused on spotting booby traps. He found two, dismantled both, and stowed them in the pack for later. Dodd posted text saying the dog collar detected no further explosives. He wasn't satisfied. Jungle fighters employed low-tech traps. He scanned the area once more, and a good thing, too. Balanced above the metal grate and concealed by waterweeds was a heavy steel plate with a razor-sharp edge, like that of a French guillotine. Once tripped, an intruder joined the ranks of Marie Antoinette. He jimmied the device. Next came Dodd's fancy can opener, and then instructions posted on the HUD along with a diagram for expanding beam width. Dodd warned to expect a slight concussive force and moderate warming of the surrounding water, though not to worry because the effects wouldn't exhibit the same force as conventional explosions.

Yeah, and what if pigs really could fly?

Billy Ray charged up the laser. He warned Lam to close his eyes and switched his dive mask to protective mode. He pulsed a single shot at the center of the grate. The high-energy beam lasted one full second, far longer than most pulsed lasers. He reverted the mask to light-enhanced. What he saw amazed him. One super-hardened metal grate, gone—vaporized!

* * *

Wiggins was about to leave the command center when a technician called out. "Master Wiggins, one of our infrared sensors just flared white."

Wiggins looked down at the technician's monitor. It was a sensor at the water treatment plant. The readings registered normal, no sign of human heat signatures. "What's the problem?"

"Unsure. The screen flashed white for point-nine seconds."

"Is there an electrical problem with your monitor?"

"It's working properly, as you can see by the picture."

“What of the other infrared sensors in the area?”

“All normal. Only this one showed an anomaly. Temperature readings also indicate a spike coinciding with visual data.”

“What was the temperature at the time of the whiteout?”

The man typed a command. The number appeared.

Wiggins stared in awe. “Impossible. That temperature only exists on the surface of the sun.”

“Technically, Master Wiggins, the sun doesn’t have a surface.”

Wiggins straightened. “Okay, photosphere,” he showed his knowledge. “Even plasma burns a magnitude cooler.”

“And plasma takes an hour to cut through our hardened grate.”

They were interrupted when Lee came between Wiggins and the technician. “Comrade, we have a problem at the main gate.”

Wiggins ignored Lee. He said to the technician, “Run a diagnostic to be sure. It was probably a lightning strike. This storm is expected to move out of the area soon, but inform me immediately of any further anomalies.”

The technician turned back to his monitor.

Wiggins faced Lee. “Now what?”

“The incident at the gate, a cameraman is setting up equipment and the reporter is about to begin broadcasting.”

“So...? Free advertising.”

“Not the kind we want. The reporter is claiming Billy Ray Jenkins is inside the park, with his hostage.”

Wiggins grabbed for his phone.

A man answered after several rings. “Front gate.”

“This is Wiggins—”

“Yes, sir!”

“I don’t care what you do, get rid of that reporter!”

“But, sir—”

“Get him off the premises, at gunpoint if you have to.”

“What about the sheriff deputy?” the guard asked nervously.

Wiggins gave pause. “Keep that reporter off the air. Invite him here to the security building. Invite the deputy, too, if that’s what it takes. I’m sending help to usher them back here.” Wiggins hung up. He turned to Lee. “Get up there, now.”

First the lightning strike at the treatment plant, and now a meddling reporter with bad information. Bad luck, Wiggins told himself. Just in case, he ordered a guard to check out the water plant. Next, he phoned somebody who could make sure the deputy at the gate posed no problems.

“Yeah?” the voice answered.

"How soon can you get here?"

"I'm kind of busy. Somebody called the emergency operator claiming they spotted Billy Ray Jenkins with the Payne girl."

"Who?"

"No idea. The caller hung up. The number belongs to a prepaid cell phone. It'll take time to track down."

"We don't have time."

"Tell me about it. Payne called in just about every cop in the state. They're closing off Big Sandy, Gladewater too. Every road in the area will be blocked or have checkpoints."

"We anticipated as much."

"Yes, but now it's times ten."

"No worries. You have control over my checkpoints."

"I'm glad you brought that up—"

"More money?"

"Yes. Another hundred—"

"Fifty—"

The voice in Wiggins' phone said, "A hundred-thousand more or the 911 operator gets another call."

Wiggins faked defeat. If a billion dollars had been requested he would've used the same bargaining ruse and then settled on the full amount. It didn't matter. The man would never see a penny. Nor would it matter what evidence the cop had collected. Wiggins only needed the first shipments to be successful. "Another hundred and not one penny more. You haven't proven your value yet."

The man began to speak. Wiggins hung up. Best to plant the seed of insecurity early, then manipulate its growth.

Wiggins went topside to receive the rabble from the front gate.

76

Billy Ray defused another booby trap inside the intake pipes and placed it in the bag with the others. The bomb had the same configuration as the previous devices. *Laziness.* He would've mixed things up, reversed the wiring on the traps at the least. Regardless, the dog collar indicated no further explosives and only two more sensors, which Dodd performed his magic on.

Twenty yards beyond the entrance, the intake began a forty-five-degree incline. It continued upward past side vents and hatch doors until coming through the floor of a lighted holding tank. He switched his mask to normal light. He felt something bump his leg, and then several somethings. Fish, undoubtedly. As his eyesight adjusted, he recognized what the creatures were. Piranhas!

The training manual had several things to say about swimming among piranha, but none heartening, except they were supposed to be good eating. If these piranhas were desperate, he and Lam were in real trouble. And they were acting rather skittish. One instruction was to make no sudden movements. Hungry piranhas were attracted by movement as much as by blood. Fortunately, neither of them had open wounds from the cattle run or else they'd be well on their way to a skeletal condition.

Blood was out. That left movement. Billy Ray turned slowly to face Lam, who could now see in the lighted tank. Lam must have spent serious time in South America. His look made it clear he knew their situation and that he, too, had read the jungle manuals.

"Lam," he said softly. "No sudden moves. We get out slowly."

Lam elected to blink his answer.

Billy Ray made for the side of the tank using smooth, fluid strokes. If any guards were present, he and Lam would be fish food for sure. He raised his head out of the water in slow motion, holding the Mark 23 SOCOM pistol at the ready-fire position.

The coast was clear.

Billy Ray hefted the dive bags over the edge and came out of the water. He signaled for Lam. Just as Lam lifted himself over the side of the tank, a piranha struck his exposed flesh. Lam yanked his legs out of the water at a speed that saved his foot. A drop of blood fell into the tank. The water erupted as hundreds of piranha rushed about searching for the source.

"That was close!" Lam forced through a whisper. He had an inch-long gash across his ankle above the rubber dive fin.

Billy Ray pulled a first-aid kit from the gunnysack. In a moment, the blood was stanched, the wound disinfected and dressed.

They removed the dive equipment. The room was bare with nowhere to hide. They pulled the gear next to a wall. Precious minutes melted away, but they were inside. Now to find a way into Wiggins' control center.

Billy Ray opted for wearing the dive mask to receive information from Dodd. A picture of the facility popped up on the HUD. A diagram showed a door and spiral staircase. He opened the door and immediately heard footsteps descending. He ran back to Lam. There'd only been the sound of one set of footsteps. He assumed the person to be a patrol. The fact he and Lam had gotten this far, and that only one guard was on the way to inspect, was a good sign, it meant they were still in the game. Bell must have been successful in creating a diversion at the gate. Stealth would be their best weapon for infiltrating the control room. Any attempt to fight the approaching guard would alert Wiggins. They needed to draw the guard into a trap and dispose of him quietly. But how?

It came to him.

Billy Ray handed Lam the silenced MK23. "Listen up," he said an inch from Lam's ear. "You get behind the door. I'm going belly-up in the tank. The guard will see my floating body and move to investigate. With luck, he'll forget about the door. That should give you the split-second you need to drop him."

Lam glanced at the tank, the look unmistakable, and began to speak.

Billy Ray cut him off. "No cop stuff. No warning. These guys are combatants. Two shots to the head and catch 'em on the way down. Got it?"

He didn't wait for an answer. Neither did he consider what awaited him in the water. What was one death over another? The fish would devour him in far less time than a dozen other forms of death this night—especially the slowest death of all, knowing he'd failed and that Rebecca was dead.

He lowered himself into the tank. The last thing he saw before going face down in a dead man's float was Lam staring at him, mouth hanging open.

Then he remembered cleaning the blood from Lam's cut.

77

The standoff at the gate began when Bell stopped the yellow jeep and demanded Ballerd get out of the car. The man at first refused, spouting his usual lines like, “I’m a news reporter,” and “I have my First Amendment Rights,” to which Bell ordered him out of the car or face arrest. He put Ballerd against the car, hands on the hood.

“Why are you doing this?” the trembling reporter demanded.

“Because you resisted my command.”

“But you’re just a deputy.”

As reward for his arrogance, Bell kicked Ballerd’s legs apart.

“That’s police brutality!”

“You ain’t felt nothin’ yet. You think you can go interferin’ with a police stakeout?” Bell made himself sound like a hick.

“What police stakeout…you mean in there?” Ballerd tried lifting a hand to point and received a slam for his effort. “Ouch!”

Bell played the part of a jacked-up rookie, unable to keep from spilling the beans. “You know what stakeout or you wouldn’t be here. You’re a vulture, always first on the scene for news.”

“What stakeout?” Ballerd repeated, his tone curious.

Time to set the hook.

“Jenkins.”

“Jenkins? You mean in there, with the hostage?”

Ballerd could hardly contain himself. Again he lifted a hand to point. Bell allowed it. “Your words, not mine.”

Let the fish run.

Cars were lining up. The gate guard finished his business with an outbound tanker truck and came toward them. After a good frisking to add credence to the act, he turned Ballerd around. “Now get back in your car and leave.”

Ballerd’s eyes told the tale—greed. The man would stop at nothing to scoop a story, to be first, to be the cock of the walk.

“What’s the problem here?” the guard demanded.

“No problem. Just a routine stop.” Bell winked at Ballerd.

Bait, set, hook.

Ballerd stepped toward the guard with his customary aplomb, pulled a business card from a vest pocket, and thrust it at the guard. “I demand to speak with the park manager!”

The guard was taken aback. “I... uh... that’s not possible.”

"Why not? I'm a reporter." Ballerd began his usual pitch.

Bell stepped back and let Ballerd take it from there. The ruse worked. Ten minutes had already elapsed on the mission clock. A diversion was in full swing and escalating. He was betting a good deal more time would tick away with the pesky reporter now running the show.

* * *

Lam stood ramrod still. The footfalls ended. The door opened halfway and held. A gun barrel rose into view and stopped. The guard must have spotted Jenkins' floating body. He chanced a quick look at the tank, hoping the ex-SEAL was good at holding his breath. The guard was cautious. If Jenkins even twitched he'd be a dead man.

Radio chatter erupted from the guard's radio. The man replied. Lam memorized the words.

Come on, he begged in his mind, *step forward.*

A little farther….

The gun barrel grew longer.

One more step….

It happened. With two pulls of the trigger, Lam deposited twenty-six grams of lead into the enemy's head. No cop, just Green Beret. He leaped forward, caught the body, and lowered it to the ground. He'd done the act before, in South America. Muscle memory served him well. But it was different this time. His law enforcement training dictated so.

Lam thought of his daughter and the cool air of justification tempered his legal mind.

Billy Ray dared not move, more for fear of the piranhas than a 9mm parabellum to the back of the head. At first the hungry fish considered him inert. Then a few piranhas began showing attention to the hand he'd used to swab Lam's blood. More creatures began bumping against him. Why he wasn't already reduced to a pile of shiny bones was owed to the disinfectant he'd used on the cut. However, a million years of evolution forced greater relevance to blood molecules than a modern compound like rubbing alcohol. It was just a matter of time.

The digital readout on the HUD said he'd been in the water five minutes and counting. Stars began popping in his brain. If Lam didn't hurry he'd be dead regardless. He felt a tap on his shoulder, the signal. Now came the difficult part, moving slowly enough to avoid becoming dinner. Another instruction in the jungle manual on piranhas was to create a diversion. Again, Lam proved to have done his homework because a bloody body splashed into the water ten feet to his right. The piranha went after the new source of food.

Billy Ray disregarded commotion and got the hell out of the water. He splashed onto the deck and sucked in lungfuls of air.

"Thanks, Army, I was about to become somebody's chum."

Lam stood guard as Billy Ray recovered. "Hey, always willing to pull a Navy guy's butt out of the soup."

The water tank boiled red behind them as they got down to business. Lam had stripped the corpse of its black uniform and now put it on. The Asian guard had been the same height though lacking in pounds. Lam cut slits in the clothing to make it fit. For the boots, he slit the toe along the sole to accommodate his longer feet. Billy Ray sorted the guard's gear—H&K MP7, ammunition, and radio. He swapped Lam the MP7 for the SOCOM pistol.

While they worked, Lam told Billy Ray about the radio call. He parroted back the words. "So what did the guard say?"

"He said, 'hold…something floats in the fish tank.'"

"That's it?"

Billy Ray poked a thumb toward the body, now sinking below the water. "I expect another call when he doesn't check back."

"What then?"

"I'll answer it. Help me practice a response. I better sound convincing enough to stall them, at least. Tell me what the guy sounded like, his pitch and cadence."

For the next minute, Billy Ray worked on a statement, repeating it as Lam pointed up or down for pitch and side to side for tempo.

The radio came to life. Billy Ray ignored it. Lam stared in anticipation.

"Get ready," Billy Ray warned. "As soon as the call repeats I'll answer. Then we grab our shit and git. Ready?"

Lam strapped his portion of the load to his back, grabbed up the MP7, and nodded. "Ready."

The voice repeated.

Billy Ray pulled the mic close to provide distortion. He pressed the talk button and began laughing and made his statement, "A dead animal." More laughter. "All clear."

The man asked him to repeat. Billy Ray did, laughter and all.

Then they ran.

78

The standoff at the gate got heated when Ballerd announced he was going live on TV to announce that Billy Ray Jenkins was holed up inside the Texas Waterland Family Park. The guard turned and ran to his booth, nearly ripped the phone off the wall to call his supervisor, then sprinted back just in time to stop the cameraman from transmitting to the world.

Things got messy when the night sky opened up and poured out the predicted rain. The guard attempted to seize the video camera. A scuffle ensued. Ballerd stepped between the two, got knocked face down in a puddle, and began screaming about his rights.

The guard abandoned his effort to impede the cameraman and assuage the reporter. He stepped back, drew his weapon, and yelled, "Stop!" Then he turned to Bell. "You just going to stand there?"

Bell pointed at the .38 Smith & Wesson. "I don't know. Is that thing loaded?" Normally he would've acted long before now, but needed to draw out the diversion as long as possible, short of somebody getting shot.

Ballerd chimed in, "Yeah, deputy, do something. Make him holster that gun. I have a First Amendment right to free speech!"

Bell didn't have to answer. The melee was interrupted when a golf cart skidded to a halt beside Bell's patrol car. A stocky Asian dressed in safari-looking clothes dismounted and took control.

* * *

The staircase ascended to a long hallway. Several doors lined either side. According to blueprints, they accessed storage and equipment rooms. Billy Ray had Dodd employ his techno-gadgets to back-feed visual data into Wiggins' camera monitors. The Korean technicians would see only empty spaces on their computer screens. Lam stood watch while he searched for booby traps. Between the dog collar and his eyes, no traps were detected.

He motioned Lam forward. "Once we exit those doors there's no turning back. The fight's on."

Lam's answer was to switch the MP7 to full auto.

Billy Ray checked his own weapon. "We have to find a way into the security building. I'll bet money there are secret escape passages somewhere, too."

"How can you be so sure?" Lam asked, always the skeptic.

"If I'd built the place, I'd want a backdoor...one near water."

"Spoken like a Navy guy. I would've chosen land."

"We're probably both right. Wiggins had years to plan."

"What next?"

"Another diversion. I'll give away my position to draw Wiggins and his men away from the security building. I think I have just the idea how to accomplish that."

Dodd's voice came over their earbuds. "Time's running out and the wind's in your face, Wolverine."

"Dolittle, your fancy computer removes my presence on the security monitors, but can it make me appear elsewhere?"

Dodd was quick. "Brilliant. Give me two minutes."

"Fill me in," Lam said.

"I'll make the far side of the park and lob some mortar rounds to get things rolling. Then with Dodd's help I'll play chase-the-rabbit with Wiggins and his men. You'll find a way underground and rescue the hostages."

"What if—"

Billy Ray cut Lam off. "There are no *what ifs.* We fail...the hostages die. It's that simple. If Dodd can make me appear to be places I'm not, the hounds will never catch me."

"Give me one shot to get my daughter. That's all I ask."

"You'll get your shot, Army. But just in case...."

Billy Ray worked out an emergency code with Lam. If either one got into trouble or were about to get their ticket punched, they were to signal using the word *Spartan* and then escape using a route decided on earlier from Dodd's maps.

Dodd said over the line, "*De Oppresso Liber.*"

Billy Ray looked into Lam's eyes. They were those of a desperate father. But he also saw resolve, and the best kind—the Green Beret kind. "As Dodd just said, *free the oppressed.* We're all Green Berets tonight, my friend. Let's go get Katie and the others."

Lam was about to reply, but Dodd came first. "Got it!"

"Got what?"

"I tweaked your idea. Wiggins will think he's playing hare and hounds. We'll give him whack-a-mole instead. I'll feed your image through cameras at various points in the park. Meanwhile, you'll pop up elsewhere and make a lethal nuisance of yourself."

"You're a genius, Dolittle."

"Don't thank me yet. Wiggins is smart, he'll catch on eventually."

"But not before Lam gets underground."

Lam noticed a change in tone. "What happens to you?" He looked hard at Billy Ray.

"Getting you inside may actually be the easy part. Getting you all to safety will be tricky. That's where I come in."

"Aren't you 'in' already?"

Dodd answered. "He means, then it's Wolverine time."

Just then, the captured radio came to life.

"Uh oh," Lam uttered.

Billy Ray chambered a round in his SOCOM pistol.

Dodd put the ball in motion. "My men are inbound. You have fifty-six minutes. So I suggest you two get on to breaking things and rescuing people."

They grabbed up the gear and weapons and busted through the treatment plant doors. Billy Ray took off for the far end of the park. Lam bolted in the opposite direction.

79

They were taken to a conference room in the main security building at the rear of the park. The reporter and cameraman were led away by Lee. Wiggins motioned for Bell to help himself to coffee and pastries on a table in the corner and then departed.

Several minutes passed. Bell began wondering if anyone would return.

There was a knock on the door.

To Bell's surprise, in walked Dixon.

"Tom! What are you doing here?"

"Heard there might be trouble, kid."

"How so?"

"You know, the Jenkins thing." Dixon looked around the room, spotted the donuts, and moseyed over to the table.

Bell was immediately suspicious. He was surprised to see Dixon so far off the beaten path. He knew for a fact Payne had ordered his second-in-command to supervise checkpoints at the edge of town, none of which were near Texas Waterland.

Dixon spoke with his back to Bell, "So what you doin' here, kid? Get lost goin' home from school?"

Bell didn't answer. He watched Dixon. Something was wrong. Like when Dixon happened to show up at the Loma Reservoir, and then afterward proceeded to get him suspended, all the while neglecting key details of the incident.

His mind raced.

"Answer me, boy!"

"You're part of this," Bell said.

"Part of what?"

"The kidnappings...the drugs. You're working for Wiggins, aren't you?" Bell addressed Dixon's back.

"You've lost your mind, kid. Sheriff Payne sent me here to pull your dumb ass out of the fire one more time."

"It all makes sense now. And I don't need an escort, I'll find my own way out."

"Actually"—Dixon spun around—"You're not going anywhere." He held a tiny Ruger handgun. The weapon was aimed straight at Bell's heart.

* * *

Reconnaissance.... Infiltration.... Interdiction....

Now it was time to destabilize, isolate, and terminate.

Billy Ray reached the far side of the park aided by Dodd's wizardry at manipulating Wiggins' security cameras. His objective was the high ground next to the replica Old West train depot. The heavy rain helped cover his advance and avoid partiers engaged in various forms of entertainment ranging from swimming naked and making out, to swigging on bottles of tequila and smoking marijuana—activities not advertised in park brochures. The women came in all sizes and colors, likely hired for the occasion. The men were all Latinos—Gallina's men.

There'd been two close calls. The first was a group of half-naked partiers. There'd been no choice, so he'd stood up and walked straight through the middle of the group as if he owned the place.

The second incident was coming upon a black-uniformed guard hiding behind a building spying on a naked couple engaged in sexual intercourse. SEAL training taught that when necessary to eliminate a sentry, an operator must consider two factors, proximity and swiftness—sneak close and kill fast. Close was easy, the man was the worst kind of distracted. Fast was achieved with a knife thrust into the base of the guard's skull. He stripped the corpse of weapons and gear and hustled off.

He arrived at the train depot attraction and got to work. It was time to announce his presence. From the larger bag, he pulled out three pieces of black ABS pipe and a pint-sized propane bottle. Then he glued the pipes together, attached a trigger assembly fabricated back at Gus' store, and ran a flexible tube to the propane bottle. Kids all across America would recognize the contraption as a potato gun. However, there'd be no "tossin' taters" this night. He had something far more lethal in mind.

He retrieved a metal case from his bag and gingerly extracted one of a dozen yellow tennis balls from the foam cushioning. The balls were filled with highly explosive acetone peroxide, or TATP, often used in roadside IEDs and makeshift bombs. TATP was extremely unstable, susceptible to accidental detonation by heat, friction, shock, or sparks and earned the name "Mother of Satan" among Islamic terrorists for prematurely airmailing bits and pieces of suicide bombers to paradise.

"I'm ready," Billy Ray said into his mic.

Lam clicked, unable to speak without exposing his position.

Egolf's voice came across for the first time on the earbuds, "Four turkeys in my sights."

Dodd said, "Let's rock and roll!"

Billy Ray said a prayer.

This night, Death rides a pale horse and Hell follows.

80

Billy Ray rolled a tennis ball down the pipe, charged the makeshift mortar, and depressed the sparking trigger.

Whumpff! The bomb shot off into the night sky.

He breathed a sigh of relief that the TATP didn't live up to its nasty reputation. He'd taken precautions by keeping the explosive cool. He'd added dry ice inside the cushioned metal case and moistened the fuzz on the tennis balls. And the rubber reduced shock until point of impact.

He fired again. The second ball was in the air before the first one hit the ground.

"Lam, get ready. The hornets are about to leave the nest."

Lam double-clicked.

Even from three hundred yards away the explosions were deafening. The low-tech cannon meant he was firing blind, able only to place the TATP tennis balls within a hundred-foot circle. No matter, the first rounds were just meant to say, *Hi There!*

"I detect movement, Wolverine. Go to position Bravo."

Billy Ray packed his equipment. Before vacating the area, he affixed mechanical detonators to two Mother of Satan bombs, set them for fifteen minutes, and attached them to the train. He located the controls, set the train in motion, and jumped off.

He headed north toward the gift stores and food court area. Dodd would show him to be elsewhere on the monitors. His plan was to pull the enemy away from the security building and get them chasing him. Lam should get an opportunity to infiltrate the underground levels. Once Lam signaled having the hostages, he would circle back and assist getting everyone to safety. At least, that was Plan A.

One worrisome matter was yet to be accounted for. The security building and underground labs were rigged to blow. Surely, Wiggins wouldn't hesitate for one second to blast the whole place to rubble if he determined his operation was compromised, then use the explosion as a diversion to aid his own escape.

Billy Ray couldn't let that happen.

He had to make Wiggins think the game was won. The key would be to use Wiggins' ego against him.

* * *

For the third time in a month, Wiggins was forced to stand before Pao. He'd put off the old man as long as he dared.

"No, it was not my idea for Angel Gallina to come here," Wiggins declared. "In fact, it would please me to shoot him for jeopardizing our operation."

The young attorney turned back from Pao. He relayed the old man's words in the usual soft monotone English. "And the hostages...why have you housed them in our secret laboratories?"

Wiggins hadn't spoken to Pao in days. Somebody on his crew was feeding the old man, but who? It had to be Lee.

"Just temporary, mate. This place is secret, remember. They'll be far away from here tomorrow."

"How will you do this? The police have the area surrounded."

"It's all arranged. No worries."

The interpreter spoke for several minutes with his master. Wiggins waited quietly, content with his own thoughts. He didn't feel the usual escalation in blood pressure from answering to these men as if he were a naughty child. Not this time. He'd won.

Operation Blood Star was at the very point of success thanks to him. Three shipments were already en route. One had left before dawn, two others between noon and nightfall. All three had passed police checkpoints with no greater scrutiny than having paperwork double-checked. After all, you couldn't hide a hostage in flesh-dissolving liquid. The police were happy to have the dangerous trucks on their way. The remaining shipments would leave on the morrow while hundreds of VIP guests and their families delighted themselves during the pre-grand opening of the Texas Waterland Family Park, including city, county and state officials. What better cover than that? Once receiving verification of the drug's arrival in all target cities, he'd blow the place and everyone in it to kingdom come and vanish.

Then let the Rapture begin.

The conference ended. The interpreter returned his attention to Wiggins. "Master Pao wishes to commend your efforts on this project. It appears that Operation Blood Star will be a success—"

The ground shook!

Then shook a second time!

Dust fell from the ceiling.

What the hell?

Wiggins grabbed for his phone. It rang before he dialed the first number. "Report!"

Lee did so. "Two Explosions, near the Wild West train depot."

"Source?"

The answer was not immediate.

"Source!" Wiggins yelled into the phone.

"Billy Ray Jenkins."

Wiggins felt his blood freeze.

Pao stared at him. He met the old man's eyes. A knowing look crossed the chieftain's wrinkled face.

"Tell us," the interpreter demanded.

Wiggins didn't bother. He bolted from Pao's room, jumped on the slimline golf cart, and gunned it toward the command center.

Wiggins redialed Lee. "Where is he?"

"Cameras picked him up at the train station firing two mortar rounds. He's now heading for the central plaza, near the Aqua Blaster wave pool. Where are you?"

"Tunnel C," Wiggins said. "Approximately two hundred yards east of the Wild West train depot. I'm returning to the command center."

"I suggest you go to the wave pool area instead, comrade. We have ten squads. What can one man do against a hundred?

Wiggins ventured a guess. At the very least, Jenkins could cause a critical delay in the timeline. At the worst, the former SEAL could cause enough commotion to draw the wrong kind of attention to the park from all of the police in the area. Things could get complicated. He made a decision. Lee was right. Stay in the field to conduct the battle. He preferred to lead from the front anyway.

"Lee, organize Gallina's men. And start the fireworks display. We need all the cover we can get against prying eyes and ears."

"This puts all our men in action. Jenkins could just be drawing us out."

"Then he gets his wish. We need to hit hard and end this thing now."

Wiggins turned the cart and headed for the action.

Two minutes later, the fireworks show began.

81

Lam made his way from the water treatment plant toward the security building. Jenkins' little deception over the radio must've worked. He didn't know the security role of the dead guard, so he walked as if on patrol, the H&K MP7 across his chest, safety off, finger on the trigger.

Suddenly everything changed.

Two thunderous explosions ripped the night apart. The dead guard's radio erupted with chatter. Men materialized from everywhere, doors and hatchways, the surrounding woods, and from the security building, just as Jenkins said would happen. He was nearly run over from behind by the very same dune buggy-looking thing Jenkins liked so well. The vehicle slid to a halt on the wet pavement at the security building door. A stocky man dressed in game warden clothes, and a black uniformed guard loaded down with weapons, ran from the building and jumped into the ATV. The guard took position on the rear platform. The stocky man claimed the passenger seat behind the hood-mounted machine gun. All three were Asian, Lam noticed. He recognized the guy in the zookeeper duds as Wiggins' assistant. The ATV sped off in the direction of the explosions.

A new voice came over the radio overriding all others. Korean words shouted, their meaning clear. Order was restored. It was a voice Lam heard only days before droning on about insurance—Joseph Wiggins.

The bastard had Katie!

Jenkins had radioed to be ready. The diversion worked, confusion began its intended reign. Wiggins' men poured from the command center. Here was his chance to get his daughter back.

Lam bolted to the security building, through the exterior doors, and then the double doors leading to the hallway he'd seen on Dodd's computer, the one with the trick floor.

He stopped. "I'm in."

Dodd's voice responded in the earbud. "Do exactly as I say."

Working from video hacked only moments earlier, Dodd guided Lam through the proper sequence of tiles along the floor.

Lam made it to the elevator. "Now what?"

"Hold tight, agent, I'm working on the remaining protocols."

"How long will that take?"

"No telling. Good news is that Palm and retina signatures are stored on computers. Bad news is that the information is encrypted."

Lam checked his watch. Forty-three minutes remained for rescuing the hostages and getting out again. He heard voices coming from the far end of the hall, beyond the double doors.

"Admiral…people coming." Lam put his back to the wall, pulled the black ball cap down low over his eyes, lifted the MP7, and posed as a sentry ready to challenge all comers.

"I have a live feed. I'll do what I can," Dodd said.

Four bodies turned the corner and stopped.

A small Korean man in a white lab coat continued forward, performing the hopscotch pattern along the tiles.

Lam snapped to attention. The technician paid him no mind, instead concentrating on security protocols. He managed a peek at the three others awaiting an all-clear at the end of the hall.

The signal was given.

The group hustled forward. It took all Lam's self-control to keep his face from registering shock. Another guard outfitted the same as him marched behind Dixon and Bell. The shock was seeing Bell led at gunpoint. If there was to be trouble, if his little ruse was to end, now would be that time. Surely, the guards knew each other.

Dodd's whispered voice said, "Steady...they're in a rush."

Lam remained at attention, weapon at the ready. He curled a finger around the trigger.

"Steady..." Dodd repeated.

The group arrived.

Fortunately, the guard took the position opposite Lam at the elevator, flanking the cops in the middle. The technician stood directly in front of the doors. Bell stood closest to Lam.

From the corner of his eye, Lam caught Bell scrutinizing him.

"Don't get any ideas, kid," Dixon said. "Or I'll put a bullet in you. Cooperate and you could walk out of here a very rich man."

So Dixon was the spy. Jenkins had said he suspected Wiggins getting help from the inside. Lam despised dirty cops.

Bell kept cool, eyes searching for opportunity. Those eyes came to rest on him again, but only for a moment, then quickly turned away.

Bell said to Dixon, "What would I want with dirty money?"

Dixon laughed. "Money is money, kid. It makes no difference."

"Well it does to me, you piece of shit!"

Bell's reward was a rap on the head from Dixon's pistol.

All eyes turned to Dixon—but away from Lam. At the same time, the elevator arrived and the group boarded, the guard going in last.

The elevator was his ride down. There was no time to discover another route. It was now or never. Lam made his move. As the doors drew shut, he extended the gun barrel, activating the safety mechanism. The doors reopened. The guard turned around just in time to witness his own death. Lam pulled the trigger on the silenced weapon. Bell reacted instantly, chopping down on Dixon's gun. Lam then slammed the deputy sheriff in the forehead with the butt of the MP-7. Dixon collapsed beside the dead guard. The technician backed against the wall, eyes wide and hands in the air.

Bell retrieved Dixon's pistol and placed it against the temple of the frightened technician. "I thought that was you."

"What gave me away?"

"Your five o'clock shadow."

Lam rubbed his chin. Sure enough, thick stubble had formed in the fifteen hours since shaving in Ulrich's precinct restroom. It was a miracle the guard hadn't reacted. Kudos to Bell for providing another distraction.

"I'm impressed, Deputy."

"Don't be. I expected to meet you or Jenkins at some point."

"Why are you here, anyway?"

"That little diversion you ordered got out of hand. I duped a reporter into thinking Billy Ray and Rebecca were in the park."

"He is—I mean—they are."

"Yes, but only Ballerd would believe such a story."

"Where's the reporter now?"

"I suspect he and his cameraman are locked up with the others." Bell changed his tone. "Whatever's going on here, it's important enough that Wiggins is willing to kill for it."

"There's no time to fill you in. Just know you're on the mark. Now let's find those hostages and get the hell out of here, before Wiggins gets his wish."

The elevator had two buttons, up and down. Lam chose down.

* * *

Billy Ray caught the exchange between Lam and Dodd, then minutes later between Lam and Bell. Good, Lam was inside. He had no idea why Bell was there, nor could he afford to give the matter further consideration. He was a little busy at the moment bolting about the park, setting explosive charges, dodging men with guns, and doing so beneath a spectacular fireworks display. The colorful starbursts provided a surreal backdrop to the mayhem on the ground.

Dodd's "wack-a-mole" strategy was working perfectly. They were using the enemy's own technology against them. He imagined Wiggins getting reports regarding the intruder's whereabouts and radioing the guards to intercept, only to come up empty.

The legendary Chinese military strategist, Sun Tzu, came to mind. Sun Tzu taught that all warfare was based on deception, and how pretending inferiority in order to encourage the enemy's arrogance was the "art of war." On the matter of deception, he and Dodd held trump. However, Wiggins was bound to catch on soon. Billy Ray's strategy actually counted on that fact.

Regarding Sun Tzu's second point, his inferiority hardly needed pretending. He was shooting at a hundred highly-trained soldiers with a damn potato gun!

Wiggins owned every tactical advantage—home turf, hardened facilities, technology, and dozens of well-armed men. In spite of all that, Wiggins possessed one glaring weakness—arrogance.

Billy Ray prayed Sun Tzu's *Art of War* still held true twenty-five centuries later, that the keys to survival and victory in battle remained the same.

He was about to implement the second phase of his plan—to encourage Wiggins' belief in his own superiority.

He would feed it.

He would exploit it.

Then he would destroy it!

82

Jenkins wasn't there. The monitors indicated he was or had been. Was there truth to Pao's warning? Was Jenkins a phantom? Wiggins laughed at the idea. He'd trained with the Soviet Union's *Spetsnaz.* They were the real phantoms. Jenkins was just a hick with military training. SEALs…? No worries, Jenkins was just one man.

Wiggins spoke into his radio. "All snipers. Report."

"One…nothing."

"Two…nothing, comrade."

"Three…clear."

"Four…nothing."

"Five…nothing."

"Wait," Four said.

"What is it, Four?"

"Something earlier, but not in the park. A laser dot appeared in my scope an hour ago. It was pointed directly at me."

"Why didn't you report the matter?"

"The laser came from two miles away, far beyond sniper range. I assumed children playing with a laser pointer."

"All snipers, your orders are to locate Jenkins and kill him."

A new voice came on the radio. It sent chills down Wiggins' spine.

"I'm coming for you."

"Who is this? Who's on the line?" Wiggins demanded.

"You know who I am. I'm coming for you."

"You're a ballsy chap, Jenkins—" The radio went dead.

* * *

The charges were set. The next wave of explosions would begin and the ground battle shift to full fury. Billy Ray had drawn Wiggins and his men away from the security building. He hoped Lam got the hostages topside soon because the mayhem about to commence was meant to clear a path to freedom for Rebecca and the kids.

Time was running out. Billy Ray lost crucial minutes confronting a new problem. Gallina's men were joining the battle. He'd already downed two cartel thugs. They'd been easy pickings, neither one having military-grade weapons. The first had possessed only a small-caliber revolver. The second *desperado* brandished a knife in one hand a broken tequila bottle in the other and fought dripping wet in a bathing suit.

He'd dropped both in mere seconds. But seconds became minutes. What Gallina's men lacked in equipment, they made up for in numbers. There were dozens more throughout the park who'd begin searching for him as word spread. He couldn't fight them all. Time was the precious commodity he was buying for Lam. Time before Wiggins discovered the deception. Time before Dodd's elimination team laid waste to the park.

He took a moment to check in. "Dolittle, how things looking?"

"Eyeballing one ATV and plus-twenty banditos closing on your six. Suggest you move to position Echo."

"Roger that," Billy Ray confirmed the directive and then gave Lam a bump. "Hey pardner, how are things in *Glocca Morra?*"

Lam's voice came back low and breathy. "Just peachy. I think we're getting close to the *pot o' gold.*"

"We...? You and Bell?"

"Yup. The guy can't keep his nose out of trouble. But I'm glad to have him." More rustling sound. Then Lam said, "I found your spy."

"Let me guess. Dixon?"

"The one and only, but he's a little out of it at the moment."

"Okay. Go get the hostages."

"About to leave the elevator now."

"Beware…life topside is about to go boom. We have thirty minutes to finish this. Radio me when you have the hostages. And if I go Spartan on you, run like hell and don't look back." He didn't tell Lam the rest of his plan, neither did he doubt for one second that Lam would refuse escape and fight to the death for his daughter. In all reality, there'd be no getting away from this battle. They were in it to the end and both knew it.

"Watch your six, Wolverine," Lam said.

Billy Ray spoke to Dodd. "Focus everything on helping Lam."

"What about you?"

"Don't worry about me. Just help Lam get the hostages out. After that, I don't care what you and your men do."

Much went unsaid. Dodd could read his meaning, that this could be the final battle for call sign *Wolverine.* With the time remaining, his every effort would be aimed at draining the enemy's morale and resources while baiting Wiggins with the sure prize of victory—the final gambit that others may live.

Explosions rocked the ground behind him.

Fireworks burst in the sky above him.

Men gathered ahead bent on killing him.

83

Lam cuffed the technician's hands and stuck a gun in his back. Bell readied his weapon. The elevator door opened. To their surprise, the way ahead lay vacant. Jenkins had drawn the bad guys out into the park. And Dodd's magic of looping false data onto the monitors had done the trick. For the moment, they met no resistance.

He pushed the technician forward. "Take us to the hostages!"

"What hostages?" the technician asked with a shaky voice.

Lam pressed the gun harder into the tech's shoulder blades.

"Wait—"

Lam clenched his teeth. "The children, the lady, where are they?"

"Master Wiggins will kill me."

Lam relocated the gun to the man's head.

"Beyond the labs, in the storage rooms," The tech said hastily.

"Lead the way."

There was no telling how long Jenkins could keep Wiggins busy. It was also likely Dodd's monitor trick wouldn't last much longer, especially at the hub of the enemy's command center. Discovery could come any moment. It turned out they didn't have long to wait.

Another technician in white lab coat and looking down at a clipboard hurried around the corner. They nearly collided. The man looked up just in time to see the butt of an MP7 collide with his forehead. Bell dragged the body back into the elevator where he stripped the white coat and hat. He put them on, grabbed up the clipboard, and rejoined Lam.

A guard and a technician...the disguises weren't much, but would suffice at first glance. A moment's hesitation was all Lam needed.

It was now-or-never time.

He pushed the technician forward. Bell brought up the rear. They passed a room filled with monitors and a dozen men concentrating on displays. The next room was a type Lam had stood in before, a war room. Men focused on monitors there, too, and a large table overlaid with maps occupied center floor. Standing with his back to the door, staring down at maps and speaking on a cell phone was a short white-haired man. He was ordering somebody on the other line to divert a shipment to Michigan.

Lam knew exactly who the man was and that the shipment would be drugs. That matter would have to wait. Lam hoped to get a second chance with Angel Gallina.

Fortunately, nobody paid them attention, absorbed instead with the havoc taking place aboveground. They turned into a cavernous room. Lam halted and reined in the prisoner. Two men dressed in black outfits receded into the far reaches of the room and vanished.

He put a hand over the tech's mouth. "You want to live?"

The man nodded up and down.

"You make one sound and you're a dead man. You got that?"

More nodding.

Lam turned to Bell. "Take point. I'll put this guy between us."

Bell led the way, gun held beneath the clipboard. The room was the length of a football field and nearly half as wide. Massive steel vats lined the length of one side, doors lined the other.

"Looks like a brewery," Bell whispered.

The tech stopped in front of the third door. It was secured with a slide bolt. Lam gave the order. Bell retracted the bolt and pushed the door open.

A dog barked.

"Daddy!" Katie called out.

Lam shut the door and motioned for quiet. He ordered the tech to sit. Katie's friend held the dog. Bell guarded the door.

"Admiral, I found my daughter!"

"Situation?"

"They're okay!"

"And the sheriff's daughter?" asked Dodd.

Lam hesitated. "No sign of her."

"The monitors give no indication you've been discovered. I suggest you get out while you can. Are both dogs with you?"

"No, just one."

"Which one?" asked Dodd.

"How should I know?"

"Try their names, Pedro and Lola."

Lam turned to the dog. "Pedro...here boy." No response. He tried Lola. The dog wagged her tail.

"It's Lola."

"Good. Notice the collar, there's a rectangular switch near the buckle. It looks like a diamond rhinestone. Slide it sideways."

Lam reached for the dog. Lola growled at the black uniform.

Smart dog.

He asked Katie's friend, "What's your name, honey?"

"Julie." She squeezed Lola ever tighter.

"I'm Katie's dad. I need your help. Please reach under Lola's chin and find her collar."

Julie did so.

"Feel for a button near the buckle. Slide it as far as it'll go."

Dodd's voice came back. "Okay, Lola's back online. Now listen, Agent Lam, you have a choice. Lola has a few minutes of power left on her collar. I suggest you use it to get those children to safety. Leave now. Lola and I will guide you."

Lam felt his stomach turn. He wanted nothing more than to take his daughter and Julie and get out of there. But that would mean abandoning the other hostage and Jenkins.

"You still there, Lam?"

"Yes. Wait one...." Lam made his decision. He turned to Bell. "I need you to get these kids to safety."

"But—"

"I know...Rebecca and Jenkins. I'm going after them. We don't have time to discuss it. I have the military background, you don't." Lam removed his earbud and mic and handed them to Bell. Then he pointed to Lola and said, "The dog and the voice on the other end of that earbud will lead you out. Get going. Save my little girls."

Katie understood and clung to her father. Lam hugged her tightly. "Daddy will join you in a few minutes. There's a nice lady I need to rescue from these bad men. Now be brave and go with Mr. Bell. He'll keep you safe. Don't make a sound, not even in the elevator. There are bodies inside and lots of blood. Just close your eyes and think happy thoughts."

The girls indicated they would. Lam hugged them both and then shook Bell's hand. "See you soon."

He opened the door. The coast was clear. Bell and the girls left in the direction of the elevator with Lola leading the way. He hoped the route to freedom through the elevator was still open. Thankfully, no elaborate security measures were required for leaving the subterranean level.

Lam turned back into the room and shut the door. He needed information from the technician.

He was prepared to beat it out of the man.

84

A shot rang out. Billy Ray dropped behind a concrete trash container. Then another shot. This time a bullet chipped the concrete near his head. He drew a mirror from his pocket, extended the wand, and peaked around the corner. He spotted a cartel member and his date dashing up the steps of a waterslide. The woman had a cell phone pressed to her ear as she ran behind her man. She had made her choice. No matter how unfortunate, she was a combatant now. He couldn't let her call go through or a hundred more cartel *pistoleros* would come rushing in to trap him.

It was a tricky shot and he was out of practice, but a shot he'd made countless times before, a target moving away and ascending. Billy Ray took a knee, sighted on the target, and aimed center mass. He squeezed the trigger.

With barely a sound from his suppressed MK23, a .45-caliber round left the gun barrel traveling 850 feet per second and slammed into the woman. She fell on her face and tumbled down the stairs.

Call interrupted.

Her date looked back for only a moment before resuming his scramble to the top of the waterslide. Billy Ray took off after the man. Upon reaching the third story landing, he stopped and looked upwards. The cartel man was aiming a pistol at him. He jumped back just as a bullet pinged off the metal hand rail.

He was about to return fire when it dawned on him what the guy was up to. The waterslide dove nearly vertical for several stories before banking hard right and disappearing into the night. The man was about to escape. Noise of a liquid torrent resonated through the fiberglass waterslide. Then came a new sound, a body plunging down the tube.

Billy Ray reached over his shoulder and drew a razor-sharp machete from its scabbard. With a mighty thrust, he jammed the blade through the belly of the slide. A moment later, the machete shivered violently. A haunting scream echoed inside the tube, then only silence but for the sound of rushing water. He yanked down on the machete and replaced it in the scabbard, its cold steel cleansed by the rushing waters. Somewhere in the park, the tube spit pieces of a human being into a receiving pool.

His next move saved his life. Hot lead from a sniper bullet passed through his shirt collar, nicking the flesh on his neck. Water sprang from a hole in the belly of the slide next to him.

When facing the specter of being sniped, and assuming you weren't already dead, immediate clues to the source of the silent killer were often unobtainable. Billy Ray, however, had two. The pass through his shirt collar gave indication of one angle and the hole in the tube provided another. He ducked out of the sightline of the sniper and called Egolf.

"Got him," Egolf announced. "Caught the muzzle flash. Mind if I bag a turkey?"

"It's open season, my friend. Go for it," Billy Ray said.

Dodd cut in. "Take them all out, Egolf."

Solid green beams of light pulsed across the night sky, darting amidst the twisting, curling starbursts of fireworks. The contrast was spectacular. Perfect beams of light stabbed through all that blocked its way.

Glorious. Relentless. Alien.

"Done," Egolf reported.

A new voice came online. "Somebody's shooting at us. I caught a bullet in the shoulder. I'm bleeding out!"

"Bell? Where's Lam?" Billy Ray demanded.

"Underground. He sent me out with the kids."

Billy Ray had heard part of the exchange with Dodd and Lola, but assumed the group had stuck together.

"Is Rebecca with you?"

"No. Lam stayed behind to find her."

"Where are you now?"

"Hold—" Bell went off-mic.

Billy Ray readied to dash to Bell's rescue. He heaved the equipment bag onto his shoulder, lighter now by several dozen pounds. Good for hauling, bad for warfighting. It meant he was low on bombs and bullets. The TATP tennis balls were gone, though somewhat to his relief. The ammonal charges he'd fashioned from ammonium nitrate and aluminum powder were attached to several major waterslide attractions and about to make the Mother of Satan look like a Girl Scout. Half of the ammo remained for Dodd's SOCOM pistol and two 40-round magazines for the H&K MP7 he'd confiscated from a dead Korean guard. He still had the three explosive charges from the water plant, which he'd hoped to return to their rightful owner. And on his person he carried his trusty dive knife, the machete from Gus' store, and two grenades from Dodd's cache—one percussion, one frag. Lastly, there was the laser gun he hoped contained enough juice for one more blast. And that was the extent of his supplies. If more were needed, he'd just have to live off the land and rob the dead.

Bell came back online. "The sign says, 'Hole in the Wall.' We're on the south end...next to a dumpster station."

"I know where that is. Hold tight, Larry, I'm coming."

Billy Ray checked in with Egolf. "Anything on Bell's shooter?"

"Nothing. I terminated four snipers. Must've missed one."

"Dolittle?"

"Just checked camera monitors...shooter's somewhere east of Bell."

Billy Ray hailed Bell. "Hang on, Larry. Jam something in that wound to slow the bleeding."

"Hurry…!" Bell's voice had weakened.

Billy Ray had seen his share of combat wounds, including his own. Blood loss and shock became the enemy.

"Dolittle, let the camera monitors show my true position."

"You sure?"

"Yes. I don't want Wiggins catching on to our camera trick just yet. Plus, I want him to think he's winning."

"Okay. Watch your ass, Wolverine."

Billy Ray bolted from cover.

* * *

"Got him!" Lee shouted over the radio.

"Where?"

"The main pedestrian path, nearing the wave pool. Wait one. I'm getting another report—"

Wiggins never doubted. It was but a matter of time. Jenkins had been a wily opponent, a rogue warrior, but a fool nonetheless, risking all for a girl—making Jenkins the worst kind of fool.

Lee's voice returned. "Comrade, sniper Five reports shooting a man fleeing with two children and a dog. He says the group is pinned down at the Hole in the Wall."

"Is the man dead?"

"Wounded only. Sniper Five says he might be one of ours."

"How so?"

"He's dressed in a lab coat." Lee relayed the details.

"Can the man be identified from the video monitors?"

"Negative. His hat is pulled too low. The face recognition software requires more data."

Wiggins felt a chill. Was Jenkins really a lone wolf or did he have a helper on the inside? It could be anyone—Gallina, Dixon, Pao, even Lee. Gallina was most unlikely, the man just took what he wanted. Dixon was a dumb ox with no access to the lower levels. Pao didn't have the assets. Lee...? His second-in-command had defied him previously, and was probably under orders to spy on him—the Dear Leader was not a trusting man. Three of his twelve lieutenants, men he trusted most of all, were no longer responding to calls. One body had already been discovered, stripped of the equipment by Jenkins. Another had been the guard he'd sent to inspect the water plant after the lightning anomaly. After radioing an all-clear, the guard hadn't been heard from since. A search turned up nothing. The last of the three posed the most troubling possibility. He'd been tasked with taking two more hostages to the underground cells and had yet to report in. Could the command center have been infiltrated while he chased a rabbit in the park? Might there be a coup in the making?

Wiggins began to order a red alert and then changed his mind. He decided to make a quiet entry at the command center, instead. He needed to know what was happening.

"Lee, issue kill orders. If it moves, it dies."

"And Gallina's men?"

"Coordinate if possible, otherwise shoot them too. Dispatch two men to retrieve those hostages. Then you take two others and go after Jenkins. I'm going to check on something."

* * *

Bell's plea echoed in Billy Ray's mind. Speed required advancing along paved pathways, stealth demanded otherwise. Deploying to Bell's position posed a dilemma. The open pathways would expose him to Gallina's hoard and Wiggins' guards, plus put him in the crosshairs of Bell's mystery sniper. Maintaining stealth would take time...time that Bell and the children didn't have...time neither he nor Lam could afford before the arrival of Dodd's elimination team.

Time became the foe.

Billy Ray chose speed.

It would be the devil's gauntlet.

85

They were coming for him now. Word of the battle had reached Gallina's men. Billy Ray could hear shouts in all directions. They appeared like locusts, suddenly everywhere. Men rode down from waterslides or cut their meals short at the various eateries. A dozen men spilled onto the causeway from the Last Stand Saloon and gathered next to a scale model of the Alamo. Others emerged from underground tunnels. No more half-naked partiers wielding whiskey bottles. These were angry men with guns, furious over the deaths of their *amigos,* each hot lead parabellum meant for him.

Billy Ray drew his first opposition at the arched bridge crossing the Lazy River. A group of eight cartel members gathered to confer and receive assignments. Some had pistols drawn. Others, just then learning of the situation, began digging for weapons. A man in the center of the gathering held a phone to his ear, receiving instructions.

He caught a break falling upon the men mainly ignorant of the battle around them. He charged straight ahead, pulling the frag grenade and yanking the pin with his teeth. He tossed it into the gathering and readied his pistol. The grenade tore through the group. Bodies flew in all directions. Flesh and blood and bits of flaming cloth landed in the Lazy River, turning the waters red. He killed two of the group with his pistol without breaking stride.

“Bad news, Wolverine,” Dodd's voice broke through the noise of battle. “Just picked up talk from your boy, Wiggins. He's heading back to his HQ.”

“Oh no, Lam and Rebecca!” he said through huffing and puffing and shooting.

Bad guys were everywhere. He sped forward, ignoring all thoughts of peril, concentrating instead on the battle and the goal of reaching Bell. He felt a bullet tear through his shirtsleeve. A dozen rounds chipped the pavement around him. He zigged and zagged to avoid offering an easy target. The rounds came from overhead, atop the Hole in the Wall waterslide. The shooters were cartel members. Wiggins' men couldn't be too far behind. It was evident the two groups hadn't yet coordinated their attacks, otherwise the cartel guys could just turn and fire down on Bell.

His role now was to draw fire from the Mexicans and the sniper. He was on the opposite side of Bell. He took a moment to catch his breath and then dashed from behind a ticket booth.

Two things happened simultaneously. A cartel member jumped into Billy Ray's path and the man's chest exploded. He dove for cover, narrowly avoiding another sniper round.

The bullet had torn away a chunk of corner trim from the ticket booth, right where he would've been. But there it was. The clue he needed to determine the remaining sniper's position. He used the telescoping mirror to peak around the corner. In its reflection, he saw the position of the downed Mexican, the placement of the fatal wound, and beyond toward the horizon. Park lights offered help, but only to the edge of the forest. The shooter was in the trees.

He estimated the distance to the tree line, noted his position when the bullet impacted the cartel man, even the placement of the kill shot. Then he calculated the approximate angle of the bullet and made a guess.

"Egolf, you there?"

"Yes, but you better hurry. This bird's about to fly."

"Scan the tree line a half click from my present position."

Dodd provided Egolf with the coordinates, determined using the dog collar and triangulating with the other data points.

A very long minute later, Egolf was back. "Got him."

A sustained burst of green laser light punctured the night. Through the reflection in the telescoping mirror, Billy Ray watched a hundred-foot section of forest instantly ignite as the beam moved across the treetops and came stationary on one point. Egolf didn't have a clean shot for a single pulse. He'd been forced to cut through to the target.

There was only one way to know if Egolf bagged his turkey. Billy Ray sprinted from his position. No sniper bullet awaited him, but a hail of lead rained down from above. Two of the enemy bullets found flesh. Billy Ray made it to the first landing of the imposing waterslide and ducked beneath.

Miracles came in bunches. One bullet had passed clean through his side. He doused a wad of soft cotton with disinfectant and jammed it into the hole. It hurt like hell, but the wound posed no immediate problem. The other shot actually hit him square in the heart, but the small caliber round had imbedded itself in the Bible he kept in the vest pouch.

Only in the movies!

The cartel members were five stories above. Judging by the bullets and trajectories, there had to be at least four shooters. An idea came to mind. "Egolf, one more time."

"Sorry, Wolverine, all packed up."

"Well unpack! I need one more shot."

There was silence.

Dodd's voice finally came on. "Do it, Egolf."

He gave a quick rundown of his plan as Egolf reassembled the blaster. Then took two of the explosive devices confiscated from Wiggins' treatment plant booby traps and combined both charges. He attached the last electronic triggering device to the bomb and gave Egolf the go-ahead.

"Wolverine, I can't guarantee how much power is left after taking out that last sniper."

"No matter, you just need to scare these guys."

"I think I can manage that."

For the final time, three rapid pulses of green laser beams shot across the Texas Waterland skyline. The first pulse burned a hole right under one of the cartel men—through his feet, the concrete, and steel. The man dropped away, his screams trailing him to the ground. The second and third pulses evaporated another large chunk of the platform. The three remaining killers jumped into a rubber raft and disappeared down the Hole in the Wall. Bad move. Billy Ray was waiting for them.

"Plug your ears, Bell!"

Billy Ray counted three and depressed the button on the electronic key fob he'd programmed to match the receiver on the bomb. A mighty blast ensued. In the span of a microsecond, the pressure wave from the massive explosion channeled upwards, getting squeezed and intensified as it went. Suddenly, three men in a rubber raft shot out the top of the slide hundreds of feet into the air. The men were killed instantly, so never knew their boat ride became part of the night's firework display.

Rub-a-dub-dub, bloodsuckers!

The blast was larger than expected. A third of the waterslide was gone and the rest beginning to lean. Billy Ray keyed his mic. "Bell, you okay?"

"What was that? Lucky we're behind these dumpsters."

It was time to move. But first, Billy Ray had one more wildcard in the deck. If he and the others had done their jobs creating asymmetry, then it was time to spook the enemy.

"Dolittle, flash my face on all monitors and trip all sensors."

"Wiggins will know you have helpers."

"I want him to. I want these bastards to feel surrounded."

"*Savoir-Faire* is everywhere!" Egolf joked for all to hear.

Billy Ray appreciated Egolf's message for what it was. A warrior had to stay loose or stress in battle took its toll. The words were meant for Bell, like a cavalry charge.

He sprinted to Bell and the girls and was never so relieved to see three smiling faces!

86

Two heavily armed soldiers in black uniforms made ready to surface from beneath the Hole in the Wall waterslide and recapture the fleeing hostages. Before they could act, a monstrous explosion collapsed the tunnel, pulverizing them, burying their bodies forever.

A hundred yards away and closing on Jenkins, Lee and two soldiers were knocked to the ground by the shockwave. The tunnel went black. Destruction radiated outward for hundreds of yards from the blast epicenter. Lee gathered his senses.

"Report!" his strained voice demanded of his two men.

He was met only with silence. He swore inwardly. The battle to stop Jenkins had gotten out of hand. How could one man do so much damage against an entire platoon of elite soldiers and advanced technology, not to mention Gallina's bandits running wild throughout the park?

The choice became abundantly clear—Kill Jenkins or suffer the total loss of Operation Blood Star...glory for the Dear Leader and riches for the homeland up in flames, and all because of Wiggins. The *white devil* had been too sure, too confident. Jenkins should've been eliminated weeks ago. Wiggins' arrogance had only led Operation Blood Star to the brink of destruction.

Two seconds after the Hole in the Wall became a giant water cannon, the ground shook and the polished pavement in the tunnel buckled and cracked. Wiggins swerved the electric cart side to side to miss broken concrete and falling debris. He jammed on the brakes. It was as if East Texas had just been struck by an earthquake.

He hit the receiver button on his radio. "What happened?"

"Explosion… tunnel… collapse…" Lee's radio cut in and out. "Guards dead… more unconscious."

Wiggins shouted into the phone. "Get back in the fight!"

The lead technician at the command center came on next. "Comrade, Jenkins is on the move."

"Where?"

"Everywhere!" the technician reported hysterically. "All park monitors are showing the American. Every sensor is going off—infrared, motion, optical, acoustic—all of them!"

"Calm down!" Wiggins had to get control, and fast. "He's getting help. Somebody has tapped into our system. Override it."

Another voice broke in, this time from his best jungle fighter guarding the park's wooded perimeter. "Comrade Wiggins—"

"Report." Wiggins forced a display of calm.

"I observed green lights in the sky moments ago."

"We're having a firework show."

"Not fireworks. I rode to sniper One's position and found his body on the ground at the base of his tree blind."

"Don't tell me he fell and broke his neck." Wiggins didn't care for anymore bad luck.

"No, comrade. There's a hole in his chest the size of my fist. It goes clean through his body—Kevlar, flesh, bone, even the tree...but no blood."

"Say again."

"There's no blood, just the smell of cooking flesh."

Lasers!

Wiggins' sense of superiority vanished. How could that be? Nobody had such weapons—nobody! And certainly not a local punk like Jenkins!

Lee's voice cut in. "Snipers down! Every one of them, dead!"

Wiggins couldn't believe his ears. "Kill Jenkins!" he shouted into his phone. "Do it now!"

He gunned the cart toward the command center. His only hope being that it wasn't too late.

* * *

It didn't take long. The technician valued his life more than he feared his boss. Driving home the point was Lam's outfit—the black uniform of Wiggins' special guards. The tech surmised that if Wiggins was to be feared then all the more somebody able to overpower a guard and infiltrate their inner sanctum. Lam bound and gagged the man and knocked him unconscious. He'd acquired Rebecca's location. He'd also learned what was taking place beneath the Texas Waterland Family Park. And it frightened him to his core!

He found Rebecca near the end of the cavernous room, beyond the last of the giant vats of Rapture. He opened the door and was met with a growl. Far worse was the sickening sight of Rebecca lying on the cold pavement, head resting in a pool of blood—but alive! As indicated by the slow rise and fall of her chest. Pedro stood beside her, licking her face. Upon his entry, Pedro reacted instantly. The dog backed up to Rebecca, assumed a defiant stance, prickled his fur, and growled. Lam dared not approach, lest Pedro attack. Harming the dog was out of the question.

He called out instead. "Rebecca...."

No response.

Wiggins would surely return soon. Furthermore, their allotted time with Dodd was nearly up. Lam hoped Jenkins was keeping the enemy busy. If not, time would no longer matter.

He thought to go find water to splash on Rebecca. He had to awaken her, and soon. Before he managed a step, the ground shook violently. The overhead light swayed, dust fell like snow.

A groaning sound came from behind him. He turned to see Rebecca stirring from unconsciousness. Her eyes opened and in a hoarse voice she said, "Johnny?"

Lam moved quickly. He assisted Rebecca to a sitting position while she spoke to Pedro. The dog growled, but didn't attack. He cut the plastic ties from her wrists and ankles, then rubbed her shoulders to get circulation back. They had to make their exodus, now. The explosion was probably Jenkins' handiwork. He'd bought them an advantage, if only for a moment.

"Can you walk?"

"I think so."

Rebecca stood with Lam's help. Dried blood caked in her hair and on her face, except where Pedro had licked it clean. A nasty bruise covered her cheek, her nose appeared broken, and her feet were bare.

She saw Lam inspecting her. "It looks worse than it is."

He wasn't so sure, but admired her courage. "Who did this?"

"Wiggins."

Lam drew his pistol, mostly to prepare for the journey ahead, but in part out of rage.

Rebecca viewed her surroundings. A worried look crossed her face. "Billy Ray?"

"He's alive, at least I think so. He just sent a message."

"Message?"

"Yeah, one big enough to register on the Richter scale." Lam helped Rebecca test her legs. "Let's get outa' here."

They left Rebecca's cell with Pedro in the lead. Lam was flying blind without communications. For lack of a better alternative, they headed back toward the elevator. He unsafed his gun. If the bodies in the elevator hadn't yet been discovered, they would be soon. They came to the door where he'd stashed the unconscious technician.

"Hold up. Let's do something about those feet." Lam went and stripped the shoes off the unconscious technician. "Here, try these."

The shoes fit.

Rebecca smiled. "You sure know how to please a lady."

They resumed toward the elevator. Pedro stopped in front of the very next room, identical to the one Rebecca had been in.

"What is it boy?" Lam whispered.

Then he heard it, muffled voices calling from inside. Lam opened the door. Two men sat back to back, hands tied and mouths gagged.

"The news reporter...what's he doing here?" Rebecca said through swollen lips.

"Let's find out."

Lam closed the door just as voices erupted from the direction of the elevator. He hoped Dodd still controlled the video feeds, but had no way of knowing. They had to move fast before their cover was blown. He made a decision he hoped wouldn't spell curtains for them all. He handed Rebecca the pistol taken from Dixon, then only loosened the bonds on the two captives.

"Hey!" the skinny reporter protested.

"Listen up," Lam said. "You two keep your hands behind your back. Keep looking like hostages. Rebecca, you stand there." Lam indicated a position beneath the surveillance camera. "All of you keep your mouths shut. This room is wired for sound. I think my group is about to lose control of the monitors, if we haven't already."

"Why? You leaving us or something?" the reporter asked.

"Briefly. I have to find another way out."

"You could shoot your way out," the reporter argued.

"Hold that thought. I assure you, Wiggins has no intention of letting any of us leave here alive." Lam watched the skinny reporter swallow hard. "If I'm not back in five minutes, consider me dead."

Three pairs of eyes went wide.

Lam faced Rebecca. "I'll knock once, then twice. You repeat the pattern. Anything other than that, shoot and run like hell!"

He let himself out and ran to the far end of the cavernous room. The men he'd seen walking away earlier had not returned. He realized now they hadn't been guards dressed in black uniforms, but rather men in dark business suits. So there had to be another way out through the underground tunnels.

Jenkins had said that the elevator shaft and entire underground facility was mined. He'd also said he believed the bombs were meant as the parting deed of a maniac, should enemy forces breach the defenses.

Lam passed by a dozen tanks holding thousands of gallons of Wiggins' poison. He was no stranger to the extreme hazards of meth lab explosions. But this would be many magnitudes worse. This witch's brew was meth on steroids laced with killer venom. Then there was the sheer volume. If Rapture was atomized by an explosion and spread on the wind, the results would be devastating for man and beast. Undoubtedly, Wiggins intended to win at all costs. He returned after four minutes, knocked once, then twice, and got the same.

"I think I found a way. Let's go."

The reporter hesitated. "But—"

Lam cut him off. "You want to live...do what I say. I'll take point. Rebecca, take rear. You two stick right on my ass and do what I say. Worry about Pulitzers and Emmys later."

The reporter found himself at the mention of the prestigious awards. Lam ignored Ballerd and turned toward the door. He shifted the backpack for balance and holstered his pistol in favor of the captured MP7 machine gun. If they were cornered he'd need all the lead he could throw at the enemy. He and Rebecca checked their ammo. Then he opened the door a crack. Loud voices echoed from the command center. Something was happening. He didn't care to wait and find out what.

"Let's go."

Out the door they went.

Pedro ran ahead. The others followed.

87

Two dozen explosions, numerous fires, and scattered corpses of cartel members littering the park had its desired effect—mass confusion. Even the heavy rain and firework display added to the distraction. The tide of battle had shifted. The enemy now had to respond to him. Billy Ray knew his next move, Wiggins did not.

He gambled on the enemy hunkering down after the Hole in the Wall explosion, expecting a secondary blast. He, Bell, and the kids bolted from their hiding place. They made good time. The elimination of Wiggins' sniper teams greatly aided their flight to safety, as did the declining number of combatants.

Bell's wound was gushing again. The young deputy was very near to slipping into shock. Billy Ray held up their escape and took refuge behind the public restrooms. He jammed another wad of cloth into Bell's wound.

"It's now or never, Larry, one final dash. Can you make it?"

Bell took a deep breath and said, "Let's roll!"

"Give me a three-second start to clear interference. Better I draw fire than you. Then all of you, run like the wind."

Three heads bobbed up and down. Lola wagged her tail.

Freedom lay a hundred meters away. An Olympic sprinter could achieve the distance in less than ten seconds. So close and yet so far. Billy Ray checked his guns and peeked around the corner. The coast was clear. He took off. Three seconds later, Bell and the girls bolted from their hiding place, Lola leading the way. Billy Ray adjusted his speed to the others. The gates were in plain sight. They were nearly home-free.

A shot rang out!

A bullet ricocheted on the ground in front of Billy Ray. It came from the guard shack thirty yards to his right, an obstacle he hadn't accounted for. Two more shots came in quick succession, this time aimed at Bell and the children!

He faced the guard shack, depressed the trigger of the MP7 at full auto, and swung the machine gun in a short arc. Half the forty-round extended magazine emptied into the shack. He ceased firing. A body crashed through the sliding window. Twelve exit holes stitched neatly across Surferdude's back.

Bell and the girls caught up with him. Billy Ray put an arm around Bell's waist and they all sprinted the last fifty yards together.

Another shot punctured the night followed by a shout. "Hold your fire!"

"Uncle Chris!" Billy Ray heard Katie yell out up ahead.

He saw women dash forward and gather up the children. Unmarked government cars blocked the gate. A dozen agents in business suits squatted behind car doors, guns drawn. Then men rushed forward to help Bell just as he collapsed. They'd made it.

Billy Ray bent down and retrieved the earbud and mic from the unconscious Bell. "Get him to a hospital, quick!"

The feds carried Bell away. One remained.

"You must be Jenkins," said a man with graying hair and a no-nonsense look. I'm Agent Dreyfus. My friend Lam is helping you."

"Good man. They don't come any better."

Billy Ray viewed his surroundings. In front, the night was ablaze with explosions from colorful pyrotechnics and dozens of fires. Behind, a new commotion joined the night. Hundreds of whirling red and blue police lights and a cacophony of wailing sirens sped toward them. Leading the way was an Upshur County Sheriff vehicle.

Dreyfus said, "I've been briefed on what's happening in the park. Can you give me a report? How's Lam?"

Billy Ray adjusted his equipment and grabbed another deep breath. His body hurt like hell, but his mind was on fire. He ignored the discomfort and reloaded his guns. He looked at Dreyfus. "I don't know how Lam's doing, but I'm going to find out." He dashed back into hell to save his friends.

He would've gone back anyway.

To find Wiggins and tear the man's evil heart out!

88

They were waiting for him. This time their efforts were coordinated. If not for the dog collar, Billy Ray would be dead.

"Dive right!" Dodd yelled through the earbud.

He dove onto the rain-soaked rubberized path and rolled behind a bulkhead just in time to avoid a second volley of lead.

"Dodd, you there?"

"Who do you think just saved you from becoming dog meat?"

"How the hell do I get out of here?"

Dodd studied his computer—maps, photos, GPS, and plotted the position of the shooters. "Bad news—"

"What...get me outa' here!"

"Can't. Not unless your name's Moses."

"What do you mean by that?"

"Look behind you."

A starburst of fireworks lit the area. It became clear what Dodd meant. He was trapped on a peninsula. The Lazy River flowed behind him. Another volley of gunfire, then shouts in Korean. Bullets pinged against the bulkhead from differing angles now. There were more Korean shouts, commands in Spanish, too. Both elements were coordinating at last. The number of rounds and differing trajectories meant proper infantry tactics were being employed, with enemy combatants leapfrogging towards his tiny rampart.

Billy Ray cursed.

He'd run straight into a kill zone!

To remain static was to die. He scampered twenty feet to his right along the low brick wall. The move saved his life as a grenade splashed into the Lazy River and exploded. Shrapnel peppered the portion of wall he'd occupied only seconds ago.

Wiggins' and Gallina's men were getting a bead on him. It had to be now or never, but what? He was trapped!

The geyser formed by the enemy grenade came splashing down into the river. Dodd's words filled his mind, *"...Moses."*

Water!

He pulled out the remaining booby trap mine, the one he'd been saving to drop down Wiggins' shorts. The bastard would just have to receive an alternate ending. He set the mechanical timer he'd crafted from a lawn watering device and attached it to the bomb. Then he said into his mic, "Did you say Moses?"

"Yes, but—"

The speakers in Dodd's van erupted with the sound of a large explosion, then the staccato of gunfire, and finally, silence.

"Wolverine?"

Dodd got no answer.

"Wolverine...! Jenkins...! Answer me, dammit!"

* * *

Lee took matters into his own hands. He hoped it wasn't too late. Either way, it no longer mattered. The honor of the nation was at stake. The Dear Leader had to be enriched and his glory magnified or he had to be protected, it was all the same. Such concerns could never be understood by Westerners. In his country, the cult of personality *was* the nation's soul. One man symbolized the lives of all. To betray the Dear Leader was to betray all.

Reports from the field were coming fast. They were losing control. Operation Blood Star was ruined. Already, seven of his closest comrades lay dead. Dozens of his operational command guards were dead or no longer reporting in. The snipers were dead. All five!

It all happened so subtly, like a woman's caress and then the hammer! The damage to the park was irreparable. Gallina had just ordered his men to prepare for an escape. Furthermore, he'd been unable to raise Pao.

Wiggins' insufferable arrogance had led to the death of Operation Blood Star!

Lee's roll became clear—protect his nation. He had to kill Wiggins and destroy as much evidence as possible. No amount of fine wine, rich food, sex, or cigars was worth his country's honor. His sacrifice for the Dear Leader would be his legacy.

He chose not to obey the order to get back to the fight. He chose instead to intercept Wiggins at the command center, before the white devil could do any further damage to his country.

Lee waited. A golf cart sped around the corner, Wiggins at the wheel. He triggered a burst of machine gun fire. Bullets chewed up the ground in front of the traitor.

Wiggins skidded to a halt. "What the hell you doing, mate?"

"I'm not your mate, none of us are. You're in this only for yourself. You've destroyed our operation and brought shame on my country!"

"We can get back on track. Blood Star can still be a success."

"Look around you. Blood Star is finished!"

Wiggins made an act of inspecting the area. While doing so, he depressed the menu button on his wristwatch. The cracked egg icon began blinking.

Lee caught the movement. He'd anticipated Wiggins going for the self-destruct button. The secret addition to Wiggins' watch had been discovered before leaving Korea.

"It won't work," Lee said.

"Sure it will, mate."

"No, the watch. It's a fake. The Dear Leader had it switched. Pao has the real one with your egg icon.

"I don't know what you're talking about."

"Yes, you do." Lee raised the machine gun and fired.

Wiggins saw it coming. With jungle cat reflexes, he dove off the cart just as a hail of bullets chewed into the seat. He rolled, drew his pistol, and fired at the fuel tank on Lee's quadrunner.

The results were devastating in the confined space.

89

Lam halted the group in front of a massive door. "This is it."

"What...a giant door with no keyhole?" Ballerd scoffed.

Rebecca ran her hand along the metal. "How do we open it?"

"I don't know. I'm assuming the door is actuated remotely from the command center."

Ballerd persisted. "Are we just supposed to wait for someone to phone in a request?"

"You got any better ideas?" Lam shot back.

Air suddenly sucked from everyone's lungs. A terrible noise filled their ears, and a large object smashed against the far side of the steel door.

"What the hell was that?" Ballerd yelled.

"Keep your voice down." Lam forced through clenched teeth.

"An explosion...Billy Ray, maybe?" Rebecca wondered aloud.

"We can only hope," Lam said, wishing like hell to have an earbud and mic so he could just call and ask.

* * *

It required perfect timing...and another miracle.

Billy Ray counted down from five and tossed the bomb into the Lazy River, then tucked tight against the concrete bulkhead and hid his face against the coming shockwave.

The explosion hit with a force so strong it nearly tossed him up and over the wall. He launched himself from the blocks and sprinted across a dry riverbed before the waters came crashing back. Guns fired from the enemy not knocked flat by the explosion.

Billy Ray never slowed, just raced full-speed in the direction of the security building. Rounding a bend at the tall sprint slides, he came face to face with one of Wiggins' soldiers. He slugged the man square on the jaw without even breaking stride. The soldier went down, dazed but conscious, then got up and gave chase.

A shot rang out. In opting for speed the soldier had chosen pistol over machine gun. He had to shake the guy. He couldn't turn and shoot, that'd only allow the enemy to catch up or opt for switching weapons. Exposed as he was in the wide area between attractions, a standoff with machine guns was a no-win bet. The soldier could afford to sacrifice his life, and was probably even under orders from Wiggins to do so. But not Billy Ray, death now would result in the slaughter of his friends.

He got his answer at the next attraction, a zip line mounted beneath the electric monorail. The sign read, The Big Zipper. The stair landings offered momentary protection from the shooter. The enemy sensed so too and stopped wasting ammo.

His longer legs allowed him to take steps three at a time and extend his lead. He reached the top, sprinted across the platform and, like a suicidal Tarzan, dove straight out into open air seventy feet above the public square. He caught hold of a zip line chair, kicked his feet outward, and pulled his knees above his head into a ball. He shot away from the platform, rapidly increasing the distance between him and the pursuer. Futile shots rang out behind him.

The Big Zipper provided three advantages, escape being most obvious. The ride also led straight to the security building. And lastly, the view was spectacular! Fireworks lit the ground below with a kaleidoscope of color. The carnage he'd caused added an apocalyptic element.

It was surreal.

A constant buzzing issued from the electrified monorail above. Then came another sound, the staccato burst of machine gun fire. His pursuer had also joined the high wire ride, though assuredly in less dramatic fashion.

Billy Ray spotted the end platform fast approaching. He lifted both feet above his head and jammed them against the steel cable. The smell of burning rubber filled his nostrils, but the added friction provided the brakes he needed. He stuck the landing on the platform with perfect tens but no time to take a bow.

Hot lead clanged against the platform. The soldier didn't need to catch up because his bullets would.

Billy Ray spotted a long metal pole with a wide hook on one end for assisting riders who pulled up short of the platform. He wound his jacket around his hand, grabbed the pole, and hooked it onto the electrified third rail above. The jacket provided insulation—the proof being he wasn't dead. Then he dropped the pole against the steel cable.

Two hundred yards away, suspended seven stories above the public square, the night erupted with its creepiest light show yet, a body catching fire and dancing violently in midair. Then ammunition in the man's gun and pockets cooked off. Finally, a grenade on the man's vest exploded and extinguished the macabre sight.

Billy Ray flew down the stairs, taking nearly whole sections at a time. He hit the ground and bolted toward the last of the monstrous waterslide attractions at the Texas Waterland Family Park, the Black Anaconda. He was betting on an underground passage to Wiggins' control center. He was also betting Gallina's men were scattered in the park, dead, or running for their lives. He hoisted the H&K MP7, switched the fire selector to three-shot burst, and opened the door he'd seen on the recon video.

He entered a world of darkness and stood still, listening, sensing, or as one SEAL buddy once called it, *tasting the air.* He was no snake, so he switched on the flashlight mounted on the side of his weapon. The room was large and presently empty. Several doors lined the walls. He half-expected Stickman to jump out from behind door number three and take a swing at him. But nothing happened. Perhaps Stickman had run off with *Carol Merrill.*

A hallway led deeper into the building, ending at a set of stairs. Billy Ray descended into the depths, slowly, carefully, one foot at a time. And then he remembered the time.

To hell with it!

He flew down the stairs until arriving at a door with the words, DO NOT ENTER. It opened to a lighted tunnel used by Wiggins' forces to traverse the park quickly and secretly. After fifty yards and another turn, the tunnel ended. There he came upon a terrifying sight, the charred and smoldering remains of two vehicles—one a golf cart slammed against the wall, the other a tangled mess that had once been a quadrunner. Two additional objects lay smoldering and seeping fluids onto the pavement, a stocky leg and a torso. Both appeared to have originated from the same body. A Danner boot and khaki material clothed the thick leg.

Billy Ray guessed the remains belonged to Wiggins' sidekick. But who did this, Lam?

The wall nearest the mangled cart was actually a massive door, the very thing he'd hoped to find. He advanced with caution and searched for a way to open it. None presented itself. The door was operated by remote control. He thumped his fist against it. It was solid steel, like a blast door in a fallout shelter. He banged again, thinking on how to get in.

A dog barked!

He tapped a message in Morse code and received a reply.

Lam! The message said, *all well…hurry…no way to open.*

"Dolittle, you awake?"

"Jenkins, you're alive!"

"Sorry for not calling you after parting the Red Sea. I had pharaoh's army hot on my tail."

"Make it snappy, then. What do you want?"

"Got a steel door...four inches thick."

"The laser has a battery reading. Tell me what it says."

Billy Ray removed the laser and turned it on. He expected to see a simple readout, like a hundred volts or something. It made no sense. "Hope you know what this means—"

"Just read what you see."

Billy Ray did.

"Just as I thought, running on fumes. It may work, but you'll only get one shot. If the door has hinges, melt through those."

"It doesn't."

"Well then, think it through. Oh yeah, nine minutes left," Dodd added.

"No pressure, right?"

"Good luck, my friend."

Billy Ray tapped instructions, *back away…shield eyes.* Lam would know what was coming. Next he chose a pattern sure to work. He imagined a chalk line on the door and blasted away. The remaining power in the laser lasted only the blink of an eye, but it was enough. The beam created a mouse hole at the base of the steel door. The edges glowed red. He didn't have hours to wait for the metal to cool. He retrieved dry ice from his pack and spread it on the pavement instead. Cooling took only a minute.

Lam was the last to be pulled through. "What now?" he asked, wasting no time on backslaps and hugs.

"First off, take these." He handed Lam the earbud and mic.

Lam brightened. "So Bell made it and my daughter's safe?"

Billy Ray nodded.

Lam donned the com gear. "Life just got more hopeful."

Billy Ray continued issuing orders. "All of you stay to your left. Fifty yards up you'll see a red door. Take it to freedom. A few of those gunmen in black pajamas remain, but your disguise should help. As for Gallina's men, I think the rats are jumping ship. You only have six minutes. Now get going!

Rebecca refused to budge. "What about you, Billy Ray?"

"I'm going after Wiggins."

Lam held up. The reporter kept going. The cameraman hadn't moved yet from Rebecca's side.

"I stay," she said with authority.

Billy Ray couldn't believe his ears. "But—"

"Listen here, Billy Ray Jenkins. I'm alive thanks to you."

Ballerd made further progress down the tunnel. Lam was backing up in the direction of freedom. Pedro danced around wagging his tail. Then before anyone could react, a large man with a knife jumped from behind the smashed golf cart, stabbed the cameraman in the chest, and dove through the mouse hole.

Rebecca screamed!

The cameraman lay dead on the floor.

Joseph Wiggins had been barely recognizable—blond hair burned to stubble, clothes in tatters, skin red and blistering. He was injured, but had strength and agility. And he was getting away!

Billy Ray took charge. "Lam, get everybody to safety—"

Rebecca interrupted, "Everybody is only the reporter."

"Do it," Billy Ray said to Lam.

Lam and the reporter turned and ran.

Billy Ray faced Rebecca. "We do it my way."

"Of course."

"Me first, you last."

"Pedro first."

Billy Ray rolled his eyes. *Women!* But she was right.

Pedro offered no warning bark. Billy Ray went through the hole next, careful not to brush the hot edges. Rebecca followed.

He took their bearings. Where to?

One if by land, two if by sea.

Lam would've chosen to escape across land. He would've chosen water. Which would Wiggins have picked?

Billy Ray stuck with water and headed for the treatment plant.

There'd been doors in the hallway, but he dismissed those as too obvious. In the pumping station, however, there'd been a hatch cover beside the main tank. He and Lam had ignored it because of the padlock and because they were ascending at the time not descending.

He felt sure Wiggins would be there.

90

Lam got lucky. There was an abandoned dune buggy just outside the Black Anaconda. He and Ballerd hopped in.

No beer cooler on the hood of this baby. There was an M-249 Squad Automatic Weapon—a gas operated and air-cooled machine gun capable of spitting tons of hot lead.

"You know how to fire one of those?"

Ballerd made a distasteful look.

"Then do you know how to drive this thing?"

Ballerd nodded up and down.

"Take the wheel!"

They traded places and Ballerd peeled off like a crazed ambulance driver. Their test came immediately.

A white limousine sped across their path. Running interference fore and aft were two red Cadillac Escalades. Men in both cars stood up through sunroofs pointing automatic weapons. A man in the front vehicle even held a shoulder-fired rocket launcher.

Gallina's entourage!

"Hold it steady," Lam Yelled. "I'm going to make some noise!"

Lam let loose a hail of bullets into the side of the passing limousine. He raked back and forth at the tires and windshields, but to no affect. Armor plating, bulletproof glass, and run-flat tires made the attempt futile. The 5.56×45mm NATO rounds just didn't have the punch of a .50-cal. He should've suspected a man as powerful as Gallina would own such a special vehicle.

Lam turned his efforts on the rear car and had better results. The Escalade flipped and exploded. Ballerd did an admirable job of avoiding the junk and gunned the ATV towards the main gate.

"Oh shit.... Stop!" Lam shouted.

The front gate was blocked by unmarked cars—his federal co-workers. Surrounding the FBI several rows deep and lining US Route 80 were what had to be a thousand cops and a million twirling lights! And here he was, dressed in the enemy's black outfit, and speeding toward them in a military ATV with a machine gun on the hood yellin' *yeehaw!*

Ballerd braked to a halt. "Why? We're so close!"

Lam pointed. "Look at all the cops. They don't know we're good guys."

"You mean they don't know *you're* a good guy."

Lam wanted to smack Ballerd, but the man was right.

Instead, he ordered the irritating newsman out of the vehicle. “Run like there’s a traffic accident up there. I’ll cover you.”

Ballerd needed no prompting. He jumped from the ATV and put his skinny legs in high gear until he reached safety.

Lam shifted to the driver’s seat and checked his watch. Dodd’s troops, or whatever they were, would begin wiping the park off the face of the earth in three minutes!

“Dodd.” No answer. “Come on Admiral, answer me, dammit!”

The voice of Admiral John P. Dodd came over his earbud. It sounded sad. “Is everyone out?”

“No, and you know it!”

“I was afraid of this.”

“Call off your men. Stop the raid. We got things won here.”

“I’m sorry. There’s far more to the matter than just winning.”

“Stall them...just ten more minutes!”

“Impossible, they’re inbound. Get out while you still can.”

“We don’t leave men behind. You should know that better than anyone. I read Jenkins’ service record, how he pulled you out of that jungle.”

“But—”

Lam cut Dodd off. “What about the dog collar around Jenkins’ neck? Could it be used like an IFF signal?”

Dodd came back immediately, his voice filled with hope. “Identification Friend or Foe—like transponders on aircraft. Genius!”

Lam cast a look at his watch.

Two minutes!

“But I still need time to get back to Jenkins. I want ten minutes!”

“You get five. And I can’t even guarantee that. The mission commander will decide. The fact Wolverine has done so much damage to the enemy operation may sway his decision. Now get going. Go get my friend!”

Lam stomped hard on the gas pedal. The ATV took off like a shot. He chose the direct route.

He hoped no gunmen lay in wait to slow him down.

91

They hustled down the spiral staircase of the water plant.

"Once at the bottom, let me open the door," Billy Ray said.

"Always the gentleman." Rebecca teased.

He had a flashback to their night leaving the Frontier Inn, and Rebecca's laughter. America's enemies would be in deep dip if the SEALs ever fielded an all-woman team. She had no fear.

They reached the bottom.

Pedro sat silently, waiting on orders. He listened at the door. Metallic clanging sounds came from inside. Billy Ray motioned for Pedro to remain still, the same for Rebecca.

Billy Ray slowly turned the knob and opened the door. At the far end of the pump station, next to the large water tank, a hideous-looking Wiggins bent over a hatch cover, his back to the door, banging hard against a padlock.

He raised the gun and rushed into the room. "Lose your keys?"

Wiggins spun around and flipped the KA-BAR knife he'd been using on the lock into his other hand, the business end pointed at Billy Ray. He was a mess, hair gone, face burned and blistered.

"Yup, a damn ballsy chap!"

"I told you I was coming for you." Billy Ray moved closer. "And now I'm going to kill you."

"I don't think so, mate. Seen your mother lately?"

"She's safe with Chief Harlan."

"Sure about that?"

Billy Ray felt confused. Was Wiggins bluffing? Undoubtedly, the ex-KGB spy had incredible sources to have gotten this far. Wiggins could easily have learned his mother's whereabouts.

"You kill me and you'll never see Lela again." Wiggins stepped forward, twisting the knife. "So how 'bout you drop that gun, mate, and we settle this like men. Whatcha' say? Wanna' try beating the truth outa' me?"

Rebecca entered. "Don't believe him, he's tricking you!"

"Ah, my little *sheila.* Back with your randy boyfriend, I see. Told you he couldn't leave a luscious *bluey* like you behind. You were the perfect bait."

"I'm not bait, you psycho."

"Oh yeah, honey pot?" Wiggins reached to his watch and pressed a button. It was a feature added *after* leaving Korea, one the Dear Leader had no control over—the doomsday trigger to blow the compound to bits.

Billy Ray caught the motion and had a sudden sinking feeling in his gut. "What are you doing?"

Wiggins looked past Billy Ray to Rebecca. "Killing the bee!" And then he lunged with the knife.

Billy Ray parried the charge with his gun, but the move had him twisting his body. Wiggins took advantage and followed with a punch to the ear and a sweep of the legs. Within a single second, Billy Ray lay flat on his back, attempting to clear cobwebs. Wiggins kicked the weapon out of his hands. It skittered across the floor.

The kick had required unequal weight on Wiggins' plant foot. Billy Ray saw an opportunity and went for it. He struck hard against Wiggins' knee. Wiggins let out a cry and went down.

Billy Ray hustled to regain his feet, but his backpack betrayed him. Wiggins caught hold of the web material and rolled, flinging Billy Ray toward the large water tank.

Fortunately for Billy Ray, Wiggins' injured knee also robbed a small amount of reaction time from his cat-like movements. Billy Ray was better prepared this time when Wiggins dove on top, knife in hand, attempting to finish the job. He caught Wiggins' wrist before the point of the razor-sharp combat knife could find its mark, and then he used his legs in bottom guard and logrolled to gain top position. Wiggins had anticipated the maneuver and kept the roll going.

They came to the edge of the tank. Billy Ray's head hung over the edge. The waters swirled beneath him.

Wiggins still owned top advantage—weight and rage and gravity his allies. Billy Ray was forced to use both hands to stop the knife, which allowed Wiggins to rapid-punch him in the head.

Bolts of lightning shot through Billy Ray's brain. His blood dripped into the tank. The dark waters began to boil. Wiggins hit him again and he felt consciousness fading, his strength, too.

Death awaited.

He could hear voices. Was it Brenda Lee? Was it Ricky? Maybe it was Edward Jones ordering him to hold the line, to fight ever onward. He couldn't tell. His mind was slipping....

BANG!

His mind awoke. A barking dog stirred his senses. Rebecca's voice, too. She held a gun and she was screaming for him!

Darkness turned to light.

Billy Ray was back. Wiggins' grotesque features, glaring red eyes, and hot rancid breath hung mere inches above his face. The point of Wiggins' knife touched his chest. Sharp steel began the plunge through cloth, flesh, bone, and heart.

"For my father!" Wiggins growled like a wild beast.

Billy Ray felt power surge through Wiggins' arms, through the burned hands, through the cold steel of the knife. Only seconds now. His life would be over. Evil would have its victory.

BANG! BANG!

The knife stopped its downward path.

"For... my... father," Wiggins repeated, losing strength.

Billy Ray bucked up and back with all his might.

Joseph Marx Wiggins somersaulted into the tank. The water erupted into a frenzied boil. Once more, black waters turned red. Wiggins managed to lift his head out of the water and loose a mighty scream before a million slashing teeth pulled him under.

Billy Ray sat upright and shouted at the red water. "No, you wicked bastard, for my brother!"

Rebecca ran to Billy Ray. "Is he gone?"

Billy Ray turned away from piranhas, from revenge, from so much pain and loss and death. "Yes."

"He beat me. I didn't know where you were." Rebecca squeezed the Ruger. Her hand turned white with the effort.

Billy Ray pulled Rebecca into him and held her until her nerves settled. He wanted to say she was safe, to rest her head on his shoulder, but couldn't. They still had a long way to go.

He checked the time.

Two minutes to midnight!

He tried hailing Dodd. It was then he realized the reason his head hurt so bad. Wiggins' punch had landed square on his ear, crushing the earbud. Blood trickled down his neck.

"We have to leave!"

"What is it?"

"People are coming to take over the park."

He stripped out of the backpack and picked up only the H&K MP7. The rest would do them no good running for their lives.

"Let's go!"

He headed for the door. Pedro bounded in front. Rebecca ran to catch up. Behind them, the roiling waters of the piranha tank suddenly calmed.

"You mean government people?" Rebecca asked as they bounded up the spiral staircase.

"I think so," Billy Ray said over his shoulder.

"Good."

"Not good. If we're in the park, we die too."

"What about the bombs that Wiggins triggered?"

The bombs! He'd forgotten about Wiggins' bombs!

"Hurry, Rebecca! There can't be much time! Bombs or secret troops, it doesn't matter. We're dead if we don't get out, now!"

Every bone in Billy Ray's body hurt. His head and face hurt. The jarring going up all the metal stairs was excruciating. He busted through the door at the top, paying no mind to potential threats. Shot to pieces, blown to bits, or obliterated by Dodd's fancy weapons, it mattered little.

He heard Rebecca scream, then it cut off abruptly. A man's voice said, "You're not going anywhere!"

Billy Ray whirled around.

Deputy Sheriff Tom Dixon stood beside the stairwell, his arm clamped around Rebecca's neck in a chokehold. He ripped the little .38 caliber Ruger from Rebecca's hand and put it against her head.

Pedro danced at their feet, barking and growling.

Billy Ray lifted the assault rifle and prepared to shoot. He switched the selector to single shot. The H&K MP7 was an accurate gun. It was his own aim he distrusted. A week of practice on the range and he would put two rounds in the man's forehead without worry of hitting Rebecca. But now, it was too great a risk.

Billy Ray lowered the gun. "Let her go, it's me you want."

"Actually, I already have you. I want her."

"But why would you want—"

With difficulty Rebecca said, "Because I know the truth."

Dixon tightened his hold.

Rebecca choked.

Billy Ray started for Dixon.

"Stop! Or I'll blow her brains out."

Billy Ray stopped, but lifted the gun nearer to ready position.

Rebecca wrestled against Dixon's arm. Pedro jumped up and down, attempting to bite Dixon and receiving a boot for his trouble. In the distraction, Rebecca managed to gain some slack.

"It was him. He was raping Brenda—"

Dixon reset his chokehold, deeper now. Rebecca struggled.

Billy Ray could hardly believe his ears!

"You...! Brenda Lee was pregnant with your child!"

"And a tasty treat she was."

"No wonder she wanted to kill herself. And you...her father's best friend...she had no one to turn to!"

"Roy Payne was no friend. He only made me a slave, like he did your daddy. I finally got smart and started taking what was owed me. And now you'll pay the price once again, if you manage to survive at all."

Billy Ray remembered the time. His watch read one minute to midnight!

In her struggles, Rebecca had managed to create some space. This time she bit down on Dixon's arm.

"Ahhh.... You little bitch! Just like your sister!" Dixon yelped and pulled his arm away. The gun came down near mid-waist. Pedro jumped up and buried his teeth into Dixon's gun hand. Dixon then slammed his arm against the cinderblock wall to loose Pedro. As Dixon did so, Rebecca twisted free.

Billy Ray pulled the trigger.

A red hole appeared in the forehead of Brenda Lee's tormentor. Dixon was dead before he hit the floor.

Rebecca rushed to Pedro. He was gone, his skull crushed.

Billy Ray grabbed Rebecca's arm. "Come on, run!"

They sprinted down the hallway of the water treatment plant and burst through the doors at a dead run.

Parked a hundred feet ahead in front of the security building was one of the most blessed sights either of them had ever seen, an ATV—*dune buggy,* Billy Ray corrected himself. And seated in the dune buggy, revving the engine, was Johnny Lam!

92

Dreyfus had nearly worn out the button on the bullhorn. "Secure! I repeat...this area is secure! You are to stand down!"

Since the moment that Upshur County Sheriff arrived, there'd been nothing but trouble. The man was out of his mind, darting back and forth rousing other officers, yelling about his daughter being held hostage inside the park by a madman running helter-skelter blowing up the place.

A dozen times already, Dreyfus had had to show his Presidential Authority ID. On two occasions, his agents were forced to draw weapons on lawmen who, apparently, possessed only third grade reading levels. *A "purdy"* picture of the President and "*fancy words*" failed to impress. Still more police arrived by the minute. The fact there actually was a man running throughout the Texas Waterland Family Park blowing the crap out of the place didn't settle matters down at all.

A strange sound began filling the rainy night air. Those on the outskirts of the police gathering noticed it first, a low hum, like that experienced near high-voltage transmission lines, only exhibiting more bass. The humming built in intensity until it canceled out other noises, including sirens from newly-arriving police vehicles. The rain was playing out, so conditions didn't favor tornadoes. So what could it be? All lights began turning off in Big Sandy then coming back on a few moments later, like a rolling blackout.

Dreyfus sensed mutiny.

He heard shouts behind him. They came from near the massive brass gates. He hurried forward to the commotion. His agents were confronting another threat. It was the Upshur Sheriff again, proclaiming he'd had enough of being told what to do "in his county." The big lawman had a scope-mounted rifle and was setting up position on the hood of his vehicle. To make matters worse, a dozen more sheriffs began following suit.

* * *

"Hey, handsome, going my way?"

Lam snapped his head around. He'd been looking toward the security building, expecting his friends to exit there. "Rebecca!"

They hopped aboard. "Gun it, Army!"

Lam poured all his skills and training into a cocktail, added a dash of bayou balls, and lit the path on fire. "Dodd gave us five more minutes."

"But Wiggins didn't. Haul ass!"

"What's that?" Rebecca yelled over the noise of the ATV.

Running away in the distance was a man with a cast on his arm and bandages around his head. Stickman!

"Lam, take me close."

As the ATV raced past the man who'd come close to killing him with a pool stick, Billy Ray lifted his foot and struck outward. With the speed of the vehicle behind his size-twelve boot, he smashed Stickman in the back of the head.

Two seconds later, half of East Texas lit up from a colossal explosion. A second after that, the shockwave caught them. The ATV was tossed around like a toy. It lifted on two wheels and nearly flipped. Lam wrestled the machine back onto all-fours.

Billy Ray chanced a look back. The security building and water plant were gone. So too was Stickman.

They had a mile to go and would make it with only seconds to spare. A red SUV sped across their path, followed by a long white limousine.

"Gallina!" Lam shouted over the noise.

Billy Ray fed fresh ammo into the M-249 SAW, then grabbed the handle and triggered a burst. "Your call, guys." He knew what side of justice he'd choose if his daughter had been stolen.

"Rebecca?" Lam asked.

"Let's get the creep!"

Lam veered toward Gallina's entourage. Billy Ray pointed at the man poking up through the sunroof of the Escalade.

Lam angled for a strafing run.

Billy Ray savaged the Escalade in a hail of lead. The red vehicle slowed and came to a stop.

He jumped from the ATV and ran up to vehicle. Of the eight men inside, four were already in hell, two paddling the river Styx, and one fleeing the scene on foot. That left only the man holding the RPG launcher, who now stared at the business end of Billy Ray's machine gun. The man simply handed over the RPG. Billy Ray turned to leave.

Rebecca shouted, "Watch out!"

Billy Ray had already expected the move. RPG guy had been reaching for a weapon upon his approach. In any event, the man had had his lucky break in life and chosen to squander it. He shot the man in the throat and got back in the ATV.

They caught up with the white limousine carrying Gallina. Billy Ray took aim with the RPG and fired. The rocket-propelled grenade zipped through the air and found its mark—a crazy old man who would be king. The white limousine exploded in a massive fireball!

Lam offered no cheers. He was too much the professional. Although, Billy Ray was certain his friend would sleep well at night.

“Take us home, Army.”

The ATV died and coasted to a stop. All lights extinguished throughout the Texas Waterland Family Park and beyond. Nothing electrical remained operable. Then all at once the night burst alive with hundreds of solid green laser beams darting in all directions. Their ears filled with a strange humming noise.

“Dodd,” Lam said.

“Who’s Dodd?” Rebecca asked,

“Another time, perhaps.” Billy Ray ended the discussion.

They got out of the ATV and walked the final thousand yards to the main gate through screams and carnage and mayhem. All around them the night was alight with confusion—fireworks, blazing destruction, a most bizarre laser show...and several large hovering discs.

Lam had warned them to stay close to Billy Ray on account of the dog collar. Billy Ray tried claiming it was because of him being the alpha male. They laughed, as people sometimes do after surviving impossible odds, saving loved ones, and avenging the dead.

A soldier in black uniform jumped from behind a building and ran at them. He was missing an arm, yet there was no blood. He looked to be in shock, but still pressing on. The soldier pulled a grenade and raised it to his mouth to pull the pin.

Billy Ray lifted the MP7 to end the threat. Before he could pull the trigger, the man’s head exploded—from within. His eyes popped out and his teeth shot from his mouth like shrapnel.

The last North Korean soldier collapsed in a lifeless pile.

* * *

A young Asian man and his grandfather sat in the back of a flatbed truck heading north on Texas State Highway 155. They wore black business suits. The driver of the truck had been kind enough to pick them up on the dark road. Their car had broken down some miles back, or so they’d said.

Pao checked the face of his Casio wristwatch. The icon of a cracked egg blinked repeatedly. Using his single finger, he depressed a button on the watch. The blinking stopped.

Pao lowered the black sleeve, stood up, and faced forward. His white hair and wispy beard fluttered in the breeze of the moving truck.

93

Billy Ray could hardly believe they'd survived. It had taken miracles, some manmade, many not. Unfortunately, the greatest miracle of all, bringing Ricky and Clarice back, was one not likely for this time. He was satisfied to have found Ricky's killer. And he could now let Dolores Richards know where her daughter was. As grisly as Clarice's death had been, to know was better than to not know. And then there was Edward Jones. The old warrior had been right all along. He was going to have to read Jonesy's diary again, more closely this time. With all that had happened, and Eva's information about her uncle's medical condition, Billy Ray wished to see the real Edward Jones in true light.

Freedom beckoned.

Just a hundred yards. The length of a football field. Only steps away.

What his life would be like once he passed beyond the gates of the Texas Waterland Family Park was yet a mystery. What he would do, where he would go, all a blur. He hoped that life would include Rebecca.

All at once, the green lasers stopped and the strange circular craft rose skyward. They shot off in unison toward the east, gone in the blink of an eye. The strange humming sound ended.

The park grew eerily silent.

Not a single soul was left alive. No one was spared the green lasers. Only they had survived, huddled tightly, walking as quickly as they could manage without tangling their feet, not caring to look back.

The fireworks had ended its finale. Even nature's downpour slowed to a gentle rain. All things electrical returned to life. The park lights came on and an automated recording played loudly over the PA system. It thanked all for coming and played a musical jingle about being *the safest place in the sun for wholesome family fun.*

Hundreds of police lights and sirens turned on at once. Billy Ray could see dozens upon dozens of cops lining the park entrance, held back by the same line of unmarked cars as before. In front of them all stood the man he'd met earlier, Agent Dreyfus. Beyond Dreyfus were more guns drawn and pointed in his direction than he'd ever seen before. Shouts came from the uniformed crowd. Billy Ray couldn't make out the words, but assumed they pertained to them.

Dreyfus' voice carried over a bullhorn. "Stand down! Do not fire! All police lower your weapons!"

"Hey, my boss," Lam said.

Billy Ray nudged Rebecca. "Look at all those cops. Your father sure does hate me."

"What was your first clue," she said.

Billy Ray realized something and stopped their progress. "Uhh, Lam, you might want to get out of those black pajamas. The boys in blue could take you for the wrong team."

"Oh, right." Lam stripped out of the uniform.

* * *

The airships and green lasers had spooked everyone except Dreyfus. He knew what they really were, and who was inside. He just couldn't tell anyone. And he certainly couldn't blame the cops for forgetting all about Jenkins and training their guns skyward against the invading aliens in their flying saucers.

Dreyfus walked the frontline repeating his commands through the bullhorn. Thankfully, nobody had taken potshots at the craft.

The officers began lowering their weapons...except one.

"There they are!" someone shouted.

"There's the hostage!" another officer yelled.

That's when matters went from bad to worse. The military saucers zipped off into the night. The humming sound ceased. And all the lights turned on at once. A moment later, a Big Sandy Police cruiser began pushing its way through the crowd, squawking and chirping its siren to clear a path. The hush that had fallen over the crowd at the sight of the saucers and lasers vanished. Voices began filling the air.

Lam and the others had just rounded a building and appeared before everyone. Then about ninety yards short of the finish line, they'd stopped.

Lam was taking off his clothes.

* * *

Lam shed the black Kevlar vest and outer clothing down to his boxer briefs and brown chest.

Rebecca made a sad face. "That's it?"

"Listen, babe, I see how your dad feels about Jenkins. I don't want him thinking I'm hitting on you, too."

Both men laughed.

Rebecca did not. She had a sudden bad feeling and began scanning the crowd.

Billy Ray said, "Hey, Dodd's boys are gone. No need for the chain-gang shuffle. What you all say we pick up the pace?" He stepped forward to lead the way.

Rebecca spotted her father in the crowd. It was simple. He was the only one pointing a weapon at them. It was a long way off, but she could see through the scope, through the eye behind it, and into the mind of a very sick man. It was a long way off, but she could see his finger slowly depressing the trigger. It could just be her imagination, but she knew her father.

Rebecca threw her arms around Billy Ray a micro-second before the bullet struck and the sound of a gunshot rang out.

Billy Ray froze!

He felt something he hadn't felt in years—something he'd hoped and prayed never to feel again—a bullet slamming into the body of a friend. This time it wasn't a fellow SEAL, but the woman he loved!

Rebecca's arms dropped and she slid down Billy Ray's body.

He caught her and held on tight. "NO! NO! NOOOO!"

Lam grabbed up the Kevlar vest and shielded them from the direction of the bullet.

Billy Ray lowered Rebecca to the ground. Tears streamed down his cheeks. "Rebecca...speak to me."

Her eyes fluttered open. "Billy Ray...."

"I'm here, my darling."

Rebecca gained a degree of strength, her eyes opened wider, her voice came clearer. "We did all right together...?"

"Yes, we did." Billy Ray smoothed Rebecca's hair.

"And the others...are they safe?"

"Yes—" Billy Ray hardly got the word out.

Rebecca eyes closed and her body went limp in his arms.

He shook her. "Hang on, Rebecca! You hear me, hang on!"

Lam draped the Kevlar over Billy Ray's shoulders and took off running.

* * *

Smoke curled upward from the barrel of Roy Payne's rifle.

Dreyfus drew his gun and bolted over to the big man. "Lower your weapon. Do it now!"

Lam came running through the park gates, mindless of being stripped down to boots and boxers. He slid across the wet hood of a blocking car and darted straight for the sheriff. The look in his eyes said it all. He was going to rip Roy Payne apart!

"No, Johnny!" Dreyfus blocked his friend's path.

The Big Sandy Police cruiser came to a stop. The police chief and a woman exited the car and hustled over to Dreyfus.

Roy Payne lowered the rifle. "What's your problem? Jenkins is a wanted criminal. I'm fully within my charter to shoot him."

Lela gasped!

Lam struggled to get around his boss. Another agent stepped in to help restrain him. Almost in hysterics, Lam shouted, "You sick bastard, you shot Rebecca!"

Payne's expression went from smug triumph to confusion.

All eyes turned in the direction of the park.

Sitting on the ground, cold rain pouring down from a black sky, and rocking Rebecca in his arms, was a truly beaten man. Billy Ray Jenkins.

Lela took off running. An agent stopped her. Dreyfus nodded and the man stepped aside.

A crowd of sheriffs and deputies gathered around the scene. Roy Payne slid down off the hood of the patrol car to stand among his peers.

Chief Harlan stepped next to Dreyfus. "If I may, Agent?"

Dreyfus nodded.

"Sheriff Roy Payne, you're under arrest—"

Payne interrupted, "Wesley, you know Jenkins is a criminal."

"Not Billy Ray. I'm charging you with the murder of Rodney "Switch" Jenkins. We found his body on your vacation property. Your caretaker has confessed."

Dreyfus raised his pistol.

Chief Harlan turned Payne around, applied handcuffs, and read the Miranda warning loud and slow for all to hear.

Roy Payne faced in the direction of the Texas Waterland Family Park. He stared at the scene in the distance where Billy Ray Jenkins held Rebecca and Lela comforted her children.

94

After Independence Day
Washington, DC

The President called the meeting to order. Dreyfus sat in the same chair as before, opposite POTUS. This time, Agent Johnny Lam sat to his left. The same cast of characters populated the remaining chairs. The Vice President was the only one not in attendance.

"I first want to tell each of you, job well done. The mission was performed brilliantly." The President turned to the woman named V and said, "The new technology worked to perfection."

The K-KEY woman offered no comment, only a nod. Dreyfus could swear a smile attempted cracking the granite corners of her mouth. Who she was remained a mystery.

After kudos to the others at the table, the President turned to Dreyfus and Lam. "The country owes you both a debt of gratitude."

Dreyfus smiled politely.

Lam spoke up, "Actually, Mr. President, we owe the thanks to the other man in the park."

"Yes," the President said. "I am quite aware of your friend's exploits. I ordered the Vice President to meet with him personally."

Lam was pleased by the President's directive, and the mention of the word *friend.*

The President continued, "Both of you have been made privy to our nation's most secret military capabilities. Merely admonishing you to remain silent is not enough."

Lam felt the group staring at him, especially the stiff gal with the dinner fork logo and only a letter for a name. He envisioned a tiny jail cell on a deserted island in the middle of the Pacific Ocean.

"Therefore, I am requesting that you both join our team." The President waved his hand to indicate the members at the table. "Beginning with you, Agent Dreyfus. My Attorney General informs me you are nearing the FBI's mandatory retirement age."

"Yes, Mr. President," Dreyfus acknowledged.

"We need an experienced legal attaché on our team. As matters call for ever-greater levels of extra-constitutional intervention within our nation's borders, I intend to see the balance between military action and justice be preserved."

"Thank you, sir, but I'm not an attorney at law."

"You have a law degree, do you not?"

"Yes, but I've taken no state bar exams."

The President smiled. "That will hardly be necessary. You will oversee all fifty states and territories. There is no bar exam for such a position that I know of, and your detective skills can aid our missions. I need someone who can narrow the field of battle...flush out the enemies within, as it were."

Lam could hardly believe his ears. Working outside the nation's Constitution? Military strikes within the nation's borders? That wasn't the America he knew.

The President caught the look and addressed it directly. "Many do not agree with this line of action, especially those in my own party. However, I have intelligence information not available to my detractors. I assure you, gentlemen, the enemies of our nation are no longer at the gates, they are inside—in our cities, our schools, our neighborhoods. And their weapons of choice are Illegal drugs. Drug abuse is epidemic. Should we fail to stop it, social disorder could soon destroy this great country. Our nation's very survival may depend on us here in this room, the K-KEY Group."

Dreyfus stared. Lam felt lightheaded.

"As you witnessed in Texas," the President continued, "the enemy came within a day of murdering millions of Americans. If not for the heavy rain at the time of the explosion that destroyed the enemy's production facility, the poison would have wiped out the local population at the very least. Joseph Wiggins and his co-conspirators narrowly missed achieving success by turning our laws, our ethics, and our morals against us."

Each of the regular attendees nodded at the President's declaration.

"I cannot—we cannot—let this happen. So yes, gentlemen, *extra-constitutional*. I don't like it. You don't like it. The country hates it. And the press would skewer me in a Chicago minute, worse even than they condemned my predecessor. But if our nation is to survive, this is what must be done."

The President stared at them, his charisma a capturing force.

Dreyfus saw the wisdom of being on the inside protecting America from the nation's enemies rather than standing on the outside protesting the methods. "You have your man, Mr. President."

"And you, Agent Lam? Those incredible flying machines you saw the other night require highly-trained operatives."

To say he wasn't intimidated would be to lie, but Lam knew his mind. He'd decided long ago who he wanted to be and what he wanted to be like. He took a deep breath and gave his answer. "Mr. President, I like my boots on the ground. I'll pass."

Lam's admission was only true in part. He also wasn't ready to depart from the wisdom of the Founding Fathers.

"I was hoping you'd say that," the President responded. "Some kids dream of flying. They dream of the stars and the craft to take them there. But alas, we have challenges right here on planet Earth, and Texas in particular. Our intelligence indicates one of the tankers carrying Rapture remains unaccounted for. How would you like to replace Agent Dreyfus in Dallas as the next Special Agent in Charge? Your first directive would be to seek and destroy the Rapture."

Dreyfus' smile was the sole vote of confidence Lam needed. "It would be my honor, Mr. President."

"It is done, then. I will have the Attorney General and FBI Director make it so, effective immediately. Dismissed, gentlemen."

As they left the Whitehouse Dreyfus said, "Well, there goes my sailboat in Florida. What about you, Johnny?"

Lam thought it over and said, "Actually, Chris, I'll be gaining something worth more than gold, silver and diamonds."

"Oh yeah, and what's that?"

"The front parking spot at the office."

"You've earned it. Now you can go back to being Clark Kent."

Lam gave Dreyfus a look. "Who's that?"

"Geez, Lam, don't you know anything?"

They walked away busting each other's chops.

* * *

The door to Cliff Michaels' office was closed. Billy Ray didn't need a sign to warn that a meeting was in progress. Michaels' volume was cranked up, getting his message through the thick head of yet another parolee with a "world-owes-me" attitude.

He picked up a newspaper. A story in the Chronicle caught his eye. A youngster had caught a strange fish using a hotdog as bait. Wildlife officials identified it as a red-bellied piranha. Citizens weren't to worry though, as piranhas weren't native to Texas. The article reminded readers that releasing pets into the wild was both illegal and potentially dangerous...blah, blah, blah.

Little did they know.

Billy Ray tossed down the Chronicle and picked up a copy of the USA Today newspaper. He unfolded it and was treated to a surprise. On the front cover was a large archive photo of the Texas Waterland Family Park and the headline "Monster Firework Display Destroys Amusement Park." Clive Ballerd's name was listed on the byline.

He read the article. There couldn't have been more than five words of truth. Ballerd went on to explain how, during the park's dress rehearsal before opening to the public, the first-ever floating platforms designed to levitate the laser light show machinery became tangled during a violent rainstorm. The equipment then crashed onto the building housing a vast quantity of fireworks for the Independence Day Grand Opening extravaganza. The fireworks exploded, shooting incendiaries in all directions and setting fire to many of the buildings. Dozens of park employees were said to have been injured or killed. Names were being withheld until next of kin could be notified. Park officials were quick to call upon the expertise of federal agents from the Bureau of Alcohol, Tobacco, Firearms and Explosives. The ATF, in cooperation with a unit of the National Guard, immediately quarantined the park and surrounding land to conduct cleanup of the dangerous explosives and residue.

There was no mention of him, Lam, Bell, or Rebecca, nor would there be. Even the matter of the statewide manhunt for Rebecca and her kidnapper got swept under the rug as an expensive hoax currently being investigated by the Texas Attorney General.

He had to laugh. Ballerd had finally gotten his big break only to be told what to write by Uncle Sam. Even if Ballerd won a Pulitzer, he'd forever know it was a load of bull. And so would a few others.

It couldn't have happened to a nicer guy.

There was sudden quiet. Billy Ray thought something had happened to his CSO. But then the door opened and Michaels' head popped out. "What are *you* doing here?"

Billy Ray stood. "Sir?"

"We don't need your kind around here."

"What kind are you talking about?"

"The innocent kind. Now get out and don't come back!"

Billy Ray dropped the paper and made to leave.

"Jenkins...."

Billy Ray turned around. "Sir?"

Michaels had a big smile. "What verse you on?"

The teasing became clear. "Tell Mosey, Revelations 21:4."

"My favorite Bible verse... *'No more death or pain.'* Cliff Michaels closed his door.

The shouting resumed.

95

Four Days Later....

Billy Ray entered the Longview Regional Medical Center. He stopped at the gift store to purchase flowers and then rode the elevator to the top floor. He made his way past two scrutinizing sheriff's deputies and into Larry Bell's room.

Bell was awake and watching FOX news.

"Hey, deputy."

"Hey yourself, Jenkins."

"So how's the shoulder?"

"Doc Hastings says I'll live, but that the Astros just lost a pitcher for the remainder of the century."

"Sounds like something Doc would say."

There was a cough from behind the curtain dividing Bell's room.

Bell looked at the flowers. "Those for me?"

"Yup. Hope you like yellow."

"I used to. Word musta got around, though." Bell pointed at two identical arrangements on his bedside table. "Tell you what, Jenkins. Give those to my roommate. The ol' bag hasn't had any visitors, and it sounds like she's coming to."

"She?"

"You think the government can afford putting me up at the Hilton?"

"After what you did, Larry, they should."

Bell blushed. "Nahh. You and Lam are the real heroes."

"Hardly. I wouldn't be standing here if it wasn't for Rebecca."

There was another cough and then a groan from the other patient. Billy Ray took that as a cue to lower his voice.

Bell pointed to the curtain. "Sneak those on over there. That woman will appreciate 'em more than me."

Bell had a big heart to go with good cop instincts. Now that the only candidate running for sheriff was in jail awaiting arraignment on murder charges, Gus Heavenor was leading a committee to recruit Bell for the job. There was no doubt in Billy Ray's mind that Larry Bell would become the next sheriff of Upshur County.

He fluffed the arrangement a bit and walked quietly around the end of the room divider. He almost dropped the flowers.

"Rebecca!"

She opened her large emerald eyes and made a valiant effort to smile. She appeared weak, her skin wan. But alive!

He went to her.

Billy Ray stroked Rebecca's auburn hair. "I thought I lost you."

She was recovering from massive blood loss. He'd thought at the time that the bullet missed her heart, but wasn't sure. When the medics rushed her away she'd had no pulse. He, in turn, had been whisked away by Dreyfus on orders from "on-high" just before a dozen square miles of East Texas was put on military lockdown by the Federal government. Countless attempts had failed to get word on Rebecca's condition, where she was, or even if she was alive. She and Bell were being isolated by the feds.

They talked quietly, affectionately. After an hour it was clear Rebecca had run out of steam.

"Where to next?" she asked, her voice breathy and weak.

"Oak Hills Cemetery. Edward Jones is being buried today."

She merely nodded.

"I attended a small memorial yesterday for Clarice Richards."

"I'm glad her parents have her back." She looked sad.

"They decided to let her remains rest at the bottom of the Loma Reservoir. Just knowing the truth was enough."

Rebecca searched Billy Ray's eyes for a long moment. She was tiring rapidly, but it was evident she still had more to say.

"I love you, Billy Ray Jenkins."

He felt a lump form in his throat. "I love you too, Rebecca—"

She touched a finger to his lips as she'd done days before. "I'll always love you. I know now what my sister saw in you, and she was right." Rebecca breathed deeply. "I'm leaving Texas for good…alone."

Billy Ray nearly lost it.

"It can't work between us. At every turn, something or somebody will be waiting to destroy us. You'll be with me every day of my life, both in my heart and on my mind until the day I die." She stopped speaking and searched his eyes, awaiting a response.

He'd fought through so many challenges in his life, so many battles—life and death. And yet, to attempt overturning Rebecca's decision seemed a war unwinnable.

For some lovers, dark spirits forever conspired.

Billy Ray loved Rebecca with all his heart. He also loved her enough to let her go—to have a chance for happiness, a career, a husband, children...peace. No such future awaited them. Their path had been spoiled by hatred. The sins of the fathers had visited upon the children.

Those sins would end with them.

"Where will you go?" Billy Ray asked.

Rebecca looked relieved by his question. Her eyelids drooped.

"Olympia... mountains... trees... water...." She slipped away.

He whispered in her ear, "Be well, my love."

Billy Ray kissed Rebecca Payne's lips for the last time.

* * *

Billy Ray stood next to an old hickory tree looking down into the valley of the cemetery. A group of mourners sat among shade and shadows. Jonesy's flag-draped casket rested beside an open grave. He couldn't make out the words, but didn't need to. He'd attended military funerals before, too many in fact.

The chaplain closed his book and stepped back from the podium. The gun salute commenced. Billy Ray felt each volley penetrate his soul. Then from far off among the rolling hills of the cemetery came the most haunting of musical tunes, a lone bugler playing Taps. Afterward, the Marine casket-team leader of the uniformed soldiers, marines, sailors, and airmen directed the folding of the flag—crisp movements of stretching, folding, snapping, and bundling. The Marine officer stepped forward with the triangle of white stars amidst a sea of blue and presented the flag to Wilhelmine Van Luven.

Billy Ray turned away. His stomach felt tied in knots. There'd been so much death, so much needless pain.

He began a slow, contemplative walk to Ricky's grave.

So much had transpired in the days since his release from prison. So much had changed, and then changed again. More than the worst enemies on sea, air, or land he feared Reverend Greer's warning. He'd been lost among briars and thorns—wandering between pity and resentment—knowing neither life nor death. Not knowing love.

Mosey had led him into the light of a savior.

But he'd chosen to go back into the darkness for a time...to find truth, to rid the world of an evil menace, and to set matters straight. He'd chosen war once again and the killing of others. So did he backslide? Or had he answered the cries of the innocent and the call of a vulnerable nation? He didn't want to be lost. He'd rather die than face the darkness again.

And then there was Rebecca. She'd come into his life for such a short time. Or had it been a visit from Brenda Lee, the spirit of his past, closure at last?

Would he ever know love again?

The sound of approaching vehicles interrupted Billy Ray's thoughts. He turned to face the distraction.

A black limousine came to a stop beside him. The back door opened and out stepped the Vice President of the United States. He waved off several men descending to their posts. The Secret Service detail responded and maintained a respectful distance.

"Billy Ray Jenkins?"

"Yes, Mr. Vice President?"

"Captain Jones' niece said I might find you here."

Captain Jones…?

Billy Ray looked closer at the VP. He was old as vice presidents went, nearly Jonesy's age.

"I've been briefed on what went on here," the VP said. "Please accept my condolences and those of the President for the loss of your brother."

"Thank you, sir." Billy Ray searched the VP's face. "His men...."

"Pardon?"

"Tears formed in Jonesy's eyes whenever he spoke of his men. You were one of his men."

"Yes." The VP straightened his back. "Captain Jones was my commanding officer in Korea. We fought together at the Chosin Reservoir. He was the bravest man I've ever known. Not many of our company survived that battle, but his actions saved possible thousands more Marines. Those of us in the company who survived—the Chosin Few as we're called—reported Captain Jones' story. He was to be given the Medal of Honor. However, when time came for him to receive the award from President Eisenhower, he was nowhere to be found. He'd been discharged and simply disappeared."

"To East Texas," Billy Ray said.

"So it seems. After a few years, the matter was forgotten and efforts to locate him ceased. A travesty, I might add. I was proud to present Captain Jones' Medal of Honor to his niece."

The VP slipped a hand inside his jacket and withdrew an envelope. It had a Presidential Seal on the front. He handed the envelope to Billy Ray.

"What's this?"

"A Presidential pardon and order for expungement of your legal record. And there's another item in there you're well-deserving of, a DD Form 214 upgrading your military discharge to Honorable and restoring your full rights and backpay. You should expect a check in the mail in a few weeks, but probably longer." The VP winked. "You know how slow government bureaucracy can be."

Billy Ray didn't know what to say, so he just nodded.

"The Navy could use a man like you."

"I'm too old."

A broad smile formed on the Vice President's face. "I find that a little hard to believe."

"We'll just have to wait and see," Billy Ray said.

They shook hands and the last of Jonesy's men departed.

* * *

Birds sang in lofty heights, squirrels chattered and scurried about, a cricket chirped as daytime lapsed into dusk.

Billy Ray came to Ricky's grave. He knelt and brushed aside a few leaves from the headstone and then spoke out loud, "Little brother, I made such a mess of things by my silence. I should have told you the truth. I'm sorry to have put you and mom through so much. You will always be in my heart—your goodness, your promise, the love you sought. I swear to you, I will never let your sacrifice be in vain."

He crossed himself.

A soft, warm hand set down on Billy Ray's shoulder. He rose from his knees and turned around.

It was Eva.

Without a word, he took her offered hand.

They began their walk along the narrow winding lane, beneath mature trees, and to the hills and valleys beyond.

EPILOGUE

Five and a half months after the failure of Operation Blood Star, the world awoke to news of the death of North Korean dictator, Kim Jong-il. A weeping newscaster announced on official North Korean State Television that the Dear Leader suffered a heart attack while traveling on a train through his beloved country. Another communist news source, the Korean Central News Agency, reported Kim's death as being accompanied:

> "...by mysterious phenomena, including a fierce snowstorm having paused, the sky glowing red above the sacred Mount Paektu, and the ice on its famous lake cracking so loud it seemed to shake the heavens and the earth."

Still further reports said that all electricity and motorized equipment in Pyongyang stopped at the very moment of the Dear Leader's passing. This was later confirmed by satellite imagery from the time in question. Many citizens claimed to have heard a deep humming sound that lasted for two hundred and sixteen seconds, during which time Kim Jong-il's soul was received into the heavens. Western news sources balked at the concept of ascension and even got the time wrong, stating it as "three minutes thirty-six seconds." It was then learned that the number 216 was the Dear Leader's lucky number, as based on his birth date of February 16. Corrections to the story appeared in the following day's editions.

Left unreported in state media were sightings of strange disc-shaped craft that appeared above Kim's train and emitted solid beams of green light. However, so secretive is the petulant regime that the world may never know the complete truth.

AUTHOR'S NOTE

A work of fiction often has its origin in fact. A case in point is Edward Jones, who I used to represent several issues of importance to my story. I wish to draw your attention regarding two of those issues in particular—the Korean War and the Medal of Honor.

The Korean War is often referred to by historians as The Forgotten War. I find this title to be offensive. Consider that nearly 300,000 servicemen and women saw action in Korea and were subjected to brutal conditions while lacking appropriate cold-weather gear. Also consider that over 40,000 Americans were killed or listed as missing in action. In my mind, it matters little what you call it—Conflict, Police Action, Declaration of War. It's all the same to the missing and the dead. Just don't call it "forgotten." God Bless their memory and God Bless their families.

July 27, 2013 will mark 60 years since commencement of the cease-fire in the Korean War. I encourage everyone to read the history of the Korean War and learn of the many stories of heroism performed in some of the hardest fought battles ever in our Nation's history. 133 Medals of Honor were presented for bravery in action in Korea, 95 of them posthumously.

I encourage everyone to go to the following websites and read the accounts of our American heroes. Their stories are humbling.

http://www.arlingtoncemetery.net/webarber.htm
http://en.wikipedia.org/wiki/List_of_Medal_of_Honor_recipients

One such story of heroism from the Korean War is that of Colonel William E. Barber, who was awarded the Medal of Honor for his actions in battle at the Chosin Reservoir. I borrowed heavily from the story of Colonel Barber's heroic actions for my Backslide character, Edward Jones. However, please note that "Jonesy" is entirely a product of my imagination and in no way represents the real William E. Barber, the full story of Colonel Barber's heroic actions, his military career, or his personal character.

Lastly, my most humble thanks to the late Colonel Barber and to all the men and women who have fought and sacrificed in wars throughout our nation's history in order that I may be free.

May America never have a *forgotten* war.

Steve Elam

About the Author:

Steve Elam was born and raised in the Grand Rapids area of Michigan. After his service in the US Navy, he settled in Olympia, Washington, where he spent more than 25 years working for the Washington State Legislature and the lobbying firm of Chiechi and Associates. Steve attended colleges in both Big Sandy, Texas, and in Olympia.

BACKSLIDE is the first book in Elam's "Enemies Within the Gates" series. The story launches the thrilling exploits of ex-Navy SEAL Billy Ray Jenkins in his personal war against evil forces seeking to destroy America from within…a cause that began with the murder of his brother at the hands of a psychopathic villain and creator of the super-drug known as Rapture.

The stakes in America are for total domination. Our nation's enemies want it all, even our souls, and they'll stop at nothing to get it. One man stands in their way!

Teamed with a cocky FBI agent, a sexy redhead, and a mysterious government operative code-named Dolittle, Billy Ray Jenkins battles to save America from impending doom!

To purchase signed copies of Backslide, leave comments, or listen to Falling Off The End Of The Middle by Mark Bowen and the incomparable Nathalie Elam, please visit: www.ElamBooks.com.